Secrets of the Tulip Sisters

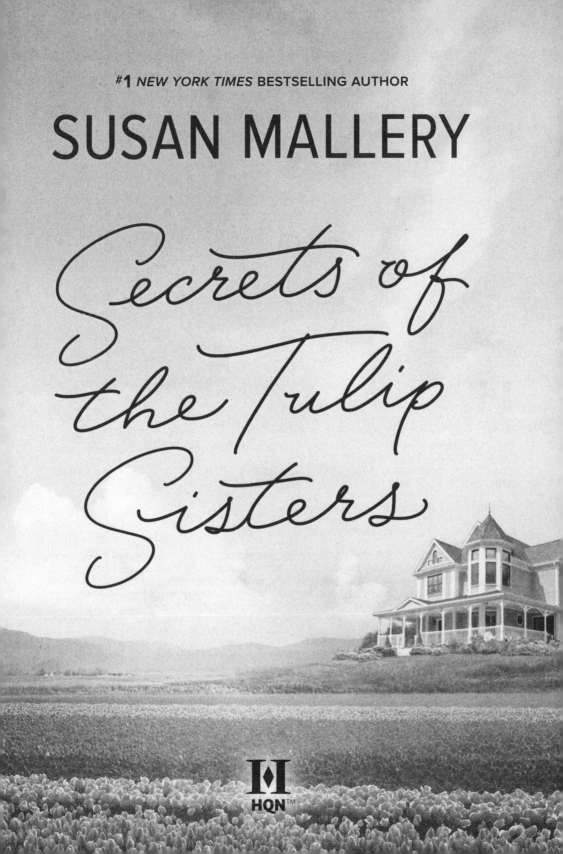

#1 *NEW YORK TIMES* BESTSELLING AUTHOR

SUSAN MALLERY

*Secrets of
the Tulip
Sisters*

HQN™

ISBN-13: 978-0-373-80276-0
ISBN-13: 978-1-335-08049-3 (Target Exclusive Edition)
ISBN-13: 978-1-335-99671-8 (Books-A-Million Exclusive Edition)

Secrets of the Tulip Sisters

This edition published by arrangement with Harlequin Books S.A.

For questions and comments about the quality of this book, please contact us at CustomerService@Harlequin.com.

www.HQNBooks.com

Printed in U.S.A.

My thanks to Lynn VL for her invaluable help when I was researching this novel. Lynn, you were fabulous and informative!! Thank you.

1

Kelly Murphy was willing to accept certain injustices in the world. That brownies had more calories than celery. That wearing white pants meant getting her period—regardless of where she was in her cycle. That her car would be low on gas only on days when she was running late. What she did *not* appreciate or accept was the total unfairness of Griffith Burnett not only returning to Tulpen Crossing, Washington, nearly a year ago, but apparently waking up last month and deciding that stalking her was how he was going to spend his days.

The man was everywhere. Every. Where. He was the aphid swarm in the garden of her life. He was kudzu, he was rain at an outdoor wedding, someone spoiling the end of a movie just as you were getting to the good part, all rolled into one.

"You're putting a lot of energy into the man," Helen Sperry pointed out in a let's-humor-the-crazy-girl tone.

"This isn't about me," Kelly told her. "I'm not the one who's always there. I'm not the one lurking."

"If you keep seeing him wherever you go, a case could be made that *you're* stalking *him.*"

"I'm not going to dignify that with a response," Kelly muttered as she pulled in front of the craft mall and parked her truck.

"Did you know Griffith back in high school?" Helen asked. "You're what? Three years younger? You couldn't have had the same friends."

"We didn't. I was a sophomore when he was a senior," Kelly admitted. "We didn't have any classes together."

But not having the same classes in no way meant she hadn't known who he was. Everyone had known Griffith Burnett. He'd been one of those godlike figures blessed with good looks, a brain and athletic talent. She'd been the slightly weird girl he'd never noticed...until he'd broken her delicate, young girl's heart.

"I'm sure him being everywhere you are is just one of those things," Helen said. "I'm sorry to use logic, but we live in a tiny, little town. You and I cross paths with each other all the time. I see you like five hundred times a day."

Kelly smiled. "But we're friends and I *like* seeing you."

"Back at you." Helen looked at her. "You okay or is there something going on I don't know about?"

"Nothing but Griffith," Kelly told her. "I'm sure you're right. I'm sure it's just a coincidence that I can't take two steps without seeing him." Words that sounded great but that she didn't believe for a second.

If she were anyone else, or if he weren't who he was, she might think he was interested in her...in a boy-girl kind of way. He always spoke to her when he saw her, and smiled. His gaze seemed to linger. But there was no way he wanted anything like that from her. Kelly had proof.

Thirteen years and some odd months ago, she'd turned a corner and had run into Griffith. She'd been on her way to AP English and he'd been...well, she had no idea what he'd been doing. For less than a second, as her books had gone flying, she and Griffith had been plastered together from chest to thigh. She'd never been so close to a boy before. Never been so aware...so *everything*.

Then he'd stepped back. He'd helped her pick up her books, winked when she'd stuttered an apology, then had lightly, and oh so gently, squeezed her hand before she'd darted off to the safety of her class.

In those magic seconds, when his fingers had touched hers and their eyes had locked together, she'd fallen totally and completely in love with Griffith.

It had been the kind of true love born only of a pure and inexperienced heart. She'd never even been kissed. From that moment on, she dreamed only of Griffith.

Just a week later, she'd walked by him standing with his friends. One of the guys had called out something about her being "doable." A gross and disgusting comment that had made her cringe, but that had been nothing compared to Griffith's casually uttered, "I couldn't be less interested."

She'd been devastated and had immediately turned and run. She'd been so upset and hurt that she'd needed somewhere to put all that emotion. That evening she'd had a fight with her mother, the kind where things best left unsaid were spoken and lives altered forever. Kelly knew in her head that what had happened with Griffith had nothing to do with her mother walking out on their family less than twelve hours later, but for her, the two incidents were forever linked.

She shook off the memories and grabbed her copy of *Eat, Pray, Love*. Their book club was discussing it tonight—for the third time—and she vowed that from this second on, she wouldn't think about Griffith ever again. At least not for the next three hours.

She followed Helen out of the truck and into Petal Pushers—the name du jour for the local craft mall the town hoped would be a tourist draw. There were booths where people could sell everything from handmade crafts to antiques to food. At the far end of the huge space was a big stage and reception area, along with a few community meeting rooms. All that was missing were the tourists. Vacationers loved to come to Tulpen Crossing for the tulip festival every spring, but beyond that, not so much.

Kelly wanted to say that wasn't her problem, but as a member of the tourism development committee, she did have a vested interest in getting people back to their small slice of heaven.

It was early on Tuesday night and Petal Pushers was closed. The long corridor to the meeting rooms was dimly lit and their footsteps echoed on the worn linoleum—Kelly's more than Helen's, actually. Probably because while Helen wore cute flats, Kelly hadn't bothered to change out of her work boots. Or her jeans. Or her slightly stained T-shirt.

One day, she promised herself. One day, she would care about clothes and buy a push-up bra and be, if not girlie, then at least vaguely feminine. She should let Helen inspire her.

Her friend was tall, with inky black hair that fell past her shoulders, and startlingly blue eyes. She had plenty of curves and always managed to look sexy, no matter what she wore. Helen worried about carrying a few extra pounds, but Kelly didn't see that at all. Helen was lush while Kelly was…boring. She had brown hair she wore in a ponytail. Brown eyes. No curves, no noticeable features at all. She was plain.

She supposed she could try to be more Helen-like but who had the time? And even if every few months she swore she was going to do something about her appearance—like wear mascara—she quickly got distracted and forgot. Until the next time.

So here she was, clumping along in boots that might or might not have mud on them. At least book club would be fun. There was always good conversation and wine.

"Did you read it again?" Helen asked, holding up her copy of *Eat, Pray, Love.* "I didn't. I figured twice was enough."

"I read it." Not reading it hadn't been an option, Kelly thought. She always read the book and took notes. She was such a rule follower. How depressing. She needed to break out of her rut or something. Maybe it was time for her to renew the mascara vow.

They walked into the community room and greeted their friends. Paula, a pretty mother of three, had already opened the bottles of wine she'd brought. Someone else had set out plates of cookies and cupcakes. Kelly scanned the sign-up sheet and confirmed that she was in charge of wine next month, and that they would be reading a memoir of Eleanor Roosevelt.

She reached for a cupcake just as a few more members arrived. Sally, a fiftysomething avid quilter who had the biggest booth at Petal Pushers, announced, "Ladies, we have a new member. And guess what? He's a man!"

Kelly looked at the cupcake she held. She wanted to take a big bite—or possibly run out the back exit. Or poke Helen in the arm while saying "I told you so" in a loud, taunting voice. Because she knew without turning around who she would find standing there. Like the Terminator, Griffith was back, and there was nothing she could do about it.

Griffith Burnett was used to being the center of attention—whether it was at a symposium on how micro housing could transform the poorest regions of Africa as well as answer the needs of the homeless in the urban centers of Europe and the United States, or at a black-tie fund-raiser for a children's charity where he was the featured speaker. He was comfortable in front of a crowd, or so he'd thought. He found himself slightly less at ease in a room filled with nearly a dozen women, all staring at him with varying degrees of interest.

No, he thought as he scanned the faces. Nearly a dozen, less one. Kelly wasn't looking at him at all.

"Everyone, this is Griffith Burnett. You should know him. He owns that tiny house company you've all seen off the highway. He grew up here. His folks are Mark and Melinda. They moved to New Mexico six months ago. Griffith here wants to join our book club."

He waited for the inevitable, "Why?" but the women only smiled and nodded. Except for Kelly, who kept her attention firmly on the cupcake she held.

"Let me introduce you to everyone," Sally said. They'd walked in together and somehow she'd assigned herself as his hostess for the evening.

She went around the room, spouting names faster than he could remember them, starting with a mother of three and ending with the reason he was here in the first place.

"This is Kelly Murphy." Sally frowned. "Didn't you two go to high school together? Or is she closer to your brother's age? I can't keep you kids straight. And what about Helen Sperry? You're the same age, aren't you?"

"I'm a year older," Helen said, offering her hand. "Hi. I think we had a social studies class together."

"I'm sure we did." He waited until Kelly had no choice but to look at him. "Hello, Kelly."

"Griffith." The word was clipped, her tone less than friendly, matching the wary expression in her big, brown eyes.

She looked good. He supposed there were some men who would be put off by the absence of frills, but he liked that about her. The sharp edges, the lack of guile. What you saw and all that. She was smart, she was determined and she wasn't going to make it easy. He'd always been the kind of guy who liked a challenge, so he was looking forward to the latter.

"Why are you here?" she asked.

Beside him, Sally stiffened. "Kelly, honey, what's wrong? Griffith wants to join our book club."

"And read *Eat, Pray, Love*? I find that hard to believe."

"Is it my reading skills you doubt or my interest in the subject matter?"

The corner of her mouth twitched. He would guess annoyance rather than humor, not that he would mind seeing her smile.

"A woman's journey to emotional and spiritual fulfillment hardly seems like something you'd enjoy," she murmured.

"Do you think you know me well enough to decide that?"

Now everyone was watching and listening. He stepped closer to Kelly. Close enough that she had to tilt her head slightly to hold his gaze.

"I find everything about a woman's journey interesting. I enjoy discovering how she's different than I expected. I like the anticipation."

Someone's breath caught. Not Kelly's. Her gaze narrowed. "Next month we're reading an autobiography of Eleanor Roosevelt."

"Lucky me. I've always been an admirer."

Liar.

She didn't say the word out loud, but she sure as hell thought it. Griffith held in a grin as he watched her struggle with her temper. He suspected she was imagining smashing the cupcake she held into his face, turning on her heel and walking away. Only she wouldn't. She would restrain herself. He couldn't wait to test that restraint in every way possible.

But not tonight. Tonight was simply the next step in his plan. He wanted someone in his life—he'd decided that serial monogamy was his road to happiness and he hoped he and Kelly could come to a mutual understanding.

"Did you think the author spent too much time deconstructing her divorce in the book?" she asked. "Should we have gotten right to the journey?"

He'd thought there might be a test, but he'd hoped it would be harder. "She doesn't deconstruct her divorce. In fact there isn't much detail as to what went wrong. She does make it clear the divorce was painful."

Something he understood personally. Screwing up was never pleasant but to mess up something that fundamental sucked in a big way.

"And the part in Thailand?" Kelly asked.

"You mean Indonesia?"

She handled defeat with grace. Instead of saying something

sarcastic, she flashed him an unexpected smile—one that hit him in the gut with the subtlety of a 2x4—and offered him her cupcake.

"Welcome to our book club."

"Thank you."

"Now if you'll excuse me, I need a glass of wine."

"He was nice," Helen said as Kelly drove the handful of miles between Petal Pushers and their respective houses.

No need to ask who "he" was, Kelly thought. She'd just endured the longest three hours of her life in the same room as Griffith. She'd listened to him analyze the book, make jokes and generally charm every woman within earshot. Except her, of course. But then she was the only one to have survived being rejected by Griffith, so she was special.

"Incredibly nice," Kelly murmured.

"Now you're being sarcastic."

"I can't help it. Doesn't it strike you as the least bit odd that he wanted to join our book club? There's that mystery one in La Conner. Why doesn't he join that one?"

"He's local, like us."

Griffith was many things but "like us" was not one of them. "Can you at least admit it's slightly odd that he showed up?"

Helen considered the question. "It's unexpected, yes. But it's not a bad thing."

"Not for you."

Helen angled toward Kelly. "Come on. Griffith is gorgeous. You have to admit looking at him isn't a hardship."

No, it wasn't, not that she wanted to admit anything of the kind. He'd always been one of those guys who captured the attention of every female in a three-block radius. Of course he was tall, with sandy-brown hair and brown eyes. But it wasn't the individual features so much as how they came together into one incredibly appealing man.

"I still wish he'd gone to the mystery book club. There are guys there. He'd feel more comfortable."

"Maybe you should tell him."

Kelly heard the amusement in her friend's voice and groaned. "You're enjoying this, aren't you?"

"A little." Helen shook her head. "Come on. Is it really so bad to have a guy like Griffith interested in you? It's been six months since you and Sven broke up. It's time to move on. Griffith is a great moving-on kind of guy."

"So speaks the woman who hasn't dated since her divorce six years ago."

"I'm very comfortable in my 'do as I say, not as I do' role in our relationship. Come on. You can't tell me you're not the tiniest bit flattered. You have to be."

"Why? Because he's staring at me? I don't know what he wants, but I doubt it's what you're thinking."

"Why would you say that?"

Kelly turned at the corner and headed toward her friend's house. "I'm very clear on my place in the universe."

"Meaning?"

Kelly waved her hand in front of her midsection. "I'm average at best. Not beautiful, not pretty, not ugly. Just regular."

If Griffith was looking for a fancier version of a Murphy, he should check out Olivia. Kelly hadn't seen her sister in forever, but she would literally bet the farm on the fact that Olivia was still gorgeous and glamorous and wearing a designer something. Not cargo pants bought on sale from an online farm equipment supply outlet.

"It's a family thing," she continued. "I take after my dad. We're sensible people. Hardworking. Ordinary. My mom and sister are the…"

"Exotic tulips in the garden that is your life?" Helen asked drily.

"Not the analogy I was going to use, but sure. It works."

"You're selling yourself short," Helen told her. "Worse, you're saying bad stuff about my friend and I don't appreciate that. You're not ordinary. You're lovely and funny and hardworking."

"It's amazing you don't want to have sex with me right now."

"Stop. It." Helen glared. "I mean it. Kelly, you're great. Griffith finally got his head out of his ass long enough to notice you."

"I thought you liked him."

"I do. I used the phrase for effect. What did you think?"

"Well done."

"Thank you." She shifted to face Kelly. "I'm serious. You're obviously over Sven. Take a chance on a great guy."

"We don't know he's great."

"I've heard rumors."

Kelly had, too. The problem wasn't Griffith. Not totally. Nor was it her still recovering from the end of a long-term relationship. She was embarrassed to admit that while Sven had surprised her when he'd said it was over, she really hadn't missed him. Or felt all that upset. Which was sad because after five years, shouldn't she have been at least a little crushed? What did it mean that she'd gone on without much more than a blink? Hadn't she been emotionally engaged at all? And if she hadn't been, what was the reason? Had he not been *the one* or was she somehow stunted?

Not a question she really wanted answered. Although Sven had pointed out that she'd never been in love with him. Which was true, if disconcerting to find out from a man.

"What's the worst that could happen?" Helen asked.

"If I slept with Griffith?" The list was really long—where was she supposed to start?

"Whoa, I was going to say if you *talked* to Griffith. I find it fascinating you jumped right into bed with him, so to speak."

"Please don't."

"Too late now. You've subconsciously told me everything."

"I haven't, and it wasn't subconscious anything. I spoke out loud." Kelly pulled into Helen's driveway.

"You're trying to distract me with facts," her friend said with a grin. "But I see you for what you are."

"I'm afraid to ask what that is."

"As you should be." Helen lowered her voice. "You're a sex-starved single woman who desperately wants to get involved with Griffith but you're afraid."

Words spoken in jest that were just a little too close to the truth. Not the sex-starved part. Sex was fine, if not the amazing, earth-shattering experience the media claimed, but still. She did find Griffith intriguing and attractive and...

"He's annoying."

"Liar, liar."

"He *can* be annoying."

"Better."

"I want him to leave me alone."

Helen sighed. "At the risk of repeating myself, liar, liar."

Kelly growled in the back of her throat. "*You're* annoying."

"That is absolutely true. Just say it. You're interested. Intrigued, even. He's hot and you have no idea why he's suddenly interested, but you don't hate it."

"What I hate is being that transparent."

Helen hugged her, then opened the passenger door of the truck and slid to the ground. "Only to me, my sweet. Only to me. My advice is simple. Say yes."

"He hasn't asked me anything. In fact all he's done is stare at me and be everywhere I am."

"Then go find out why. Oh, and start keeping condoms in your purse. Just in case."

With that, Helen waved and walked into her house. Kelly waited until the living room lights came on before backing out of the driveway and heading home.

Kelly had no plans to take the condom advice, but confronting Griffith might not be such a bad idea. Maybe she could find out what he was up to. Because as nice as it would be to think he was interested in her, she knew for a fact her luck wasn't that good. Besides, he was Griffith Burnett. Even if she got him, she would have no idea what to do with him. Sad, but true.

Most people thought the main difference between a tiny house on wheels and one that wasn't had to do with size. But Griffith Burnett knew differently. It was about weight. If you were going to be pulling your to-hundred-square-foot tiny home all over the place, you didn't want to be weighed down. No granite countertops, no thick wooden flooring, no wrought iron railings on the upper deck. But if your two-hundred-square-foot home was going to stay in one place, then he knew a great hard-surfaces vendor who could hook you right up. And because your tiny home was…well…small, you could get first-class material at remnant prices.

He stood in the center of what could, in a pinch, be called his manufacturing facility. In truth it was two warehouses connected by a covered walkway, but not only was it a start—it was his.

The bigger of the buildings held six houses in progress. Two were headed for San Francisco, one to Portland, Oregon. Two were for a family compound in eastern Washington—or as a frustrated middle-aged woman had put it, "My sons are never leaving home. I just can't stand stepping over them every day. I'll accept that they're staying put if I don't have to deal with them and their mess."

The last was going to be an elegant guest cottage at a quirky Texas B and B.

That side of GB Micro Housing made the money. Whether

you wanted to spend thirty thousand or a hundred and thirty thousand, Griffith could build you a tiny home pretty much to your specifications. Single level, two levels, lofts, upper-story decks, high-end finishes or everything recovered from tear-downs. You name it. It was all about weight and how much money you were willing to spend.

He had orders for the next couple of years and the waiting list continued to grow. He'd hired two more full-time employees, bringing his total to ten.

He supposed a money person would tell him to use his other warehouse to fulfill the paying orders, but he wasn't even tempted. That second, smaller space, well, that was where the real work happened.

In the smaller warehouse, he experimented, he played, he dreamed. He would never make a cent from that work, but it also meant at the end of the day, he could know he'd done what was right. That made sleeping at night a whole lot easier.

He went into the break room to pour himself some coffee only to find his brother sitting at one of the tables. Ryan leaned back in a chair, his feet up on a second one. His eyes were closed as he listened to something through earbuds.

Griffith resisted the urge to kick the chair out from under his brother's feet. Maybe that would get his attention, although he had his doubts.

Ryan was currently unmotivated. The only reason his brother had come back to Tulpen Crossing was because he'd had no-where else to go. When Ryan had blown out his shoulder, the Red Sox had cut him loose. After two years of paying more attention to baseball than college and nearly four years in the minor league, Ryan wasn't exactly skilled labor. He'd needed a job and Griffith had offered him one—on the line, building tiny houses. It was a decision Griffith was beginning to regret.

He nudged his brother's arm. Ryan opened his eyes and smiled.

"Hey, bro."

"Hey, yourself. Break ended a half hour ago."

"What?"

Ryan blinked and looked around, as if genuinely surprised to find everyone else was back at work. "Huh. Sorry. I was listening to the game. I guess I got distracted."

Griffith could guess how the conversation had gone. One of the guys would have said break was over. Ryan would have said he would be there in a minute. Had the twenty-five-year-old been anyone else, the shop supervisor would have been notified. But Ryan was the boss's brother. No one was sure if the rules applied—not even Griffith.

He briefly thought of his parents who had always insisted he look after his baby brother—no matter how inconvenient it might be—sucked in a breath and told himself he would deal with Ryan another time.

"Get back to work," he said. "Now."

"Sure thing."

His brother got to his feet and ambled toward the door.

Griffith watched him go and told himself any annoyance was his own fault. Ryan had never hustled—unless he was on the baseball field. There he could be little more than a blur of activity, but in life, not so much with the speed.

"I love it!"

Olivia Murphy basked in the delighted tone and happy words of her client. Jenny was a sixtysomething recent widow who needed to sell the family home to fund the rest of her life. Getting top dollar was a priority.

The ranch-style three-bedroom, two-bath wasn't anything fancy. In fact hundreds of them existed in the older neighborhoods of Phoenix. Adding to that challenge were the lack of updates and the time of year. June wasn't exactly peak selling season in the desert—not when midday temperatures routinely topped a hundred degrees. No one wanted to be looking at homes if they didn't have to be. Winter was far more active in the real estate market.

But Jenny couldn't wait until winter, which meant making a splash on minimal budget. Olivia had spent hours on Pinterest, had haunted thrift stores and had begged and borrowed everything else. For less than five hundred dollars, she'd transformed the aging, very ordinary rambler into a cute, welcoming Cape Cod retreat.

"I just can't believe it's the same house," Jenny crowed. "Look at what you've done."

"I know," Marilee Quedenfeld said, her tone a combination of modest pride and look-at-me. "It's wonderful, isn't it? The second you walk in, you feel the cool, ocean breeze."

Olivia kept her smile firmly in place. There was no point in saying anything. Working for Marilee these past four years had taught her that. If there was praise to be had, it went to Marilee. If there was a complaint, well, that went anywhere else.

"You're a genius," Jenny told Marilee. "Everyone said you were the best, but I didn't expect this. Thank you!"

"You're welcome." Marilee put her arm around her client. "I know what you've been through and this is the least I can do."

Words Jenny would take at face value, Olivia thought, while Marilee was probably thinking something along the lines of *Dear God, why doesn't this woman take better care of herself?*

The contrast in their appearances was startling. Jenny was short, frumpy and had obviously surrendered to the aging process. Marilee, by contrast, wore an Akris punto polka-dot A-line dress and Valentino pumps. Her hair was a sleek, shoulder-length, dark blond bob, her makeup emphasized large eyes and smooth skin. She was close to fifty, looked thirty-five and occasionally tried to pass herself off as even younger.

"Let's go look at the rest of the house," Marilee suggested. "You're going to love everything I've done."

"I know I will."

Olivia stayed in the kitchen. It was safer there—she wouldn't be tempted to blurt out a fact only the designer would know. While the momentary satisfaction would be great, she would pay for it later.

Olivia had joined Marilee's successful real estate business right out of college. She'd started as a secretary and had worked her way up to designing all the company's marketing. As that wasn't a full-time gig, she'd tried her hand at selling homes, but had discovered she didn't have the right kind of personality. Marilee didn't, either, but she was better at faking it.

In an effort to keep from having to fill her day with secretarial duties, Olivia had started taking design classes. She quickly discovered she had a knack for more than putting together a great outfit on a budget and transforming a plain house into something wildly appealing. So far she was offering her staging services for only the cost of supplies, but she was toying with the idea of starting a real business and had the savings account to prove it. This house had been her biggest project by far. She might not be getting the credit, but she had plenty of before and after pictures for her portfolio.

Jenny and Marilee left the house to return to the office. Olivia stayed behind to lock up and look around one more time.

"Your assistant is such a pretty girl," she heard Jenny say as they walked to Marilee's Mercedes. "We should all be so young."

Olivia winced. Marilee would not appreciate being lumped into Jenny's over-sixty age group, nor would she like Olivia being complimented. But that was for later.

She checked that the rear slider was locked, pausing to admire the Adirondack chairs she'd found at a garage sale for all of ten bucks each. She'd set a thrift store tray on top of a ratty plastic end table. A few shells in an old mason jar with a little sand transformed the tired poolside into something beachy.

Inside she'd covered Jenny's lumpy sofa with an off-white

slipcover, then added throw pillows in gray, blue and pale aqua. A textured throw rug in beige and cream covered most of the 1980s floor tile.

In the master she'd recovered the headboard with striped gray-and-white sheets. She'd splurged on a new comforter, then had rearranged the furniture. A few accessories—starfish, a clock in the shape of a lighthouse and piece of driftwood—continued the theme.

The master bath was pure illusion. Rolled towels and pretty jars of bath salts distracted from the outdated tile. A quick coat of white paint added a sense of freshness. She'd found a darling silk flower arrangement and put it into a child's sand bucket. The touch of whimsy drew the eye away from the ugly tub.

Her phone chirped. She glanced down and saw she had a text from Logan. They'd met over the weekend and he'd been trying to get together with her ever since. Honestly, Olivia just wasn't in the mood. Yes, he was Kathy's boyfriend and stealing him would be good fun, but for some reason the idea didn't appeal.

She scrolled through other texts and paused when she saw the one that had really caught her attention.

You should come home for a visit. We could hang out. Miss you, babe.

Every woman had her weakness. For some it was brownies, for others it was shoes, for her it was Ryan Burnett.

The man made her crazy. She knew the reason—they'd never had their chance. She'd been cruelly ripped from his arms before they could become the most popular couple in high school. Later, at college, he'd been more interested in baseball than her, something he still had to pay for.

She wanted to forget him and couldn't. He was the promise of what could have been, of what *she* could have been. When she was with him, she finally belonged. She needed that—needed him. Ever since he'd moved back to Tulpen Crossing three months ago, he'd been asking her to come up for a visit. Which was ridiculous. That was the last place she wanted to be. Except for Ryan…

She dropped her phone back in her bag and walked outside. After making sure the key was in the lockbox, she checked the front door, then drove back to the office. She arrived in time to hear Jenny raving about the marketing campaign Olivia had prepared.

"I don't know how you do it all," Jenny gushed. "Marilee, you're amazing." She turned to Olivia. "You must learn so much working for her."

"I do. Every day." She turned to Marilee. "The house is ready to go live. Shall I take care of that for you?"

"Please."

Olivia retreated to her small, windowless office. She went online and uploaded the listing she'd already prepared. Then she checked on their other listings, which didn't take very long. The number of houses they were selling would pick up again in September, but until then, they were in the real estate dead zone.

An hour later, Marilee buzzed for Olivia to come to her office. Olivia smoothed the front of her sleeveless dress before walking down the carpeted hallway. Marilee sat on the leather sofa in her large, corner office.

"That woman is so tiresome. I thought she would never leave. At least she liked the staging, although I have to say I was a little disappointed." She wrinkled her nose as best she could, considering the Botox. "Really, Olivia? Starfish and a sand bucket? Is that the best you could do?"

Olivia felt herself flush. "I had a budget of five hundred dollars. There weren't a lot of choices. I think the unique style will appeal to buyers."

"We'll see. Jenny was happy at least, although that's not saying much." She leaned back and closed her eyes. "How hot is it out there? Over a hundred?"

"It's close."

"I can't wait to get out of here. Roger's place in Colorado is going to be heavenly. The views are amazing. You should go away for a few weeks, Olivia. There isn't much business over the summer and it would save me having to cut your hours."

The not-so-subtle hint wasn't new. Marilee was forever threatening her employees with reduced wages or being fired. The fact that she owned the most successful real estate firm in the city gave her power and she knew it.

When she'd first joined the firm, Olivia had been immune to Marilee's pettiness and whims, but lately that had changed. Maybe it was inevitable with the passage of time. Maybe it was the fact that Olivia had caught Roger staring at her legs. No matter how much Marilee did to slow the clichéd ravages of time, the truth was she would be fifty in a couple of years. Whatever the reason, Olivia wasn't Marilee's favorite anymore. She was just like everyone else.

A familiar ache filled her chest. It had started when she was twelve years old and her mother had simply left. Olivia had been devastated. She and her mother had been so close. They were the two who got each other. Kelly had always been Dad's favorite and Olivia had been Mom's, one each, the way it was supposed to be. But when Mom had left, Olivia had been alone.

Ever since then, nothing had been right. There had been moments when she'd felt safe, as if she belonged, but only moments. Except with Ryan. When she was with him, she always knew that she was going to be okay. With him, she could believe in herself, in the future.

She thought of the messages on her phone. The meaningless parties she could waste time on, the women she hung out with. They, like Marilee, were more frenemy than friend. What did she have keeping her here? Kathy's boyfriend? A career that was going nowhere? She had no idea what she wanted, which meant she was never going to achieve anything. She needed time to think and maybe, just maybe, the chance to make her life perfect again.

She couldn't go back to being that twelve-year-old girl again, but she could take Ryan up on his invitation. Go back to Tulpen Crossing. That would give Marilee something to chew on and wouldn't that be fun? Plus she could finally get her man. Because with Ryan, everything was better.

"You know what, Mom? You're right. I *should* take some time off."

Marilee's expression tightened. "I've told you not to call me that. Especially at the office. I'm nowhere near old enough to have a daughter your age."

"Good thing Kelly doesn't work for you. She's even older than me."

"I have to say I don't care for your attitude."

"Sorry. I should probably get out of here, then. I need to pack and close up my apartment."

"You're actually going somewhere?"

"Uh-huh. Home. I'm going home for the summer."

Marilee sat up. "Home? To that backwater town? Are you crazy?"

"No. I think it will be fun. I haven't visited in forever. I'll let you know when I'm heading out. And I'll make sure Kathy has all the information she needs for the listings we have."

"You can't simply leave me. You have responsibilities."

"You'll be fine, Mom. You always are." Olivia smiled. "At least this way you don't have to cut my hours."

Reporting for work at 5:00 a.m. was not for sissies but there were a few things that could mitigate the horror. One was the smell of freshly baked cinnamon rolls hot out of the oven. The other was Billy Joel blasting at a volume just short of hearing loss.

Helen Sperry walked in the front door of The Parrot Café at two minutes to five. Being on time wasn't difficult what with her basically living around the corner. She paused to inhale the glorious, gooey scent, then smiled when she heard the opening line to "Uptown Girl."

"I'll bet Billy can afford to buy all the pearls he wants now," she called as she flipped on lights. "What do you think, Delja?"

There was no answer from the kitchen, but that was okay. Delja America wasn't much of a talker. Instead she expressed herself through her amazing cooking and baking.

Helen hummed along with the song as she walked into the kitchen. "Morning. Everything okay?"

Delja had been with the diner since she graduated from high school nearly forty years before. She was barely five feet tall, but had the build of a linebacker. The muscles of one, too. She could flip a fifty-pound bag of flour onto the counter like it was a small baggie filled with grapes. And the things the woman could do with eggs bordered on miraculous. She was a widow, with one son—the current mayor of Tulpen Crossing—and a daughter who lived in Utah.

Delja looked up at Helen and smiled. Helen crossed the kitchen to receive her morning hug—the one that nearly squeezed the air out of her body. She hung on as tight as she could, trying to return the body crushing with equal force, but suspected Delja was not impressed by her upper body strength.

Delja released her, then held her at arm's length.

"You good?"

The question was asked in a low, gruff voice. It was the same one Delja had asked every single morning for the past eight years—ever since Helen had taken over the diner from her aunt.

"I am. Did you talk to Lidiya? Are you going to stay with her this summer?"

Every year Delja visited her daughter for three weeks. The entire town wept as the supply of cinnamon rolls dried up. Tempers grew short and people counted the days until Delja's return.

"September."

"Okay, then. You'll email me the dates?"

Delja nodded once, then turned back to frosting the rolls.

There was more they could discuss. Their personal lives, what supplies might be running low, whether or not the Mariners were going to have a winning baseball season, but they wouldn't. Delja preferred a single-word response to actual conversation and did most of her communicating via email. If something had to be ordered, she would have already sent a note to their supplier.

As for checking on her work, Helen knew better. Delja started her day at two in the morning. By five there were biscuits in the oven, all the omelet extras had been prepped and oranges squeezed. At The Parrot Café, the back of house ran smoothly— all thanks to Delja.

Helen went to her office and tucked her handbag into the bottom drawer of her desk. She glanced in the small mirror over the sink by the door. Her black hair was pulled back in a French braid, her bangs were trimmed and her makeup was subtle. All as it should be. The fact that she couldn't see below her shoulders meant she didn't have to notice that her last diet had failed as spectacularly as the previous seventeen. Which was not her fault. Really. How could she be expected to eat Paleo while living in a world that contained Delja's cinnamon rolls?

She returned to the front of the store and started the morning prep. There were place settings to be put out and sugar shakers to be filled. Silly, simple tasks that allowed her to collect herself for her day. And maybe, just maybe, give her a second so that the butterflies in her stomach calmed down from their current hip-hop to a more stately waltz.

The Parrot Café (named for parrot tulips, not the bird) had been around nearly as long as the town. Helen's aunt had inherited it from her parents and when she'd married, her husband had joined the team. From what Helen could tell, the two of them had been very happy together. The café was open from 6:00 a.m. until 2:00 p.m., seven days a week. Until Helen had come along, the childless couple had shut down every August and had traveled the world. Then Helen's parents had been killed in a car accident, leaving the only child an orphan. There had been no other family, so Helen had come to Tulpen Crossing.

She supposed her aunt and uncle had tried. As much as her world had been thrown into chaos, theirs had been, as well. They'd done what they could to make her feel welcome, but she'd known the truth. They hadn't wanted children. It had been a choice—yet they were stuck with her.

She'd done her best to not be any trouble, and to learn the business. By the time she was thirteen, she was already waiting tables. The patrons loved her and no one knew that she cried herself to sleep every night for the first three years after her parents had died.

Her parents had been poor but happy—both musicians. That meant there hadn't been any money for, well, anything. The only thing she still had of her parents' was the piano they'd played and their wedding rings. She kept the former in her living room in her small house and had had the latter made into a pendant she wore every day. She hadn't inherited much of their musical gifts, but like them, she did love Billy Joel. He was her connection to the past.

By five thirty Helen had the coffee brewing. The rest of the wait staff showed up at five forty-five and the first customer would walk through the door exactly at six. By seven thirty every booth would be full, as would the counter seats. There was always a lull around ten that lasted until the lunch crowd showed up. By then Delja had clocked out and the culinary students from the school up in Bellingham were hard at work in the kitchen, prepping for lunch.

It was a system that worked. The students got to practice in a real world restaurant, her customers had an opportunity to try new and fun food, along with traditional favorites, and she had a steady supply of labor. Many students signed up for weekend shifts and those who lived local often wanted a job with her for a couple of years to get experience for their résumés before moving on to somewhere a lot more elegant than The Parrot Café.

Helen glanced at the clock, then reached for a mug. She was still pouring coffee when she heard the front door open. Her butterflies started a quickstep and for one brief second, she thought her hands might actually shake. Which was ridiculous. And right on cue, the recorded sound of breaking glass was followed by the opening chords of "You May Be Right."

"I may be crazy," Helen whispered to herself before turning around and smiling as Jeff Murphy walked toward her. "Morning."

"Hi, Helen." Jeff winced slightly. "Does it have to be this loud?"

"Billy is my rock-and-roll boyfriend. A love like that demands volume."

"Uh-huh."

Jeff set paper-wrapped flowers on the counter before pulling out his phone and tapping the screen. It only took him a second to find the Sonos app and lower the volume to the level of background noise.

"One day Billy's going to kick your ass for doing that," she told him.

He grinned. "I'm willing to take the chance."

It was a variation on the conversation they had nearly every day. One she looked forward to with ridiculous anticipation. Billy might be her rock-and-roll boyfriend, but Jeff was, well... Jeff was the reason her heart kept beating.

Stupid, but there it was. The truth. She was wildly, desperately in love with Jeff Murphy.

The man was gorgeous. He looked a little like the actor Jason Bateman, with shaggy hair and big brown eyes. He was tall, fit, funny, kind and he could play guitar like nobody's business. In a word—irresistible.

He was also single, so what was the problem? Why couldn't she simply tell him how she felt? Or ask him out to dinner? Or rip off her clothes and smile winningly? Jeff wasn't a dummy. He would get the message.

Only three things stopped her. One, he was older. Sixteen years, to be exact. While she didn't care, she thought he might. Two, the extra thirty pounds she carried. She was currently subscribing to the when-then philosophy—distant cousin to the if-then concept. *When* she lost weight, *then* she would be brave and throw herself at Jeff.

She acknowledged that pending moment of disaster might be the reason she seemed in no hurry to commit to a weight-loss plan but she wasn't sure.

Reason number three—which was probably the most important and therefore should be the first—Jeff was her best friend's father.

Yup, Jeff was Kelly's dad, which added a whole layer of complicated to the situation. Because should she ever confess the truth to said best friend, there would be a conversation filled with "WTF" and "Are you kidding me?" All of which would be screamed rather than spoken.

Oh, wait. There was a fourth reason Helen hadn't thrown herself at Jeff. He'd never once made a move in her direction. All the more reason to bury her unrequited love/lust in a warm cinnamon roll.

"Let me show you what I brought you today," he said, unrolling the paper. "Havran."

Helen stepped closer to study the beautiful tulips. They were deep purple with a slightly pointed petal. The stems were pale green and smooth.

"They're lovely. Thank you."

She knew better than to offer to pay for them. She'd tried a couple of times, but Jeff had simply shaken his head. "I grow tulips, Helen. I want to do this."

She'd tried reading something into his words but weeks, then months, had passed with nary a change in their relationship. Not by a whisper, look or touch did he ever hint that he thought of her as more than a friend. She'd learned to accept the flowers as a kind gift. The man was a tulip farmer, after all. It wasn't as if he'd bought them for her.

She collected a tray filled with small vases, along with clippers. Together they loaded the vases and put them on each table. When she returned to the counter, he held out a small wrapped package the size and shape of a single stem.

"For you. Don't tell Kelly."

Humor danced in his dark brown eyes. Eyes she would very much like to get lost in. Maybe while he slowly undressed and reached for her as they...

"Helen?"

"What? Oh, thanks. Although I'm not sure I should thank you for stealing from your daughter's private greenhouse."

"She's not going to notice one flower missing."

"You take one every week. At some point she's going to catch on."

He winked. "She hasn't yet."

No, she hadn't. Because Kelly would have mentioned the thefts, had she spotted them.

Yes, it was true—father and daughter worked together on their tulip farm. In addition to growing millions of blooms for florists and grocery stores, Kelly had a small, private greenhouse where she cultivated special flowers. Flowers Jeff occasionally stole and brought to Helen.

Today's offering was red with a yellow base. But what was most remarkable were the long, slender petals that came to a needlelike point. They were delicate and exotic and incredibly beautiful.

"*Tulipa acuminata,*" Jeff said.

Helen didn't know if the words were Latin or just scientific, but hearing him say them made her girl parts sigh in unison.

"It's stunning," she said. "I'll put it in my office and not tell my best friend, which makes me a bad person and it's all your fault."

"I do what I can."

He took a seat at the counter. His regular seat. The one she thought of as Jeff's chair. When she had a moment between customers, it was where she later sat. Sad, but true.

"Want to see a menu?" she asked.

He raised his eyebrows. "Is that your idea of humor?"

Because he'd been coming to the café all his adult life and knew everything they served.

"I'm trying to mix things up," she said.

"I'll have an omelet."

"With bacon, avocado, cheese." A statement, not a question.

"You know what I like."

If only that were true. If only she knew the words or moves to get him to see her as more than a friend. Unless, of course, he wasn't interested. Which he probably wasn't, because he was a decisive man. So she should get over him and move on with her life. Only she didn't want to get over Jeff. She wanted to get into him. Or have him get into her, or...

"I need more coffee," she muttered. And a hormone transplant. Or maybe just some more Billy Joel.

3

Leo Meierotto, the fortysomething site supervisor, stuck his head in Griffith's office. "Boss, you've got company." Leo's normally serious expression changed to one of amusement. "Kelly Murphy is here."

Because Leo was local and in a town the size of Tulpen Crossing, everyone knew everyone.

"Thanks."

"Think she wants to buy a tiny home?"

Considering she lived in a house her family had owned for five generations, "Doubtful."

Maybe she'd shown up to serve him with a restraining order. Or did that have to be delivered by someone official? He wasn't sure. Avoiding interactions that required him to get on the wrong side of law enforcement had always been a goal.

He told himself whatever happened, he would deal, then walked out into the showroom of the larger warehouse. Kelly stood by a cross section of a display tiny home, studying the layout.

He took a second to enjoy looking at her. She was about five-five, fit, with narrow hips and straight shoulders. A farmer by birth and profession, Kelly dressed for her job. Jeans, work boots and a long sleeved T-shirt. It might be early June, but in the Pacific Northwest, that frequently meant showers. Today was gray with an expected high of sixty-five. Not exactly beach weather.

Kelly's wavy hair fell just past her shoulders. She wore it pulled back in a simple ponytail. She didn't wear makeup or bother with a manicure. She was completely no-frills. He supposed that was one of the things he liked about her. There wasn't any artifice. No pretense. With Kelly you wouldn't find out that she was one thing on the surface and something completely different underneath. At least that was what he hoped.

"Hey, Kelly."

She turned. He saw something flash through her eyes. Discomfort? Nerves? Determination? Was she here to tell him to back off? He couldn't blame her. He'd been too enthused about his plan when he should have been more subtle. She was going to tell him to leave her alone.

Not willing to lose without a fight, he decided he needed a distraction and how convenient they were standing right next to one.

"You've never been to my office before," he went on. "Why is that?"

"I don't know. You've been back about a year. I guess I should have been by." She turned toward the tiny homes. "You build these?"

"I do. Have you seen one before?"

"Only on TV."

He grinned. "Gotta love the free advertising." He gestured to the model next to the cross section. "Micro housing is defined as being less than five hundred square feet. They serve different purposes for different people. In sub-Saharan Africa, micro housing provides sturdy, relatively inexpensive shelter that can be tailored to the needs of the community." He pointed to the roof. "For example, we can install solar panels, giving the owners access to electricity. In urban settings, modified homes can be an alternative to expensive apartments. They can also offer shelter to the homeless. For everyone else, they fill a need. You can get a single-story house for an in-law or a guest cottage with a loft. You can take it on the road, even live off the grid, if you want."

She studied him intently as he spoke, as if absorbing every word. "I like living *on* the grid, but that's just me."

"I'm with you on that. Creature comforts are good. Come on. I'll show you where we build them."

He led her around the divider and into the back of the warehouse where the actual construction was done. Nearly half a dozen guys swarmed over the homes. Griffith saw that Ryan was leaning against a workbench, talking rather than working. No surprise there. He ignored the surge of frustration and turned his attention to Kelly.

"Clients can pick from plans we have on hand or create their own. If it's the latter, I work with them to make sure the structure will be sound. A house that's going to stay in one place has different requirements from one that will be towed."

She nodded slowly. "You'd have to make sure it was balanced on the trailer. Plus it can't be too high. Bridges and overpasses would be a problem. Maybe weight, as well."

"Exactly. A lot of people think they want a tiny home but when they actually see what it looks like, they're surprised at the size."

"Or lack of size?" She smiled. "I can't imagine living in five hundred square feet."

"Or less. It takes compromise and creative thinking."

"Plus not a lot of stuff."

They walked back to the show area. She went through a completed tiny house waiting to be picked up.

"I can't believe you fit in a washer-dryer unit," she called from inside.

"Clothes get dirty."

"But still. It's a washer-dryer." She stepped back into the showroom. "It's nice that you have this setup for your clients. They get to see rather than just imagine."

He nodded as he looked around. There were photos of completed projects on the wall, along with the cross section. He had a small selection of samples for roofing, siding and hard surfaces. All the basics.

"What?" she asked.

"It's okay," he admitted. "I want to make it better, but I don't know how to do the finishing touches." He could design the hell out of three hundred square feet, but when it came to things like paint and throw pillows, he was as lost as the average guy in a housewares department.

"I wish I could help, but I can't." She flashed him a smile. "I'm totally hopeless at that kind of thing, too. Now if you want to know the Pantone color of the year, *that* I can do."

"The what?"

"The color of the year. Every year the design world picks colors that are expected to be popular. You know, for clothes and decorating."

"Why would you know that?"

"Um, Griffith, I grow tulips for a living. If I don't get the colors right, nobody wants them at their wedding or on their coffee tables."

"Oh, right. I didn't think of that." He frowned. "Don't you have to order bulbs before you plant them? What if you get the colors wrong?"

"Then I'm screwed and we lose the farm. Which is why I pay attention to things like the Pantone colors of the year. It's not so much that people won't buy yellow tulips regardless of what's popular, it's that I'll lose sales by not having the right colors available when my customers want them. I like being their go-to vendor when they need something."

He'd known she cared about her business, but he hadn't thought of her as competitive. Better and better.

"Do you focus on having the right colors in the field flowers as well as those you grow indoors?"

She studied him for a second, as if surprised by the question.

"They're different," she admitted. "What we have for the annual tulip festival are more focused on popular colors as well as types of tulips. I use the greenhouses for wedding seasons as well as for the more exotics. It's easier to control the process when you don't have to deal with Mother Nature."

"I hear she can be a real bitch."

Kelly laughed. "If there's a spring hailstorm, I won't disagree. Ten minutes of hail can ruin an entire crop."

He winced. "That sucks."

"Tell me about it."

They smiled at each other. He had a feeling she'd forgotten about why she'd come to see him, which was how he wanted things.

He'd known who Kelly was since high school. She'd been a couple of years behind him, but he'd seen her around. She'd been relatively quiet. Pretty, but not in a flashy way. Her freshman year, they'd worked on the yearbook together and he'd gotten to know her. Still, he'd been *that* guy and she'd been younger. He hadn't known if he wanted to make his move or not. Then things had blown up with her mother and he'd hurt Kelly's feelings and, before he could figure out what to say or do, he'd graduated and gone off to college.

To be honest, he hadn't thought about her all that much until he'd moved back to Tulpen Crossing, but now that he was here, he found her on his mind a lot. Her five-year relationship had conveniently ended six months ago. He figured there'd been enough time for her to have moved on. Now all he needed was to get her to buy into the plan. And if the lady said no, well then he would back off.

"Come on," he said, motioning to the door leading to the walkway between the warehouses. "I want to show you something."

Her expression immediately turned wary. "Etchings?" she

muttered, then flushed. "Sorry. I didn't mean to imply…" She cleared her throat and stared at the floor, then back at him. She sucked in a deep breath, then asked brightly, "What did you want to show me?"

"Just the other warehouse."

"Okay."

Her voice was doubtful, but she followed him along the covered walkway, then into the second building.

It was smaller and currently unoccupied. There were piles of material around the perimeter, plans tacked to the walls and empty pallets next to a small forklift.

"Is this for overflow when you get really busy?" she asked as she walked over to a stack of boxed solar panels.

"No. This is why I do the other work." He shoved his hands into his jeans pockets. "Don't get me wrong. I enjoy designing homes for people. They're so excited and enthusiastic. It's just there are other places, other people, who are desperate for shelter. That's the work I do here."

Her brown eyes widened. "What do you mean?"

"I work with several nonprofits. They collect materials and ship them to me. When I have enough, I ask for volunteers and we put together micro housing in kit form. It's then sent to wherever it's needed most." He pointed to the solar panels. "Those are for sub-Saharan Africa. They'll be self-sufficient as far as electricity. I'm working with a guy I know in Oklahoma who's experimenting with different ways to purify water. Right now the units are too big and too expensive, but eventually we'll be able to send them with the houses. These are more basic than what I sell here, but they're still shelter."

He walked over to the designs on the wall. "One of the organizations has me build tiny houses for homeless shelters. Same premise, different materials, depending on which part of the country they're for. A couple of times a year, they send me interns to coordinate everything. We're getting ready for a build next month. I'll be putting the word out for volunteers."

Her mouth wasn't exactly hanging open, but it was close. Good. Griffith didn't do the work for the attention, but he wasn't above using it to impress Kelly. Because when it came to a woman like her, a guy had to be willing to take advantage of whatever the gods offered.

"I'd like that," she told him. "To help. This is a great project. All of it. I had no idea you were doing this." She shifted her gaze from the materials to his face. "It's amazing. Everyone always says they want to make a difference, but so few of us have the opportunity to do so directly. With this, there'll be homes for families when there weren't homes before. That could mean the difference between life and death—literally."

"You get it," he said before he could stop himself.

She smiled. "Doesn't everyone?"

No. Jane hadn't. His ex-wife had gone along with him when he'd moved to Africa to work with his mentor, but she hadn't liked it one bit. She'd made that clear on a daily basis. He supposed he had culpability in the problem. He'd been the one who was supposed to join an international architectural firm and design museums and elegant skyscrapers. Instead he'd fallen hard for micro housing. Jane hadn't approved.

"You'd be surprised how many only want to write a check," he said instead. "Not that I'm knocking the check writers. They provide the funds."

"It takes both sides of the equation. Without your work, the check would be meaningless."

"My thoughts exactly."

She stood a comfortable distance from him. Her posture was relaxed and open. She'd forgotten why she'd come to see him. Which probably meant it was time to remind her.

"What did you want to talk to me about?"

She blinked in surprise, then her whole body changed as she

remembered her mission. "Oh, right." She cleared her throat. "I, ah… Well, the thing is…"

He waited patiently. "Yes?"

"You are, um, around a lot. Around me."

Around was better than stalking. A lot better. He gave her his best smile again, hoping it would help.

"You're not imagining things," he said quietly. "I've been trying to get to know you without being too obvious. I guess I suck at the spy thing, huh?"

She relaxed. "Kind of."

"Sorry if I've made you uncomfortable. I didn't mean to." Now it was his turn to be nervous. Kelly didn't play games so he wasn't going to, either. He was going to put it out there.

"When I moved back, I noticed you right away. You were with Sven, so I figured I had to let it go. Then you two broke up. It's been six months, so I'm hoping you're over him."

Her eyes widened. "Okay." The word was drawn out to three syllables.

"So here's the thing. I want us to get to know each other. I think we could have fun together. If I'm right, I'd like us to take things to the next level." He looked into her eyes. "I'm a decent guy. I believe in serial monogamy. I'm not looking for love or marriage or happily ever after. But I am looking for a long-term girlfriend. I'm hoping you feel the same way and we can work something out."

Her mouth dropped open. She closed it before taking a step back. "Friends with benefits?"

"Something like that, although I was thinking more lovers who are friends."

"You want to have sex with me?"

He grinned. "Kelly, pretty much every guy who sees you wants to have sex with you, but to be clear, yes. I would like that very much."

"I don't understand." She held up her hand. "I take that back. I understand what you said. It's just... Wow."

Wow was better than *drop dead* or *hell, no* so he would take it. "You probably want some time to think about it."

"Yeah. That would be great." She looked more than a little shell-shocked. "You read *Eat, Pray, Love* to get me into bed?"

"No. I read it because your book club was reading it and I thought it would be something we could talk about. I don't just want to sleep with you, Kelly. I meant what I said. I'm looking for a relationship."

"But not love or marriage."

"Right."

"You're very up front and honest."

"That's the goal. You'll think about what I said?"

"I would imagine it's going to be hard to think about anything else."

"No means no. If you decide to break my heart, I won't bother you again." Not that he wanted her to say no, but nothing about his invitation was supposed to scare her.

She nodded slowly, as if stunned.

"Why don't I walk you to your truck?"

She nodded again and began walking. He fell into step with her. "Thanks for coming by."

"Uh-huh."

They went outside. Kelly glanced around as if she wasn't sure where she was. He pointed to her truck.

"Over there."

She glared at him. "You're enjoying this, aren't you?"

"Just a little. Wouldn't you if you were me?"

"Maybe." Her brown eyes turned wary. "This isn't a joke, is it?"

The softly worded question cut him more deeply than he would have expected.

"Kelly, no." He moved close and took her hand in his. "I'm

not kidding. I meant what I said. About wanting to get to know you, about us having potential together, about no meaning no. All of it. I swear. Please believe me. I have no reason to want to hurt you."

"Okay. Thanks."

She got in her truck and backed out of the parking lot. It was only after she'd turned onto the highway that he remembered what had happened in high school. How he'd dissed her in front of all his friends. He'd done it for the best possible reason but at the end of the day she'd been humiliated and it was all his fault.

Well, hell. No wonder she didn't want to trust him now.

It was rare for anything to keep Kelly from a good night's sleep, but her conversation with Griffith had done that and more. The man had made it clear he wanted to sleep with her. In a way more troubling, he wanted her to be his girlfriend.

Who talked like that? She'd never had a guy come up and baldly state his intentions. Not that she had huge experience with men. She wasn't exactly a guy magnet. She'd had the requisite college boyfriend where she'd lost her virginity and had doodled *Mrs. Elijah Mellon* in her notes, but by her senior year, she'd realized she was more excited about returning to the farm than getting married.

A couple of years after graduation, she and Sven had started seeing each other. Their relationship had started slowly. They'd been friends for nearly a year before they'd taken things "to the next level." After becoming lovers, they'd settled into a comfortable, albeit not very exciting, relationship. She'd never pushed for more, nor had he. Still, she'd been surprised when he'd ended things six months ago. Not heartbroken but surprised. Which was too bad because on paper, she and Sven were well suited. She grew tulips, he grew plants for nurseries up and down the West Coast.

So that was her romantic past—Elijah and Sven. Did she want

Griffith as her third? And what did it say about her that Griffith thought she would be okay as only a girlfriend with no promise of more? Which she was, but why did he know that?

She finished making her bed, then walked back into the Jack and Jill bathroom she'd shared with her sister growing up. After brushing her wavy hair into submission, she pulled it back in her usual ponytail, then studied herself in the mirror.

Why her? She wasn't pretty or glamorous. Now if she were her sister, Olivia, she could understand Griffith's interest. Of course if she were Olivia, Griffith would have to get in line because there were always men interested in her younger sister.

Not that Kelly was interested in that kind of attention. She didn't want passion or the drama that came with it. She'd seen what uncontrolled passion did in the form of her mother's destruction of their family. Kelly wanted something different. Not quiet and not sensible, just…safe. She wanted to feel safe. In her mind that was way more important than some fleeting hormone-induced excuse to destroy and abandon.

She left her bedroom and walked down the hallway to the kitchen. The Murphy house was nearly a hundred years old, built when the land was originally homesteaded. All remnants of the classic farmhouse had been remodeled away until what remained was a U-shaped rambler.

The front of the house had a big family room, a large kitchen and formal dining room. To the left was the study her dad used, and beyond that were the master bedroom and an en suite guest room. To the right of the main living quarters was another, shorter hallway, leading to two good-sized bedrooms with the Jack and Jill bathroom at the end of the hall.

Funny how she and her sister had never fought over that shared bathroom, or much of anything else. At least not when they'd been younger. Despite their parents' troubled marriage, the constant fighting and the way each parent had claimed one child as his or her favorite, Kelly and Olivia had been buddies. They'd played together, hung out together and had been close. That had changed. Kelly wasn't sure when exactly, but by the time their mother had left, Olivia was different. Or maybe Marilee's departure had caused the shift—which meant Kelly had even more responsibility for what had happened.

She could tell herself she'd been a kid and it wasn't her fault, but she knew the truth. Her fight with her mother had pushed Marilee into leaving and Kelly was the reason Olivia had been sent away.

"Deep thoughts for a weekday morning," she murmured as she crossed to the coffeepot.

The coffee was already brewed—her father would have started it before he left for the diner. She poured a mug and inhaled the delicious scent before taking her first sip. In a matter of minutes caffeine would flow through her veins and her world would slowly right itself.

She took another swallow before starting her breakfast. While the instant oatmeal heated in the microwave, she made a protein shake with frozen berries. When her cereal was ready, she stirred in a few walnuts and a spoonful of brown sugar and carried everything to the kitchen table. She got her tablet from the shelf by the window and checked her email while she ate.

By the time she'd finished, she'd scanned the digital headlines, browsed two farm equipment ads, and had chuckled at a kitten playing with a laser dot on a Facebook video.

She rinsed her dishes and put them in the dishwasher, then poured a second mug of coffee. She had to figure out what she was going to cook on her days this week. She and her father alternated that particular chore.

They'd come to terms with their unusual living arrangement fairly easily. They each had a wing in the house. He went out for breakfast at Helen's diner five days a week, they had someone in to clean the house, and they traded off cooking the evening meal. Their schedules were posted on a large wall calendar in the oversize pantry, so each would know when the other wasn't going to be around for dinner. Every now and then Kelly thought that maybe she should move out and get her own place, but each time she mentioned it, her father told her he liked having her around. As for her, well, she didn't seem to be in a big hurry to go anywhere.

The back door opened and Jeff Murphy walked in.

"Hey, Kitten."

"Hi, Dad. How was breakfast?"

"Delja cooks a mean omelet. If I thought I was man enough, I would marry her in a second."

Kelly laughed. "I don't think she's your type."

"Probably not, but a guy can dream." He hung his jacket on the hook by the back door and crossed to her for a quick hug. He poured himself coffee, then leaned against the counter.

"We have two more Christmas orders," he said. "If this keeps up, we're going to be shipping half a million tulips in December. Plus you know some idiot's going to call in November and ask if we have any extras."

"I'm ready. We can go as high as six hundred thousand, then we're out."

"I'll be sure to let our distributors know. Also, that fancy yellow one is selling real well in Los Angeles. Connie wants to know if you can make those in any other colors."

"Da-ad. *Those yellow ones?* Is that really what we're reduced to these days?"

"You go ahead and use their fancy names. I'll stick with yellow."

Jeff knew the names better than she did. He'd been growing tulips since he was a teenager. When Kelly had graduated college and joined the farm full-time, they'd talked about how to handle things. Jeff was tired of being responsible for all the growing and Kelly had no interest in dealing with distributors or clients, so they'd split the duties. Like their living arrangements, it was a system that worked for them.

Sometimes she wondered if he'd ever wanted more than life in a small town. He was a relatively young man—not yet fifty—but he hadn't remarried after his divorce. As far as everyone was concerned, he'd never even dated. Every few months he disappeared to Seattle for a long weekend. Kelly assumed he met someone for a brief affair, but that was it.

As for herself, she had no idea what she was going to do about Griffith. Being someone's girlfriend again sounded nice, but shouldn't she want more? Shouldn't she want to fall in love and have babies and live happily ever after?

She supposed the problem was she didn't believe in happily ever after anymore. If she ever had.

4

Jammin' Madame Lefeber—named for the tulip, not a person—took up about a third of what had once been a grocery store, long since defunct. The other two-thirds were a bowling alley, with both businesses sharing the ample parking lot. On the upside, neither business cared if the other made noise. On the downside, despite thick layers of insulation and sound-deadening drywall, the crack of bowling balls hitting the pins could still be heard. It was a low and arrhythmic beat and could distract even the most professional of musicians.

Helen walked into the foyer a couple of minutes early. Pictures of former students covered the walls. Some were classic studio poses while others showed bands playing live at a venue. She smiled when she saw Jeff and herself in the background of many of the band shots.

JML was a music school that focused more on guitar and drums than the more classical instruments. As part of the services, students could put together a band. An instructor would help them learn a handful of songs, then arrange for a showcase onstage at Petal Pushers or somewhere else. To help the fledgling bandmates get their sound together, near professional-level musicians played along.

The work didn't pay much. Helen did it for the fun and to get the chance to play keyboard every now and then. The bands were interesting, although rarely gifted. Still, it was better than playing piano alone in her living room. Adding to the pleasure was the fact that she and Jeff frequently worked as a team. The man played a mean guitar. More than one fourteen-year-old had been left slack-jawed at Jeff's rendition of "Stairway to Heaven."

Thinking about Jeff got her chest to fluttering. She reminded herself of the importance of appearing cool, even if she didn't feel it, despite the fact that her feelings for the man bordered on a rock-star crush.

She knew that he'd played in a rock band in high school, then had quit after he'd gotten married. She wasn't sure when he'd taken up the guitar again. She'd started working with the students at JML years ago—shortly after her divorce. In fact, that was where she'd first noticed Jeff. She'd fallen for him during an off-key Beatles retrospective—specifically "Hard Day's Night."

Before she could dig up more swoon-worthy memories, Jeff appeared in the foyer. Her throat immediately tightened and speech became impossible. What was it about a man in a plaid shirt? Okay—not any man—just this one. Or maybe it was the worn jeans that hugged his narrow hips and long legs. Or the way he held his guitar case with such confidence.

Jeff smiled as he approached. "Heard anything about our latest bandmates?"

"Isaak said they're fifteen-year-old twins who got guitars for their birthday."

Jeff winced. "Why do parents do that?"

"Someone has to be the next generation of rock music."

Isaak, a tall, curly-haired man of mixed heritage, walked into the foyer. "You're here," he said, sounding grateful. "Adults. Thank God."

"How are the new students?"

"You honestly don't want to know. They're arguing about whether to play Atreyu or Pop Evil."

"Are those bands or songs?" Jeff asked.

"Bands," Helen told him. "You really have to pay attention to music from this century."

"I like Coldplay."

"They started in the nineties."

"But they have songs out this century."

"You're hopeless."

"Probably." Jeff turned to Isaak. "Give them the approved music list."

"That's less of a problem than them having trouble grasping what a chord is. Can you give me a few minutes?"

Jeff looked at Helen who nodded.

"We'll wait," Jeff told him.

The music director retreated to one of the practice rooms. Jeff and Helen walked to the break room in the back. Jeff pulled several dollar bills out of his pocket and walked to the soda machine.

"Diet Coke?" he asked.

"Thanks."

He got them each a can, then joined her at the round table by the window. One wall thumped from uneven drumming while another vibrated with an overly enthusiastic bass guitar.

"We should have brought earplugs," he told her.

"You always say that. The students get better."

"Not today."

The table was small, forcing them to sit close enough for their knees to bump. With every casual contact, Helen felt a jolt of awareness zip up her leg. Talk about stupid.

"I can't believe you mocked Coldplay," he said.

"I didn't. I simply pointed out you're not a fan of contemporary music."

"No one's better than the Rolling Stones."

"Billy Joel is better."

He looked at her over the can. "You have a thing for him so you can't be impartial."

"My thing for Billy is nothing when compared to your slavish devotion to that British band."

"Mine doesn't have a sexual component. That makes it more honest."

"Because sex isn't honest?" she asked with a laugh.

"You know what I mean. I'm not blinded by lust."

"It's not lust." Of that she was sure. Her love for Billy Joel was different than her feelings for Jeff. Now if he really wanted to talk lust, she was all in.

"Next time he's in Seattle, I should take you to a concert," he said. "Unless you're going to throw yourself at the stage. I'm not sure how I'd feel about that."

There was so much unexpected information in that brief statement, she didn't know what to say. Was Jeff asking her out? No, it was a friendly invitation, but still. But there was something… Or was that just wishful thinking on her part?

She clutched her can of soda for courage and decided to go with it. "Wouldn't that cramp your style?"

"What are you talking about?"

"Your trips to Seattle. When you go to…" She made air quotes. "A Mariners game."

He put down his can, then picked it up again. "I do go to games. I like baseball."

"Uh-huh. No one is fooled. You go in for a long weekend to see a game, but sometimes the Mariners aren't even in town. There's a woman. Or women. I'm not sure."

Nor did she want to be talking about this, only it was going to be hard to change the subject now. Plus, she couldn't help thinking that if they could get into something slightly more personal he might see her as more than just a buddy.

"What do you mean everybody knows?"

"It's understood," she said. "I don't talk about it with your daughter, if that's what you're asking, but she's a bright girl."

She met his wary gaze. "It's not a bad thing, Jeff. You've been divorced a long time. It's nice that you have someone."

No, it wasn't. It wasn't nice at all. It ate her up inside. It made her want to scream and beg and wish she had the courage to say "What about me?"

Jeff swore under his breath. "I didn't think anyone knew." He swore again. "It's not like however you're thinking. It's just sometimes a man—"

Had needs? Because she could help with that. But before she could figure out how to offer, Isaak joined them.

"This is going to take a while. Are you two willing to come back in a couple of hours or do you want to call it a night?"

Jeff glanced at the clock on the wall. It was nearly six.

"Buy you a burger?" he asked Helen.

"That would be great. Thanks."

Jeff returned his attention to Isaak. "We'll be across the street."

"Great. I'll come get you there."

Jeff locked his guitar in his truck before they headed across the highway to the Tulip Burger restaurant. While Helen didn't mind that their town was all things tulip, she felt the new owners of Tulip Burger had taken things too far. There were stencils on the wall, a tulip-shaped blackboard with specials and tulip-printed napkins. Cute, but not necessary. Tourists already knew where they were—there was no reason to drill home the point.

They took a seat at a booth in the back. Helen knew better than to read too much into the dinner invitation. New band disagreements were frequent, which meant she and Jeff often had time to kill between sessions. What she didn't know was whether or not she wanted to return to the previous topic. While it might help get her closer to her goal of being his love slave, there was also the risk of him saying something like, "I will only ever see you as my friend."

Helen stared at the menu. They had a really nice grilled chicken salad. If she asked for dressing on the side, she would have made it nearly twelve hours on her new low-carb, low-fat diet and wouldn't that be special.

"Want to split the bacon cheeseburger?" Jeff asked.

Because while the decorations might be tacky, the food was amazing and the bacon cheeseburgers were huge and delicious and, well, damn.

Helen's stomach grumbled, which she took as a vote of "yes, please." Oh, why did she have to be weak? Or fat?

"Sure," she murmured, then waited for the wave of guilt.

Their server came over. Jeff ordered for them, asking for extra fries and suggesting a chocolate milk shake. In deference to the now broken diet, she said she would just have water.

"We're getting Christmas orders," Jeff said when their server had left. "It's June. What are they thinking, waiting so long? We have to grow the tulips from bulbs, which we have to order. It's not like we can put on an extra shift in the factory."

"Maybe if you put up inspirational posters they'd grow faster."

"Are you sassing me?"

"Actually I believe I was sassing the tulips." She sipped her water. "I get that you're growing flowers, but it's still strange to me that flower distributors have to order flowers so far in advance. The most I have to do is make sure my food orders are done two weeks out. What if the bulbs don't work?"

"They'll be fine."

"Still, it seems risky. You put a bulb in the ground and expect there to be a flower. You even know exactly which one it is. That's a lot of trust."

"It's farming, Helen. Don't make it into magic."

"I think there's an element of magic. I mean, come on. Eggplants. Who saw that coming?"

A burger and more fries than Weight Watchers would approve of later, Helen pushed her plate away. The chef had tossed a little avocado on their burger, taking it from delicious to heavenly. She would, she swore, start her diet tomorrow. Again.

Jeff moved his glass of iced tea in a circle on the table. He looked at her, down at his drink, then back at her.

"Before you were asking me about the women I sleep with."

Had Helen been drinking, she would have choked. As it was, she tried not to flinch and still had to clear her throat before speaking.

"That's one way of putting it," she murmured. "I was just wondering about, you know…"

"Not really."

She tried desperately to think up something to say. If she wasn't desperately in love with him, what would she want to know?

"How do you do it?" she asked, then held up a hand. "The logistics of finding someone. I know how to have sex."

He smiled. "I would hope so."

"It's the other stuff."

"Why are you asking?"

Because I want you desperately and I'm hoping you'll make the jump from friends to more than friends, pull me close and ravish me with a fiery passion. She glanced around the diner. *Okay, maybe you'll just suggest we go back to my place.*

"Helen? Why are you asking?"

"I've been divorced for years and I need to do something."

"You don't want to date anyone in town?"

"Um, well, that's hard to say. There aren't a lot of single guys. Sven is Kelly's ex, so that would never work. Griffith is into Kelly, so again, a problem. Now that I think about it, your daughter is creating trouble in my personal life."

"You want to date Sven and Griffith?"

"No, but blaming Kelly means it's not my fault."

"I respect that. There's Ryan."

Helen wrinkled her nose. "Thanks, but no. He's flaky and not my type."

"Plus he's too young for you."

She glared at him. "Excuse me? He's what, five years younger than me? That's a perfectly acceptable age gap." Jeez, if Jeff didn't think five years was okay, what was he going to say about their sixteen-year difference?

"You're an old soul. Ryan isn't."

"That's amazingly similar to calling me old."

"You know I didn't mean that. You're on a tear tonight."

"Not really. Just sassing you."

"You said it was the tulips."

She grinned. "I lied."

"You don't have to sound so cheerful about it."

"Why not? I'm a cheerful person. Now about your women... How does it happen? Do you go to bars? Is there a website? And why haven't you ever brought someone home? Don't you want to get married again? I know things with Marilee weren't great, but it's been forever. You're still a relatively young man. Don't you ever want more? Someone to care about you and be a part of your life?"

His steady gaze warned her that she might have gone too far with that last bit, but she figured Jeff would chalk it up to enthusiasm rather than a plea for attention.

"Helen," he began, then stopped. His tense expression relaxed.

She turned and saw Isaak walking toward them.

"Timing bites," she muttered.

"Depends on how you look at it."

"You *would* say that."

Isaak slid in next to her and reached for a fry. "We have made our musical selections."

"Great." Jeff was already standing. "Can't wait to hear what they are."

"Someone's enthused."

Isaak grabbed two more fries, then rose. Helen followed, then moved close to Jeff.

"Chick, chick, chicken," she chanted softly.

"You know it."

★ ★ ★

Kelly spun back and forth on the stool at the counter. Helen stood at the cash register, making change for her last customer of the day. It was a little after two and the diner was quiet. The kitchen staff had cleaned up and gone for the day.

Helen walked Mrs. Pritchard to the door and held it open, then closed and locked it. She turned to Kelly.

"You could have texted me or something. I can't believe you confronted Griffith and waited all this time to tell me."

"It's been less than two days."

Helen put her hands on her hips. "That's like eight years in best-friend time. Are you mad at me or something?"

The question was more teasing than serious. Helen always had a dramatic flair. She was so alive and present in her life. Not in a scary way, like Kelly's mother or sister, but from a place of positive energy. Being around Helen always made Kelly feel better about everything.

"I'm not mad and you know it. I just needed to process."

"Let me grab us drinks, then you're going to tell me everything. You'll start with you said hi and he said hi and go from there. Remember, no detail is too small."

"I promise you will hear them all."

Kelly moved to a booth. Helen got herself a diet soda at the dispenser, then made Kelly an Arnold Palmer and carried both to the booth.

Her dark blue Parrot Café shirt brought out the deep blue of her eyes while her black jeans emphasized her curvy hips. Her long black hair was pulled back in a French braid. She was sexy and voluptuous and by comparison, Kelly felt practically two dimensional.

Helen rested her elbows on the table. "Start talking."

Kelly drew in a breath before exhaling slowly. "I went to see Griffith, which was, by the way, your suggestion."

"Yes, I'm the brilliant friend. Go on."

"He said…" She still had trouble wrapping her mind around what he'd said, let alone repeating it. "He wants us to get to know each other with the idea of entering into a long-term relationship. But he doesn't want to fall in love or get married. So we'd be friends having sex in a committed way." She sipped her drink. "Committed to each other, not the sex."

"You don't actually know that," Helen said, before leaning back. "He really said all that? Just blurted it out?"

"He didn't blurt as much as explain. He's not interested in getting married again and he's not a one-night-stand kind of guy. He wants a long-term monogamous relationship. With me."

"Of course with you. You're amazing. He'd be an idiot to pick anyone else, but jeez. Nobody just *says* that."

"I know."

"It's interesting."

Kelly could have come up with about twenty-seven other words. "Interesting? How?"

"It's kind of your thing. You were with Sven for five years and you never once thought of taking things further." Helen stared at her intently. "You never did think of it, did you? Because I asked all the time and you kept saying you didn't want to marry him."

"I didn't, I swear. He was great and all, it's just, I wonder if maybe I wasn't exactly in love with him." A thought that had haunted her since the breakup. They'd been together five years. Shouldn't she have been crushed when he ended things?

"Not everyone has to fall in love and get married. People have wonderfully happy relationships without going that route. And some of us who do get married choose incredibly badly and end up divorced." She smiled. "What did you say?"

"That I would think about it."

"And?"

"It's been less than forty-eight hours. I don't know what to do or think or say." She picked up her drink. "What do *you* think?"

"What went wrong with Sven? Why wasn't he the one?"

Kelly blinked at the question. She'd thought they would be discussing the pros and cons of Griffith.

"I'm not sure. On paper we were the perfect couple. We have similar interests and all but there wasn't any spark." Sven had been way too into sex. "He liked to walk around naked. That didn't make me comfortable."

"Just randomly naked?"

"After sex."

"Well, sure. He has the body for it. You couldn't appreciate the show?"

"Not my style." She shrugged. "He was nice and all but there wasn't anything special between us. Not that Griffith is offering me magic, either."

"Do you want magic? You're always so careful when it comes to guys."

An excellent point, Kelly thought. "I guess I want more than I had with Sven. I want to be intrigued and have fun." All within the careful confines of being sensible. "I should tell Griffith no."

"Why? Don't say that. He might be exactly your style. Maybe he dresses after sex. Come on, don't give up without trying. You need someone in your life."

"Why? You don't date."

Helen reached for a napkin from the holder and began to wipe the table. "That's different. I was devastated by the end of my marriage. Not because he broke my heart, but because I was an idiot to trust him the way I did. Griffith is a great guy. Aren't you the least bit tempted?"

"Maybe a little." More than a little, she thought. If she were being honest.

"Then at least continue the conversation. What have you got to lose?"

"You're right."

"My two favorite words ever."

Kelly laughed. Maybe she should talk to Griffith again and figure out if he meant what he said. She supposed there was no harm in that. As for what had happened in high school—she couldn't hold that against him forever. It didn't speak well of her.

"Maybe it's time for you to start dating, too," she said. "Sven's available."

"Let me think about that." Helen tilted her head. "No. Did I say no? No. He's your ex. That would take us places neither of us wants to go." She raised her voice. "And that little mole on his inner thigh. Isn't it darling?" Her voice returned to its normal pitch. "I love you like a sister, but there are some things we simply aren't meant to share. Although I could totally get into Sven being naked. When it gets hot and he takes his shirt off…" She sighed. "You could bounce a quarter off his stomach."

"I never tried."

Helen pointed at her. "See, if you'd been in love with him, I'm sure you would have tried. It's a sign. Go take advantage of Griffith, then tell me all about it. I want to live vicariously through your exciting life."

"It's not exciting yet."

"That is just a detail."

5

Kelly left the diner and drove back to work. She passed the acres of tulip farmland long before she reached the main offices. Only a few weeks before, the blooming flowers had been a sea of color. After the harvest, there was nothing left but dark soil and the promise of flowers next spring.

It was a ridiculous waste of land, she thought as she turned into the driveway. Not only was the crop uneatable, the ground lay fallow nearly nine months out of the year. Still, the Murphys had grown tulips for five generations. The flowers were in her blood, so to speak, and she had no interest in doing anything else.

She pulled into the parking lot and saw Griffith's truck in the spot next to the one she generally used. The man himself leaned against the driver's door. As she pulled to a stop, he straightened and walked around to greet her.

In the few seconds it took him to make the trip, she found herself feeling oddly flustered and out of breath. Did he expect her to make a decision right that second? She needed time to know what on earth she was going to do.

He pulled open her door and smiled. "Kelly."

"Griffith."

"You had an overnight package." He held out a small box. "It was delivered to me by mistake. I thought it might be important."

She stared into his brown eyes and found herself oddly unable to speak. What on earth? No. No way. She might be interested in dating Griffith and possibly sleeping with him, but there was no way she was going to fall for him. That would be the complete definition of stupid.

She took the box from him and recognized the mailing label and return address. Her nerves immediately calmed and her throat unconstricted.

"I have no idea how this got to you, but thank you for dropping it by."

"It's important?"

She smiled. "It is to me, but I doubt you'd agree."

"Now I'm intrigued."

He stepped back so she could get out of the truck, then he followed her into the building.

The farm offices were in front of one of the largest greenhouses. They were basic at best, with only a half-dozen offices and a small waiting area. The real work was done elsewhere. At least Kelly's was. Her dad handled sales and scheduled deliveries, so he spent plenty of time in his office, while she did her best to always be out in one of the greenhouses or in the fields.

They didn't employ a receptionist, nor did they have a company phone system. If someone needed her, they called her cell phone. The same with her dad. Most of their orders were done online. Only special orders or panicked begging happened on the phone.

She dropped her battered, woven handbag on the counter and reached for a pair of scissors sticking up from a juice can of pencils. She slit the tape on the box and opened it.

Inside lay a half-dozen bulbs. They were on the small side and nestled in cotton. There was nothing special about them, nothing to indicate what they would be. A card had been taped to the inside of the box: 8756-43.

"That's a letdown," Griffith told her.

"For you. I'm all aquiver."

"Seriously? Over bulbs?"

"Not just any bulbs, Griffith. These are special. A hybrid or maybe a new color or shape."

"You don't know?"

She showed him the card. "That's as much information as I have." She picked up the box and nodded toward the back of the office. "Come on. I'll show you."

She led him through to the big wooden door in the rear, then out along a gravel path. When they reached the smallest of the greenhouses, the one that was hers alone, they went inside.

The temperature was warmer, the air thicker and more humid. The scent of plants and life and water filled every breath. There were tables lined with square trays and in each tray were rows of bulbs.

"In the main greenhouses, each of these can hold up to a hundred and fifty bulbs," she said. "We only have a single level of planting here, but there are farms where they have tall buildings with roofs that open and close and machines that raise and lower pallets of plants."

"Somebody has greenhouse envy."

"You know it." She motioned to the various trays. "These are all experimental tulips. Different horticulturists develop them, then send them to me to grow them. I keep track of everything that happens to them—from how much water, to the nutrients used, to the amount of light and ambient temperature. I document the life cycle and report back my findings."

He pointed to the box she held. "What is that going to be?"

"I have no idea."

"They don't tell you?"

"No." She laughed. "That's part of the fun. I haven't got a clue. It's like unwrapping a present."

"Only it takes a couple of months to get to the good part."

"That's okay." She touched the bulbs. "They email me basic

instructions, letting me know how long they think I should refrigerate the bulb before bringing it out to root, but that's it."

"You refrigerate the bulbs?"

"They have to think it's winter before they can think it's spring."

They left the greenhouse and walked into one of the barns. There were huge cooling rooms filled with thousands and thousands of bulbs.

"Holy crap," he said as he looked around. "You're going to grow all these?"

"In less than a year. I have a computer inventory program that helps me track when the bulbs are put into cold storage and when they'll be ready to come out. Depending on the type of bulb, I know how long for them to root and from then, how long until they flower. We work backward to fill our orders. Some of the tulips—the kind you can get at any grocery store or florist year-round—are always in production. We vary the volume based on the season."

She pointed to labeled boxes of bulbs. "Those are red and white tulips for the holidays."

"Now you're messing with me."

She laughed. "I swear. Come back in five months and I'll prove it."

She put the new bulbs from the box into a square dish on a shelf by the door. After writing down the date on the card, she tucked it next to the dish. They walked back outside.

"Impressive," he told her.

"It's not housing for the homeless, but I like to think my flowers will make someone happy."

"They will."

They stood facing each other. There was a confidence about him, as if he knew his place in the world and was happy about it. Sven was plenty confident, too, so that couldn't be what made Griffith feel different.

"I'm sorry about what happened in high school," he said quietly.

The words were so at odds with what she'd been thinking that at first she had no idea what he was talking about. When she managed to find context and remembered that horrible day, she flushed and wanted to run away. Instead she forced herself to stay where she was. Her chin came up.

"All right."

He looked at her. "I panicked. I knew your mom was in her room with Coach and I was pretty sure I knew what they were doing. I didn't want you to walk in on that."

Because her mother had been having an affair with the football coach, along with countless other men. Everyone had pretended not to know, all the while being acutely aware of what was happening—Kelly most of all.

As a teacher at the high school, Marilee had had a permanent classroom. One where the door was often locked at lunch. Kelly hadn't even been thinking as she'd approached. She'd been too distracted by seeing Griffith with his friends.

"I was stupid to say what I did," he continued. "I know it was a long time ago, and this is late, but I'm sorry for what I said. I didn't mean it."

"You couldn't just ask me a question about homework? You had to announce you weren't the least bit interested in me?"

"I totally blanked, which is the truth, not an excuse."

She liked that he continued to hold her gaze, as if he wanted her to know he meant what he was saying. And the apology was nice, too. Yes, very late, but still.

"I was humiliated," she admitted. "Then my mom left and everything changed at home and what you'd said didn't seem that important."

Her mom hadn't just left, Kelly thought grimly. They'd fought. She still remembered the anger between them.

"Why can't you just be like everyone else?" Kelly had demanded of her mother. "Why do you have to be this way? You're so selfish. You have a family. You're supposed to take care of us."

What she'd really meant was that her mother was supposed to take care of *her*, but she hadn't been able to say that.

"I'm not like other mothers. Someday you'll understand."

"I won't. I hate you. If you're so unhappy, why don't you just leave?"

"Is that what you want?"

"Yes. Go away. You're horrible. We won't miss you at all."

Marilee's green eyes had darkened with an emotion Kelly couldn't understand. "Be careful, darling. Wishes like that can be dangerous."

The fight had ended then. Kelly had cried herself to sleep—an embarrassing truth for a fifteen-year-old. She told herself it was wrong to hate her mother, to wish her gone, but she couldn't seem to think any other way. The next day, Marilee had left Tulpen Crossing forever.

That was when everything had changed for all of them. Without Marilee, the dynamics had shifted. They'd all been in pain and reacting. Looking back, Kelly wondered if she hadn't just lost her mother that day—if she had lost her sister, as well.

"I'm sorry about that, too," Griffith said. "I know it was tough for you and your sister."

Olivia had suffered far more than Kelly. While Kelly had wrestled with guilt, she'd still had her dad, and the relative peace that had followed. But Olivia had always been their mother's favorite. With Marilee gone, she was alone. Jeff's awkward attempts to fill the void had not been enough.

Kelly knew she should have stepped in, should have done more. Why hadn't she? A question that still had no answer.

"What I said didn't help," he added.

"It's okay," Kelly told him. "I appreciate the apology." She managed a slight smile. "I guess based on our previous conversation, I should assume you're over your distaste."

His brows rose slightly. "There was never any distaste."

"You say that *now.*"

"You're going to make me pay, aren't you?"

"I think a little, yes."

"Okay. I've probably earned it. Thank you for the tour," he added. "I liked seeing where you work."

"You should come by when we're harvesting. It's pretty exciting."

"I'd like that."

"Me, too," she said before she could stop herself.

He smiled and took a step toward her. For a second she thought he was going to kiss her. She had no idea how she felt about that or what it would be like. Anticipation quickened in her belly right before he lightly touched her upper arm, then turned and walked back toward the parking lot.

She stared after him in disbelief. That was it? What had happened to him wanting to sleep with her? Why hadn't he made his move?

She put her hands on her hips and glared at his retreating back. Men were stupid. All of them, but mostly Griffith.

Helen finished locking the front door of the diner. The downside of her job was starting so early in the morning. The upside was she was usually out by three in the afternoon—earlier if she could get her food orders in during the mid-morning lull.

She dropped her keys into her bag and turned to find Jeff standing a couple of feet away.

She pressed a hand to her chest. "You startled me." Which was the truth and also better than her next thought, which was more along the lines of how good he looked. All manly in his plaid shirt and jeans.

"Were we supposed to go to JML or something?" Because while Jeff was a regular at the café, he'd already been by for breakfast. He wasn't generally an afternoon kind of guy.

"No. I wanted to talk to you."

For a second she allowed herself to hope that he'd finally come to his senses, realized he was madly in love with her and was here to declare himself. Or at least try to get in her pants, but she was okay with that, too.

"I've been thinking about what we talked about before," he began. "About the women I see in Seattle."

Yes? Yes? She did her best to look completely normal when on the inside she was doing a competition-worthy cheer routine. Oh, please, oh, please let him want sex with her. Wild, crazy, hot monkey sex.

"You caught me off guard with your questions. I didn't know what to say." He raised one shoulder. "I guess I was embarrassed."

"About what?"

"I don't know. People talking."

"No one's talking. I observed." Although she did think other people had noticed, she wasn't going to tell him that.

"My point is, you're right. We're friends. Good friends. So ask me what you want to know and I'll do my best to answer your questions."

The hot, glowing sex bubble inside of her burst with an audible *pop*. "That would be great. Probably not right here."

He looked around at the empty café parking lot. "Probably not."

They walked the quarter block to her small house, the one she'd bought after her aunt and uncle had moved away. It was just over fourteen hundred square feet, with nice light and an updated kitchen. But what had sold her on the place was the oversize living room with the perfect space for her piano. The small upright was one of the few things she had from her parents. The piano had to be on an interior wall, away from drafts, vents and the sun.

She unlocked the front door. Jeff followed her inside. They

gravitated to the kitchen, as people always did, and settled on the bar stools in front of the main counter.

Unsure of the protocol for a conversation like this, she asked, "Do you want something to drink?"

"I'm fine."

They were sitting about two feet apart, angled toward each other. Helen set her purse on the counter, then didn't know what to do with her hands.

"I have a couple of bars I go to," he began. "I've also used a dating website or two."

She told herself that whatever he said, she was going to keep her mouth firmly shut. And act natural. No snorts, no gasps, no blushing, although the latter would be hard to control.

"I make it clear I'm not looking for anything long-term or involved. No serious commitments."

"Why not?" she blurted before she could stop herself. "See, I don't get that. I know you and you're a commitment kind of guy. You love your routine and the rhythm of the seasons. Why would it be different with a woman? Why wouldn't you want to be with someone long-term?"

"It's complicated."

"It's not. Kelly wouldn't care. She worries about you being alone. One day she's going to move out and then you'll be in that big house all by yourself. You can't sell it—it's been in the family too long. I guess you could move out and Kelly could..." She cleared her throat. "I'm going to stop talking now."

He gave her a brief smile. "Want to bet on that?"

She grinned. "No. Anyway, you were saying it's complicated."

"Maybe that's not the right word. With my past..."

He meant Marilee, the bitchy, unfaithful ex-wife. "You know what she did wasn't your fault. It wasn't about you, it was about her. Something inside of her." She pressed her lips together. "Sorry."

"It's okay. You're right. There *was* something in her." He

shifted on the bar stool. "When we first started dating, I knew she wasn't long for this town. That as soon as she graduated from high school, she was gone. Then she got pregnant. I was shocked when she told me and even more surprised that she wanted to have the baby. We got married and Kelly was born and Marilee went to college and got her degree and started teaching. For a while things were okay between us. Then they weren't."

He looked at her, then away. "I never knew how to make her happy enough."

Happy enough that she wouldn't cheat, Helen thought. She'd had a similar thought herself. With Troy. She'd kept thinking that if only she were prettier or thinner or more adventurous in bed, he wouldn't cheat on her.

"Like I said before, it's not about you. It was never anything you did. It was always her."

"You telling me or yourself?" he asked gently. Because, of course, Jeff knew about her past. Everyone in Tulpen Crossing did.

"Both."

"I agree with you, at least in theory. My head tells the story, my gut is less likely to believe."

"And because of that, you won't get involved?"

"That's part of the reason."

"What's the rest of it?" That he was secretly in love with her? If only life were that convenient.

He leaned toward her. "This conversation is supposed to be about you. Here's my advice. Make sure you like the guy. Keep yourself safe. Listen to your gut and make him wear a condom. Don't take any crap about how it doesn't feel good with a condom. It feels just fine. You deserve someone who looks out for you."

Like he was doing now, she thought dreamily. Only he wasn't talking about himself. He was giving her advice on how to sleep with someone else. Not exactly the act of a man secretly in love with her.

Another dream dashed. It appeared she was never going to have her way with Jeff—not if she couldn't get him to be the tiniest bit jealous.

"I appreciate the advice," she told him.

"Good." He stood. "I need to get back to the office."

She rose and walked him to the front door. He turned and smiled at her. Before she could catch her breath or react, he pulled her close. Like in a hug. Not that they hadn't hugged a billion times before, but maybe this was different. Maybe he was finally going to—

He leaned in and kissed her. On. The. Top. Of. Her. Head. WTF?

Helen forced herself to smile tightly as he drew back.

"I'll see you soon," he said.

What she said was, "Absolutely." What she meant was, "Not if I see you first."

6

Kelly lowered the seared pot roast into the pressure cooker, then added broth and the vegetables. While most people were Crock-Pot fans, she'd never taken to it. The thought of having to get up first thing in the morning and dice or chop or even assemble was too daunting. A pressure cooker gave her the same kind of flavor in a significantly shorter period of time.

She put on the lid and set the timer. In ninety minutes they would have pot roast—one of her dad's favorites.

She supposed a psychologist would have a field day with the fact that she was still living at home at the ripe old age of twenty-eight. Every now and then she thought about moving out. She just wasn't sure when that was going to happen. Or if there actually was a reason to. In some societies, multigenerational families were the norm. She and her dad could start a trend.

She smiled at the thought, then rinsed off the cutting board. A quick glance at the clock on the wall told her that dinner would be ready at six. She was halfway to her dad's study to tell him when the front door opened and a semi-familiar voice called, "Hi, Dad. It's me. I'm home."

Had Kelly been holding more than a dish towel, she would have dropped it for sure, because standing right there in the living room was her sister, Olivia. The same Olivia who had left at fifteen and never returned.

Okay—that wasn't fair—Olivia had been sent away. As for

not coming home, at first she'd refused to come back for holidays and summer vacation. Kelly remembered that. What she couldn't recall was if or when she and her father had stopped asking her to come home.

Kelly took in the stylish, beachy, wavy hair, the perfect makeup, the casual-yet-elegant tunic over leggings and the brightly colored athletic shoes that were obviously all about style rather than sports. She was acutely aware of her own battered cargo pants and faded University of Washington sweatshirt.

On the surface, she and Olivia looked a lot alike. They were the same height, with brown hair and eyes. At least they'd started out that way. Today Olivia's hair was more golden than brown and her eyes had a distinct hazel cast to them. Kelly realized she wasn't the before picture so much as the cautionary tale.

Her sister stared at her. "Kelly? What are you doing here?"

"I could ask you the same question."

"I came to see Dad."

Just like that? As if she hadn't been gone over a decade? Because although Jeff made regular pilgrimages to see his daughter and Kelly had tagged along more than once, Olivia had, to the best of Kelly's knowledge, not been back to Tulpen Crossing in over a decade.

"I'm making dinner," Kelly said.

Olivia frowned as she glanced around the kitchen. Her expression cleared and she laughed. "Oh, that's right. Dad told me you were still living at home."

Jeff walked into the kitchen. "I heard someone…" He stared at his youngest daughter. His eyes widened and his mouth formed a happy grin. "Olivia! When did you get here?"

"Just now. Hi, Dad."

Jeff held open his arms. Olivia rushed into his embrace. Kelly fought against a sense of resentment and foreboding.

"I've missed you so much," Jeff said as he held her tight. "I can't believe you're here."

"I've missed you, too."

They stepped back and smiled at each other. Jeff pulled out a chair and they both sat at the kitchen table. Kelly stood awkwardly by the island, not sure what she was supposed to do. Join them? Bolt? She settled on hovering.

"Tell me," her dad said. "Why are you here?"

"I thought it was time for me to visit," Olivia said with a brilliantly white smile. "Phoenix gets so hot in the summer and the real estate market pretty much dies. I had some vacation time, so here I am. I hope it's okay."

"Of course it is. Better than okay."

Kelly reminded herself to smile when Olivia glanced at her. She was trying to remember the last time she'd seen her sister. Five years ago? Six? They rarely had any contact at all. The occasional birthday text or an awkward phone call, but that was it. Jeff and Olivia visited more regularly, but still not that often. Jeff had gone to Olivia's college graduation. Kelly had been sick and stayed home.

"You're selling real estate?" she asked.

"No, I work in marketing. I design the brochures and handle the advertising for the individual houses and the company. I've also recently started a staging business. I help people set up their homes so they're more appealing to buyers. It's fun."

"That sounds great," Jeff told her.

"I like it. It's amazing what you can do when you rearrange furniture and add some accessories." The bright smile returned. "I've been working a lot so I'm looking forward to taking a couple of months off."

A couple of months? Kelly held in a groan, then reminded herself that Olivia was her sister. It would be nice for them to get to know each other again. They weren't teenagers anymore. They were adults and would get along fine just like they had when they were little. Although the entire situation made no sense at all. Olivia had never liked being a small-town girl.

"This will be fun," Jeff said. "My two girls under the same roof."

"I know." Olivia smiled again. "I can't wait to get together with my friends. Everyone's going to be so excited. I was texting with Ryan and—"

Kelly groaned. "You have got to be kidding me," she said before she could stop herself. "You came back for your high school boyfriend?"

Her sister's mouth formed a prim, straight line. "Of course not. You're being ridiculous. I want to see *all* my friends. Ryan is just one of them."

"Sure."

Kelly wondered whose idea the visit had been—Olivia's or Ryan's. Last she'd heard Griffith's younger brother was going hot and heavy with someone else.

Olivia stood and moved to the counter. "I mean it, Kelly. I've moved on. Started a career." She picked up her sister's hand and shook her head as she studied Kelly's short, ragged nails. "Gotten a manicure. You're the one still living with Dad."

Kelly told herself to ignore the dig, but that didn't stop heat from flaring on her cheeks.

"Girls," Jeff said mildly. "I know you haven't lived together in a while, but come on. We're family."

Kelly snatched back her hand and nodded. "Of course. It's so nice to have Olivia back."

Her sister winked at her. "I know. It's great, isn't it?" She turned to Jeff. "Daddy, do you mind if I stay here?"

"Of course not." The man couldn't have looked happier. "Your old room is just as you left it. Kelly will show you where the clean sheets and towels are. Stay as long as you'd like. I'm sorry I won't be able to visit with you after dinner, but I have a gig tonight."

Olivia laughed. "What does that mean?"

"I'm in a band." He chuckled. "Okay, not a real band. I work with a music school that helps people learn to play instruments and then perform."

"He's the ringer," Kelly added. "Dad and my friend Helen are the professional musicians who help. They perform in showcases every few weeks."

"That's fun." Olivia wrinkled her nose. "I think I remember you playing guitar when I was little. It was nice."

"Come with me. We can talk between sets."

"Thanks, but I'm meeting friends later."

"Next time, then." Jeff hugged Olivia and Kelly. "My two girls back at home. Who would have thought?"

Yes, who, Kelly thought to herself. Certainly not her.

For reasons not clear to Griffith, the sign at the craft mall/community center had been changed. When he'd shown up for the book club, it had been called Petal Pushers. Now there was a new sign: The Dutch Bunch. He figured it was an homage to the tulips they grew in the area, but still. Kind of strange for the Pacific Northwest where Native American names gave visitors tongue-twisting trouble.

He always enjoyed listening to tourists trying to pronounce places like Snohomish, Issaquah or Cle Elum, or his personal favorite, Stillaguamish. Not that he knew anything about naming a craft mall.

He'd shown up for a musical showcase where local bands performed for friends and family. It was the audible equivalent to a train wreck—you really didn't want to look and see anything bad, but it was impossible to turn away. In this case, there was the faint possibility of hearing something passably good, with the more likely outcome of wincing through the butchering of a perfectly good song. Or twenty.

Griffith wouldn't normally bother coming. He had plenty to fill his time. But Leo's son was playing tonight and Leo had asked Griffith to attend. Leo rarely asked for anything, plus he'd sounded so proud when he'd told Griffith about the showcase.

Apparently the band was going to perform a Beatles retrospective. Griffith hoped the Beatles who had already left the earth had reached a state of grace and forgiveness. If they chose to exact punishment for what was about to be done to their songs, there was no telling what could happen.

The room would hold a couple hundred people. There were about sixty there already. Leo and his family had claimed the entire front row of tables. Griffith waved at him, then settled in for what he would guess was going to be a very long evening.

The event was BYOB. He'd grabbed a six-pack of beer. As he found a seat at one of the tables, he wondered if he should have brought something stronger. Or more of it.

He'd just opened his first bottle when he saw Kelly walk in and look around. At first he thought she was looking for friends to sit with, but then he noticed she seemed tense and on edge. When she glanced in his direction, he waved her over.

Her look of relief was gratifying.

"What are you doing here?" she asked as she approached. "I didn't think anyone came without being obligated. You know the music is going to be awful, right?"

He stood and held out a chair. "I do. Leo, my floor supervisor, has a kid playing. He asked me to come. What's your excuse?"

"I couldn't stay home." With that she pulled a bottle of vodka out of her large tote bag. "They still serve sodas and stuff here, right?"

He eyed the full bottle, then pointed to the concession stand by the wall. "Sure. What do you want?"

"A large glass with ice. Tonic water if they have it, otherwise club soda and a lime."

"I'll be right back."

"Thanks."

The room was filling up and the noise level rising. They were going to have a full house tonight. He walked over to the serve-yourself concession stand and filled a large Solo cup with ice and three inches of tonic and added a couple slices of lime. When he returned to their table, Kelly sat staring at the far wall. Her eyes were unfocused and her mouth trembled slightly.

He sat next to her and handed her the cup. "What's wrong?"

"Is it that obvious?" She poured a healthy serving of vodka, then swirled the ice in the cup. "Don't ask. I know the answer. It's just… I don't know. Everything was fine, you know? Sure, my life isn't that interesting, but I like it. I have a good job and good friends and then bam, something smacks you upside the head."

For a second he wondered if she was talking about what he'd suggested. No, that had been several days ago and when he'd seen her at the farm, she'd been friendly enough. It was something else.

"Olivia's back," she said flatly.

It took him a second to figure out who Olivia was. "Your sister?"

"That's her. She's home for the summer." She took another drink. "I'm being punished. I get that. It's fair, but damn. I don't know how I'm going to get through it. She's so perfect. Her clothes, her hair. Plus the way she talks about everything in Phoenix. Only if it's all so great, what is she doing here?"

He had no idea what she was talking about, so he kept his mouth shut. Kelly needed someone to listen—him knowing or not knowing the subject seemed unimportant.

"It's been so long. She was fifteen when Dad sent her to boarding school and I was eighteen. Getting ready to start college. I was so excited and—"

She looked at him. Tears filled her eyes. "I'm lying. Dad didn't send her away. Okay, he did, but it was my idea. I'm the one who said she was acting out in school. She and Ryan were dating and it was getting serious and I was so scared she was going to be like our mom. I was worried for her, but mostly for myself. I knew if she screwed up and got pregnant, I would be stuck dealing with it all and I just didn't want to. I know that makes me a horrible person."

He shifted his chair closer and put his arm around her. "No, it doesn't."

She blinked away the tears. "It does. I was selfish."

"Because you didn't want your sister to get pregnant at fifteen? Yeah, you were a real bitch."

"But we sent her away."

He thought about his brother and the women in his life. Griffith had been away at college when his brother was in high school, but he'd heard plenty of stories.

"You did the right thing for both of them."

"You're being nice. Thank you." She leaned against him and took another drink. "Now she's back and she's already mentioned seeing him."

"Ryan has a girlfriend."

"That's what I thought. I'm not sure Olivia knows, but that's not my rock. I just don't know how I'm going to deal with her for the summer. Biologically we're sisters, but in reality, we're strangers."

"Want to move in with me?"

She looked at him. "Wow, there's an invitation."

He grinned. "I meant into your own room. The house is big enough."

"I'm not sure jumping from the frying pan to the fire is a good idea, but thank you for the offer." She sighed. "Dad is happy. She's his baby girl and now he has both of us together under one roof. Maybe this is a sign that I should get my own place."

"Maybe you should see how things are going to go first."

"Logic. How like a man."

She poured more vodka into her cup. Griffith rubbed her arm and wondered how this was all going to turn out. It did seem strange that Olivia would simply leave everything for the summer. As for Ryan, God knew what trouble he was in now, what with his current girlfriend and his former girlfriend all in the same town. Maybe he would try to escape the trouble by showing up to work on time. Unlikely, but a guy could dream.

The band played for nearly an hour, although it seemed much longer what with their lack of understanding about music and staying in tune. When they were done, Griffith's ears were ringing. He hoped the condition wasn't permanent. He congratulated Leo and his son, then went back to the table and collected Kelly.

"That was great," she said brightly as she tucked what was left of her vodka into her bag. "I think by the end, they were getting the hang of it."

"I think you're drunk."

"Maybe. But that's okay. I'm an adult."

"You're an adult who's not driving home."

She wrinkled her nose. "Probably not. I'll get a ride with my dad." She looked around, took a step, stumbled, then started to laugh.

"Okay, then." He drew her close and started for the stage. "Let's go find him together."

"That's nice." She smiled. "Are you going to kiss me?"

There was a non sequitur. "Nope."

"Why not? You want me as your girlfriend. That means kissing, Griffith."

"Yes, it does and while I look forward to kissing you, I'm a firm believer in the woman being sober. Or at least not as drunk as you. Call me old-fashioned."

"I didn't know there would be rules."

"There are always rules, Kelly. The trick is knowing which ones it's okay to break."

"I don't break rules. I should. Maybe I'd be more like Olivia. She's so pretty. I want to be pretty, too."

"You are."

"You're just saying that for the sex, but it's still nice. Have you seen her clothes?"

"Not yet."

"And her hair. It's so shiny. She was wearing makeup and everything. Plus, she has boobs. I never got mine."

His lips twitched. "You are so going to regret this conversation in the morning. When you get home, drink a lot of water."

"I'm perfectly fine."

"You say that now. Come on. Let's go find your dad."

7

Olivia's bravado had lasted through the three-day drive up from Phoenix and walking into the house where she'd grown up. But as the evening progressed, it had slowly faded until now she was left with nothing but a gnawing sense of not belonging anywhere.

She walked through the empty house, trying to find some connection to her past. Funny how she'd assumed the old place would feel like home. It was where she'd grown up, but whatever part of her had been left behind must have gotten swept up with the dust.

The living room was different. New furniture and a bigger TV. The layout was all wrong, but that wasn't her problem. The kitchen had been remodeled, as well. Whoever had done the design had used the space well and in the day there would be plenty of light.

Her bedroom was exactly as it had been. The same pale lavender walls, the books and yearbooks in the bookcase. She recognized the stuffed animals, but felt no need to hold them close. They were cute and all, but no longer a part of her.

Tucked into the big mirror over her dresser were several photos of her with friends. She looked impossibly young, with horrible makeup and hair. Thank goodness she'd learned how to make the most of what she had. Unlike her sister, who was determined to be as low-maintenance as possible, as if that were a point of pride. Olivia had already spotted her bargain shampoo-and-conditioner 2-in-1 bottle in the shower, along with a bar of generic unscented soap.

There were no lotions on the counter, no hint of makeup had ever been allowed past the hallowed doorway. Kelly was odd, but then they'd always been so incredibly different. She wondered how much of that was personality and how much of it was how they were raised.

She sat on the edge of the bed and tried to figure out if she could really stay here. And if she didn't, where on earth would she go? Her dad had been happy to see her, which was nice. Kelly had just looked shocked and panicked and why not? They were strangers.

She tried to remember the last time she'd seen her sister and couldn't. She and her dad had met up in San Francisco three years ago. Before that, he'd come to her graduation from Arizona State University. Marilee hadn't—she'd gone on a cruise instead.

Olivia fingered the hideous floral bedspread, then stood and crossed to the mirror. Tucked in the corner was an old picture of her with her sister. Kelly didn't look all that different from how she did now. In the photo, they were laughing together, as if they'd just shared a joke. As if they liked each other.

Olivia knew that at one point they had. They'd been close when they'd been younger, but after Marilee had run off, everything had changed and then Olivia had been sent away.

That part of her past was a blur. One second she'd been a diva in her high school and the next she'd been flying to an all-girls boarding school in Colorado. It had been mid-semester, when the cliques had already been established and no one gave a shit about the new girl.

She'd been so scared, so hurt. That first spring break, she'd refused to go home, out of spite. When someone had invited her home for the summer, she'd accepted, mostly to punish Kelly and their dad. She'd waited for them to call and beg her to come back, to be with them…only they never had.

She tossed the picture onto the dresser and stared at herself. She willed any hint of weakness from her eyes and squared her shoulders. She'd come a long way from that frightened teenager, abandoned by both her parents. She wasn't going to let anyone control her destiny ever again. She was strong and in charge. If she wasn't sure if coming home for the summer was a good idea, then she was going to damn well find out.

That decided, she went to her closet. She flipped through the dresses she'd unpacked and hung, stopping when she found a sleeveless little knit number that was exactly what she was looking for.

She touched up her makeup, fluffed her hair, then stripped down to her thong. The dress was snug, requiring her to tug and shimmy it into place. It dipped low in front and back and barely came to mid-thigh. Probably a little much for Tulpen Crossing, but she didn't mind. Far better to cross the line than not be remembered at all.

She put on dangly earrings and several gold bangles and slipped on a pair of sandals with four-inch heels. When she was done, she stood in front of the mirror.

The dark green dress made her eyes look more hazel than brown. She checked herself from the rear, then faced front again. She adjusted her breasts to make sure they were even before pinching her nipples several times. Her nipples hardened and became clearly visible under the knit fabric.

Excellent, she thought as she reached for her small clutch. No straight guy would be able to turn away. It was just one of the tricks her mother had taught her. On the drive to the bar, she would turn the AC to frigid, ensuring plenty of nipple when she arrived. When one might be facing a battle, one had best show up armed. For her, that meant sex, or at least sexual interest. You could always control a man with his dick.

★ ★ ★

Olivia pulled into the parking lot of Candy Cane—the poorly named bar in town. Ryan had mentioned more than once he liked to hang out there with his friends.

She was already shivering from the air-conditioning, but took a second to pour cold water from a bottle on the inside of her wrists. She shuddered at the cold. Oh, yeah, this was going to be good.

She crossed the parking lot and walked into the bar. It was fairly typical with plenty of tables, a few booths and some guys playing pool in the back. The men at the bar turned to look at her. Three of them nearly fell off their stools while a fourth stared at her openmouthed. She ignored them and looked around. Tension left her when she spotted Ryan.

He stood by a large table, talking to his friends. He was tall and gorgeous, a beer in one hand. Anticipation combined with satisfaction. If all went well, they would be naked in less than thirty minutes.

As she approached the table, she felt everyone turning to look at her. She thought she recognized a couple of his friends and smiled at them. Someone said something and Ryan turned. His eyes widened and his expression turned practically feral. Oh, yeah. Starving man, meet your buffet, she thought smugly.

"Olivia? What are you doing here? I can't believe it. Jesus, you're stunning."

He put down the beer and moved to her side. Dark hair, blue eyes and a dimple. Whatever more could she want?

"You're really here," he said.

She smiled. "I'm really here. How are you?"

"So much better now."

He reached for her. She arched her back and watched his gaze settle on her breasts. His intake of air was audible.

"Ryan!"

The shrill single word cut through the charged moment and

brought Ryan to a halt. Terror was followed by guilt, with a regret chaser. Olivia watched a pudgy blonde approach and step between them and knew her plans had just been flushed.

"Ryan, what do you think you're doing?" the blonde asked.

"I, ah, I…" His gaze locked with Olivia's. "This is Autumn."

"Is it?" Olivia's voice was cool. She looked the other woman up and down, taking in the worn, ill-fitting jeans, the unflattering too-tight top and the hair in desperate need of styling. "How unfortunate."

Autumn raised her eyebrows. "Yes, it is unfortunate. Ryan's with me. I don't know who you are, but he's with me."

"You do keep saying that, as if we all need to be reminded." Olivia paused. "Ryan especially."

Autumn flushed. "Tell her to go away."

"Autumn, she's a friend. I've known her since high school."

"Yeah, well, I don't care."

Olivia forced herself to smile casually. "Ryan, don't worry about it. There's no need to upset her. I'm going to be in town for a while. We'll have plenty of time to…catch up."

Autumn glared. Ryan grinned.

"I'd like that," he said.

"I'm sure you would."

Olivia maneuvered around Autumn, put her hand on Ryan's chest, then kissed his cheek. As she drew back, she whispered, "Too bad, because I'm naked under this." She smiled at a gasping Autumn. "So nice to have met you."

"Stay away from him, you hear me?"

"Oh, honey, I'm not the one you have to explain that to."

With that, she turned and walked to the door. A couple of guys approached, but she waved them off. She made it to her car before she began to shake. Tears burned. She willed them away as she drove back to the house.

Damn Ryan. He'd invited her here even though the bastard had a girlfriend? Okay, maybe *invited* was stretching things, but he'd told her he missed her and that she should come see him. She'd believed him.

Fine. If that was how he wanted to play it, game on. She had no doubt he would come crawling to her. And when he did, she was going to punish him. Not in a happy way, either. While Ryan would get the girl in the end, first he was going to have to pay. The only question was how.

Helen poured Jeff's coffee as he sat at the counter. She did her best to wrap her mind around his news. Not only the shock of his youngest daughter's return, but the fact that Kelly hadn't called and told her.

"I never thought she'd come home," he said. "I know it's just for the summer, but still. She's here." He looked around. "I wanted to bring her this morning, but she was still asleep."

"It's 5:45 in the morning. Most people are." She studied him. "I can't tell if you're happy or not," she admitted.

He looked at her. "I'm happy. Of course I am. She's my daughter." He dropped his gaze. "I sent her away, Helen. I sent my own daughter to boarding school when she was fifteen. I can never forgive myself for that."

She glanced at the clock and saw they only had a few minutes until her early regulars started showing up. She sat on the stool next to his.

"It's not as if you got tired of her and wanted her out of the way. She's not a puppy you returned to the pound."

He shrugged. "Maybe, but still." He turned so he was facing her. "I was terrified she was going to turn out like her mother. Marilee had always kept her close and after she left, Olivia was lost. I could see it, but didn't know what to do. I tried, but hell, I'm sure I failed her a dozen ways to Sunday. As she got older, I could see more and more of Marilee in her. I told myself I was making the right decision, but sometimes I wonder if I took the easy way out instead."

Every now and then she told herself the only solution to her problem was to fall out of love with Jeff. To figure out his flaws and focus on them. And then he went and did something like admitting his faults and regretting them. Because so many people ignored what was wrong. So many people simply pretended they were always right and everyone else screwed up.

"You wanted what was best for your daughter," she pointed out.

"I sent her away."

"You sent her to a well-respected school where she was able to be with girls her own age and grow."

"I sent her away."

"Yes, you did and saying that over and over again doesn't change what happened. If you really believe you were wrong, tell her and apologize. If you made the best decision you could under the circumstances, then get over it."

One corner of his mouth turned up. "That's telling me."

"I didn't have a choice. You were turning into a girl."

He chuckled. "You always surprise me, Helen. And I mean that in a good way. You're smart, you're determined, you speak your mind. When your ex cheated on you, you booted him out on his ass. I admire that. I should have done the same thing with Marilee. Instead I put up with her ways for years. What lesson did that teach my girls?"

"At least you got married for a fairly noble reason."

"Because I knocked her up?"

"You know what I mean. You did the right thing. I can't even say I did that."

"Why did you marry Troy?" He held up a hand. "Sorry. I shouldn't have asked that. You were in love with him."

She stared into Jeff's brown eyes and knew she had to come clean. If not for him, then for herself. To say the truth aloud meant it wouldn't have power over her anymore.

"He was the first person to say he loved me after my parents died. No one else ever had. I'm sure my aunt and uncle cared about me, but they weren't the type to say the words."

"Helen."

His tone was gentle and caring. For a second she thought he was going to reach for her, but there was only the single word. Alas.

"They weren't bad people," she continued. "But it made me sad, so when he said he loved me, I married him." She grimaced. "And then he cheated, so I threw him out." She held up a hand. "I take that back. The first time, I gave him a chance. The second time, I threw him out."

"Admirable."

Before she could say anything else, the front door opened and a couple of customers walked in. Helen felt the tenuous connection between her and Jeff snap as she rose to greet them.

Customers were seated, orders taken. She poured coffee and chatted and before she knew it, Jeff was waving goodbye. She gave him a quick smile as she went to pick up several breakfasts.

The work was familiar, she thought, and all she'd known for years. Funny how she hadn't planned to stay in Tulpen Crossing. She'd saved like crazy for college, thinking she would get her degree and leave town. She'd been considering nursing—the kind of skill that meant she could get a job anywhere and always support herself. Because that was important. Her parents had died broke, leaving her little more than memories and a piano. Her aunt and uncle had made it clear that once she turned eighteen she was on her own. If she wanted to continue to work at the diner, then she could still live with them. Otherwise, she was expected to leave.

She'd chosen the most sensible path—working full-time at the diner and taking classes at Skagit Valley College, all the while saving every penny she could for when she transferred to a four-year college. She'd met Troy her second quarter. They'd started dating and somehow she hadn't had the time for her third quarter. An embarrassing truth, but there it was.

Instead she'd told herself she was in love and had accepted his proposal. They'd moved in together, had a small wedding and life had gone on with her working at the diner. Dreams of leaving town had been put on hold. After the divorce, she'd been too hurt and embarrassed to do much more than get through her day. And just when she'd been thinking of going back to college, her uncle had suffered his first stroke.

While he'd recovered from that, his second stroke had left him much more debilitated. Her aunt had offered to sell her the diner at a reasonable price. Helen had spent two weeks considering her options before coming to the realization that she had nowhere else to go. No family, no connections. Everyone she knew in the world lived in Tulpen Crossing. Ironically, Troy had left town after the divorce.

So she'd made the decision to stay. To buy the diner and make her life here. She'd taken up playing the piano again and through that had started working with JML, and had fallen for her best friend's father. And here she was, all these years later, still in love with him.

She wasn't sure if that made her slightly foolish or mortally idiotic, because to date she had no evidence that Jeff saw her as other than a friend.

Which left her with only two options—get over him or take a chance and be willing to live with the consequences. Because if he turned her down, well, then she would have nothing at all.

Kelly couldn't remember ever having a hangover. She wasn't one to get drunk very often, or ever. She enjoyed the occasional cocktail or glass of wine, but she was fairly confident she'd never downed half a bottle of vodka before.

Most of the details of the concert were hazy. She knew she'd hung out with Griffith and had said some fairly unfortunate things. What exactly wasn't clear, although she did have a humiliating recollection of complaining that Olivia had boobs and she didn't.

Somewhere around 2:00 a.m. she'd gotten up to drink more water and had promptly thrown up in the kitchen sink. That had been attractive. She'd stayed up, sipping water until nearly four when it had seemed safe for her to go back to bed. She'd slept until six thirty.

One shower later, she was feeling almost human. The pounding in her head was pretty awful but wouldn't be fixed until she could down an aspirin—something that couldn't happen until she ate. The thought of food was enough to make her want to kill herself, only she didn't think she had a choice.

She pulled on jeans and a T-shirt, then ran a comb through her wet hair. Maybe dry toast, she thought. Or a banana. She thought she'd read somewhere that a banana was good for a hangover because of the potassium.

She stumbled to the kitchen and put a slice of bread in the toaster. Her father, a great, great man, who had warned her she was going to feel awful this morning, had started coffee before he'd left for the diner. She poured herself a cup and did her best not to notice how her hands shook.

The first sip had her system relaxing just a bit. When the toast popped, she grabbed it and took a bite. Her stomach was silent.

Kelly offered a prayer of thanksgiving before finishing the slice and her coffee. Only then did she down an aspirin and start to believe that yes, she was going to be all right. Except for what she might or might not have said to Griffith.

She also had to deal with her truck. She'd left it at the craft mall. When her dad got home, she would ask him to drive her out there. Yet one more check mark in the embarrassing column.

"Good morning."

The happy, loud voice made her wince. She turned and saw Olivia walking into the kitchen. Her sister also wore jeans, but aside from the basic concept, they were nothing like Kelly's. The denim was darker and the fit tighter. Olivia's jeans were long, coming to the heel of her stylish boots. A purple sweater with a deep V exposed just enough cleavage to remind Kelly of her shortcomings.

Olivia's hair was still all wavy, beachy, and she had on the kind of makeup that emphasized her perfect features. It was annoying and intimidating and made Kelly want to throw coffee in her pretty face.

"Morning," she mumbled instead, when what she really wanted to ask was "Is everything you own either pretty or beautiful?" There was no point as she already knew the answer. Not that cute, stylish clothes were practical. Kelly was a farmer, after all. She would spend her day grubbing and hauling, but jeez, it was so depressing. And unfair.

Still, she wouldn't say any of that to her sister. To be honest, none of what Kelly was thinking was Olivia's fault, which made her feel guilty, so she said, "Are you getting settled?"

"I am. It's strange being back."

"I would imagine. Did you have fun last night with your friends?"

Olivia hesitated. "It was great. How was the band?"

"Awful. They usually are. They had their own vocalist. She was okay, but my friend Helen is way better."

Olivia poured herself a cup of coffee. "Are you going to the farm today?"

"I'd planned to, why?"

Olivia studied her for a second. "I thought maybe we could spend some time together. After all, we're sisters and we barely know each other."

Guilt flooded Kelly. Guilt because she'd been the one to suggest sending her sister away. Guilt because she'd never wanted to be friends with the person she saw as their mother incarnate.

"Some of the reason is that as I grew up, you were always mad at me," Olivia went on. "I get it. I was a pain in the butt and you thought I was too much like Mom."

Kelly felt her mouth fall open. She carefully closed it. "I never said that."

"You didn't have to."

Say it! Tell her! The voice in her head was so loud and spoke in time with the pounding of her headache. This was the moment, she thought, to come clean and say that she had been the reason Olivia had been sent away. Only the words got stuck and wouldn't move.

"We've always been different," Olivia said.

"I know. I take after Dad and you…" Kelly sipped her coffee.

"I don't take after Mom that much." Olivia glanced away.

There was something about the way she said it—as if she knew one way or the other.

"Do you ever see her?" Kelly asked.

Olivia sipped her coffee. "Ah, sometimes. Not all that often."

Wow—there was information. Once Marilee had taken off, Kelly had never wanted to spend time with her mother again. Of course she and her mom had a very different relationship than Olivia and Marilee.

"You and I were always on opposite sides," Kelly said. "Me with Dad and you with Mom."

"Soldiers in their war."

"Is that how you saw it?" Kelly asked. "I never did. Dad didn't fight."

"He should have. Things would have been better if he'd stood up to her."

"I know. I think he was trying to get along." Not that she wanted to say anything bad about Jeff. He'd been a good dad—always there for her.

"I was asking about the farm before because I thought we could hang out together. After work."

"That would be great," Kelly said automatically, then wondered what on earth they were supposed to do together. She doubted she and Olivia had anything in common and it wasn't as if there was a ton to do in Tulpen Crossing. Part of the reason they had trouble attracting tourists in the off-season.

"I have a tourism board meeting tonight," she said. "We're trying to update the local craft mall and figure out ways to get more tourists to come to town. Maybe you could help us brainstorm."

She expected Olivia to roll her eyes at the suggestion. Instead her sister nodded eagerly.

"I'd like that a lot. I worked with a couple of charities in Phoenix. Maybe some of the things we did there will work here."

Kelly didn't know which was more surprising—her sister's enthusiasm or the fact that she'd volunteered for something. Which wasn't fair, she reminded herself. Olivia wasn't a teenager anymore. She'd grown up, graduated college and had created a life of her own away from her family. Of course she was different.

"That would be really helpful." Kelly smiled.

"I hope so. I'll see you after work."

"You will."

Kelly poured coffee into a to-go mug and grabbed her bag. She opened the back door just in time to remember that she had no transportation, only to find her truck sitting where it was supposed to be. The keys were in the ignition and a bottle of aspirin was on the front seat with a note that said, *Hope it's not too bad this morning. G*

Griffith had somehow arranged to return her truck to her. Talk about above and beyond, she thought happily. She might not be sure about what to do about her sister, but her decision about Griffith's suggestion was getting more and more clear.

She slid into the driver's seat, then reached for her purse when she heard her phone chirp. The text message was from Helen.

Your dad just left. Olivia's back? Are you still in shock?

Yes. Shocked. Stunned and seriously hungover. Missed you last night.

I heard the band was awful. I didn't miss hearing that. Need to talk?

I'm okay. I'll fill you in on everything tonight. Oh, Olivia's coming with me.

Why?

I honest to God have no idea.

8

Olivia tidied the kitchen after her sister left, not that there was much to do. Kelly had only eaten toast and coffee and Jeff had left her a note that during the week, he ate at a local diner. The scrawled PS offered to take her along, but the "I leave at 5:30" had her shuddering. Um, no thanks.

They all had lives, she thought as she poured her second cup of coffee and leaned against the counter. They had their routines, time had moved on. While she knew that in her head, she was still surprised. Part of her had expected life in Tulpen Crossing to be exactly as she had remembered it, with no one changing but her. How silly.

The back door opened and her dad walked in.

"Hey, sweetie."

"Hi, Dad. How was breakfast?"

"Good, as always. Did you sleep well?"

"Uh-huh. The bed's still comfortable."

"I'm glad to hear that."

He poured himself a mug of coffee and smiled at her.

Her dad looked good—trim and fit, with only a few wrinkles around his eyes. While Marilee held back the hands of time with Botox and fillers, her dad could pass for a decade younger than his age all on his own. The product of great genes and clean living, she supposed.

"Kelly already gone?" he asked.

Olivia nodded.

He flashed a grin. "She got a little drunk last night, so I would guess she's not feeling her best today."

A hangover? "Does she get drunk a lot?" Kelly didn't seem the type.

"Not usually. I brought her home. I was going to help her get her truck, but unless she walked to the farm, someone took care of that for her."

"Her truck was here this morning."

"What are you going to do with your day?" her dad asked.

"I thought I'd explore the town—see what's changed. I'm excited that it's not already ninety degrees."

"How do you stand the heat?"

"You get used to it." Although in the middle of summer, no one enjoyed 108 degrees with a low of 95.

"I'm glad to have you home." Jeff kissed her cheek. "You let me know if you need anything."

"I will, Dad. Thanks."

There hadn't been a lot of fanfare, but that was okay. Olivia trusted her father's steady acceptance more than any parade. Marilee had been welcoming at first, but lately that had changed and Kelly had no idea why. Nor did she know why she'd lied about how much she saw her mother. Instinct, maybe. Being sent away had taught her that the only person she could trust was herself.

She rinsed her mug and set it in the sink, then went back to her room to check email. She'd been in touch with her clients before she left, but wanted to make sure they were all okay.

By ten she'd finished with email, had played three games of Solitaire and was wondering how on earth she was going to get through a whole summer with nothing to do. Her dad had long since left for work. Everyone had somewhere to be but her. She grabbed her bag and walked out to her car. The air was cool, the sky cloudy. She had a feeling it might actually rain.

Up here that wasn't anything but ordinary. If she stayed long enough maybe she would start to take the rain for granted, just like everyone else.

She drove to the end of the street, then merged onto the main road. The town had grown just enough to be slightly unfamiliar, as if it had somehow shifted out of focus. She saw a few new stores. The library had been refurbished. What had been an old grocery store was now a bowling alley and some kind of music school. She kept driving until she reached the edge of a huge field, then pulled to the side of the road.

For as far as the eye could see was flat, groomed earth. She wasn't sure how many acres her family owned, but it was a lot. Murphy Tulips were sought after all over the country. They were known for quality blooms, delivered on time. The main crop was traditional tulips in a variety of colors, but the company also had a small but growing exotic collection. If you wanted Russian Princess tulips for a dinner party, Murphy Tulips was the one to call.

Even though she'd never been interested in the family business as a kid, she couldn't help learning a few things by virtue of where she'd grown up. She knew that every fall bulbs were planted in the fields and come spring they would grow and blossom into beautiful flowers. Once they were harvested, the bulbs were dug up and sorted. Those deemed healthy and hearty could be reused, a process different from hothouse tulips.

Olivia pulled onto the road and drove back toward the highway and turned into what looked like a big antiques mall. They had a couple similar malls in Phoenix and she'd always found them a great place to shop for staging projects. She could often find unusual pieces at a great price.

She parked in front. Despite the fact that The Dutch Bunch had been open for a couple of hours, there was only one other car in the lot. That wasn't good for business, she thought.

She walked inside and was immediately overwhelmed by several large, busy displays with too much information. There were notices about activities, posters for a couple of local hotels and restaurants and a corkboard covered with business cards. Flanking the disarray were mock room settings filled with ugly furniture and too many decorations in a tulip theme. There were tulip pictures and tulips slipcovers. Wooden tulips on a table covered in a tulip-print tablecloth. A tulip rug, tulip stenciled bassinette. Even someone who loved tulips would find it all overwhelming. No wonder there weren't a lot of customers— Olivia imagined most of them had turned and run in terror.

She walked past the horrible tableau and went down one of the main aisles. Here things were more like she expected. Different booths featuring different items for sale. Some were craft-based while others were antiques and a few had nothing but junk.

She stopped in front of a booth filled with quilts. The work was lovely—beautiful and well-made, but the display was terrible. Only two quilts were hanging. The rest were stacked, with only a bit of the design showing. Olivia would guess the owner wanted to display as much of her work as possible, but nothing about this was working. She should hang three or four quilts, then have a binder with high-quality pictures of her inventory. A pretty chest could hold several dozen of them, so a customer had choices.

She continued wandering the aisles only to find herself forced to make a sharp right turn that ended in a blank wall. She went back the way she'd come and realized she'd missed several rows of booths. The flow of the mall was all wrong, she thought. There would be booths and vendors that no one would see. There had to be a better way. She wondered if there was someone she could—

"Don't bother," she murmured to herself as she headed back to the front of the building. As her mother had told her countless times, no one cared what she thought. They never had.

★ ★ ★

The scent of blueberries and sugar and something baking filled the café. Helen's stomach growled, despite the fact that she'd managed to grab a salad at eleven, before the big lunch rush. Still, it had been small and dressing-free and whatever was happening in the kitchen needed to be tasted.

"What are you doing, taunting me like that?" she asked as she walked in back.

Delja stood at the stove with Sven by her side. They were each stirring a large pot. Here the delicious smell was intense to the point of being heady but what really caught her attention was the contrast between the two friends.

Sven topped Delja by at least a foot. He was broad-shouldered and chiseled, some from his job and some from working out. Delja was short and round. He was blond-haired and blue-eyed. Delja had dark hair and eyes. He was Nordic, she was Russian, but they came together over their love of cooking.

Sven had shown up in the diner's kitchen shortly after he'd moved to town and asked if he could use the large stove. He'd been so charming, no one had thought to tell him no. Every few weeks he would arrive with interesting ingredients. Together he and Delja would create something amazing for the following day's special.

"You're killing me," Helen said as she peered into the pots and saw early blueberries simmering in a thick sauce.

"She's on another diet," Delja said, rolling her eyes.

Ack! Did her friend have to choose this moment to start speaking in more than single words?

"Sven doesn't need to know that," Helen said quickly, hoping she didn't blush. After all, Sven was the poster boy for physical perfection.

"You're beautiful," Delja told her. "Don't change."

"I agree." Sven held out a spoon coated in thick, dark purple sauce. "Try this."

She hesitated for a second before taking the spoon and putting it to her lips. The explosions of flavors—sweet blueberries, something tart and a hint of butter and brown sugar had her groaning.

"You're the devil."

"So I've been told," Sven said with a grin. "Tomorrow you'll have blintzes and crepes on the menu."

Helen held in a whimper. How was she supposed to exist on plain salad while surrounded by blintzes?

"I have a meeting at JML," she said. "You two will lock up when you're done?"

Delja nodded. She motioned for Helen to move close, then hugged her tight.

"Beautiful girl."

"Thanks. You're always good to me."

Delja smiled.

"Come here, you," Sven said, surprising her by pulling her into his embrace.

Helen didn't have time to wonder if Sven had decided to see her as more than a friend. Before she could gather any thoughts at all, he'd squeezed all the air out of her and then ruffled her hair.

"You're fine. Stop trying to change."

"Thanks," she said between clenched teeth. "Great advice."

Ruffled her hair? What, was she five? Apparently no one saw her as a sexual being. It was incredibly disappointing. Not that she wanted Sven but still.

She drove to JML and walked inside. It was too early for lessons, so the building was blissfully silent—except for the occasional smack of a bowling ball hitting pins. But when compared to the indignities the untrained could inflict on an innocent guitar, the sound was almost welcome.

She found Isaak in his office. She waved as she plopped down in one of the visitor chairs.

"Let me guess," she said with a grin. "You have a new group that wants to learn every song from the Foo Fighters."

"I wish, but no. I'm hosting a showcase."

"You're always hosting a showcase. I heard the one last night was particularly challenging for those attending."

He groaned. "Tell me about it. You were lucky you didn't have to be there. But this is different. There are a couple of other music schools that do what we do. We've been talking about organizing something together. It's going to be up here at Petal Pushers."

"They changed the name. It's The Dutch Bunch now."

"Whatever. I can't keep up. Anyway, the venue is great and we're each going to bring our best bands and players. I thought you and Jeff could do a duet."

Naked, she thought dreamily. That was the duet she was most interested in. Naked Jeff and naked her. Not onstage, though. In her bedroom. Yup, that would be fantastic. Just their bodies touching and rubbing and—

"Helen?"

"What? Oh, sorry. That would be great. We can do our usual."

Isaak sighed. "Not everyone likes Billy Joel."

"Everyone should. He's an icon and my personal piano hero."

"I thought you could try something different." He passed over sheet music.

She picked it up and glanced at the title. As she didn't know if she should laugh or scream, the sound that escaped had a snort-like quality to it.

"You're kidding."

"Nope. You'd be great."

"It's not a duet."

"It could be."

Helen briefly closed her eyes. "'*Wrecking Ball*'? I doubt Jeff knows who Miley Cyrus is and I know he's never heard the song. It's not his style."

"Neither is Billy Joel but Jeff does it for you. I think 'Wrecking Ball' has potential." Isaak winked. "Plus, he'll love the video."

Helen winced. No offense to anyone, but having Jeff watch that particular video was not going to get him in the mood to have sex with her. Miley was too beautiful, too perfect, too everything. Ordinary, plump women wouldn't stand a chance.

"I'll talk to him," she said.

"Your lack of enthusiasm is inspiring."

"I still think we should stick with what works."

"No Billy Joel."

She took the music and stood. "I'm going to tell Billy you said that and he's going to come beat the crap out of you, so there."

Isaak laughed. "I'm willing to take the chance."

9

By the time Kelly was due to leave for the tourist board meeting, she was back to her regular self.

In deference to Olivia and not because her sister made her feel frumpy and androgynous, Kelly dug out a pair of relatively new jeans and a long-sleeved white shirt she rarely wore because it required ironing when it was washed. She took an extra couple of minutes with her hair, releasing it from her usual ponytail and fluffing it with her fingers. She thought briefly about mascara, but was afraid the single tube she owned might be well over a year old and God knew what could be growing in it. She settled on swiping on a little Burt's Bees lip balm and called it a night.

When she stepped into the hall, she caught sight of her sister and thought maybe she should have risked an eye infection. Olivia had changed into a dress. Not just any dress, but a pretty sleeveless one that was white at the top and bottom with wide bands of different shades of pink and red in the middle. The dress had a relatively high neck, was fitted to the waist, then flared out to just above Olivia's knees.

Her bare legs were toned and tanned and she wore a high-heeled nude pump. Her hair was pulled back into a French braid. She had on pearl studs and the kind of makeup that made her look sophisticated and competent.

Kelly felt her meager confidence shrivel and die as she turned from normal human to genderless country mouse. Telling herself she didn't care about things like clothes and makeup didn't help. Not when faced with a living, breathing example of what both could accomplish.

Olivia smiled. "Hi. I'm ready. You said six thirty and I didn't want to keep you waiting."

"You're right on time," Kelly said, hoping she didn't sound as bitter as she felt. It wasn't Olivia's fault Kelly felt inept when it came to things like fashion.

"I'm really interested in the meeting tonight," Olivia said as they walked out to Kelly's truck. "I spent the afternoon researching tourism in the area and in other towns similar to this one. There are a lot of things that can be done to draw in tourists." She opened the passenger door. "Don't worry. I'll only take notes and give you my thoughts later. You can use them or not."

Kelly put her key in the ignition. "What do you mean?"

"It's your meeting. I'm not going to butt in."

"Trust me, any ideas would be welcome. We're all at a loss. The tourist season around here is way too brief. Once the tulips are gone, so are the people. The hotels are full all summer long, but everyone is busy going somewhere else. We have the same weather as the rest of western Washington. It's pretty. Why not spend the weekend here?"

"You wouldn't mind if I said something?"

"Of course not. Is that what you did today? Computer research?"

"I drove around this morning. There are a few changes, but not that many. I went to The Dutch Bunch."

"What did you think?"

"It has a lot of potential, but right now it's a mess. That display by the door is overwhelming and way too busy. It's going to frighten people away. And the layout of the booths is odd. There are entire sections you can't get to without knowing where you're going. How does anyone make any money?"

"I'm not sure anyone does."

Kelly had to admit she'd never much thought about how the craft mall was laid out.

"Did your friends seem different?" she asked. "Or is everyone the same?"

"A bit of both."

"I know you mentioned wanting to see Ryan. It's possible he's dating someone. Just so you're prepared and all." She glanced at her sister, then back at the road. "I'm saying that to give you a heads-up. Not to hurt you or anything."

Olivia stared at her. "Why would you think I'd assume you wanted to hurt me? I know you don't. We might not have been close since we were little, Kelly, but you're still my sister. I'm going to assume the best about you until you prove to me I shouldn't."

Wow—that was mature. And nice. And unexpected.

"Ah, me, too." Great, so not only was Olivia the prettier sister, she was also more mature and gracious. Kelly sighed. "Okay, don't get mad, but I thought you'd be more like Mom. Not that I know anything about her now, but I thought you'd be like how she was before."

"Cruel and slutty?"

"Not that, exactly. It's just you two were so close and it was hard on you when she left."

Olivia stared out the window. "It was hard on you, too. You might not have gotten along, but she was still your mother and you were only fifteen."

"You were twelve. She was your world. I know you were devastated." She drew in a breath. "I'm sorry I wasn't there for you more. You know, when she left. I should have been more understanding."

"You were going through your own thing."

"It was my fault she left," Kelly said quickly.

"No, it wasn't. She was going to leave anyway. Even I knew that. You don't actually believe you drove her away, do you?"

"Sometimes. I wish I didn't, but every now and then I wonder if I pushed her over the edge."

"She was already there."

Kelly hoped that was true, then shook her head. That wasn't right, not sure how to explain it, even to herself. Everything with Marilee was complicated.

"You said you see her," Kelly said. "Are you close?"

"I barely know her."

"I wonder where she is now. What she's doing. Did she remarry?"

Olivia shook her head. "She's not the type."

"I guess not. I never hear from her. After she left, I kept waiting for her to get in touch with me, but she never did."

"I kept waiting, too." Olivia's tone was bitter. "I'm the one who reached out to her. It's not as if she missed having a daughter around."

Kelly pulled into the parking lot. When she turned off the engine, she faced her sister. "I really am sorry about all you went through."

"We both went through a lot." Olivia wrinkled her nose. "I keep telling myself to get over all the childhood drama. It happened a long time ago and I'm a different person now. Only I can't seem to let go of all of it, you know?"

"I do," Kelly said slowly, pushing down the guilt swelling inside of her. Olivia wasn't just dealing with the fact that her mother had left. She had the additional trauma of having been sent away when she was only fifteen. A decision Kelly had been a significant part of.

"This place has potential," Olivia said, pointing to the building. "Who manages it?"

"The craft mall doesn't have a manager. It just sort of runs itself. You apply to rent a booth and when one opens up, it's yours. We pay by the quarter for our booth." She tried to think of a few other facts. "Oh, the tourist board is in charge because the craft mall is supposed to attract tourists to the area."

Olivia looked from the building back to her. "Seriously?"

"Maybe it's not doing a great job."

"You think?" Olivia got out of the truck.

Kelly joined her and they walked inside. As they passed the entrance to the booth part of the building, Kelly glanced at the main display and winced. Olivia was right. It was a mess and kind of overwhelming. Maybe someone should clean it up or something.

They walked back to the community room. Rows of chairs had been set up facing the small stage. Judging by the number of seats provided, someone was expecting a large crowd. Kelly had a feeling that was more about optimism than an actual likely head count. There were about six people in the room and she would be impressed if they even doubled the number of attendees.

Olivia excused herself to use the restroom. When she'd walked away, Kelly spotted Helen.

She crossed to her friend who met her by the chairs.

"OMG!" Helen said, giving her a quick hug. "She's really here. Wow, she looks great. I love the dress. Oh, to be that thin and gorgeous. Why didn't you call me? I would have thought the unexpected return of your long, lost sister was call-worthy."

"I know, I know. I'm sorry. I was in shock and didn't know what to do, so I ran. I came here for the showcase because I thought you were playing with Dad. I forgot the band had their own vocalist."

"How was she?"

"Awful."

Helen grinned. "Oh, good. More work for me." Her smile faded. "Are you okay? How's it going? Is it weird?"

"More than weird." Kelly glanced over her shoulder and saw Olivia chatting with Sally.

"What's she like?"

"I don't know. In some ways really nice. She's all grown up. It's been eleven years, but I didn't expect her to be so mature."

"Your dad's excited," Helen told her. "He was practically giddy this morning." She pressed her lips together as if she didn't want to say too much.

Kelly could read between the lines. No doubt her father wrestled with the same guilt that she did.

"Ladies."

Kelly turned as Griffith joined them. Her heart gave an unexpected little bump in her chest and she suddenly didn't know where to put her hands. In her pockets, behind her back, on Griffith's chest? All options that left her flustered...especially that last one. Which was curious because she wasn't the type to be...

A hazy memory of her asking if he was going to kiss her stirred. Heat burned her cheeks as she ducked her head. No. That couldn't have... She hadn't...

The need to run exploded but by then he'd reached them and there was no way to escape.

"How are you feeling?" he asked Kelly. "All recovered?" He looked at Helen. "Our girl here drank a fair amount of vodka."

Helen's brows rose. "In celebration of your sister's return, no doubt. Did you hydrate?"

"Yes, and I took aspirin and I feel fine. It was nothing." She cleared her throat. "Thank you for bringing my truck back."

"You're welcome. You owe me."

The teasing tone did a number on her stomach, not to mention other parts of her. Ack! She had to get a grip.

Griffith looked over to where Olivia was now talking to a larger group of people. She said something and everyone laughed.

"Your sister, I presume. I see the resemblance."

Kelly laughed. "If you mean we're both female, then sure. Otherwise, she's the sophisticated Disney princess and I'm the unremarkable face they draw for the background."

Both Helen and Griffith swung their attention back to her.

Kelly realized a second too late that the words might have sounded more bitter than she'd intended.

"Um, what I meant was—"

Griffith stared at her. "Kelly, I like you just fine the way you are but if you're not happy, you should make a change."

She flushed. "No, I didn't mean that…exactly."

Helen kept her mouth shut but looked plenty knowing. Kelly was sure there would be talk of this conversation later.

Sven walked into the room and waved to her.

"The competition," Griffith murmured. "You're trying to make me jealous."

"Oh, please. You know it's long over."

"Just checking. I don't want to be your rebound guy."

"I'm not the rebound guy type."

"This is just so interesting," Helen said. "You two do remember I'm standing right here, don't you?"

"You're best friends." Griffith winked at her. "You already know everything. There's no point in pretending otherwise."

"A wise man." Helen laughed. "I'm intrigued and can't wait to see how this plays out."

Olivia joined them. She smiled her perfect, pearly white smile. "Hi. I'm Kelly's sister, Olivia."

Kelly introduced Griffith and Helen, then kept her eye on her non-boyfriend to see how he would react to the sensual power that was her sister.

"Nice to meet you," he said, shaking her hand. "You used to date my brother, didn't you?"

Kelly relaxed. There was no obvious tension in his body and his tongue wasn't hanging out, so hey, a win for her.

"Some in high school, then later in college." Olivia sounded disinterested at best. "Who's that guy?"

"Sven," Helen said with a grin. "Isn't he beautiful?"

"I'll say. Yours?"

"The man ruffles my hair when he hugs me, so no. As far as

I know, he's completely single." She looked at Kelly. "Unless you know something I don't."

Kelly knew that her friend was making sure she didn't mind if her sister made a play for her ex, which was lovely and supportive.

"He's not seeing anyone," Kelly told her sister. "It's a small town. We all know when someone sneezes, let alone dates."

Olivia nodded slowly. "I'm going to have to go introduce myself. Just to be neighborly."

"Is that what we're calling it these days?"

Olivia grinned. "In mixed company, yes." She made a beeline for Sven.

"She's not awful," Helen whispered after she was out of earshot. "You must be relieved."

"I am. But the sister thing is strange."

Sally walked to the podium on the stage. "It's seven o'clock, everyone. Let's get the meeting started."

Helen and Kelly started toward the chairs. Griffith joined them and sat next to her. Olivia settled on the other side of Helen, then shocked the hell out of Kelly by pulling a small notebook out of her purse.

Kelly leaned across Helen. "What's that?"

"I did some research this afternoon. Demographics on the town and the surrounding counties, that sort of thing. It would help a lot if we were on the sound. Waterfront communities always brings in a crowd."

"Not something we can easily change," Helen said.

"I know." Olivia sighed. "Unless there was a really big earthquake and the western part of the county fell into the sound. But that's probably not something I should wish for."

"Death and destruction," Griffith whispered in Kelly's ear. "I'd go see the movie."

"You're such a guy."

"You wouldn't want me any other way."

★ ★ ★

Despite the tall blond Viking god sitting at the edge of her peripheral vision, Olivia paid attention to the woman leading the meeting. Ryan might have been part of her returning home game plan but she knew he was someone she could manage. Sven, on the other hand, was an unknown. The last thing she needed was a messy affair mucking up her summer. But if the opportunity presented itself, she might be willing to change her mind, just not tonight.

After a slightly rambling introduction, Sally had gotten to the point of the meeting. Getting more tourists in town.

"Maybe some kind of summer festival," one person suggested. "The old Johnson farm is growing potatoes."

"No one wants to take pictures of potatoes," Sally said. "Pumpkins are attractive. Is anyone growing pumpkins?"

"I have a couple of vines in my garden."

"I doubt that's going to attract many people."

"What about opening up the tulip fields to tourists?" Olivia asked.

Everyone turned to look at her.

"Excuse me?" Kelly asked. "Open it up for what?"

"Planting. Bulbs are planted in the fall. We could invite people to come plant."

"I don't think so. I don't want a bunch of people who have no idea what they're doing anywhere near my farm."

"I'm talking about a couple of acres near the road. You wouldn't miss them at all. People would make the trip for a big planting party. It would give them ownership. They could sign up for a newsletter and get updates on how their bulbs are doing. Then they'd for sure want to come back in the spring."

"She's right," someone called. "It could be fun."

"Not for me," Kelly grumbled. "This is how I make my living, people."

"It's a couple of acres," Olivia repeated. "Seattle is about an hour away. The population of the metro area is nearly four million people and they all ignore us except when the tulips are blooming. We need to change that. I've been researching what other small towns are doing to attract tourists and their dollars, and the list is impressive. We have to work with what we have to be more appealing."

She motioned to the space around them. "This craft mall, for example. It has potential but it needs to be updated. I walked through it today and the flow isn't user friendly. There were booths I couldn't get to without looking at a map and backtracking three times."

"I told you," an older man said. "It's not set up right."

"The bigger problem is the roof," someone in the back yelled. "No point in putting lipstick on a pig. If we don't get a new roof soon, we won't have a craft mall."

The room went silent. Sally sighed. "Yes, the roof. You're right. That is the bigger problem."

"What about a bake sale?" a woman offered. "Or a car wash?"

Olivia raised her hand. "How much is the new roof?"

"Thirty thousand, give or take."

"You're not going to get there on cupcakes."

Sally raised her eyebrows. "You have a better idea?"

Olivia felt everyone turning to stare at her. She knew what they were thinking. She was an outsider—she didn't belong. The only reason they were listening was that she was Kelly's sister.

"An auction," she said confidently. "A big evening with a nice dinner. A silent auction during cocktails and a live auction during dinner."

"We don't have the money to pay for that," the old man grumbled.

"Get a couple of sponsors and price the tickets at seventy-five dollars each and you don't have to."

"Seventy-five dollars?" the old man asked, his tone outraged. "Who pays that for dinner?"

"A lot of people. I'm not talking burgers and fries." Olivia smiled at Helen. "No offense."

"None taken. I actually like the idea of an auction. We haven't done anything like that before. There are people with money around here. They don't want to be bothered with a lot of donation requests, but I'll bet we could get them to come to an auction. It would be a matter of offering the right items."

The unexpected support gave Olivia courage. "I've done this sort of thing before for a women's shelter, and it was very successful. Helen's right. It's about getting the right kind of donations to draw a big crowd."

"You could donate one of your tiny homes," Kelly murmured to Griffith.

"It would be cheaper to just pay for the roof." He looked at Olivia. "I'll donate a custom design and a five-thousand-dollar gift certificate."

Several people gasped.

Olivia had a feeling she looked as shocked as Kelly.

"Thank you," she managed to answer.

"I'll donate the garden for the house," Viking-god Sven said loudly. "And a thousand dollars' worth of plants for someone else."

"Oh, all right," the older guy grumbled. "The missus and I have season tickets to the Seahawks. We're going on a cruise and will miss one of the games. You can have those."

Seattle was a rabid football town, Olivia thought as she scribbled in her notebook. If she could put together a package with a hotel and dinner at a nice restaurant, she could have a great item.

Several more people offered suggestions. Olivia wrote them all down. Sally called for a vote.

"All in favor of letting Olivia here plan an auction to help pay for the roof, raise your hand."

Every hand shot up.

"Then that's what we're going to do." Sally looked at Olivia. "I want a comprehensive plan in ten days. Can you do that?"

Olivia felt a flush of pride. "I can." She hadn't expected to walk out with a job, but she would take it. As for the no pay part, that was a detail.

"Good."

They moved on to other business, then the meeting ended. Olivia approached Sally and got her contact info.

"Let me give you my cell, as well," Olivia said. "I'm hoping word will spread and people will want to call me to donate things."

"Oh, honey, you have no idea. Brace yourself. There's going to be junk."

"There always is."

"How did your event in Phoenix go?"

A simple enough question. Olivia had gotten involved with the women's shelter at Marilee's request. Her mother had wanted to bring attention to the real estate company—helping battered women was simply the delivery device for what she saw as earned media.

While Olivia had started out with the same attitude, she'd quickly found herself enjoying the work. She liked convincing people to give more than they'd planned and had enjoyed the overwhelming details of helping put on a fancy dinner for five hundred people. Unfortunately after two years, Marilee had complained the event was taking too much time and she wasn't getting enough in return.

"The second year, we increased our donations for the night by thirty percent," Olivia said proudly. "It was nearly a million dollars."

"I see. So thirty thousand doesn't intimidate you."

"Not at all."

Olivia walked back to her seat. Griffith rose and pulled Kelly to her feet. "Give your sister your truck keys."

"Why?"

"Because she's going to drive herself home. You and I are going out."

Kelly looked surprised, then flustered. "I can't. It's only Olivia's second night here. I should go home with her."

Olivia rolled her eyes. "I'm perfectly fine on my own." She held out her hand. "I know how to drive a truck. Hand over the keys." She smiled. "You're insured, right?"

Kelly flinched. "You're kidding."

"It's a small pickup with automatic transmission, sis. Not an eighteen-wheeler. I'll be fine."

"Okay. I won't be late."

Griffith winked. "She'll be late."

They walked out together.

Olivia watched them go. While part of her *had* wanted to spend the rest of the evening with her sister, she'd said what she had because of the Marilee lie. Guilt was a powerful motivator, she thought.

She wasn't even sure why she'd avoided the truth—something she was confident a psychologist would have a field day with. Was it because her relationship with her mother was so strained these days? Or was she embarrassed by the fact that she'd gone looking for her mother in the first place? Questions that would not be answered tonight, she told herself.

She felt a small twinge of something she was afraid might be envy. Not because she wanted Griffith for herself but because he seemed nice. He wouldn't have an agenda or a wife waiting at home. He wasn't interested in arm candy or status. He was just a regular kind of guy who was smitten with her sister. It was the kind of relationship Olivia had never had before. Men looked at her and saw—

To be honest, she had no idea what they saw but it wasn't anything close to being smitten. Men wanted to sleep with her, to show her off, to claim her, but no one had ever loved her. Especially not Ryan.

So why had she come back for him? What did she think was going to happen?

"It doesn't matter," she whispered as she walked to her sister's truck. She was here now. She could figure out what she was capable of without having to worry about what Marilee would do or think. She was free. The auction would be a success or failure completely due to her. This was her chance to prove what she could do. To the world and maybe to herself.

10

Griffith took Kelly's hand and led her out to the parking lot. She stopped by his truck and stared at their joined hands.

"Technically you never asked," she told him. "About tonight or any of it. You're assuming I said yes to your proposition."

She looked good in the dim light of the parking lot. All big eyes and pouty mouth. He also noticed that while she made her complaint, she didn't bother pulling her hand away.

"I'm not assuming. You did say yes."

"When?"

He grinned. "When you asked if I was going to kiss you."

"That never happened. And if it did, it was the vodka talking."

"Oh, I know it was the vodka, but it was also you." He opened the door to his truck. "Get in."

She climbed onto the passenger seat. "Where are we going?"

"My place."

"Should I be worried?"

He grinned. "Yes, but not for the reasons you're thinking."

He was still chuckling when he climbed in beside her.

He liked how things were going between them. Slow was fine. Slow was better. He was the kind of man who could appreciate anticipation as much as victory.

He liked Kelly—he thought they had a lot of potential. He wanted to see where that went, as long as neither of them wanted to fall in love. Griffith wasn't a man who failed at much, but he'd failed at his marriage and he wasn't going there again. He was determined to keep things simple. If a promise wasn't made, it couldn't be broken.

It only took a couple of minutes to drive to the older neighborhood where he lived. He pulled into the driveway of the nearly hundred-year-old quasi-Victorian he'd bought seven months ago.

Kelly got out before he could walk around to hold open her door. She stared up at the house.

"Not a tiny home? Are you rejecting the very work that brings you fame and fortune?"

"It brings me neither, and no, I didn't plan on buying the house. I was living in one of my own designs when this place came on the market. A developer was going to buy it and tear it down. I couldn't stand to see that happen."

"You're softhearted."

"Don't sound surprised."

"I am, a little. Are you going to restore it?"

"Every inch. I figure it will take me about ten years."

"That's a long time to live with construction."

"I don't mind."

They went inside.

He'd already started work on the front parlor. He'd taken off the hideous paneling and replaced it with beadboard and a chair rail. Era-appropriate wallpaper was on order and he'd sanded the floors.

She paused to study the room. "What are you going to use this for?"

"I'm not sure. It's a parlor, so a formal living room makes the most sense. But I'm not a formal living room kind of guy. Maybe a study or a home office."

She wrinkled her nose. "Not at the front of house. You'd have to keep it too tidy. Go with the formal living room. Women will love it."

"Because I'm going to have a stream of them coming through?"

"You never know." She smiled. "I'm here, after all."

"Interesting. Thanks for the advice."

He led her toward the kitchen. It had been updated in the 1960s and featured avocado-colored appliances, except for the refrigerator, which was from the 1990s.

He switched on the coffeepot, then collected a can of decaf and scooped out enough for a couple of cups.

Kelly prowled the kitchen before moving to the family room. She studied the worn sofa that had come with the house and the magazines scattered across the coffee table. She pulled out one and held it up.

"For the articles?" she asked sweetly.

He glanced at the *Sports Illustrated* swimsuit edition and shook his head. "Not mine. You'll have to talk to Ryan about that."

She put down the magazine. "That's right. He lives with you. How's that working out?"

A question for which he had no answer.

When his brother had blown out his shoulder, Griffith had been in the house about a month. Offering Ryan a place to stay had seemed like the right thing to do. The same with offering him a job. But things hadn't turned out the way he'd expected.

"Sorry," Kelly said as she walked back to the kitchen. "It wasn't supposed to be a hard question."

"Family."

"Tell me about it. You have Ryan and I have Olivia."

"I don't think you have to worry about Olivia. She had some good ideas at the meeting tonight."

"Yes, if she can do it. Putting on a fund-raiser like that is a big deal. Do we know if she really has the experience to pull it all together?"

"You're concerned."

"Wouldn't you be?"

He didn't know enough about Olivia to answer the question. He suspected Kelly didn't, either.

"What are you going to do?" he asked.

"Nothing." Kelly leaned against the counter. "I don't know enough to go barging in to help, and maybe she'll be fine."

He poured them each a mug of coffee. "You sound doubtful."

"I am and that's not fair. I should let her mess up before I judge her." She sighed. "That sounded incredibly snotty and I didn't mean it to be."

"I know. Milk? Sugar?"

"Just black." She flashed a smile. "You forget, I'm a farmer. We're hearty stock."

They carried their mugs into the family room. Griffith was pleased when Kelly sat on the sofa instead of one of the chairs. At least she wasn't trying to get away from him. It was one thing for her to ask him to kiss her when she was drunk and quite another to deal with him while she was sober. He was confident that she'd already made up her mind, but didn't want to push her. Better for her to be the one urging them to the next step. He settled beside her on the sofa, but not too close.

"Has any other part of the house been remodeled?" she asked.

"The master bath and bedroom."

"I wouldn't have thought a house this old had a master bath."

"It does now. I took what was the nursery and had it converted. The main bedroom was a good size. That was easy. A little paint, refinished floors and a big throw rug. The bathroom was more complicated."

"If it was just a nursery, I would say complicated doesn't begin to cover it. You would have to run plumbing and all kinds of stuff."

"Don't be impressed. I traded with a friend. He did my bathroom and I built him a tiny home."

"You could have let me think you did it yourself."

"Except I didn't. Besides, one day you might ask me to help you tile something and then the truth would come out anyway."

"Your parents would be very proud of your honesty," she teased.

"My mom especially."

"How are they?"

"Good. Loving New Mexico. They're enjoying the weather and have made a lot of new friends. My mom is helping at a wild horse refuge. I keep waiting for her to slow down, but I'm starting to think it's never going to happen."

Kelly smiled. "They are such nice people. Your dad used to put air in my bike tires every summer."

Griffith's parents had owned a gas station in town. Technically *the* gas station for a number of years. His dad had a couple of guys to help with the auto repairs. Both he and Ryan had worked at the station in summers to earn spending money.

Theirs had been a traditional, middle-class upbringing. There'd been plenty of family time, a ranch-style house and two cars in the garage. Had either of the brothers wanted to go to community college and then transfer to a state school, there'd been savings for that. Instead Ryan had gone to college on a baseball scholarship and Griffith had headed to Harvard on an academic one.

Once his parents had realized the college fund wasn't necessary, they'd sold the gas station and the house and had bought a place in New Mexico to live out their retirement.

"Yeah, he's a good guy. He has a huge workshop where he's restoring an old '68 Mustang. He texts me pictures every week, showing me what he's done."

"My dad will be just like that when he retires," she said with a grin. "Which is years away. It's nice that your parents are still together." She grimaced. "Not that I want my parents to have stayed married. It was not a successful union."

"Some aren't."

She looked at him. "I wasn't implying anything."

"I know. I didn't plan on getting a divorce."

"I don't think anyone does." She set her coffee on one of the magazines. "I'm sure it was painful."

Griffith didn't want to talk about his failed marriage or his ex-wife. Neither spoke well of him. But if he was looking to get involved with Kelly, then she had the right to know at least the basics of what had happened.

"And a surprise," he said slowly and set his mug next to hers. "I met Jane in college. She was an English major and planning on getting her master's in political science. She was smart, from a good family. On paper we had a lot in common. I planned on joining an East Coast architectural firm when I graduated. I was going to design hotels and museums."

He raised a shoulder. "Shallow, right?"

"We all need somewhere to stay when we go on vacation." She met his gaze. "What happened?"

"I went to a lecture about tiny homes. It was mostly so I could tell my professors that I'd attended. They like that sort of thing, and it was a chance to learn. What I didn't expect was to be blown away by the possibilities." He leaned toward her. "There's so much we take for granted here in our country. Like access to clean water and sanitation. Did you know that in the world today over two billion people still don't have access to toilets as we know them?"

Her eyes widened. "Are you kidding?"

"I wish I were. I didn't study the kind of engineering that can build a sanitation system, but I can at least provide housing to people and with that housing, give them a toilet, whether it's self-sustained or hooked up to plumbing."

He knew this was a ridiculous topic. Not many women found a discussion on poverty and toilets arousing. But he couldn't seem to shut his mouth or change the subject.

"That's what got me excited. I was accepted for an internship in Africa. I spent two summers building tiny homes there. Jane expected me to get it out of my system. I was offered a place at a New York firm and another in London. I turned them both down to go back to Africa."

"Were you married by then?"

"Oh, yeah. Jane came with me and stuck it out for two years. When we returned to the States, I was supposed to take a job in New York. Instead I accepted a position at a nonprofit in LA, designing shelter for the homeless. That was it for Jane. She left."

He paused. "Okay, that makes it sound like I was a saint and she's a horrible person. I don't mean that. She and I had other problems and I'm sure most of them were my fault. She's very sweet, but she had expectations that I didn't meet."

"What about now?" Kelly asked. "Would she like what you're doing?"

He smiled. "Tulpen Crossing isn't exactly her speed."

"But we have the craft mall. How could she not love it here?"

"I'm confused, as well." He thought about what had happened when Jane told him she wanted a divorce. "I didn't see it coming," he admitted. "I knew she wasn't happy but I figured we'd work it out. That she wasn't willing to try shocked the hell out of me. I couldn't get past how I'd made such a bad decision. Of course I'd changed the rules, so maybe she's the one who was shocked. Either way, I'm bad at love and bad at marriage."

"That's a fairly harsh assessment after a single failed relationship."

"I don't like making mistakes."

"No one does, and I'm not judging. It's not like my five years with Sven made any sense. He's a great guy, but I don't know. I should have missed him more, you know? He ended things and I felt bad, but I wasn't crushed."

She grabbed a throw pillow and pulled it against her midsection. Even in his guyness, he was able to recognize the gesture as protective.

"Were you in love with him?" he asked.

"I'm not sure. While we were together I would have said I was, but after it was over, I just kind of went on with my life. I missed the concept of our relationship more than the actual man himself."

"Good to know." He put his arm on the back of the sofa and rested his hand on her shoulder. "So, Kelly Murphy, what's it going to be? Now that we've confessed our failed relationships, you want to see where things go between us?"

She looked down, then back at him. "No falling in love, no forever. Just dating."

"And sex."

She rolled her eyes. "Yes, and sex. I'm clear on the expectations."

Her phrasing surprised him. Why expectations? That made it sound as if it would all be about him and not her. Didn't Kelly like sex?

Before he could ask any questions or figure out a way to pursue the topic, she drew in a breath.

"Yes."

His mind screeched to a halt, then skipped back to what he'd asked.

"You're in," he confirmed.

"I'm in."

He thought maybe she was going to say something else, but decided not to give her a chance. Instead he pulled the pillow away and tossed it on the floor, then scooted a few inches closer, cupped her face in his hands and kissed her.

Her mouth was warm and soft and yielded immediately to his. Her lean body was temptingly close, but he wasn't going to rush things. His gut told him slower was better where Kelly was concerned. He wanted her to trust him.

He kept his lips on hers for three full beats of his heart, then slowly brushed back and forth. Just a little. Just to get the feel of her.

Heat burned in his chest before moving lower to the traditional spots, but he ignored the expected reaction to kissing a woman he was interested in, instead focusing on her.

Her hands fluttered, as if she wasn't sure what to do with them. One finally landed on his shoulder. Her breathing quickened slightly. Just when he was about to draw back, she parted her lips.

The invitation was clear and not one he could resist. He slipped his tongue inside, just for a second, and let himself enjoy the taste and feel of her. Her fingers dug into his shoulder and she leaned closer. He circled her tongue with his, felt his blood heat then, regretfully, broke the kiss and straightened.

Her eyes were half closed. She blinked and looked at him. He smiled and brought the hand on his shoulder to his mouth. He kissed her palm.

"It's late. I should get you home."

"Oh. Okay."

He debated asking her to spend the night, but instead rose and helped her to her feet. He was a man with a plan. No matter the temptation, he was going to stay focused. He didn't want one evening with Kelly—he wanted a lot more and he knew he was going to have to earn that.

Olivia parked in front of The Parrot Café. She wasn't that hungry, but a childhood memory of an Oreo cookie milk shake had her mouth watering.

She didn't actually need the billion calories, but she could run them off later. One of the advantages of being back in the Pacific Northwest was the balmy temperatures. She didn't have to get up at five to run before the sun was up, nor was she concerned about it getting over a hundred by midafternoon.

She went inside. It was a little after one o'clock and much of the lunch crowd had dissipated. She took a seat at the counter and was surprised when Helen, her sister's friend, appeared and handed her a menu.

"Oh, hi," Olivia said. "You work here?"

"Actually, I own this place. I bought it from my aunt and uncle a few years back."

"I didn't know that. I'm sorry—we weren't in the same grade at school, so you're kind of a mystery to me."

Helen laughed. "That's okay. I'm what, six years older? When you were in high school, I was already working here full-time. I would have seemed ancient."

"Maybe just really mature." Olivia pushed away the menu. "Do you still make Oreo milk shakes?"

"We do and they're delicious."

"I'll take one."

"You've got it."

Helen took the menu and entered the order on a small computer on the back counter. Olivia glanced around at the booths and tables, the cheerful prints on the walls. Big windows let in lots of light. The restaurant wasn't fancy—more diner than bistro—but it had a welcoming feel. It was a place you'd want to come back to.

Helen returned with a napkin and a long-handled spoon. "How are you settling in to being back in town?"

"Pretty well. So much is familiar, but every now and then there's something I don't remember." She tilted her head. "I sort of remember you weren't born here. Is that right?"

"I moved in with my aunt and uncle when I was eleven."

Olivia wanted to ask why, but told herself it wasn't her business. "And you stayed. That's nice. So many people want to be somewhere else."

"Like you?" Helen grinned.

"I suppose. Although I didn't so much make a choice not to stay as to not come back." After all, being sent away when she was fifteen hadn't been her idea. "Your diner's really nice. I like the way the wall color complements the booths and the artwork."

"Thanks. I've made a few changes since buying the place."

A bell softly chimed. Helen turned and collected the tall milk shake, then brought it over.

"Here you go."

Olivia stared at the black-and-white ice cream mixture, the fudge poured over the top and the whipped cream.

"It's so beautiful. I'm having a moment."

Helen laughed. "Should I leave you two alone?"

"No, I'm good. How on earth do you not eat one every single day?"

"Oh, there are plenty of temptations in this place. I swear I start and break a diet every other day."

"I would, too."

"Yes, but you're skinny." Helen held up a hand. "Sorry. That's my curvy bitterness manifesting. No offense."

"None taken." Olivia dipped her spoon into the milk shake and tasted it. "Oh. My. God. It's amazing."

"Another satisfied customer. I'll pass along your praise to my cook."

"Please."

A family walked to the cash register to pay their bill. Helen assisted them, then returned to sit by Olivia.

"I'm going to donate three or four gift certificates for the auction," she said. "I'm trying to decide if I want to do a dollar amount or breakfast for four. I'm not sure which would be easier for the winner and for me."

"Would you be willing to have one of the breakfast gift certificates be part of a package? I'm going to talk to one of the local hotels for a two-night stay. Being able to add breakfast here would make it even more desirable."

"Sure. That works."

"Thanks. Oh, and if you want me to design a gift certificate, I can do that. You could even use it for other purposes. Get it printed out on a nice card stock for holidays or something."

"We've never had gift certificates. I hadn't thought of selling them, but that could be a good idea. I appreciate it."

"No problem. I love doing all kinds of design work." Olivia put the straw in the milk shake. "In Phoenix I do marketing for the real estate firm where I work, but it isn't exactly full-time, so I've branched out. I've done a little interior design and lately I've been doing more and more staging. So if you ever want your living room spruced, I'm your girl."

"I'll keep that in mind. Have you gotten a lot of people offering items for the auction?"

"Not yet. I'm starting to get the word out. You wouldn't happen to have any contacts with a hotel in Seattle, would you? I want to make the Seahawks tickets a really big item."

"Like you mentioned for the hotel here. Bundle the tickets with a hotel and maybe a restaurant?"

"Uh-huh."

"I don't," Helen told her. "You might want to talk to Griffith. He's done a lot of work for clients in Seattle. He'd be your best bet."

"Thanks. I met him last night. He seems like a good guy."

"He is."

More customers waited to pay their check. Helen excused herself and went to help them. Olivia sipped her milk shake.

This was nice, she thought. The town, the people. She liked that she was being accepted. In a way she could start over—no Marilee, no past, just her and her family. And wouldn't that be nice.

11

Helen took a deep breath for courage, told herself that she was strong and self-actualized and that there was absolutely no reason to be nervous, then she walked into Jeff's office at Murphy Tulips and felt her knees knock together.

He sat at his desk, the phone pressed against his ear. When he saw her, he smiled and waved her closer.

"Give me a minute," he mouthed. She nodded and went to the window.

From where she stood, she could see two of the huge greenhouses that grew their "off-season" tulips. They were between harvests, but in a few weeks, nearly three dozen workers would descend on the place to harvest and wrap tulips to be delivered up and down the West Coast.

"Let me see what I can do," Jeff was saying. "It's late in the season to be placing orders, but I'll do a count and figure out what we have available."

Christmas tulips, Helen thought with a grin. Someone else had been caught flat-footed, realizing too late red-and-white tulips were required for whatever they had going on.

"Give me until tomorrow. I'll call you in the morning. Uh-huh. Bye." He hung up and stood. "Idiot."

"Don't you hate people who don't plan ahead?"

"Mostly they just annoy me. What's going on?"

She pulled the sheet music from her bag and waved it. "Isaak wants us to do a new duet."

"Are there any Billy Joel songs we don't already know?"

His voice was low and teasing. Helen's stomach fluttered, along with the rest of her.

"It's not Billy Joel."

Jeff held out his arms. "Do you need a hug?"

She did and more, but they were talking about different things. "I'm trying to breathe through my disappointment. He suggested a Miley Cyrus song instead. It's not a traditional duet, but he thinks it has potential."

"I know that name," he murmured. "Give me a second."

"Her publicist will be so proud."

She set her phone on the docking station he had on his credenza and pressed play. She adjusted the sound as the first notes of "Wrecking Ball" filled his office.

Jeff sat on the corner of his desk as he listened. At the end he reached for the sheet music.

"We could do this in harmony," he said absently. "Decide who starts the song. Would you play it again?"

As the opening notes began, he started scribbling on the paper.

"You'll start," he told her. "That's what people will be expecting. I'll join in here, then take over after the chorus."

"We could try it."

"Is there a video?"

Her heart sank. Literally. It fell to her feet and flopped around, whimpering in pain.

"Helen?"

"Oh, there's a video."

"Why do you say it like that?"

Why? Why? "Because it's so unfair. She's beautiful and the rest of us mortal women don't stand a chance."

He dropped the sheet music to the desk and studied her. "What does that mean?"

Her throat tightened as she recognized that this was one of those make-or-break moments in her life. She could tell him exactly what she was thinking and see what happened or she could continue to wish without doing a damned thing to make her dreams come true.

She sucked in a breath for courage and raised her chin. "Jeff, I—"

"There you are," Kelly said as she walked into the office. "I saw your car in the parking lot and knew you had to be somewhere. What's going on?"

"Isaak wants me and Helen to try a new duet," Jeff said, glancing at his daughter.

Helen held in a scream. She forced herself to smile at her friend because none of this was Kelly's fault.

"Miley Cyrus."

Kelly grinned. "Do you even know who she is, Dad?"

"I'm going to find out. Helen says there's a video."

Kelly took a step back. "I so don't want to be around when that happens. Ew."

"Now I'm even more intrigued," he said.

Of course he was. And then he was going to have Miley Cyrus stuck in his head and then what chance would she have, assuming she'd ever had one at all. Life was not fair.

"I don't want to interrupt," Kelly said. "Come see me when you're done."

"We're finished." She waved at Jeff and walked out with Kelly, not sure if the universe was trying to protect her from heartbreak or having fun at her expense.

Olivia hung up and pumped her fist in victory. The PR department of the Seattle Mariners had been more than helpful. Thanks to them, she would be able to get excellent tickets to a baseball game, which she would add to the football tickets that had already been donated. Creating a sports extravaganza, as she was thinking of calling it, would increase the value of the auction item.

In the past couple of days the reality of what she'd taken on was starting to sink in. She didn't doubt her organizational abilities, it was more that she was working in unfamiliar territory. She didn't know all the nuances of the town and how it worked, nor was she a favorite local kid doing good. Still, she was going to do everything possible to make the auction a success. Her goal was to raise enough money for a new roof and a major sprucing up of the inside, as well.

Her phone buzzed. She glanced down and saw a text from Ryan.

Miss you. Can we get together?

Bastard. Did he think she was going to spend time with him after what had happened at the bar?

Just the two of us or will Autumn be coming along? Want me to ask her?

She doubted Ryan would respond to her sarcasm, which was fine. What really pissed her off was feeling unsettled about him. Their relationship had ended through external forces and had never run its course. While her sensible brain could guess they would have eventually broken up and gone their separate ways, her teenaged heart was less sure. Being with Ryan was her un-realistic antidote to everything that had gone wrong back then. She knew he wasn't anything close to what would make her feel better about herself, but she couldn't help wanting him back in her life. Or at least the *theory* of him.

She pulled on workout capris and a tank top, then laced up her running shoes and pulled her hair back into a ponytail.

Five minutes later, she was jogging along the big park about a half mile away. It was nearly eleven in the morning, but not hot at all. She'd forgotten what it was like to not have to worry about things melting in the heat of summer.

Not that she'd paid much attention to the weather when she'd lived here as a kid. She'd had more important things on her mind. Like Ryan.

She thought about his stupid text and grimaced. No way she was going to forgive him anytime soon. He needed to be punished and for more than just his current girlfriend.

Back in high school, they'd been the perfect couple—at least before she'd been sent away. According to her friends it had taken Ryan all of fifteen minutes to get over his supposed broken heart and take up with someone else. Two years later he'd gotten a full ride to Texas Christian University. When she'd found out, she'd applied and had been accepted. He'd been surprised but pleased when she'd walked into his English class. It had been a scene straight out of *Legally Blonde*. But unlike Elle Woods who'd had the good sense to fall for someone else, Olivia had set her sights directly on Ryan and had never turned away.

Oh, she'd played hard to get for the first month, but once Ryan had won her back, she'd been his...until he'd dumped her for the Red Sox farm team, leaving with barely ten minutes' notice. She'd transferred to ASU and had finished her degree there.

Frying pan meet fire, she thought grimly. She'd gone from dealing with Ryan to dealing with her mother. Not much of an improvement.

She reached the park and started along the main jogging/bike path. After a couple of minutes she picked up the pace. Her breathing was regular, her mind starting to clear. This was the part of her run that she liked the best. When the rest of the world started to fall away and she could simply be in the moment.

About a half mile later, she saw another jogger running toward her. He was tall and blond, with broad shoulders and a body that would stop traffic in any major city. She started to enjoy the show only to realize she'd met him at the tourism board meeting a couple of nights before. It was the Viking god, Sven.

She was prepared to simply say "Hi" and jog past, then saw he was slowing, so she did the same.

"Hello, Olivia."

"Hi, Sven."

They came to a stop.

"You're a runner," he said.

"I am, and it's much nicer here than back in Phoenix."

"Less sweating."

She grinned. "You know it."

"Want to run together?"

"Sure."

She wasn't the fastest runner, but she had a steady pace and great endurance, so if he didn't turn the outing into a sprint, she should be able to keep up.

They started back the way he'd come, matching their strides as they jogged.

"Thank you again for your donation for the auction."

"You're welcome."

"You're from around here?" she asked.

"I've lived here seven years. I grew up in San Diego."

"How on earth did you get from San Diego to here and why?"

He laughed. "You say it like you're surprised."

"I am."

"My great-uncle had a small nursery here and left me his house and land when he died. I'd met him a couple of times when I was young and must have made an impression. He knew I'd been working for a large nursery in San Diego and wanted to start my own business."

"People up here sure like to grow things."

"Like your sister." Sven glanced at her. "She never talks about you."

"Not a surprise. We're not that tight and I haven't lived here for years. So do you grow tulips, too?"

"No. Other kinds of plants. I leave the tulips to the professionals. I do believe in beautiful gardens and I've been experimenting with mat gardens. You unroll it, water it and plants grow."

"I think I've seen them on an infomercial."

He dismissed that with a wave. "Simple designs with common plants. I want to make something more special. I've developed a different growing material that allows me more leeway with what I plant. I'm getting ready to launch them online, but I'm having trouble with my website."

Sven-the-viking-god.com?

"What kind of trouble?"

"My web designer Alison wants content."

"Most women do."

He shot her a grin. "Yes, they do, but what is the point of a web designer if she won't fill the pages?"

"Okay, so a web designer is like a house builder. They build the house, but they don't furnish it. You have to buy your own furniture, meaning you have to tell her what to put on the pages."

"I'm no good at that. She also wants me to pick the colors. It's plants and flowers. Those are the colors."

"Such a guy," she murmured. "Would you like some help? I have a bit of a design background and I've worked on web content before. It's not difficult. How big is the website going to be?"

He stared at her blankly.

"How many pages?" she clarified. "Will you have drop-down menus or just…" She shook her head. "Never mind. I'm happy to help."

"Thank you. I have no idea what I'm doing. I'm much better with my hands than on the computer."

Yes, she was sure he was, she thought with a grin, knowing he meant working in his nursery while she was thinking something else entirely.

They came out the other side of the park and crossed a street, then ran along a dirt road lined with trees. Apples, she realized, surprised to see them growing there.

"I didn't know someone was growing apples," she said.

"I am."

"These are yours?"

"Yes. I also grow blueberries. About half my blueberry crop goes directly to consumers while the rest is processed, as are the apples."

"You ship over the mountain to eastern Washington?"

"No, I ship north to Canada. They're both turned into sweet wine for the Asian market."

She came to a stop and stared at him. "Apple and blueberry wine?"

He smiled. "It's a huge market. I'm doing very well with my exports."

A Viking god with a brain and big hands. Talk about a sparkly day.

He motioned to the small farmhouse about a half mile up the road. "That's me. We've run nearly five miles. Why don't you come inside for water, then I'll drive you home?"

Five miles? Plus the nearly two she'd already done that day? Her normal workout was about four miles.

"Water would be great. Thank you."

She wondered how sore she was going to be in the morning, then decided she didn't care. Sven was interesting and she'd enjoyed running with him.

As they approached the house, she saw the large garden

sprawled in every direction. There were roses to the east, some kind of orchid or lily garden to the north and what looked like a jungle of vines and bushes to the west.

"I assume there's a plan?" she asked.

"Yes. I'm experimenting with hybrids and different soil." He flashed her a sexy grin. "Some I grow because I like it."

They went inside. Olivia hadn't been sure what to expect. From the outside, Sven's home was a traditional farmhouse but the living room was a different story.

Walls had been removed to create a completely open floor plan. Large windows offered views of the garden and let in tons of light. The furniture was modern—chrome-and-glass tables with sleek, dark leather sofas against pale-colored hardwood floors.

The kitchen had been remodeled with stainless steel appliances and poured concrete counters. The upper cabinets opened by lifting up instead of out and the pantry doors were frosted glass. There was no clutter, very little art. An iPad sat on the kitchen island and there was a bowl of cherries on the counter. Otherwise, there were no signs of life.

She could have been in a San Francisco or New York loft rather than a Tulpen Crossing farmhouse. She supposed there would be people who would find the house sterile, but she liked the clean lines and openness.

Sven watched her, his blue eyes unreadable. She admired the sculpted chairs in the eat-in kitchen and touched the glass table.

"I love it," she told him. "The design is totally unexpected, which is a lot of the appeal, of course, but everything flows so well. You've made this your own."

"Some people think it's too cold."

"Some people are idiots."

"Thank you."

He got two glasses from an upper cabinet and walked to the refrigerator. He poured water from a pitcher, then handed her a glass. She swallowed several gulps before telling herself to slow down. She didn't want to throw up by drinking too fast, because hey, not very sexy.

"Did you design it yourself?" she asked.

"I had a basic idea, but I hired someone to help with the finishes. The whole house is like this. I put a sauna in the bathroom."

"Of course you did," she said with a laugh, then finished her water.

"More?"

"I should be getting home. How far is it?"

"Six miles when you don't cut through the park. I'll drive you."

The house really was great, she thought. And the sauna would be delicious. Naturally it would be even better with Sven soaking up the heat with her. The man was very easy to look at.

"You're smiling," he said.

"I find life amusing."

"You're very beautiful."

The unexpected statement surprised her. She knew how to clean up well, but that was for when she wasn't exercising. She wasn't even wearing mascara.

She looked up at him. Literally up—she was barely five-five and he was over six feet. She'd never been the blond hair, blue eyes type, but was starting to see the appeal. He watched her with the kind of interest a man shows a woman he wants to sleep with, but he didn't make a move. She sensed the decision was up to her. She could say "thank you" and he would take her back to her place. Or she could say something else and things would progress. What was a girl to do?

She thought he was nice and it was obvious her body was more than a little interested. She wasn't seeing anyone and sleeping with Sven would certainly be good for her morale, not to mention teach Ryan a lesson.

"Are you involved with anyone?" she asked.

"No. I was in a long-term relationship but it ended several months ago. I haven't dated anyone since. What about you?"

"There's no one."

"What about Ryan?"

She felt herself flush. "I don't know what you're talking about."

"I was at the bar the other night. I saw you there with Ryan."

"Oh." She hadn't noticed him. She'd been too focused on her old boyfriend. "He's seeing someone, which makes him much less interesting."

"How long since you slept with him?"

"That's a blunt question."

One shoulder rose and lowered.

"Six years."

"It's time to get over him."

"I agree."

"I could help with that."

She stared into his eyes and saw desire there. In response, her belly clenched. "I'm sure you could."

"I'll be right back."

He walked out of the kitchen and down the hall and returned less than a minute later. He tossed a box of condoms on the island.

"I have a fantasy about making love with a woman in this kitchen. I want to take you on the counter."

She glanced from the poured concrete to his body and saw the height would be about perfect. "That seems very doable, but why haven't you made that happen before? Is the kitchen new?"

"No, it's three years old."

Which meant the old girlfriend wasn't the kitchen counter type? Her loss.

So many women didn't get it. Sex was easy—it was emotions that were a bitch. Something Olivia had learned very early on. She moved close to Sven and pulled off her tank top. Her sports bra followed. He drew her close and kissed her. At the first sure stroke of his tongue, she let herself sink into his embrace. Sven was a capable guy—she was sure he knew what he was doing, which meant she got to relax and let him do the driving.

12

Kelly stood in front of her closet and was torn between swearing, throwing herself out the window or giving up before she started. Swearing wouldn't help at all and her bedroom was on the first floor, so hey, empty gesture. Which left her with giving up, but she really hated to quit anything. How hard could it be?

Apparently too hard for her, she thought glumly and turned away, only to find Olivia standing in the doorway to her room, an orange in one hand.

"What?" Olivia asked.

"Nothing."

"You don't have nothing face. You have something face. What is it?"

Kelly took in her sister's jeans. They were fitted to the point of being tight, but somehow they looked great. She had on a T-shirt, but it had a nice neckline and a cute shirttail and was in a great shade of green. Instead of work boots, Olivia wore simple flats. Technically Kelly and her sister were wearing the same thing yet they couldn't have looked more different, and that was before she got started on the whole hair-makeup thing.

"Kelly, should I worry?"

"No. It's nothing."

"We've been down the nothing road already. What's going on?"

"You look nice."

The compliment was grudgingly given. Kelly wanted to stomp her foot as she said it, or throw something. This was all Griffith's fault because, dammit, she wanted to look good for him.

There. She'd thought it. She wanted to look nice for a man. She collapsed on the bed. "I'm so pathetic."

"Why?"

"Griffith. I want to look nice for him."

Olivia moved into the room and sat on the chair by the small desk. She set down the orange. "Why is that pathetic? You have a great boyfriend. Of course you want to look nice for him. Not that he was first attracted to you for your fashion sense."

"Ha ha."

"Stand up."

"You don't get to boss me around," she muttered even as she stood.

Olivia moved her until she was in front of the full-length mirror on her closet door. "What do you want to change?"

"Everything."

"You don't mean that. You have no interest in dressing any differently for work. You'd tell me it was stupid. That what you wear is practical."

Kelly met her gaze in the mirror. "You don't know that."

Olivia simply raised her eyebrows. Kelly sighed.

"Fine. I like what I wear to work. It's practical and easy."

"Then keep it. What do you want to be different when you're with Griffith?"

Kelly had no idea. She just knew that ever since he'd kissed her, she'd had a hard time thinking of anything else. Except...

"I want him to think I'm pretty," she admitted, then wanted to claw the words back into her mouth.

Olivia smiled. "He already does."

"You don't know that."

"I'm fairly sure. Not a lot of men date women they don't find attractive."

"Oh." Kelly had never thought of it that way before. Griffith liked how she looked? She smiled.

"And people thought you were the smart one," Olivia grumbled as she walked into the closet. "Let's see where we're starting."

She handed Kelly armfuls of clothes with instructions to put them on the queen-size bed in stacks.

"Jeans, cargo pants, tops, dresses. We'll sort from there."

Twenty minutes later the rack was empty and the bed was covered with what even Kelly could see was a fairly pathetic inventory.

"You have one dress," her sister said. "Who only has one dress? And could you possibly own more ratty jeans and disgusting cargo pants?"

"They're for work."

"Even if I accept that, what do you wear to business meetings? You don't have a single pair of nice pants. Something in black. You don't have a blazer or a skirt. You own one blouse that buttons."

Kelly tried not to get defensive. "I don't have meetings. Dad handles all that. Sometimes I meet with the direct shippers but they don't care what I wear. I'm a farmer."

"That's not an excuse to dress badly outside of work." Her expression turned stern. "Stay right there."

Olivia walked out of the room and returned less than a minute later with a bright yellow sleeveless dress.

"I don't know why I brought this one with me. The style's all wrong for me and I think my hair's too light for the color. Put it on. I'll be right back."

She disappeared again. Kelly stared at the dress, then at the doorway.

"This is beyond stupid," she grumbled, even as she pulled off her T-shirt and stepped out of her jeans. Her boots and socks followed. She drew the dress over her head and was fumbling with the zipper when Olivia returned.

Her sister had several banker's clips in her hand. She zipped up the dress, then began fussing with it in the back.

"Just like I thought. You're what, a size four? I can't tell you how much that bites. I run five miles a day and I'm a solid size 8."

"I'm skinny because I don't have breasts. You have breasts."

"Boys do like breasts," Olivia admitted. "However, you can wear a lot of cool backless things that make me look trampy. Now, *this* is what I'm talking about."

She turned Kelly to the mirror. Kelly stared at herself and couldn't believe it.

The dress fit perfectly. It hugged her torso before skimming over her hips. She looked tall and almost elegant. The color made her skin glow and added golden highlights to her hair.

"I don't understand," she whispered.

"Nice clothes make a difference," Olivia said. "Clothes that fit. The right colors. You don't have to spend a ton, but make a little effort." Her gaze narrowed. "You have no idea what I'm talking about, do you?"

Kelly shook her head.

"That is just so typical." Her sister walked over to Kelly's handbag and pulled out a credit card. "I'm going to order you a bunch of stuff. You'll try it on and keep what you like. After we figure out your basic style, such as it is, I'll sign you up for a shopping site where they send you a package every couple of months. I'll be the one filling out the questionnaire, just to be clear. Then you keep what you like and return the rest. It will allow you to build up a non-work wardrobe over time."

Kelly was torn between being uncomfortable and grateful at the same time. The two emotions did not sit well together.

"I don't know what to say," she admitted.

"That, I believe." Olivia eyed her. "We have got to do something about your hair. How curly is it?"

"It's more wavy than curly."

"Then stop trying to tame it. You either start blowing it out every morning with a round brush, which we all know you're never going to do, or you embrace it fully. You need a good cut. A layered one."

"You're not cutting my hair."

"Do I look like I'd know what I was doing when it comes to cutting hair? Of course not. I'll find someone decent in the area, although we may have to drive a bit. It's all about a great cut and the right product." She put her hands on her hips. "I'll tell you what to buy and you'll buy it. I'm also going to take you makeup shopping. We need an Ulta or Sephora."

Kelly stared at her blankly. "I don't know what they are."

"No one's surprised. I'll find the closest one and we'll do that when you go get your hair done. Oh, I'm going to email you some YouTube videos. They'll be on basic makeup application. Watch them all. I mean it. All of them. All the way through."

The combination of bossy and caring was unexpected.

"How do you know all this?" Kelly asked. "Who taught you?"

"Friends. Older sisters of friends." Olivia looked away. "I, um, read a lot of magazines. They always have tips. The basics aren't hard. You're going to have to practice, though. And don't tell me you don't have time. You do. Tulips do in fact grow themselves."

"Thank you."

The simple words didn't begin to describe what Kelly was feeling inside. Confused, mostly. Overwhelmed, yes, but more than that. For the first time since Olivia had returned, she thought it might be nice to have a sister again. That now that they'd grown up, they might be able to get along, like they had when they'd been little.

Back then they'd been different, too, but it had worked between them. Now Olivia was sophisticated while Kelly was the country bumpkin. Like knowing about makeup. Had that been what she'd been learning all the times she'd spent summers with friends rather than coming home?

"You're welcome. I really like doing this kind of thing. It's like staging a house. I can see the potential, then make it happen."

She walked over and unzipped the dress. "Does your dry cleaner do tailoring?" She held up a hand. "Never mind. You don't have a dry cleaner, do you? I'll talk to Helen and ask her. We'll get this taken in so you can wear it."

Kelly spun to face her. "You can't give me a dress. It had to have been expensive."

"I don't want it. It's yours."

Kelly believed in living her life on an even emotional keel. She didn't like a lot of highs and lows—most likely one of the reasons she'd stayed with Sven for so long. There hadn't been any drama.

Now she felt a flood of emotion that she couldn't name and didn't know what to do with. Her throat got all tight as words formed, then faded. For one horrible second, she thought she might cry.

"You're being so nice to me," she managed to say.

"I know. I'm shocked, too."

Kelly chuckled, then choked. "I appreciate your help. I wish…" The feelings swirled and separated, then merged into one overwhelming sense of guilt.

"I'm sorry."

Olivia's expression turned quizzical. "About?"

"Before. When—" Tears formed but Kelly pushed them away. She shouldn't talk about it. Couldn't. Except—

"I'm sorry I talked to Dad about sending you away," she said quickly. "It was my idea."

Her sister's eyes widened as color drained from her face. "What?"

"You were so crazy about Ryan and I was terrified you were

going to end up pregnant and then what? It would have all been on me and I just couldn't stand to watch you turn into Mom. Plus, I didn't want to get stuck with your baby. I wanted to live my own life. But you're nothing like her and I was wrong and I'm sorry. Olivia, I really am."

Her sister stared at her for three heartbeats before turning on her heel. "Go to hell," she yelled before she ran out of the room.

Olivia was up at five—not that she'd slept very much. She waited until there was enough light that she wouldn't get side-swiped by a passing car, then went out for a run. By the time she returned, both her father and her Judas sister were gone, which was good. What wasn't was the fact that she didn't feel the least bit better.

Running was supposed to clear her mind. When she ran she was free. But despite the four miles she'd clocked, she was just as hurt and confused as she'd been before.

Kelly had been the one. Olivia had always been so pissed at her dad. Pissed and hurt and betrayed. She'd blamed him, had hated him and a few years ago had realized she had to forgive him or deal with the fallout of being angry for the rest of her life. She'd made peace, in a way. And now that peace was shattered.

Nearly as bad, there was no one to talk to. No one to call and say "You'll never guess what my bitch sister just admitted." She didn't have friends. There were women she hung out with, but they were more frenemies than people who cared about her.

She certainly couldn't call Marilee. She and her mother weren't speaking right now and if they were, Marilee honestly wouldn't give a damn. She only cared about herself—something that had taken Olivia a while to realize. It was that knowledge that had forced her to self-heal about her dad.

She showered and dressed, then stared at the credit card still sitting on the desk in her bedroom. She thought about booking herself two weeks in Aruba, all compliments of Kelly's VISA.

Her sister had her sent away. She'd made the decision that Olivia wasn't welcome, then had talked their dad into making it happen.

She opened her computer and pulled up a travel website, then began a search of all-inclusive five-star resorts. She was about to click on one when she got an email notice. She clicked on the small envelope.

The email was from someone in town offering a weekend on a forty-five-foot yacht for the auction. Olivia nearly fell off her chair. Talk about a score. She wrote back immediately, accepting the generous gift, then read the rest of her mail. Most of it was from locals wanting to donate physical items for the silent auction.

It was a lot of stuff. A quilt, several bottles of wine, three large planters. The list grew as she opened more emails.

"I'm going to need somewhere to store all this," she murmured, absently closing the travel site. Renting a storage unit would be pricey. Maybe she could find someone to donate space in a warehouse or something.

There might be room at the farm, but Olivia wasn't in the mood to ask her family for anything right now. She thought about Helen, but that was too much like asking Kelly. On a whim, she searched the number for Sven's business, then called. He picked up on the second ring.

"It's Olivia. I'm getting a lot of people emailing me about donating to the silent auction and I'm going to need a place to store it all. I wondered if you knew anyone who had extra garage space for me."

"I have a barn you can use. Why don't you come over and see it when you have time?"

"Thank you. I can come over right now."

"I'll be here."

Two hours, one barn viewing and an orgasm later, Olivia sat at the island in Sven's kitchen while he made pancakes. He had a small black apron tied around his waist but otherwise was completely naked.

She'd pulled on panties and one of his oversize T-shirts. The hem hit her midthigh—a very flattering post-coital length, she thought. She'd already set the table with plates, butter, syrup and a blueberry compote he swore he'd made himself.

Music played from hidden speakers. It had a very New Agey tone to it, but somehow it suited the man and the house. The view wasn't bad, either, she thought, watching the muscles in his back bunch and release as he flipped pancakes.

"Do you do this a lot?" she asked. "Have midday sex and then pancakes?"

He smiled at her. "This is a first."

"Which?"

"The pancakes after sex."

"It's nice that you cook. I never learned. I suppose I should. It's traditionally female to cook."

"Is that why you don't?"

"Maybe."

He piled pancakes on a plate, turned off the burner, then handed her the stack. As she carried it over to the table, he unfastened his apron and walked naked to claim a chair.

He was so unselfconscious, she thought. So beautiful. She wanted to run her hands up and down his body until they were both aroused. But first, pancakes.

"Thank you again for the offer of the barn," she said. "It's really going to help."

"You're welcome. What are you going to do with the extra money?"

"What extra money?"

He put two pancakes on her plate and took four for himself. "You're well on your way to making the auction a success. You're going to raise more than what's needed for the roof. What will you do with the extra?"

It was rare for someone to have that much faith in her, she thought. "It's not mine. I guess the tourism folks will decide. They should use it to fix up the craft mall. Right now it's a disaster and it doesn't have to be. It has a lot of potential."

"You should tell them."

She took a bite and chewed. The pancakes were light and fluffy, the blueberries just sweet enough. "Delicious," she told him when she'd swallowed. "They don't know me from a rock. Why would my ideas matter?"

"You're obviously smart and you know what you're doing. Why wouldn't they?"

She nearly dropped her fork. "You think I'm smart."

"No. I know you're smart. Beautiful, too, but that's on the surface. Although it's easier, isn't it? People don't expect as much."

"Because you trade on your looks?" she asked.

"My body more than my looks, but yes." He smiled at her. "Ironically, my last girlfriend didn't care about my body. She didn't look at me the way you do."

Olivia glanced at her plate and willed herself not to flush. "I do enjoy the show."

"There's nothing wrong with that. I enjoy looking at you, as well. Your face is perfect. Your smile draws me in and when your breasts move under the T-shirt, I get hard." He raised his shoulders. "We like what we like. It took me a long time to figure that out."

"Is that when you ended your last relationship?"

He nodded. "What about you? Tell me about your great loves, aside from Ryan, of course."

She rolled her eyes. "Ryan isn't a great love. In fact I haven't had one. There have been men, but no one I really loved."

"Because of them or because of you?"

"What do you mean?"

His blue gaze was steady. "Either you deliberately chose men who wouldn't touch you or you wouldn't let them touch you."

He held up a hand. "I don't mean your body. I'm speaking of your heart, Olivia. I can see what you're doing. You deliberately keep things superficial so you won't be hurt. I'm not going to ask who wounded you, I promise. If you want to tell me, I'll listen."

The unexpected words, so kindly spoken, undid her. She'd been prepared for flip or casual conversation—not for a man who could see all the way down to her soul.

He'd guessed the truth about her, about why she was the way she was. She had to win at nearly any cost, all without letting anyone in. Because people who were supposed to love you betrayed you over and over again.

She started to speak and realized she couldn't. Worse, tears burned in her eyes.

Horrified, she dropped her fork and started to stand. Before she'd made it all the way to her feet, Sven was at her side, pulling her close. He wrapped his strong arms around her and held her tight. At the same time he kissed her.

He tasted of blueberries and maple syrup. Their tongues met in a dance of hunger and need. In seconds she was wet and ready.

Even as he lifted her onto the counter and drew off her panties, a part of her brain pointed out that escape was only temporary. Eventually she was going to have to face what she was feeling. Then he drew off the T-shirt and cupped her breasts. As he entered her she was able to pretend once again that absolutely nothing was wrong.

13

"You're happy," Griffith said as Sven whistled softly.

"I'm a happy man."

Griffith knew his friend to be even-tempered but he rarely whistled. "You're freaking me out a little."

Sven grinned. "Then I'll stop."

They were in Griffith's office, going over different garden designs for the most popular tiny homes. Griffith had decided to offer mat gardens as an option and needed pictures for his website along with a few posters for the showroom. He and Sven had taken pictures and were now choosing the best ones.

"I heard from my cousin Lars," Sven said. "He'll have the custom pieces to you by the end of the month."

"I look forward to seeing how they work."

Lars was a carpenter who had designed several multipurpose pieces for the tiny homes. Chairs that folded down into beds or staircases with hidden storage. They were well-made from reclaimed wood. Not cheap, but there was a market for them.

"I'm going to ask him to donate something to the auction," Sven added.

Griffith chuckled. "Trying to impress the new girl?"

Sven winked. "You know it. She's very different from her sister."

"I'll take your word on that." Griffith couldn't imagine anyone being more interested in Olivia than Kelly, but that was just him. "Kelly's more my style."

"She likes you." Sven flipped to another picture. "You're one of the reasons I broke up with her."

Griffith stared at his friend. "Me?"

"I saw how she looked at you when she thought no one was watching. She never looked at me like that."

Griffith didn't know what to say. Shouting with delight and pumping his fist seemed to be in bad taste. "I, ah—"

"I know you didn't do anything while we were together. I'm glad you're dating her." He hesitated. "We were never meant to last as long as we did. There wasn't enough chemistry. Kelly's very quiet and I'm not."

In bed.

The words weren't said aloud, but they hung there all the same. Holy shit. They were guys. They didn't talk about that kind of stuff. Not without being drunk first. No one wanted to know what his buddy was like in bed. Gross. How was he supposed to get "not quiet" out of his head?

"I think this picture," Sven said, tapping one of them. "And the other one."

"I agree. I'll get them printed up. You want me to send you the pdf file?"

"Thanks. It'll give me content for my web person."

Sven left and Griffith collected the rest of the pictures. He was still stuck on the quiet in bed remark. What did that mean? That she wasn't a screamer? He was okay with that. Not everyone had to tell the world everything what was happening. Or was it more than that?

Before he could decide, Leo knocked on his open door. One look at his foreman's face told him there was trouble.

"What's the problem?" he asked, motioning to the chair by his desk.

"We have two late deliveries this week. I've already talked to the suppliers. They have good excuses, but I'd rather have the material. I want to look for other vendors."

Griffith nodded without speaking. He'd worked with Leo long enough to know that when bad news was delivered, his foreman started with the easy stuff first, which meant there was more coming.

"We're behind on one of the homes we're building," Leo continued. "If I put on an extra shift, we'll be close, but I'm not sure we can meet our deadline even then."

Griffith felt his jaw tighten as frustration swept through him. Dammit all to hell.

"Which house?"

"Two twenty-seven."

Griffith had considered a number of ways to keep track of the homes he built and had settled on the simplest of systems. Year two, house twenty-seven. The house Ryan worked on.

"It's my brother, isn't it?"

Leo glanced at the papers in front of him. "He's a good guy. Everyone likes him."

"Sure. He's always willing to talk or take an extra ten minutes at break, turn lunch into an hour and a half. The other guys see he gets away with it, so they start doing it, too. You can't just discipline Ryan, so the whole project goes to hell."

Leo didn't say anything. He didn't have to.

Maybe giving Ryan a job had been a mistake. Maybe what his brother needed instead was a kick in the ass.

"I'll talk to him," Griffith said. "His free ride is over. From now on, you treat everyone the same, Leo. Ryan doesn't get special treatment. If he's not back from his break or lunch on time, dock his pay. If he mouths off, give him a warning. If that doesn't help, suspend him."

"You sure, boss?"

"Yes. I should have done this a long time ago. I'm sorry I put you in a difficult situation."

Leo relaxed. "No problem. I'll tell the guys that I'm going to be on them and we'll take it from there."

"Thanks."

They both rose. Griffith went in search of his brother. He found the entire crew standing around, laughing. When they saw him, they all scurried back to work—all except Ryan who stretched and walked toward him.

"Hey, Griffith. What's up?"

"We have to talk."

His brother rolled his eyes. "You sound like a woman, bro. What's up with that?"

Griffith stepped into the utility closet where they kept cleaning supplies, a couple of buckets on wheels and several brooms. Ryan stopped in the doorway and raised his eyebrows.

"What's up?"

"You need to do your job," Griffith said bluntly.

"Jesus. I put in my eight hours. What more do you want?"

"You put in about four. You're paid for eight. Two twenty-seven is behind and you're the reason. You've been getting away with goofing off because you're my brother and that's going to stop. You'll show up on time, work your full shift or your pay will be docked. If you're going to work part-time hours, you'll get a part-time paycheck."

Ryan folded his arms across his chest. "What's got your panties in a bunch?"

Griffith took a step toward him. "I realize what happens here isn't important to you, but it is to me and the people who bought the house. They're waiting for it. Every day they wonder how construction is going and they're telling their friends and family about it. I'm not calling them to say it's going to be late because my lazy-assed brother can't bother to show up. I have a business to run, bro." He emphasized the last word. "Either participate or quit. Am I clear?"

"You're a dick."

"That may be but I'm also your boss. I mean it, Ryan. I gave you this job to help you out. If you don't want it anymore, you know where to find the door."

"Go to hell."

Ryan turned and walked away. Griffith had no idea if his brother had just quit or not. He figured they would all know in the morning. If he had to bet, he would put money on Ryan showing up. His younger brother needed the money and Ryan wasn't one to do without.

Helen sat at the piano, but instead of playing, she turned to look at the living room. Everything was in its place—the surfaces were all clean. She liked her house—it was convenient and suited her purposes. So why did she feel so restless?

She got up and went to the kitchen and got a glass of water, then returned to the living room, but didn't sit down. For some reason sitting down felt like giving up, and wasn't that the weirdest thing?

She had to snap out of this, she told herself. While the café wasn't her dream job, she enjoyed working there. She had security and modest financial freedom. Shouldn't she be doing something with that? Planning a trip? Falling in love? Taking a two-week road trip to the Rock & Roll Hall of Fame?

She heard a knock on the front door a second before it opened and Jeff stepped inside.

"It's me," he called, then smiled when he saw her. "Ready to tackle Miley?"

"Hi. Sure. Let's have at it."

He came to a stop and studied her. "What's wrong?"

"Nothing."

"There's something. I can see it in your eyes."

Seriously? He could see that she was upset but hadn't once noticed her almost throwing herself at him? Was the man dense or simply giving her his answer in a very gentle way?

"I'm restless," she admitted. "About my life and what I do." She held up a hand. "It's not any one thing and I can't explain it more than that. When I pick things apart, they're all fine. I do like the café. I enjoy my employees and the customers. There's a sameness, but that comes with every job. Routine is part of getting things done. I'm just…"

She drew in a breath. "I hate the master bathroom."

"I know a good contractor. You could get it redone. What else?"

"Nothing." Nothing because she was a coward who couldn't say what she was thinking about the man she was in love with. "I think that's pretty much all my whining. We should work on our song. Did you finish with the arrangement?"

He set sheet music in front of her. "I did. It's a really good song."

She glanced at him. "And the video?"

He sighed. "What is it about young women today? They don't get it. Naked out of context is just naked. Miley's far more sexy in the T-shirt and boots, but then I'm just some old guy. What do I know?"

Helen felt the restlessness fading as humor took its place. "And the sledgehammer?"

Jeff grimaced. "That was weird. Why lick it?" He held up his hand. "I get the symbolism, but come on."

"Your parents said the same thing about your music. New music is one of the ways the generations separate from each other. It's part of the growing process."

"You're making that up."

"I'm not. I read it somewhere."

"Always the smart one." He settled next to her on the bench. "All right, Helen. Let's see what we can do there."

She began to play the opening chords of the song. Jeff's shoulder brushed against hers and when he started singing, she felt the vibration of his voice all the way down to her toes.

The problem wasn't her master bath or restlessness in her life. The problem was her. What was that old saying? It was time to put up or shut up. She was tired of wishing. Action was required and then she would know. If the results were a disaster, then she would take that road trip to Cleveland and along the way, she could figure out what was next.

Kelly rested her head, shoulders and arms on the counter of the café. "I'm a horrible person," she said, realizing that confessing all hadn't made her feel the least bit better. Usually telling Helen what was wrong had a cleansing effect, but not today. Maybe her sin was too great.

"I know what you're going to say," Kelly continued. "That I was only eighteen and it was my dad's decision to make, which is true only he wouldn't have thought of sending Olivia away if I hadn't mentioned it. I'd even researched schools. I practically shoved her out the door. I'm a terrible sister and a worse person. You're not going to want to be my friend anymore."

"Dramatic much?"

Kelly raised her head. "You're turning on me in my hour of pain?"

"Yes. Get over yourself. You're feeling guilty but Olivia's the one who was sent away. She's the one who had to start over somewhere that wasn't her home. You got to keep doing your thing here, only now you just had to worry about yourself."

Kelly sat up. "Ouch."

"I'm sorry to be blunt, but the facts are pretty much the facts. Let me be clear—I don't judge you for what you did. You're doing a great job of that all yourself. You're my friend and I love you. If you really want to make this better, you have to admit what you did and ask for forgiveness. Wallowing isn't going to make it go away."

Harsh words that were, unfortunately, very true. Kelly had been wallowing for the past few days and she still felt like crap.

Sometimes she was able to convince herself that it wasn't her fault. That she'd just been the sister, making suggestions. The decision had been Jeff's, and Olivia had been the one going at it with Ryan like they were rabbits. Pregnancy had just been one slip-up away. And then what?

But the rest of the time, she knew that she'd been far less than innocent. That she'd been terrified of what her sister might do and how that doing would impact Kelly's life. She hadn't been willing to take the risk and because of that fear, Olivia had been sent away.

She and Helen were alone in the café. It was nearly two thirty. All the customers and staff had left. Kelly had come seeking solace. Instead she was getting a well-deserved kick in the butt.

"Olivia's been in touch with our mother," Kelly said. "You'd think I would be jealous and want to know things, but I don't. I'm glad she's gone and I don't ever want to see her again."

"Based on what you've told me about her, I'm not surprised. Are you sorry Olivia came back?"

Kelly considered the question. "No," she admitted. "I like her way more than I would have guessed."

"So that's good."

Kelly looked at her friend. "Do you still love me?" she asked in a small voice.

"Yes. Double yes. You're my best friend, Kelly. I think you're amazing, but we all have flaws. You obviously think you screwed up with Olivia. She's mad, you're upset and the only way to fix it is to fix it. Talk to her. Tell her you're sorry and see if the two of you can start over."

"You're so rational."

"It's easy to see what's wrong with other people. It's correcting our own lives that's hard."

Kelly straightened. She didn't like what Helen had said, but she recognized the truth and wisdom of it.

"I have to talk to her," she whispered. "I have to suck it up and apologize and take whatever happens." She stretched her arms toward her friend. "Come with me and hold my hand."

Helen laughed. "You have to do this all on your own. Otherwise it won't count."

"There are so many rules." Kelly stood. "Okay, I'm going to do it. I'm strong and brave and she's my sister. It's all going to be fine." She paused. "I'm so lying."

"Yes, but you look good doing it."

Helen hugged her. Kelly thanked her for her advice, then got in her truck and drove the short distance to the house. With luck Olivia wouldn't be home and she could—

Kelly turned the corner and saw her sister's BMW parked in the driveway. So much for a reprieve. She parked next to the car and gripped her keys in her hand.

She found her sister standing in the middle of the living room. The furniture had all been rearranged. Several pieces had been brought in from other rooms. Olivia adjusted an end table, then straightened.

"What do you think?"

Kelly's first instinct was to protest. How dare Olivia change how the room had always been? Then she took a second and saw that the flow was better and the conversation area had gotten bigger, even though there were the same number of seats. Now you could talk to anyone without have to twist your head into an uncomfortable position.

"It's so much better," she admitted. "How did you know what to do?"

"I do staging. It's a thing."

"A good thing."

Kelly dropped her bag onto an end table, then put her hands on the back of a wing chair. She looked at her sister and told herself to just say it. She owed Olivia that.

"I'm sorry," she began. "I'm sorry for what happened and my part in it. I'm sorry I was uncomfortable with you and Ryan having sex. Not that I cared about the sex, it was that I thought you were going to get pregnant and it was just a matter of when. I shouldn't have assumed you would or that I would get stuck, and I'm sorry I worried that you were just like Mom, and I'm even more sorry I thought about myself more than you. I shouldn't have gone to Dad and suggested he send you to boarding school. I don't think he would have thought of it himself. It's all my fault and I was wrong."

Olivia stared at her for a long time. Kelly had no idea what she was thinking.

"Did you really think I was going to be like Mom?" Olivia asked.

Kelly hesitated before nodding. "You two were so close. You had so much in common. You were both beautiful and outgoing and nothing like Dad and me. When you started dating Ryan, it was like watching her all over again. I was so scared."

"That I would end up sixteen and pregnant?"

Kelly nodded.

"You're probably right."

Kelly gaped at her. "What?"

Olivia sat on the sofa and sighed. "We were young and stupid, so getting pregnant seems inevitable. To be honest I don't know if I would have had the kid or not. And if I had, you're right. You would have been stuck, one way or the other. After all, you're the responsible sister."

Kelly didn't know what to do with the information, nor could she read her sister's mood.

"I'm sorry," she said cautiously as she sat down.

"I got that." Olivia gave her a brief smile that faded quickly. "I'm not saying it didn't hurt. Of course it did. My own sister wanted to get rid of me." Her mouth twisted. "But the thing is, I kind of understand why."

"Thank you for saying that."

"You're welcome. We both know better now," Olivia told her. "I accept your apology. We can move on."

"I'd like that. I'm glad you came back. Are you?"

"Mostly."

"Do you miss Phoenix?"

Olivia shuddered. "Not at all. I honestly don't know if I'm going back. My job isn't going very well." She glanced at her hands, then back at Kelly. "My boss is a bit of a nightmare. Everything is about her, which is exhausting. I've been thinking I need to make a change. Now I can get serious about it."

Kelly started to ask where she would go when it occurred to her that Olivia might want to stay here.

Her first response was to insist that not happen. Tulpen Crossing was hers—her sister wasn't welcome. But that was the teenager inside of her. On second thought, having Olivia around might not be that bad.

She remembered when they'd been little and how Olivia had cried when Kelly had left to go to kindergarten. Kelly had done her best to remember everything that had happened during the day and had told her sister all about it the second she got home. Three years later Olivia had been the best prepared kid in *her* kindergarten class.

When had all that changed, Kelly wondered.

"I really am sorry," she whispered.

"I know. It's okay. You saved me from being a teenaged mother, so that's good."

"Are you seeing anyone in Phoenix?"

"No. I don't have many ties there, which is ridiculous considering how long I've lived there. I don't have ties anywhere."

"You have us. Dad and me."

"Thanks for that."

Kelly pressed her lips together, then couldn't help asking, "Are you still hoping to get back together with Ryan?"

Olivia sighed. "I don't know. He's dating Autumn. I'm sure

he'll dump her eventually but then what? Do I want a guy who'll dump someone for me? Doesn't that mean he'll dump me for someone else later?"

"Technically yes, but seriously who could that be?"

Olivia laughed. "It is hard to imagine anyone more sparkly and wonderful. How are things with Griffith?"

"Confusing. Good."

"I'm glad."

They smiled at each other. Kelly felt the guilt ease. Some of it would linger, but steps had been taken. She and Olivia weren't exactly close, but there was potential. Potential and promise.

14

Olivia emptied the contents of her grocery bag. She had a rotisserie chicken, mayo, mango chutney, curry powder, celery, walnuts and grapes, along with a loaf of freshly baked bread. Every now and then a girl had to celebrate her life with a curried chicken salad sandwich.

She barely finished shredding the chicken when she heard a truck pull up to the house. The driver would either be her dad or her sister, and for once, Olivia was okay with either. Whatever anger she'd had at her dad had long since faded and having Kelly apologize so sincerely had made things right between them.

The back door opened and her dad walked in.

"Hey, sweetie. I thought you might be home. I came by to buy you lunch."

She motioned to all the ingredients on the island. "How about if I make you a sandwich instead?"

"Even better." Her dad crossed to the sink and washed his hands, then set the table. "What else can I do?"

"Keep me company."

He leaned against the counter. "How are you settling in? You remembering what it's like to live here?"

She smiled. "Yes and no. It's different, what with not being in high school. I'm hoping to meet up with a few friends." Assuming she still had any in the area. When she'd last lived here, everything had been about Ryan rather than her girlfriends.

"You're not running from something, are you?" her father asked.

"Oh, Dad."

His gaze was steady. "Not an answer, Olivia."

Ten years ago the paternal tone would have had her bristling. Today it made her feel taken care of.

"I'm not in trouble, if that's what you're asking. There's no scary boyfriend, no loan shark. Business really is slow in the summer and I wanted some time to think. I'm not loving everything about my life."

"Such as?"

She dumped the shredded chicken into the bowl, then started halving grapes. "There's no one special. I think maybe I'd like someone special."

"Make sure he's a good guy. You want someone kind and capable. I know all you young girls want a good-looking guy with a hot car, but looks fade. Be more concerned about his character than his bank account."

Good advice, she thought sadly. Advice she should have gotten when she was seventeen, not twenty-five. Only she hadn't been here at seventeen.

"There are less good guys out there than you'd think," she told him. Ryan certainly didn't count. She wasn't sure about Sven, not that they had a real relationship.

"Besides," she added, "a man is kind of the least of it right now."

She diced celery, then stirred the ingredients before adding the mayo and chutney. She folded in the walnuts last.

"I'm not sure I like my job." She got plates and put them on the island. "I take that back. I really don't like my job. Any part of it."

"You do marketing for a real estate company?"

She nodded. "I design the campaigns for each of the houses. I set up targeted advertising on social media, format the print ads, design the flyers. It's okay, but there's a real sameness to it. Plus, it's not totally full-time, which means I spend the rest of my day being a secretary."

"There's nothing wrong with honest work."

"I agree. I just want to do more. I've done some interior design work on the side and I've started staging homes for selling. That's fun."

She scooped the salad onto the bread, then sliced the sandwiches in half. Her dad collected bags of chips from the pantry and poured them each iced tea from a pitcher in the refrigerator. They sat at the table.

"Is there room for advancement?" he asked.

She laughed. "Ah, no. It's a real estate company owned by one individual and she's not the nicest person around." A second too late Olivia reminded herself not to say more about Marilee. Talk about flirting with danger.

She battled with guilt—she should just fess up that she worked for her mom. But then what? Easier to keep quiet.

"I did try selling real estate," she added quickly. "It's not for me. I'd rather be doing other things than tagging along on the house-buying adventure." She sighed. "I think that's part of my problem. I don't want to do any one thing. I want to do all of them."

"Why can't you?"

"Because it's traditional to have a single job."

"Since when have you been traditional?"

An interesting question, she thought as she took a bite of her sandwich.

"What do you like doing best?" her dad asked.

"I like helping people," she said automatically, shocking the hell out of herself and possibly him. "Okay, that was weird, but it's true. Like the staging. I can take a plain house and make it so much more. I don't need a big budget. Just some rearranging, a few flea market finds and I'm good and the people selling the house get a higher offer."

"I like what you did in the living room."

"Thanks. It's really fun. I also like doing interior design so people can enjoy their homes more and I would love to get my hands on the craft mall. Oh, I'm enjoying the work for the auction. I want to be a part of things."

"Then that's what you should do."

"That's not one job."

Her father smiled at her. "No, it's not. But it could be one company. You could offer many services, all similar in nature. There's a lot of things that fall under the decorating umbrella. The same with the fund-raiser. Isn't it a type of party planning? Granted, we live in a small town, but what about helping businesses attract more tourists? Or talk to Griffith about his micro housing. Is he doing all he can to market them? You have a lot of options, Olivia. Not everyone has to be a fifth-generation farmer. The world only needs so many tulips."

She smiled. "Don't let Kelly hear you say that."

"I won't say anything if you won't."

"Deal."

Saturday morning Kelly was up at her usual time. Normally she tried to sleep in, but today was her first time volunteering at GB Micro Housing and she didn't want to be late. She walked into the bathroom only to find her sister was already dressed.

"Hi. You're awake early."

"I know." Olivia rolled her eyes. "I think it's the birds. They're so noisy at daybreak, which this time of year means five thirty. I couldn't get back to sleep. What are you doing up?"

"Griffith is holding a volunteer event. He's been collecting materials to build tiny homes for a charity that supports the homeless. We're going to build several tiny homes today. They'll be delivered where they're needed."

"I didn't know he did that. Want another pair of hands?"

"Absolutely. Can you be ready to leave in twenty minutes?"

"I can be ready in ten."

Olivia was as good as her word. Eleven minutes later they were driving to Griffith's warehouse.

"He said there would be breakfast there," Kelly said. "It's donated. I've never done one of these before, so I don't know exactly what to expect."

"You haven't done this before? I thought you two had been dating a while."

"No. Not that long."

Kelly wasn't sure they were really dating now, but she wasn't going to admit that. Griffith had said he wanted them to get together and he kissed her in a way that had made her toes curl, but she wasn't sure that made them a couple.

They pulled into the parking lot. There were hardly any spaces left and most of the cars looked unfamiliar.

"This is a crowd," Olivia said. "He must really put out the word. I wonder if he's on a volunteer email loop or if the charity he works with has contact with someone with a database of volunteers. That would make the most sense."

"Thinking of starting a charity?" Kelly asked, her voice teasing.

"No, just thinking about ways to get people together. Information is always good."

They went into the main warehouse. There had to be at least fifty people there. The regular houses had been moved out and in their place were stacks of material. Kelly saw the build was going to have an assembly line quality to it. Supplies were lined up in order. House frames at one end and finishes at the other.

Several huge posters hung from the walls. There was a detailed floor plan of the 8x12 home: to the left of the door were a two-burner stove and a small refrigerator, along with a small sink. To the right was a sofa that folded out into a twin bed. At the back were a toilet and a shower.

There were a few cabinets for storage above the stove and sink and above the sofa bed. Solar panels provided electricity and the toilet had a holding tank that could be emptied into an RV waste dump.

"Not bad for less than a hundred square feet," Olivia murmured. "Because of the width, the house can easily be towed."

"How do you know that?" Kelly asked.

"I've done some research on all the major employers in town. Griffith's company is one of them."

Her sister continued to surprise her, Kelly thought.

Helen hurried over and greeted them. "Breakfast is in the other warehouse," she said. "You check in there, as well. They assign tasks based on your skill level." She showed them her blue badge. "I'm screwing in things like door handles and doing a final clean. I begged for drywall installation. I mean, that's a skill I could really use, but did I get it?"

"Is there drywall on the walls?" Kelly asked.

"No. They use some special lightweight material instead. Another hope dashed. But I'm thinking I'm going to have to take some kind of basic home repair course if I don't want to always get stuck with cabinet knobs and cleaning."

"I guess we'll all be cleaning," Kelly said.

"I know how to do some plumbing," Olivia told her.

Kelly put her hands on her hips. "Are you serious?"

"In college I had an apartment with a bunch of leaky faucets. The landlord was never around, so I learned to do it myself." She smiled smugly. "Let's go register."

"Show-off," Kelly grumbled, more impressed than she wanted to admit.

They walked into the second warehouse. People were eating breakfast and introducing themselves to each other. There were several groups Kelly didn't recognize and she wondered if they'd come up from Seattle to help. Through the open back doors she saw the trailers that would carry the completed homes to their final destination.

She and her sister registered. She, too, was given a blue tag while Olivia's was orange. Olivia waved it.

"I get to install kitchen sinks," she said happily. "And the faucets. Not the toilets or showers, though. Those require licensed plumbers. I wonder what it would take to get a license."

"I'm impressed," Helen said. "Let's get some breakfast before we get started."

The buffet of eggs, bacon and sausage were from a catering company in Bellingham. Griffith joined them in line.

"Morning," he said.

Kelly felt herself get a little swoony at the sight of him. Ridiculous. It had just been a couple of kisses. She was stronger than that. Only not, apparently, around Griffith.

"Not buying local?" she asked, pointing at the name on the side of the food trays.

"I ask for the food to be donated at cost," he told her. "Which means whoever provides it is losing money. The catering company is owned by a large corporation. I figured they can afford it while it would be tough on Helen. She would never refuse me and I didn't want to put her in an awkward position."

It was too early for him to be that sweet, Kelly thought. She hadn't even had coffee. How was she supposed to resist him when he talked like that?

"You're a good guy," she complained. "Nice even."

"So I've heard."

"Aren't you going to be upset that I said that? Don't most guys want to be bad?"

He put his hand on the small of her back and eased her forward in line. "I'm not most guys. You like nice. It makes you feel safe, ergo I like being nice."

"Ergo?"

"I'm very cosmopolitan."

He was a lot of things, she thought happily. "I'm stuck with a blue badge," she said, showing him. "I have no construction skills. That's depressing."

"You can be on my team. We're installing solar panels."

"You'd trust me with that?"

"We need someone to make sure we don't run into anything as we're raising the panels. You can do that." He leaned close and whispered, "If anyone asks, just tell them you're with the band."

She laughed. "Thanks."

Olivia spent the day installing sinks in tiny homes. She had to run the pipes first, set the sinks in place, connect everything, then test her work. A little before noon, as she crawled out from under the third sink, she got the idea that maybe she'd been chosen more for her size than her skill level. None of the male plumbers could have fit in the cramped space.

At lunchtime Helen came and got her.

"Are you feeling superior?" Helen asked. "With your mad skills?"

"I'm mostly feeling like a pretzel. How about you?"

"I have applied door handles to the best of my ability, vacuumed and wiped down entire homes. I'm smug in my goodness."

They collected sandwiches and salads and took them outside to sit on the grass. Olivia noticed Kelly hanging out with Griffith.

"Someone's crazy about her new boyfriend," Olivia said in a singsong voice.

"I'm glad. Kelly deserves a great guy."

"Don't we all." She looked across the lawn to where Sven sat with a group of the construction guys. He caught her gaze and winked. She smiled back, then turned to Helen. "What about you? Is there anyone special lurking in your bed?"

"I wish." Helen sighed. "I'm divorced, which is fine. Troy was a jerk and I shouldn't have married him."

"I'm sorry."

"Me, too, but it's done. And now..." Her voice trailed off.

Olivia studied her. "What?"

"Oh, there's this one guy, but I'm not sure he sees me as more than a friend."

"If he doesn't, he's stupid."

Helen laughed. "Thanks. I just don't know what to do. Do I tell him and risk losing the friendship? Continue to pine? Get a cat?"

"You should go for it," Olivia told her. "Regretting not acting is the worst. You're stuck with the could-have-beens. If it doesn't work out, then at least you know you tried. Plus, you'll know he's an idiot and you can move on."

"You think?"

"I'm totally and completely sure."

"I want your level of confidence one day."

Olivia grinned. "I'm mostly faking it."

"You're doing a good job."

Conversation shifted to the upcoming auction and all the items that were being delivered. They brainstormed ways to bundle them together so the silent auction was more appealing, then tossed their trash and headed back to work. On the way a woman about her age stopped by Olivia. She was petite, with dark hair and green eyes.

"Hi, Olivia. I'm Eliza. We went to high school together. Do you remember me?"

Olivia had a vague recollection of a quiet, shy brainiac who always aced tests. "Sure, Eliza. It's nice to see you."

"Thanks. I wasn't sure you would. Remember me, I mean. We didn't exactly hang out in the same circles. I was with the smart kids and—" Eliza slapped her hand over her mouth. "I'm sorry. I didn't mean to imply that you weren't smart."

Olivia laughed. "I know. It's okay. I'll forgive you if you honestly tell me whether or not I mean-girled you in high school."

Eliza grinned. "Nope. You ignored me completely."

"Thank God. So you still live around here?"

"I just moved back a few months ago. I graduated from Washington State University vet school and I got a job with the local vet here. It's challenging but fun."

"Come along, ladies," one of the volunteers called. "Work first, talk later."

"Maybe we can get lunch sometime and catch up," Eliza said.

An unexpected shot at friendship, Olivia thought. "I'd love that. Let's plan on that for sure."

15

The forklift carried bins of rooted tulips from the cooling rooms into the greenhouse. Kelly inspected the trays as they were shifted into place. Around her, a couple of guys worked the watering system. The tulips would be given a day to warm up to the greenhouse's constant sixty-seven degrees, then the special water-nutrient mixture would be added to the trays. In exactly twenty-one days, they would be harvesting this batch of tulips.

Olivia arrived and walked over to where Kelly was working. Kelly instantly felt dowdy in her green coveralls.

"Hi," Olivia said. "I saw all the cars in the parking lot and came to check it out. What's going on?"

Kelly motioned to the forklifts and the stacked trays ready to be put onto the tables. "Over the next two days, we're going to start forcing about a hundred thousand bulbs."

Olivia laughed. "You're kidding." Her humor faded. "You're not kidding. How is that possible and why?"

"August weddings. These bulbs are already purchased by a big distributor on the West Coast. Pink, yellow and orange are very hot this year and we have the best color saturation."

"Wedding flowers? That's so cool." She eyed the trays of bulbs. "What if they flower late?"

"They won't. They will be ready in exactly twenty-one days, give or take twenty-four hours."

"How on earth do you pick that many so fast? You must need dozens of people."

"I do. We have some mechanization, but a lot of it is done by hand. I have a group of regulars who come in. Mostly stay-at-home mothers who work for me every couple of months. They're long days, but I pay well enough that they make the schedule work."

Kelly was willing to offer the extra money in exchange for not having to employ full-time people. It was much cheaper for her.

Olivia looked into one of the trays. "There's a little stem already."

"I root them while they're still cold. It speeds up the forcing time and allows me to know exactly when they're going to be ready. Between now and when they bloom, they'll live in a perfect sixty-seven degrees with plenty of light and nutrients."

"Do you grow more for Mother's Day?"

"We deliver about six hundred and fifty thousand stems."

"Don't you worry about something going wrong?"

"Every time I plant."

Olivia frowned. "And here I thought farming was boring."

"It's a lot of things, but boring isn't one of them." The guys continued to put trays on tables. "I need to go back to my office and take care of a few things. You can stay and watch if you want."

She expected her sister to refuse, but instead Olivia nodded. "Thanks. I'm going to walk around for a while. I'll stay out of their way."

"Have fun."

When Kelly was back in her office, she slipped off her coveralls. She checked her email, then opened her scheduling program to confirm she would have enough workers when the tulips began to bloom.

Her dad walked in and took a chair across from hers.

"How's it going?" he asked. "I saw you're moving the bulbs into the greenhouse."

"All hundred thousand. We're on track for our deliveries."

"I'll put out the word. Brides across the west will sleep easier."

"Somehow I think they have more to worry about than tulips."

"Have you seen that Bridezilla show?" He shuddered. "They worry about everything."

"When have you ever seen a show about Bridezillas? How do you even know what that word is?"

"I hear things."

"You have a whole secret life, don't you?"

"Telling would mean it wasn't a secret."

She laughed. "Olivia's out there, watching the trays being put on the tables. She's fascinated."

"It's all new to her." He looked at Kelly. "I like having her back."

"Me, too."

"Do you? I wasn't sure at first."

Kelly sighed. "I was shocked when she showed up and more than a little resentful because I thought she would get in the way, but we're all different now. I guess growing up has a way of changing a person."

"I hope so. If not, there's a bigger problem."

She leaned toward him. "Does she remind you of Mom?"

"Olivia? Not at all. Why?"

"I just wondered. When we were kids she was with her all the time."

"I'm sorry about that," he said. "Marilee and I screwed up as parents in every way possible. The fact that you two are the least bit functional is because of you, not us."

"You didn't screw up."

"Sure, I did. We each had our favorite child. That was wrong. We were rarely a family—we were two teams. When Marilee left, Olivia had no one. I didn't know how to relate to her at all. I should have been there for her as much as I was there for you."

Kelly understood his point, but what she wanted to say was if her dad had been more involved with Olivia, he would have been less involved with her and then she would have had no one. It wasn't as if her mother would have picked up the slack. But that sounded petty and immature.

"I don't think we should have gotten married," he admitted. "I never thought she'd say yes. I should have taken you myself and raised you as a single father."

"Then you wouldn't have had Olivia."

"You're right. It's complicated. I know the divorce was hard on you. All the fighting, your mother doing what she did."

Kelly rolled her eyes. "You're always so nice when you talk about her. You never call out her crap."

"Whatever I think of her is my problem. Marilee will always be your mother. I respect that."

"You're a good man."

He grinned. "Thanks. Just don't tell your mother you said that."

"As I haven't spoken to her since I was fifteen, I don't see that as a real problem."

Olivia stopped running long enough to shrug out of her jacket and tie it around her waist. She checked for traffic, then crossed the street on her way to the park. Her breathing was steady, matching the rhythm of her stride. Her mind cleared of all the general crap, leaving her able to focus on what was important.

Since the volunteer day, she'd received more calls and emails about items people wanted to donate. At this rate she was going to be using a lot more of Sven's barn than she'd first thought. She was also going to have to figure out how to bundle various items so the number of bidding opportunities was manageable. If there were too many items, people wouldn't be able to make a choice. Or they'd go bargain shopping and that wouldn't help anyone. Fewer items that were more exclusive meant bidding wars.

She had one more meeting with a caterer and then she would make her decision on the dinner menu. The tourism board had given her an advance to use as a deposit. As the event was being held at the craft mall, she wouldn't need to pay for the space, but she did have to organize some burly help to move booths out of the way, opening up a large area for the silent auction.

Tickets would go on sale at the end of the week. The city had an online site she was able to use for collecting the money. Two of the local high school teachers had offered students in need of their volunteer hours to graduate for her to use as free labor. While the project was still at the "Am I going to pull it off" stage, she was feeling relatively positive.

A truck pulled up behind her. In that split second before she turned, she found herself smiling. Sven, she thought happily, hoping he would invite her back to his place. She could use a little mind-clearing sex, followed by great food. Honestly, his last girlfriend had been an idiot. Who wouldn't want to be with a guy who was that good in bed *and* could cook? The walking around naked part was good, too. Dinner and a show.

She was still grinning as she turned around and saw the driver wasn't Sven at all. It was Ryan.

She let the smile fade as she walked toward him. Technically Ryan was one of the main reasons she'd returned to Tulpen Crossing. She was supposed to get closure and he'd really hurt her feelings that first night she'd sought him out. Since then, she'd thought of him less and less. But as she got closer and she saw his familiar face, she wondered if she'd just been fooling herself. Ryan had always been the one. The dream guy.

He rolled down the window and leaned toward her. "God, you're beautiful."

She stopped a couple of feet away. "Hello, Ryan. Shouldn't you be at work?"

"I'm good. Besides, if I was at work, I wouldn't be talking to you. How are you? I never see you around." His expression turned serious. "I miss you, Olivia."

"Do you?"

"Every minute of every day. I've been thinking about you a lot. About how we were, back in college. It was the best ever."

She'd thought so, too, until he'd been offered a spot on a farm team. He'd left within the hour, barely bothering to tell her where he was going. He'd promised to stay in touch, but he hadn't. He'd just been gone.

He reached out his hand to her. "I should have taken you with me when I left college."

"You probably should have."

"You're the best thing that ever happened to me."

"No doubt."

He smiled. "I respect that you're making me work for it, babe. You're worth it." He nodded toward the passenger seat. "Want to spend the day together? We could drive to Seattle, walk on the waterfront. Check into a great hotel and get to know each other again."

He was offering her everything she was supposed to want. There was only one slightly overweight catch. "Is Autumn coming with us?"

He grimaced. "That's over."

"You broke up with her?"

"Yes. I swear."

I swear. Ryan's favorite phrase.

"I swear I'll love you forever."

"I swear I'll pull out before I come."

"I swear I'll never leave you."

She had a long list of *I swear* broken promises.

"Does she know you broke up with her?" she asked.

His gaze flickered. She rolled her eyes.

"See you," she called as she turned and ran in the other direction.

"Dammit, Olivia, why are you acting like this?" he yelled after her.

She didn't bother turning around or answering. He was a jerk. She knew he was a jerk. She wasn't sure she even wanted him in her life. It was just that stupid nagging sense that they weren't done. That he'd always been the one, and that she should try at least one more time to see if they could work it out.

When she'd been alone and sad, Ryan was the guy she'd dreamed about. In college, he'd almost proposed. If he hadn't been drafted or whatever it was called, he would have. They could be married now, with a kid. They could be happy. More important, she would belong. She'd never belonged—not since her mom had run off all those years ago. Ryan was the dream of finally having a place that was hers alone.

The only problem with that seemed to be the man himself. Or maybe it was her. Maybe she was hanging on to the wrong thing, or learning the wrong lesson. Or maybe she just needed to give Ryan a chance.

Jeff held open the door to JML. Helen walked out into the early evening and breathed in the cool air. The stillness surrounded her, easing the tightness in her body. Her ears throbbed from both the volume and the horror of the evening session but that would fade with time and distance.

"They were awful," Jeff said with a sigh. "Possibly the worst band ever."

"I agree. No one should butcher country music that way without being prosecuted." She shuddered. "I'm going to call Isaak tomorrow and tell him we can't help them. They are, in fact, beyond help and should take up another hobby."

Not words she said lightly, but honest to God, there was no way she could survive another practice session.

The clients were a father, mother and ten-year-old twin girls. None of them could play an instrument to save their souls and that lack of ability wasn't even close to how awful they all sang. With years of instruction they might make it all the way to tone deaf, but even that would be a stretch.

Jeff opened the trunk of her car and put her keyboard inside. It was something he always did, like holding open doors or paying the check if they went out. He was a polite man. Polite and kind and funny.

They walked around to the driver's side and he held open the door. "You'll probably want to take an aspirin when you get home," he told her.

"There's a thought."

She looked up at him, liking how he was taller. There were a few laugh lines by his eyes, but other than that, he wore his age well. He was a physically active, attractive man and she desperately loved him. While she didn't think she was ready to confess that, it was long past time to say *something*.

She sucked in a breath, felt herself flush and suddenly wanted to run away. Only she couldn't. She'd been doing that for far too long.

"Jeff," she began.

He stared at her expectantly.

She opened her mouth, then closed it. "I like how you play."

"You couldn't hear me tonight."

"I know, but the rest of the time. I like how you play guitar."

Ack! Talk about lame. She had to get it together.

"What I mean is you're really nice and we're friends and I've thought a lot about what you said about Seattle and finding a guy there, but it's so not anything I could do. I want to be with someone I know and I like and who likes me back. I want to be friends with the guy I sleep with. I want that guy to be you."

Nothing about him changed. He continued to study her and for the life of her, she had no idea what he was thinking.

"I wanted you to know that if you wanted to start something with me, I'm open to it. Anytime."

He still held his guitar in his left hand. He shifted it to his right, looked at the ground, back at her, drew in a breath and exhaled.

She could hear the highway about a half mile away and the faint crash of a bowling ball smashing into pins. Her face burned and she knew she was beet red, but there was nothing to be done. She wasn't going to call back the words. They had to be said.

He finally looked back at her. "Thanks for telling me, Helen. Have a good night."

Then he turned and walked to his truck. He got in and drove away. Just like that.

When she was alone in the parking lot, she blinked back tears before getting into her car.

She wasn't going to be sorry, she told herself firmly. Or apologize or feel bad. She had the right to feel how she felt and to want what she wanted. If he didn't agree, then he was a fool. Which all made sense, only as she drove home she couldn't helping thinking that the only fool right now was her.

"We just can't wait," Penny Kerr said with an excited smile. "This is going to be the perfect summer house for us. When my grandfather left us the lot on the lake, we had no idea how we were ever going to afford to build a house and after two years of camping all summer, let me tell you that gets old."

Her husband, Ben, nodded in agreement. "Once the twins came along last year, it was impossible. My job allows me to work from a remote location but a tent doesn't cut it."

The Kerr family had chosen one of Griffith's largest models. The house would be twelve by twenty-four feet, with a loft. The main level included a kitchen and small bathroom at the back, a combo eating area/play area in the middle and a living room up front. The loft contained two twin beds over the kitchen and a queen-size bed over the living room.

"There are just so many decisions." Penny bit her lower lip. "The flooring, the fixtures. Is there someone who can help us figure this out? I want the house to look nice, but with our twins, everything is going to have to be durable."

It was the question Griffith always dreaded. He could design the hell out of four hundred square feet, but he had no idea how to decorate it.

"I can show you pictures of what other people have chosen," he said. "I also have a list of vendors."

"But no in-house designer?"

"No. Sorry."

"It's okay. We'll figure it out." Penny handed over the deposit check. "You'll let us know when you start construction so we can drive up and see the house?"

"Absolutely."

"Thanks."

The young couple left. Griffith walked back to his office. The Kerrs weren't the first clients to want help with their tiny home. While some clients had a clear and detailed vision, more often than not, they expected direction from him. A problem that wasn't going to be solved today, he told himself.

He'd barely settled in his chair when Ryan burst into the room. His brother waved a piece of paper as he stalked over to the desk.

"What's this?" he asked. "Do you think it's funny? You're an asshole, Griffith. I can't believe you did this to me."

Griffith leaned back in his chair. "I have no idea what you're talking about."

"My paycheck. Where's the rest of it?"

So Leo had taken him at his word, Griffith thought. Good. Ryan needed to learn a lesson.

Griffith stood and faced his brother. "You were paid the hours you worked. Simply being in the building isn't enough. You take ninety-minute lunches and show up late. When you do work, it's half-assed most of the time. If you weren't my brother, I would have fired you already. Consider this a warning."

Ryan glared at him. "You can't do that."

"I can and I will. You've always had it easy. Grades, girls, baseball, but you never learned consequences. The lesson is coming late, but I'm hoping you'll figure it out."

Ryan took a step forward. "You're a sanctimonious bastard. I know what this is about. You're jealous. You've always been jealous. I had everything and you had nothing. You're just some guy. I was the star. You can't let that go, so you're punishing me."

His sympathy faded in the face of his brother's inability to take responsibility for his decisions. While his shoulder blowing out hadn't been Ryan's fault, everything after had been of his own making.

"Whatever story you have to tell yourself to make it through the night, kid." He pointed to the door. "You see that out there? It's a successful business. *My* business. I started it from nothing. I have a good life, Ryan. I get you're still dealing with what you lost, but it's time to suck it up and move on. Baseball is over. That's unfortunate but you can still be—"

"Fuck you," Ryan screamed. "I hate this crap town and this job and you and everything. I'm not supposed to be here. I'm not supposed to be like everyone else."

"Too late. You are. Now figure it out. You want to get paid, you need to work. If you don't, then quit. Whatever you decide, spend some time thinking about your next act."

"Go to hell."

Ryan turned and left. Griffith noticed his brother was careful to take his paycheck with him.

He settled back in his chair and wondered which way things were going to go. Ryan could either get it and move on, or he could spend the rest of his life being a has-been. There was no way to know. The irony was Griffith was just as guilty as his brother, only his weakness didn't show.

Ryan had lost his baseball dream and couldn't cope. Griffith had failed at marriage and decided to turn his back on the institution. If he couldn't be good at it, he wasn't going to try again. Having found Kelly, he didn't have to. He could have it all—or at least as much as he could handle. He supposed that made him lucky.

But even as he had the thought a part of him wondered if instead he was being lulled into a false sense of security. If fate was somehow simply waiting for him to get complacent before jumping up and biting him in the butt. Only time would tell.

By ten the next morning, Helen knew that Jeff wasn't going to be coming into the diner. Actually she'd known at five forty-five that morning, but had kept hoping that someone would burst in and say that the roads had all washed out and he couldn't get to the café, or that he'd been beamed up by aliens, but had left her a lovely note. Instead there was only the usual morning rush that kept her running and a growing sense of dread in her stomach.

Once the regular post-breakfast, pre-lunch lull started, she slipped out back and sat on the rear steps in the watery sunlight. She honestly didn't know what to do or what to think. She'd told him what she wanted and he'd disappeared.

They lived in a small town—there was no way to avoid him. Did he pity her? Would he not want to be friends? What about their singing and their mornings together? She didn't know if everything was lost or what was going to happen next.

"I shouldn't have said anything," she whispered.

What if he started telling people what had happened? What if everyone knew and then laughed and pointed? While she wanted to believe he would never be cruel, she was scared and hurt and—

"No regrets," she whispered. It wasn't wrong of her to like someone, to tell him. She'd been honest and polite. He might not share her feelings, but she wasn't a bad person for what she'd suggested.

She wrapped her arms around her midsection, as if to hold in all the emotions swirling inside of her. She breathed in and out to the count of ten, then rose and walked back into the cafe. Whatever was going on in her personal life, people would be expecting lunch. The world kept turning and there was absolutely no way for her to step off.

16

Olivia spent a ridiculous amount of time trying to figure out what to wear. She wanted to look pretty without being over-dressed. Plus, it was Tulpen Crossing—not exactly the fashion capital of anywhere.

She settled on white crop pants, a lightweight boatneck sweater layered over a matching tank, and flats. Her makeup was natural, her hair wavy. She grabbed a straw clutch, then walked down the hall and found her father sitting in the kitchen, a magazine open in front of him. In that split second before he noticed her, Olivia would have sworn he was incredibly sad. But before she could say anything, he looked up, saw her and smiled.

"You look nice. Going out?"

She grinned. "I am. I'm meeting Eliza. She and I went to high school together."

"I'm glad you're hanging out with your friends again."

She didn't correct him. She knew he assumed she'd been with friends that first night, because she'd said what she was doing. She was also lying about her mother and her job and seriously, she needed to come clean at some point. Just not today.

"I won't be late," she called as she walked to the back door.

"Have fun."

Eliza was waiting for Olivia when she got to Tulip Burger. They got a booth by the window and sat across from each other.

Eliza wrinkled her nose. "You look really nice. Ignore the

cat hair all over me. I was leaving work when there was an escape from the boarding area. I had to help with the roundup."

"You look fine."

Olivia said the words automatically, even though she was thinking that the huge print on Eliza's T-shirt totally overwhelmed her, and the shirt itself was way too big. The shoulder seam hung a couple of inches down her arm. But she was here to make friends, not give fashion advice.

"Thanks for suggesting this," she said instead. "I've been looking forward to hanging out."

"Me, too. How long have you been back in town?"

"A couple of weeks. I'm staying the summer."

"Then you go back to… Is it Phoenix?"

"Yes, and to be honest, I'm not sure I'm going back. I don't really like my job there." Or her boss, and she didn't want to talk about that, either. "What about you? When did you move home?"

"January. I graduated in June of last year, then took an internship before accepting a job here."

"We're the same age. How did you get through college and vet school so quickly?"

"I graduated high school early and got in to WSU. I always knew what I wanted to do. I spent my summers volunteering at the vet clinic where I work now." She flashed a smile. "I think the vets there hired me out of self-defense. They were afraid I was simply going to camp out in the parking lot until they gave me a job."

"They're lucky to have you."

"I'm really the lucky one," Eliza told her. "It can be tough to get a job after graduation. My internship helped. When we graduate, we don't really know anything. I mean there's a lot of learning but very limited practical experience. One of the great things they have at WSU is a partnership with Seattle Humane.

You get to spend time at the facility, working with the surgical team. It's invaluable training."

She pressed her lips together. "I'm babbling. I'm sorry. I guess I'm nervous."

"To have dinner with me?"

"Yes. You're, you know, Olivia Murphy."

"Hardly notable."

"It is to me. You were always so popular in high school. Look at what you're doing now. You've been back less than a month and hey, you're raising money to put a new roof on the craft mall. That's impressive."

"It's not saving a life."

"I couldn't do it."

"I couldn't do what you do, either. How about if we agree to be impressed with each other and just have dinner?"

"I'd like that." Eliza leaned forward. "The burgers here are still delicious. It was always one of my favorite places to come as a kid."

"Mine, too." Although her mother had always complained about the lack of choices and how everything was so provincial. Funny how now Olivia could see the charm of Tulpen Crossing. She'd grown up enough to realize her mother's issues with the town had nothing to do with geography and everything to do with whatever demons she carried with her.

"Are your folks still here?" Olivia asked.

"Of course. They'll never leave. My two sisters live only a couple of blocks from my parents and are popping out babies left and right. I can't get a date. It frustrates my mom." Eliza lowered her voice. "I'm the first member of my family to go to college. They don't know what to make of me."

"They're proud."

"I hope so. It's hard being the baby of the family, you know? Plus, I'm small. I look like I'm twelve. I wish I were elegant, like you."

Olivia laughed. "I'm not elegant."

"You are. The way you dress. Your confidence."

She thought of her lack of direction and how she'd come back for a guy she wasn't even sure she liked. "That is mostly faked."

"I don't think so. When I meet with the pet owners, I never know how to talk to them. Half the time they don't believe I'm really a vet or they want to see one of the other doctors." Eliza pressed her lips together. "Would you mind giving me some advice about what to wear and maybe how to put on makeup? I never learned. I'd ask my sisters, but they're more into glitter than what I'd be comfortable wearing to the office."

Olivia thought about the fun she'd had buying clothes for her sister. In a way, the makeovers were a lot like staging a house. You started with the bare bones and fluffed.

"I'd love to help. I'm looking for a good hairstylist. When I find her, I'll give you the name. The first thing you need is a great haircut. The rest will be easy."

"You think?"

"I can have you looking like you're fifteen in no time at all."

Eliza laughed. "That would be great. Then we can aim for twenty."

"Oh, don't get too wild. Besides, in twenty years you'll be thrilled to look younger."

"I'll hang on to that thought."

"What is wrong?"

A fairly wordy question coming from Delja, Helen thought, doing her best to smile brightly. "Nothing, why?"

"No smiles."

"I'm smiling right now."

Delja rolled her eyes as if to say that no one was fooled. She crossed her arms over her ample chest and stared. The message was clear. She was in this for the long haul.

It was after two. The café was closed and Delja seemed in no hurry to move on. There was no way Helen was going to explain that she was beyond sad that she hadn't seen Jeff in two days. Two! The man hadn't been by or texted or anything. Whatever he was thinking, it couldn't be good.

But that didn't solve her current problem.

There was no way to explain about Jeff. Okay, technically there was, but she felt she'd had more than enough humiliation in her life for one week. She thought about what else she could say, then felt a flash of inspiration and tucked crossed fingers behind her back so the lie wouldn't count.

"I'm having a lot of cramping with my period. It's getting better, but I haven't felt well."

Delja studied her for a second. "Yes?"

"I'm fine otherwise. I'll be better in a day or so."

Because she would have to be. She couldn't keep pretending to have her period indefinitely. She would give herself the night to mope and eat more ice cream and then she would move on. Jeff was great and yes she was desperately in love with him, but he obviously didn't want anything to do with her romantically. That was his decision. A wrong decision, but still. His to make.

She would put the disappointment behind her. The good news was she'd been brave and *yay her*. If he was too stupid to see what a catch she was, then blah, blah, blah.

Delja hugged her. "Feel better."

"I will. Have a good rest of your day."

The cook waved and left. Helen pushed aside the guilt she felt for lying, then made sure everything was turned off in the kitchen and that the back door was locked.

Starting tomorrow, she would come up with a plan, she promised herself. She would start exercising. She'd seen Olivia jogging all over the place. Maybe she could talk to her about how to begin a walking program. Walking was healthy. She would give up sugar and daydreams about men who didn't appreciate what was offered. Then she would go online and find someone who was even hotter and who wanted her with a fiery—

She walked into the front of the café and stopped short when she saw Jeff standing by the counter. She stared, aware of the silence except for the ticking of the old-fashioned wall clock.

They looked at each other. His expression was unreadable, his body language tense, which didn't make her feel as if he'd shown up to tell her anything she wanted to hear.

"How did you get in? I know I locked the front door."

"I have the key you gave me."

That was true. She *had* given him a key in case of an emergency. Because they were friends and she trusted him. At least she had.

She raised her chin and squared her shoulders. She was self-actualized, or she would be once she got her plan working. She could get through whatever he had to say.

"We need to talk," he told her. "Can we go into your office?"

No. Whatever it was, she didn't want to hear it. He was going to hurt her. He was going to rip out her heart and stomp on it. He was going to leave her gasping and bleeding and a lot of other things that were incredibly painful.

She led the way. After flipping on the light, she stood in front of her desk, close enough that she could lean on it if she had to, and waited for him to talk.

He stood by the open door. His arms hung loose at his side. His dark gaze was more intense than before. His jaw clenched.

"Did you mean what you said?" he asked, his voice low. "About wanting me?"

"Yes."

"In bed?"

She wasn't sure where he was going with this. Did he want more details so he could humiliate her more completely? She sucked in a breath.

"Yes."

"You're sure?"

"Oh, my God. What's wrong with you? What are you try-ing to get me to say? Yes, I want to sleep with you. Yes, I think you're incredibly hot and while I like being friends, I want more. I want you in my bed and I want to be in yours. I like you and I want to make love with you. Is that what you wanted to hear?"

"Every word."

He closed the distance between them, cupped her face in his hands and kissed her. She was so shocked, it took her a few seconds to respond and when she did she couldn't help throw-ing her arms around his neck. Which turned out to be a good thing because when Jeff kissed her, he did it with heat and need and tongue, the result of which left her more than a little weak in the knees.

He dropped his hands to her shoulders, then lowered them down her back to her butt. He gently squeezed the curves, which made her instinctively arch against him. Her belly came in direct contact with what felt a whole lot like a very large, very hard erection.

I… You… What?

Helen drew back enough to stare into his fire-filled eyes. "I don't understand."

He reached for the front of her shirt and started unfastening the buttons. "What's not to understand?"

Any answer got lost when he leaned in and began kissing along the side of her neck. Tingles joined the confusion. There was a brief tussle for dominance, then the tingles won. They were joined by heat and need and a growing sense of *Holy crap, this is really happening.*

It took him all of five seconds to get her shirt off. Her bra followed, then he was kissing her breasts, licking, loving and sucking until she was clinging and begging him to never stop. Somehow his shirt was off. He put her hands on his chest and then she was stroking everything she'd dreamed about. Okay, not everything, but a lot of it and he felt good. All muscles and heat.

He kept stopping to kiss her over and over, his tongue dancing with hers. Their lips clung, their hands reached. Without really trying, she found herself naked and sitting on her desk. His hand was between her thighs rubbing her to a fast, hot orgasm that had her writhing in pleasure.

He pulled a condom from his jeans front pocket, put it on, then pushed home. By the second stroke she'd wrapped her legs around his hips and was pulling him as close as possible. Their eyes locked and she came all over again.

When they were both breathing like normal people again, Jeff leaned his forehead against hers and sighed. "You have no idea how long I've wanted to do that."

"For real?"

He smiled. "Let's get dressed and head back to your place. I didn't intend to start things this way. I had a slow seduction all planned."

"We wouldn't want that to go to waste, now would we?"

He kissed her. "Absolutely not."

"I don't understand," Helen admitted nearly an hour later, when she could breathe again.

They were lying in her bed, in her room, naked. Completely and totally naked, which wasn't nearly as surprising as the fact that the reason they were naked was that she and Jeff had just had sex. Again.

She turned her head and stared into his brown eyes. "What happened?"

He smiled, then leaned in and kissed her. "You're so beautiful. I've wanted to tell you for months now, but wasn't sure I should. And if you have to ask what just happened, then I've been doing it wrong all these years."

"You're not. I'm still dealing with aftershocks." Little jolts that zinged through her girl parts, up to her breasts, then made a happy return trip. "But I really don't understand."

He supported his head on one hand and rested the other on her belly. Not her favorite place to be touched, what with it being, you know, not flat, only the light pressure of his touching her felt too good for her to complain. Plus she was already totally naked, something she generally avoided. She was a master draper. Nightgowns, sheets, you name it, she could drape it such that very little actual nakedness was ever seen. But somehow with Jeff, that had all gone away. Here she was, in the middle of the afternoon, buck naked in her bed. And they'd already done it in her office, on her desk, where she'd also been naked. So much for her draping skills.

"You mean when did I first realize I liked you?" he asked as he leaned in and kissed her.

She closed her eyes and reveled in the warmth of his mouth on hers, in the way passion quickened and how it was perfectly okay for her to put her fingers on his face or his shoulders or his chest or his dick. Although technically she hadn't really touched the latter, except to guide him inside, so she slid along his thigh until she could take him in her hand and lightly stroke him. He flopped back on the bed and groaned.

"I need at least an hour."

"I'm just playing."

He pulled her against him so that her head rested on his shoulder. He settled his hand on her hip.

"I've always thought you were sexy as hell," he admitted. "From the first day you showed up at JML to play keyboard. It was cold and raining and you had on a blue sweater the exact color of your eyes. I couldn't figure out where to look first. Your face or your chest."

She raised her head and stared at him. "You were looking at my boobs?"

He grinned. "Every chance I got. Still do."

"I never noticed."

"I try to be subtle."

"You're successful." She liked this game. "Then what?"

"Then I told myself you were my daughter's friend and way too young for me and I tried to stop looking. Then you and I became friends and it was nice. I didn't want to screw that up."

"How would we screw it up?"

"Helen, I'm going to be fifty soon. I'm sixteen years older than you. We live in a small town where everyone knows everything. I didn't want to mess with that. Plus, I wasn't sure how you felt about me."

She was going to ignore the messing up part—that wouldn't be fun to talk about, but the rest of it was nice to hear. He ran his hand from her shoulder to hip, then back again.

"Sixteen years isn't that much difference," she told him. "The Kelly thing is complicated. She doesn't know I have the hots for you and it's not like she and I were friends in high school, so you didn't know me when I was a kid. I had no idea if you saw me as anything but a friend and I couldn't stand the humiliation of her knowing her father had rejected me."

"Only a fool would reject you."

She thought of Troy, but decided not to mention her past. Or Jeff's.

"Why did it take you two days to get back to me?" she asked. "I thought you were thinking of fifty ways to tell me no."

"I was thinking it through. This is a big step for me." He shifted so he could look into her eyes. "Helen, I've never gotten involved with anyone in town. If this ends badly, we're both going to be sorry. We can't escape each other. You get that, right?"

A sensible conversation, but not one she wanted to have. "I know."

"You're okay with that?"

She nodded.

"Good. I am, too." He lightly kissed her. "I'm not seeing anyone else. I hope you're not, either."

He was being serious, but his words made her laugh. "Oh, my God. When would I be seeing anyone? I believe this all started because I was complaining about my lack of seeing someone. Which, by the way, wasn't me interested in dating. It was me trying to get you to ask me out. Either I'm not very good at hinting or you're totally oblivious. I'm going with the latter."

"Probably the right decision. So we're in this? You and me? We're together, exclusively?"

It was an awful lot like him asking her to be his girlfriend. Her breath caught and she nodded. "I'm in."

"Me, too. Do you want to tell anyone or keep it quiet for a while?"

By anyone she was pretty sure he meant Kelly and Olivia.

While she knew that telling her best friend was inevitable, she mostly didn't want to have to deal with that. Not yet. Not when everything was new and sexy and fun. She just wanted to be with Jeff, at least for now.

"Can it just be us until we figure it out?" she asked. "I'm not saying forever, but a few weeks?" Mostly because she had no idea how Kelly would take it. Would her friend be happy for her or too caught up in the ick factor of Helen and Jeff being an item?

His expression turned stern. "You want me to lie to my children?"

Well, crap, when he put it like that…

One corner of his mouth turned up. "Of course we'll keep it between us for now. This is the fun part, Helen. I want what you want."

Oh, please, oh, please, let that be true, she thought.

He kissed the top of her head. "Want to order in pizza?"

She was weak from their lovemaking. Every cell in her body had been pleasured and she knew she was going to hurt in happy places that hadn't seen action in forever. He was a thoughtful, sexy lover who knew how to push all her buttons. If they were this in tune after a single afternoon, imagine where they would be in a month or two when they'd really started exploring each other. The possibilities were incredible.

"You want to stay for dinner?" she asked.

"If it's all right with you."

It was more than all right. It was magical.

She smiled. "Can we get extra cheese? You need to keep up your strength."

"Sure, but we both know that's not the part you want to keep up."

She was still laughing when he pushed inside of her.

17

Olivia knew it was time to get things straight in her mind and her life. If she didn't like where she was with her job, she needed to change that. If she didn't like where things were with Ryan, she had to change that, as well. Fixing her job was going to be the more complicated of the two—what with her not being in Phoenix at the moment, but the Ryan problem could be solved with a simple conversation.

With that in mind, she drove to GB Micro Housing and parked by the main entrance. She was very aware that any conversation she had with Ryan was going to be strange and complicated. While technically he'd invited her to visit him, his invitation had been casual at best. The fact that she'd jumped on it as an excuse to return home was her own problem. Still, they'd been an item and she'd once thought he was her reason for living, so she needed to get clear on them.

Not that she wanted him to break up with Autumn for her. That wouldn't speak well of him at all. And if she started going out with him after that, then she was stupid and deserved whatever happened to her.

"Self-awareness sucks," she muttered as she walked into the warehouse and looked around.

The showroom—put away for the volunteer weekend—was back in place. She could hear the sounds of construction and smiled as she thought briefly about offering her services. After all, she installed a kitchen sink with the best of them. She glanced down at her summer dress and heels. Not that she was dressed appropriately, but still. Maybe they were hiring.

Leo, the shop foreman, saw her come in. "Olivia, nice to see you."

They'd met on the volunteer day. Leo had been in charge of the volunteers. He'd likened it to herding cats.

"Happy to have your trained crew back?" she asked with a smile.

"I don't know. My Saturday folks have a lot more enthusiasm. What can I do for you?"

"I'd like to talk to Ryan if that's all right. Only for a second." Because it was the middle of the workday and hey, he had a job to do.

Leo grimaced. "He's not here. He called in sick." His tone made it clear that he assumed Ryan was lying.

"I didn't know. Sorry to bother you."

"No bother. We're just finishing a house. Why don't you come see what we can do when we have more than a day?"

"I'd like that."

She followed him into the warehouse. The sound of construction made conversation difficult. There were at least a half-dozen tiny homes in various stages of completion. She saw cabinets ready to be installed, three toilets lined up against a far wall and stacks of flooring. Big display boards had designs on them, along with lists of materials and notes about the finishes.

When they reached the back of the warehouse, they walked outside and she saw two nearly finished homes.

"We're waiting on a refrigerator for that one," he said, pointing to the one on the left. "It's a special order. This one still needs the built-in furniture installed. It was a custom order and their guy is late."

The houses were about the same size. She slipped off her shoes and walked barefoot through the first one.

"They're both twelve by sixteen, with a loft," Leo told her. "This first one is designed to be self-sufficient. The refrigerator can run off the solar panels or use ice."

The finishes were rustic, as was the furniture.

"Reclaimed wood?" she asked, touching the kitchen table. "This looks like the side of a barn."

Leo glanced at her. "You're right. This guy wants everything eco-friendly. He has a flush toilet inside, and will be installing a septic toilet outdoors, along with an outdoor shower."

"I hope he's not moving to Minnesota," she murmured. "That could be one chilly shower."

There was a queen-size mattress in one loft and storage in the other. The shelves, bins and cabinets confused her.

"Did he say what he was storing?" she asked.

"Six months' worth of food."

"I want to ask why, but I won't. If there's an apocalypse, we all know where to get a sandwich."

The second tiny home was nearly the exact same floor plan but the execution was totally different. The finishes were high end, the cabinets smooth and elegant. She saw complicated-looking electronics and built-in speakers. While there wasn't any furniture, she could see where it was going to go.

"I never realized you could do so much in such a small space," she told Leo. "I see the appeal of both styles. How on earth do people figure out what they want?" She held up a hand. "Never mind. I would guess they show up with a detailed plan."

"Some do. Some want us to help them make decisions. Griffith's great on the design of the home but picking out furniture isn't his thing."

"Is it yours?" she asked, her voice teasing.

"I leave that to my wife."

"A wise, wise man."

"I've been married a long time and I've learned a thing or two."

They walked back through the warehouse. She thanked him

for the tour and got in her car. On the way to the craft mall, she thought about all the staging she'd done and how a few small details could make a room. Was that also possible in a tiny home? With space at a premium, you couldn't toss around a few pillows and put out a lot of knickknacks. Still, a house, regardless of size, needed to feel homey.

Armed with a notebook and a camera, she walked around the craft mall and took pictures, then made notes. Some of the booths were well laid out but a few were awful and most could use help. She paused by the quilt display and felt her heart sink. Sally's skill level was incredible, but no one could see it. And her prices were ridiculously low for the custom work she did. Not that anyone was asking Olivia, but still.

An hour later, she was home in front of her computer. She'd already uploaded the pictures and now carefully composed the first letter. She would start with Sally and see how that went. If the experience was positive, she would move on to other booth owners.

She glanced at her notes, then started her email. She explained how she admired Sally's work, then pasted a picture to illustrate her point about the clutter. She made a few suggestions for making the quilts more visible in the display and offered to help prepare a book of pictures of her inventory, along with rearranging the booth. Before she lost her nerve, she hit Send.

Once it was gone, she opened her browser and typed in "decorating tiny homes." Because you just never knew.

Kelly stared at the stack of boxes on the front porch. There were five and a couple of them were huge. Even more confusing, they were all addressed to her. She carried the first three inside, then went back for the other two. As she studied the return address labels, she realized these were the clothes Olivia had ordered for her. With Kelly's credit card.

"Not exactly something I'm going to thank her for," she

muttered to herself. She should have stopped her when she was doing it. Now she was going to have to return everything. And hadn't her sister signed her up for some kind of clothing delivery service? That would be a disaster. She worked on a farm—she didn't need high fashion. Besides, she was hungry. She should fix some dinner first, then deal with the Olivia-created mess. Only the boxes seemed to call to her.

Grumbling under her breath, she opened the first box. Inside were two dresses, a couple of shirts and a pair of pants. The fabric looked nice enough, she supposed, but where would she wear dresses?

She took the box to her bedroom and stripped down to her bra and panties, then took the first dress out of the packaging. It was a simple sleeveless style that wasn't much to look at. The white-and-purple pattern was interesting, but honestly, she wasn't a dress person.

Except when she slipped it on, she could see how there was more pattern in the middle and less at the top and bottom, which gave her the illusion of an hourglass figure. In this dress she actually had hips and almost breasts.

She opened her closet and stared at herself in the full-length mirror. She had to admit the dress looked good. She took it off and tossed it on the bed, then reached for the next one.

The second dress was a soft moss green, also sleeveless, but more of a halter style. She had to take off her bra to keep the straps from showing, which made her feel both sexy and uncomfortable. When she put the dress on, she realized she wasn't showing much more than an extra inch of shoulder and yet... She felt good.

"Dammit, Olivia, what did you do?"

There was plenty of time to find out, she thought with a grin. Her dad had texted to say he was having dinner with friends and would be home late. Her sister was who knew where.

She ran barefoot to the kitchen and collected the rest of the boxes. Twenty minutes later, she was surrounded by piles of clothes and couldn't help grinning like a fool.

Olivia had done good. Better than good. Okay, there were a few duds. She wasn't a hoodie girl and refused to try on the two her sister had bought. There was a calf-length skirt that made her look like she was auditioning to be an extra in a Western, but other than that, the choices were…fantastic. There were at least a half-dozen really cute T-shirts, both long and short-sleeved, that she could wear to work, along with ridiculously expensive dark wash jeans that she should instantly reject but couldn't help noticing how good they looked on.

There were ankle-length and cropped pants in different colors with coordinating flirty tops, four dresses and a jean jacket that cost as much as a car payment, but made her whimper with its cuteness.

Three of the shirts and two of the dresses required her to go braless, something Kelly would have sworn she would never do. Only the clothes were so pretty and she felt so good wearing them, she wasn't sure she had a choice. Besides, at some point, not having breasts should work in her favor.

She turned in front of the mirror, checking out a fitted black-and-white-plaid short-sleeved dress. It was both casual and pretty. As she looked at herself from the back, she wondered if she had any decent sandals tucked in some corner of her closet.

"How the mighty have fallen."

She looked up and saw Olivia standing in the doorway to her bedroom. Her sister smiled at her.

"I knew you'd look good. Admit it. The clothes are nice."

Kelly glanced at the huge pile on the bed. "You spent nearly three thousand dollars. On my credit card."

"They're your clothes. Plus the last time you bought something that wasn't a pair of cargo pants was 1969."

"I wasn't alive in 1969."

"You get my point. You never shop. And yes, you can use the excuse that while the local Costco has some lovely options, they are limited. But hello, use the internet. You're easy to fit and even Tulpen Crossing gets mail delivery. I like the dress a lot."

"Me, too."

"Try it with the jean jacket."

Kelly frowned. "I can't. The dress is black and white. The jacket is denim."

"And?"

"They don't go together."

Olivia rolled her eyes. "You're so provincial. Jean jackets go with everything. Hold on."

She walked through the bedroom to the bathroom and returned with a set of hot rollers. After setting them on the desk, she plugged them in, then picked up the jean jacket.

"Try it on," she said as she held it out.

"Those curlers better not be for me."

"Of course they're for you. I already did my hair this morning. I want to make a point. You know I'm going to help my friend Eliza with a makeover and she's a lot more cooperative than you."

"You spent three thousand dollars."

"I believe we discussed that already. Put. It. On."

Kelly did as instructed. Olivia turned the collar up, then stared at her.

"You need a black patent leather belt. I don't suppose you have one, do you?" She shook her head. "Never mind." She found a pad of paper on the desk and started writing. "Shoes. You're going to need shoes. Lots of them. Did you try those on?"

Those were a pair of taupe-beige suede shoes that weren't exactly sandals and weren't exactly booties and weren't exactly anything Kelly had seen before. They had a peep-toe and a sling back with a three-inch heel. They covered the top of her foot, except for the tips of her toes and while they looked sexy, they were also two and a half inches more heel than she was used to.

"I can't do heels."

"You *don't* do heels. There's a difference. Try them on." Olivia pointed to the chair. "Sit there and try them on or I'm going to start singing. Trust me, no one wants that."

Kelly did as she was instructed. The neutral color looked pretty on her skin and there was plenty of padding. She stood and was surprised to find that they weren't as hard to walk in as she'd first thought.

"They're nice," she admitted, crossing to the mirror.

"They have a platform, so they only look high. You'll need to practice getting around in them, but they're a fairly classic style and they'll go with everything. You and I are going to have to go to the outlet mall one afternoon and buy you a bunch of shoes. I'm not having you ruin everything I bought by wearing them with your horrible work boots or ratty athletic shoes. Now get over here and let me curl your hair."

Twenty minutes later Kelly's waves were actual curls. She liked the shorter, bouncy look. She and Olivia sorted through the clothes and agreed on what was to go back. While the dresses were cute, right now Kelly only needed a couple. She was forced to admit that she loved all the cropped pants and cute tops and was delighted to realize that yes in fact she could wear the jean jacket with everything.

She stood in front of the mirror admiring herself in tan ankle pants, her new shoes, a cute lightweight, sherbet-orange sweater and her jean jacket. She would never be like her sister, but this was really, really good.

Her phone buzzed. Olivia reached for it and grinned. "Someone wants to buy you dinner."

Kelly felt her stomach quiver. "Griffith?"

"Unless you're two-timing your boyfriend, who else would it be? Shall I tell him you're available?"

Kelly grabbed the phone. Let me bring over takeout, she texted back.

Can't wait.

Olivia sighed. "You're just like the guys I date. You get what you want and then you abandon me. It's fine. I'll recover."

"Are you serious or are you messing with me?"

"Messing with you. I've got some work to do tonight. Design research. Plus I heard back from Sally on her booth and I want to work up a couple of sample floor plans. You kids have fun."

"I might be late," Kelly said as she started out the door. "Don't wait up."

"Oh, my God. Stop!"

Kelly froze. "What?"

Olivia walked to the desk and opened drawers until she found a pair of scissors. "You still have tags. You might grow the most beautiful tulips on the West Coast, but you are ill-equipped to deal with normal life."

She snipped and tugged, then said, "Now you can run off to have sex with your hot boyfriend."

Kelly flushed. "We're having dinner."

"I really don't want details."

Kelly thought about explaining that she and Griffith hadn't done more than kiss, only she knew Olivia wouldn't believe her. Plus, Griffith was waiting.

Impulsively, she hugged her sister. "Thank you for all this."

"You're welcome. Tomorrow we'll pick a couple of online shopping sites and sign you up for delivery service."

"I'd like that a lot."

Olivia smiled at her. "Me, too."

18

Kelly went by the Chinese place because there weren't a lot of take-out choices in Tulpen Crossing. She ordered small amounts of several entrees, along with fried rice and egg rolls, then drove over to Griffith's place.

As she got closer, she felt more and more nervous. Were the clothes too much? The hair? She didn't want him to think she was trying too hard, only even as she thought that statement, she realized the ridiculousness of it. They were supposed to be a couple. Having him think she liked him was hardly bad.

She parked and walked to the porch. The front door opened as she approached and then Griffith was moving toward her. He took the large bag of food from her, leaned in and kissed her.

She felt the impact of his mouth on hers all the way down to her toes. The kiss was light, but he lingered and she started to get a little breathless.

"Hi," he said as he drew back. "You look beautiful. Thank you for coming over."

"Thanks for asking me."

They went inside. He'd set two places at the table in the dining room and had a bottle of white wine chilling in an ice bucket. Music played from hidden speakers.

"Ryan's out," he said as he set the food on the table. "We're currently not speaking so I don't expect him home for a few days."

"What are you fighting about? Or would you rather not say?"

"The usual. He rarely shows up to work on time, doesn't put in his hours, but is shocked when I dock his pay. His attitude is rubbing off on the team. I told him he's got to get his act together and he told me that I'm an asshole. Brother stuff."

"I'm sorry."

"Me, too, but it is what it is. I hope he figures it out." He poured her a glass of wine. "And now we're going to talk about something more pleasant. How are you?"

"Good. Busy. We just planted a hundred thousand bulbs for the late summer wedding season."

They sat across from each other and began passing cartons back and forth.

"Your hundred thousand tulips put my production schedule to shame. Wedding flowers based on the Pantone colors of the year?" he asked, his voice teasing.

"You remembered."

"I remember nearly everything about you."

She ducked her head. "Yes, well, I based my planting on my orders. A lot of pinks and peaches, some reds. Late summer weddings tend to have more color in them. I have no idea why. Christmas is a lot of red and white, of course, and don't get me started on Valentine's Day."

He picked up his wineglass. "That's February fourteenth, so you'd have to ship what, by the seventh?"

"Depending on how far the flowers are going, no later than the eleventh."

"So you're planting mid-January and getting the bulbs in to root in late December."

"Someone's been doing online research," she said as she picked up an egg roll.

"A little. You spent a whole Saturday learning about what I do. I wanted to return the favor."

Which was very fair and so like Griffith. "You should come

by when we're harvesting," she told him. "It's pretty insane, but also interesting. At least I think so. Shipping out a hundred thousand blooms in two days might not be everyone's idea of fun."

"I'll be there," he told her. "Have you been to Holland?"

She laughed. "No, and I want to go, of course. Can you imagine seeing how they grow tulips there? I've seen a bunch of YouTube videos. Some of the mechanization is incredible."

"You'd have farm equipment envy."

"On a huge scale."

"We should look at taking a trip."

The casual statement nearly made her choke. Her mind went blank before being filled with a thousand questions. They'd barely kissed—how on earth could they travel together? When would they go, and she'd never really been away with a man. She and Sven had spent a weekend together in Portland once, but that was it.

"Why would you want to go to Holland?" she asked, because it seemed the safest and most reasonable of questions.

"To look at architecture. They're doing interesting work with micro housing in Europe."

"Oh."

"Oh, that sounds interesting and if things work out I'd like to go with you, or oh, what on earth are you talking about, Griffith? Everything about you annoys me?"

Some of her tension eased. "That's a broad range."

"I believe in options."

"I think it's an intriguing idea."

"Good." He studied her. "I want to clarify the ground rules. About us and how things are going to go."

The man was nothing if not thorough, she thought humorously. "We've been over them already and this is the strangest relationship I've ever been in."

"Strange good or strange bad?"

She laughed. "Strange good."

"That's what I like to hear." He cleared his throat. "We're getting to know each other with the idea of a long-term connection that will not end in marriage or even love. Just like and mutual respect."

She wanted to ask if he really thought he could control his feelings that much. To her, emotions could be so volatile. However, Griffith might feel safe in his statement because he knew there was no way he would fall in love with her, which was wildly depressing and not a place she wanted to go.

Not getting married seemed okay. She wasn't sure she ever wanted to risk that. Her parents' marriage had been a disaster from the beginning. Helen's marriage had ended painfully. She didn't mind giving up marriage. She was less sure about children. She'd always sort of thought she would have kids, although the idea had been vague at best. Sort of an unformed "one day" scenario.

But love… She had to admit the love thing had her stymied. She didn't want the scary passion her mother had experienced. The swing of emotions that left destruction in its wake. But love was different. She believed in love. The good kind. Friendship and a parent's love for a child. She knew her dad had always loved her and she loved him. She loved Helen and…

She frowned. Was that it? Her dad and her best friend? Shouldn't she love more people? And what about her sister? Did she love Olivia? The more she got to know her, the more she respected and liked her. Was there a family thing, where she had to love her sister? If so, that was different than choosing to care.

"Kelly? You still with me?"

"Sorry. I was thinking."

"I can tell. Want to tell me what about?"

She looked at him. Griffith was nice-looking and funny and she enjoyed being around him. She wasn't super excited about the sex but that was more her than him and maybe it would be better than her past experiences. As for the rest of it…

"I'm fine with the no marriage clause," she told him. "With getting to know you and having this potentially be a long-term thing. I think you're fooling yourself if you think you can control falling in love. I believe it just happens, which can be both good and bad."

"I don't want to fall in love with anyone."

Which was a less harsh way of saying he didn't want to fall in love with her. Words that could have hurt, only she respected the honesty of them. While she liked the theory of love, she'd yet to let herself experience it. Something else she could blame on her mother.

"I'm a good boyfriend," he added. "I'll be attentive and faithful."

"Me, too. Not the boyfriend part."

"Good, because while I respect the other team, I don't want to play for them."

She smiled. "I'll keep that in mind."

He picked up his fork. "If this was high school, I'd give you my letterman's jacket or something."

"Didn't they used to have pins a million years ago? Didn't you pin a girl?"

"It sounds painful for the girl."

She laughed. "You know what I mean."

"I'll get you a pin."

"I'm all aquiver."

"Then my work here is done."

They finished dinner and moved to the family room. Kelly liked how Griffith listened when she talked and that they were both interested in each other's work.

"When does your dad play again?" he asked.

"Because you want to hear another awful band?"

"Sure. They're fun. And sometimes they're not terrible."

"You could write advertising copy," she teased, and made

air quotes. "Download this band's song. Sometimes they're not terrible."

"I'm supporting the arts."

They sat on the sofa, not all that far apart. They'd brought the wine in with them although she had her doubts about them finishing the bottle. Not at the rate they were going, which was also fine.

He reached out and tugged on a strand of her hair. "I like the curls."

"That was my sister's doing."

"How's it going with her?"

"Really good. I'm glad she and I have worked through our issues. Now there aren't any more secrets. It's better that way."

"Not a fan of hiding the truth?"

"It makes things too complicated. You have to remember what you can and can't say. It's hard to keep straight."

She started to say more but before she could speak, he shifted closer and kissed her.

The move was just unexpected enough to steal her breath away. Or maybe it was the kiss itself. Or the man.

He leaned in and pressed his mouth to hers. The touch was gentle, almost teasing. He kissed her again, his mouth more firm this time. His lips were warm, not yielding, but not taking, either. He held back just enough that she found herself easing toward him, increasing the pressure and moving back and forth.

One of his hands settled on her waist. Her sweater rode up a little and his fingers rested on her bare back. The contact was nice. A little arousing, a little unexpected. This was the good part. The before. If only it could go on forever.

He felt good… No, they felt good together. There was a rightness in the kiss. She liked how he went slow and how his hands made her tingle just a little. Her breathing quickened as anticipation swept through her. The sensation was thick, as if it would take a while to warm up, but it was there and it felt nice.

Unexpectedly, Griffith drew back. "I should let you get home."

The words made no sense. Weren't they going to do this for a while? She liked doing this. It was the best part. Later, they would move on to sex and while that would be fine, it wasn't the same.

"You meant what you said about taking it slow," she murmured.

"I did. Is that annoying?"

"Just a little." She spoke without thinking, then held in a groan. She didn't want him to believe she was hoping they would go further than they had. "What I meant was—"

He kissed her again. Lightly. Teasingly. "I know what you meant."

She doubted that but didn't bother trying to explain.

He stood and pulled her to her feet. "This was nice. I'm looking forward to seeing you again."

"Me, too."

More than she would have thought. There was something about Griffith. Something she liked a whole lot.

He walked her to her truck, pulled her close and kissed her one last time.

"Think of me tonight," he whispered.

"I promise."

Easy words—what else could she possibly think of except him?

Olivia printed out another picture of a quilt and put it into the plastic sleeve. She was preparing a sample notebook to demonstrate to Sally how the quilts could be photographed to show the details and colors. Better to have only a few quilts displayed and pictures of the others available than to have a constant mess as people dug through stacks of them. Plus, unattended inventory would get dirty and then be difficult to sell. Sally's work was exquisite. People needed to respect that.

Olivia had already drawn up several floor plans for the booth. That had been the easy part. A quick trip to the local Target for supplies had meant she could put together the notebook. This, after working on some ideas for decorating tiny homes. Her back was sore and her hand was a little cramped from drawing, but that was okay. She liked what she was doing.

She got up and stretched as she wandered into the kitchen. Her dad was still out with his friends and Kelly was still on her date. Given how hot she'd looked when she left, Olivia wouldn't be surprised if Kelly didn't make it home much before dawn.

Olivia supposed she could have been bothered by being alone, but the old house was friendly enough for her to feel safe. She'd heated up some leftovers for dinner. Now she took a cookie from the jar on the counter and walked into the living room.

It was nearly nine—quiet with the sun just going down. She crossed to the window and looked out onto the front yard. Her BMW looked out of place. If she stayed she would have to replace it with something more sensible when the lease was up.

If she stayed…

There was an unexpected thought. Stay here in this tiny town? She hadn't been able to find full-time marketing work in Phoenix. There was no way she could earn a living here.

She finished her cookie and flopped onto the sofa. Okay—that wasn't completely true. She could have found full-time work if she'd left Marilee's firm and gone out looking for a job, only she hadn't. There were a thousand reasons, none of them especially impressive.

She'd been afraid. She'd doubted herself, which was nearly the same thing. Somehow her mother had always sensed when she was getting ready to quit and gave her a raise or a different opportunity that kept her in place. Marilee was good like that— she could see what was happening and twist circumstances to suit herself, the rest of the world be damned.

"Don't think about her," Olivia said aloud as she stretched out her legs and put her feet on the coffee table. It was still early and she wasn't tired. She would finish Sally's notebook, then draw up a tiny house loft bedroom design before switching on the TV.

She started back to her room. Car headlights swept across the wall, distracting her. Her dad or Kelly. Olivia smiled as she realized she wanted it to be her dad. That would mean Kelly was still out and having a good time with Griffith. The fact that she wanted the best for her sister made her feel good about herself. She could have carried a grudge or been sullen, but neither had happened. Maybe she wasn't as terrible a person as she'd feared.

She went back to the living room, arriving just as the front door opened. But it wasn't her sister or her father. Instead, Marilee walked into the house.

"I saw your car parked out front and knew you were home." Her mother smiled. "Hello, darling. I know, I know. I'm a surprise." She glanced around. "It all looks the same. So very cozy. I see Jeff still isn't locking the front door. That man."

The words made sound, but for Olivia it was as if she was hearing them from far away, or underwater. Olivia told herself to turn and run, or to pinch herself and wake up from the awful, scary nightmare. Only she wasn't dreaming. She was living this moment, which meant there was no escape.

"What are you doing here?"

Marilee set her Valentino handbag on the sofa table and continued to study the living room.

"You said you were enjoying your visit. It got me to thinking about how long it had been since I spent time with your father."

"You shouldn't be spending time with him," Olivia whispered, barely able to speak through the horror of it all. "You're divorced."

Marilee waved that factoid away. "Ancient history. He was always such a handsome man. So dependable. Not like Roger. Two weeks into our vacation and he grew so tiresome. He accused me of flirting with one of the waiters at his country club. Can you imagine?"

Easily, Olivia thought. The question wasn't whether or not her mother had flirted, but if the flirting had gone any further. It wouldn't surprise her at all to hear Marilee had ducked into a linen closet with said waiter for a quick round of slap and tickle.

Which wasn't the point. The point was Marilee was *here*. She couldn't be here. She had to leave right this second.

"Mom, what's going on?"

"I told you. Your texts got me to thinking about the past and made me want to see your father. And you, of course, I've missed you. Oh, and Kelly. She must still be around. She did love the farm. She wouldn't go far." Marilee sighed. "My girls back together. It's a wonderful thought."

Bile rose in Olivia's throat. No. No! Marilee couldn't be planning on staying. If she talked to Jeff or Kelly, she would say things. Like the fact that she was from Phoenix and that she and Olivia had been working together for nearly four years. Something Olivia hadn't mentioned at all.

"Mom, no. You have to leave."

"No, I don't. This is my house, too."

"You left. You and Dad got a divorce."

"So you keep saying. I'm very clear on my marital status, Olivia. Don't be tiresome." Her gaze sharpened. "Or is that not the problem? What did you tell them about me?"

Olivia swore silently. Marilee always knew what she was thinking. It was so frustrating and beyond annoying.

"You haven't said anything about me, have you?" Her mother laughed. "Oh, that's brilliant. I can work with that. Do they think we've been in touch at all?"

"Yes." She bit her lower lip, thinking about what she and Kelly had talked about. "Some."

"But not that we work together. Wonderful. I can get to know both my girls at the same time."

Not a scenario Olivia liked, but what choice did she have?

Marilee wandered into the kitchen and glanced around. "Not the remodel I would have chosen, but nicely done. How's your father these days?"

"He's fine."

"Is he seeing anyone?"

"Mom, no. Leave him alone."

"That's hardly your call, Olivia. Do I have to remind you that you kept secrets from Kelly and your father? How sad if they had to find out about your deceits. I doubt they'd want to have you around if they knew."

Before Olivia could figure out what to say, she heard a truck door slam. Someone was home.

Her stomach flopped over, as she broke out in a cold sweat. Nothing good was going to come from any of this, she thought frantically. Disaster loomed and she honest to God didn't know how to stop it.

The front door opened and Kelly walked in. She was flushed and smiling.

"Hi. It's me."

She looked like a woman who'd been well satisfied, Olivia thought, wishing there was a way to warn her off, or at the very least, protect her.

Kelly saw her and grinned. "How was your evening?"

Marilee stepped out of the kitchen. "Hello, darling."

Kelly came to a stop. The color drained from her face as she took a step back, then another. Her eyes widened, her mouth opened and closed as she tried to speak.

"Mom?"

"Yes, it's me. Surprise."

Surprise? After being gone thirteen years, after walking out on her family, all her mother had to say was *surprise*? Kelly stared

at the woman standing by the kitchen and did her best to rec-
oncile what she remembered with what she saw.

Marilee looked much as she had then—as if the passing years
weren't an issue. She looked more polished, her hair more sleek,
her makeup more subtle. She wore tailored pants and a clingy,
low-cut blouse. There were no signs of physical aging, but
Marilee had always been one to defy convention.

"What are you doing here?"

The question came out more harshly than she'd intended,
but she didn't add anything to soften it. What *was* her mother
doing here? Why now? Why did she have to come back at all?

"Do you need money?"

Marilee laughed and stepped toward her, as if they were going
to embrace. Kelly took a step back, prepared to put furniture
between them if necessary.

"Oh, Kelly, I'd forgotten how you could be so funny." She
smiled. "I came to see you and your father." She turned to
Olivia. "I came to see both my girls."

"You knew Olivia was here?" Kelly glanced at her sister.
"You told her?"

Olivia nodded.

Panic flared. Kelly found herself confused and afraid—as if
she were that fifteen-year-old again. The one who had fought
with Marilee and caused her mother to abandon them all.

No, she told herself. It hadn't been her fault. Her mother had
wanted to leave. Kelly had provided an excuse. Marilee had
chosen an extra cruel way to go, that was all.

Her mother approached. Kelly forced herself to stand her
ground. Marilee touched her shoulder. "You're all grown up.
When did that happen? How old are you? Twenty-five?"

Kelly shrugged away from the contact. "I'm twenty-eight.
Olivia is twenty-five. Dad is nearly fifty. We've all managed to
keep on living, even without you. I know that's shocking. I'm
sure from your perspective we should be exactly where we were,

waiting for your return. But it doesn't work that way. We got on with our lives. We're all fine."

Aware that she was practically shouting, Kelly pressed her lips together.

Marilee blinked several times. "You're still angry with me. Oh, darling, I'm sorry if I hurt you. That was so very long ago."

Kelly wanted to scream that she wasn't hurt, she was furious. Olivia moved to her side.

"Mom, this is an unexpected visit," Olivia said. "Does Dad know you're here?"

"No, and I'm so excited to see him. How is he?"

Kelly's senses went on alert. "Why do you ask?" She glanced down and didn't see a ring on her mother's left hand. "No," she said forcefully. "No. You're not getting back together with him. He's happy without you. We all are. You need to go right now."

The front door opened. Kelly spun around as her father walked into the house.

"There's a rental car in the driveway," he said when he saw her. "Who—"

Marilee stepped around her daughters and walked to her ex-husband. "Hello, Jeff," she said, her voice low and sexy. "It's been a long time."

Kelly wanted to scream at her dad to take cover. She wanted to throw herself between them. Nothing good could come of this.

"Marilee?"

"I know." Her laughter was a soft trill. "I've missed you."

"All right."

He seemed as shocked as Kelly felt, as confused.

Marilee tilted her head. "Have you missed me at all?"

Olivia stepped between them. "Did you rent a car at the air-port?"

Marilee raised her eyebrows. "Yes, I did, then drove up." She turned back to Jeff. "I was with friends in Colorado. Olivia and I text occasionally. She'd mentioned she was here and I just couldn't stop thinking about the town. I remember it all so fondly."

"You left," Kelly blurted. "For years you talked about leaving, then you walked out on your family."

"Kelly." Jeff's tone warned her.

"No." She put her hands on her hips. "This is ridiculous. It's been thirteen years. *Thirteen*." She glared at her mother. "You walked out on us. There was no warning. One day you were here and then you were gone. You cheated on Dad over and over again. You made our lives hell and then you disappeared. We never heard from you again. You never bothered to get in touch with me at all. I'm your *daughter*."

She felt her eyes start to burn and blinked away the tears. No way she would give Marilee the satisfaction of knowing any of this affected her.

"Then you show up here with no warning? It's outrageous."

Marilee's mouth trembled. "Kelly, I'm so sorry. I obviously hurt you. I'd hoped…" A single tear slipped down her smooth cheek. Her shoulders slumped. "I was wrong. So very wrong."

Jeff cleared his throat. "Kelly, it's fine. Your mother is always welcome to visit."

The tears vanished. Marilee brushed her cheek, then beamed at him. "I knew you'd understand. I'm so happy to be back with my little family."

"Where are you staying?" Jeff asked. "There's a new hotel in town. I hear it's nice."

Marilee's mouth formed a perfect circle. Her eyes widened with shock. "I thought I'd stay here."

"No," Kelly and Olivia said at the same time.

"To get to know my girls," she added. "You've had them all this time. That hardly seems fair."

Kelly had no idea how her mother managed to twist everything, but she was a master.

"Dad," she began, only to have her father quiet her with a look.

"You can stay in the guest room," he said. "Kelly, would you please get your mother clean sheets and towels?"

Just like that, Kelly thought, outraged. Because no matter what, her father had never said a word against Marilee. Not when she'd cheated, not when she'd left, not in all the years since.

She supposed it was some absurd code by which he wouldn't trash talk his daughters' mother in front of them. While she respected the theory, in practice, it made him annoying as hell, and now they were stuck with Marilee in the house.

Kelly walked out of the living room and into the hallway. The main linen closet was by her room. Olivia followed.

"This isn't a good idea," her sister began.

"I know that, but what are we supposed to do? It's his house and she's his ex-wife. I can't believe this."

"Me, either."

"You had to tell her you were here? You couldn't have said you were at Disneyland?" Kelly saw her sister flinch and groaned. "I'm sorry. I didn't mean that. It's not your fault. Of course you would mention that you were here. It's just, I don't want her here."

"Me, either."

They walked back the way they'd come and down the hall leading to the master and the guest room. Marilee was already in the latter. She examined the queen-size bed and the small en suite bathroom.

"This is so nice," she told them.

Jeff appeared with her suitcases. "I hope you'll be comfortable here," he said as he put them down, then left.

Kelly watched him go. She didn't like anything about this. Her mother was back and in the house. She had a horrible feeling that once in place, Marilee would be impossible to remove.

"Good night," she said brusquely, before retreating to her own room. She sat on the edge of her bed and told herself to breathe. That she would be fine.

A lie, she admitted to herself. Worse, the evening's events had killed her Griffith kiss-induced buzz and how fair was that? Speaking of Griffith...

She pulled out her phone and started to text him, then dropped her phone back in her bag. She had no idea what to say. What a nightmare. Marilee was back and there didn't seem to be a damn thing she could do about it.

19

Kelly had a hard time falling asleep. It was after midnight by the time she dozed off, so she didn't appreciate someone shaking her awake a little after five. She opened her eyes and saw her father standing by her bed. He looked tired, as if he'd slept even less than her.

She sat up. "Are you okay?"

"Kitten, I need you to do me a favor. Can you go to the diner and tell Helen I won't be in this morning?"

"What?"

"I guess you're going to have to tell her what happened. About your mother."

Kelly hardly needed an explanation on the "what happened" front. "Sure. I guess. Can't you just text her or something?"

"I can, but I want you to tell her."

An odd request, Kelly thought as she swung her feet onto the floor, but her dad didn't ask for much. Besides, she would really appreciate the chance to get her friend's perspective on the situation.

Given the early hour, Kelly passed on a shower. She dressed, brushed her teeth, combed her hair and was in her truck by five thirty. Ten minutes later she parked in front of The Parrot Café and thought longingly of coffee. At least three cups, she told herself. Maybe more.

Her mother was back. That hadn't changed. There'd been no

waking up with that blissful *it was all just a bad dream* feeling. Instead there was reality—ugly, why-did-she-have-to-come-back, reality.

Helen's happy smile faltered when Kelly walked into the café.

"Hi," her friend said. "Was I expecting you?"

"No. My dad sent me." She made her way to the counter and sank onto a stool. "You will never in a million years guess what happened."

Helen seemed to go pale. "Is Jeff okay? Did something happen to him?"

"What? No. He's fine. I doubt he slept much, but then none of us did." She leaned forward and pointed to the full pot. "Can I have a cup?"

"What? Oh, sure. Let me get it." Helen poured a mug and set it on the counter.

While she was off getting a small pitcher of cream, Kelly inhaled the nurturing smell. "My mother's back."

The creamer slipped from Helen's fingers and fell, spilling cream on the Formica. They both reached for napkins.

"That was dumb," Helen said with a lighthearted laugh. "I must be especially clumsy today. What did you say?"

Kelly poured in the last of the cream, then handed over the empty container. "My mother showed up last night. I was out with Griffith and when I got home, there she was, in the living room. I mean, come on. Seriously? It's been thirteen years. I don't get it."

Helen swallowed. "Marilee is back? How does she look? How did Jeff, um, your dad take it? Was he happy? Shocked?"

"I think it's pretty safe to say we're all stunned. Who does that? Shows up like that with no warning? I'm beyond pissed. My dad's not happy. Olivia's been in touch with her some over the years, so she would know her the best."

Helen poured herself a mug of coffee and took a sip. "I don't know what to say."

"Me, either. My dad wanted you to know. Honestly, I'm surprised he didn't come over and tell you himself. As a way to escape her."

"Escape? She's staying at the house?" Helen's voice was nearly a shriek. "Are you kidding me?"

Kelly rolled her eyes. "Beyond strange, right? We made up the guest room for her. She's still all smiles and 'I'm so perfect.' I don't want to hate her because that means I'm devoting too much energy to her. I want to not care. I need to find my Zen center."

"You need to get her ass out of your house."

Kelly frowned. "I don't think that's happening. Are you okay?"

Helen gave her a tight smile. "I'm fine. Why?"

"I don't know. You seem upset."

"You're my friend. I'm Team Kelly all the way. I know you and your mom never got along. This is so terrible for you and Olivia. And your dad."

Kelly nodded. "You're right. I'm sorry. I'm exhausted. I didn't sleep. I'm guessing no one did, except of course Marilee. I'm sure she slept like a baby."

"She um, still looks good? I mean she was always very beautiful."

Kelly thought about the elegant clothes, the way her mother carried herself. "She looks good, I guess. Not older, which is a little creepy. She looks like Olivia's sister while I look like a troll." She sighed. "Wow, I *am* tired. Listen to me rambling. What time is it?" She glanced at the clock. "I should let you get back to work. I know you have customers showing up in a few minutes." She managed a smile. "I'm going to go home and face my mother, all the while chanting *kill me now.* Or her. Maybe killing her would be better. Not that I'd like prison."

"Thanks for coming by," Helen said. "We should talk later. And please let me know if I can help."

"With the killing?" Kelly teased.

"Sure. I'm all in on that one."

Helen's response made her laugh. "Thank you for pretending to be bloodthirsty. Oddly enough, it makes me feel a whole lot better."

Helen figured she had less than five minutes between the time Kelly left and the first customers arrived. There was plenty of work to be done and she should be running around, prepping. Instead, all she could do was stand behind the counter and wonder if she was going to throw up.

How was any of this fair? Did the universe really hate her that much? Was God sending her a message? How on earth was it possible that less than twelve hours after she and Jeff had actually found their way to each other his ex-wife showed up? And *moved into his house*? If someone tried to write that into a movie, they would be told it was implausible. Ridiculous, even. But here it was—happening to her.

She didn't know what to do. Screaming seemed good. Crying. Later, there would be blintzes for sure, but how much good could sugar do in these circumstances? What she needed most was to see Jeff. To have him hold her and tell her none of this mattered. That he wasn't interested in Marilee, no matter how beautiful or skinny she was. That their shared history was meaningless. That he wasn't lying awake thinking about his gorgeous ex-wife in bed just a few feet down the hall.

Only Jeff hadn't been the one to tell her. He'd sent Kelly and while she could sort of think that was thoughtful, part of her wondered if he was simply trying to escape having to face her.

At one minute to six, the first of several cars pulled into the parking lot. Helen hurried into her office, to check her face in the mirror hanging by the file cabinet. She was shocked to see tears on her cheeks. She quickly brushed them away, gave herself her best smile, then went back to the front of the café.

In her pocket, her phone buzzed. She pulled it out and glanced at the text from Jeff. Sorry I couldn't be there myself. I'll be by as soon as I can to explain.

That was it. Not "I miss you" not "I want you." Nothing on which to hang her battered and frightened heart.

Yet another day for Kelly to be grateful she didn't have the kind of job that required her to make life-or-death decisions, she thought as she pulled in front of the house at five that afternoon. She hadn't had to suit up and run into a burning house, or perform surgery or work some arm on the space station. No one's life was affected by the fact that she'd spent the better part of eight hours checking on bulbs and hating her mother.

She stared at the house. There were hours yet until sunset, so no lights were on. She couldn't see inside, but based on the rental car, her sister's BMW and her father's truck, she had a fair idea who she would find when she went inside.

Kelly thought briefly of bolting. She had gas in her truck and a zero balance on her emergency credit card. She could simply go. Drive any direction but west and be somewhere else. Okay, without her passport, best not to head north to Canada, although being arrested by the border police would be a great excuse to miss dinner. If only, she thought regretfully as she got out and walked up the front path. This was her father's fault. He'd raised her to be responsible.

She braced herself, then opened the door.

"I'm home."

"We're in here, darling."

The sound of her mother's voice made her jaw clench. She consciously relaxed, set her bag on the table in the entryway and walked into the kitchen.

Olivia and Marilee sat at the kitchen island, a laptop between them. As Kelly approached, Olivia closed the computer and offered a slight smile.

"Dad's in his study," her sister said. "He's paying bills or something."

Marilee sighed dramatically. "He always did take life so seriously. I never understood why."

"Someone has to," Kelly pointed out. "Someone has to make sure there are things like food in the refrigerator and that the electric bill gets paid so we can have light and heat. Someone has to stay behind and clean up other people's messes. Not everyone gets to walk through life, destroying everything as they go."

Marilee's eyes widened slightly, then she shook her head. "Kelly, sweetie, you need a man. I'm going to take a bath before dinner. What time do we eat?"

"In about an hour," Olivia murmured.

Kelly wanted to point out there wasn't a tub in the guest bathroom, but before she could say that, she realized her mother planned on using the tub in the master bath. Not anything she wanted to think about.

"I guess we're cooking," she said when their mother left. "Any ideas?"

"I bought a couple of pork tenderloins at the grocery store. I have an easy recipe for baking them. It's plenty of food and Marilee doesn't eat beef."

"Why not?" Kelly held up a hand. "Never mind. You deal with the pork, I'll look at sides."

She washed her hands, then opened the refrigerator. There were brussels sprouts and cauliflower in the vegetable crisper, and a bag of red potatoes in the pantry.

She washed the vegetables, then began cutting the Brussels sprouts in half and the cauliflower into florets. After tossing them with olive oil, salt and pepper, she dumped them onto a cookie sheet.

"How long does the pork cook?"

"Forty-five minutes at 350."

"Perfect. These can go in with them. They'll caramelize. I'll get the potatoes ready now and we can start them closer to dinner. Does Marilee like mashed potatoes?"

"As far as I know." Olivia put everything in the oven, then crossed back to the counter. "Are you okay?"

"Not really. What the hell is she doing here? Why now? It's so awful. I don't like having her around. She's not a nice person."

"You're right. She's exactly the same. Selfish and cruel. I don't want her here, either."

"Dad won't throw her out," Kelly complained as she started peeling potatoes. "I can't figure out if he's the nicest guy on the planet or a total sucker."

"I think he wants her here for us."

"What? That's ridiculous. Why would he think...?"

Because her mother had walked out when she was fifteen, Kelly thought. Because even though Marilee had been a nightmare, she'd been a presence in the house. Because Kelly had felt both relieved and abandoned when her mother had left.

"I should talk to him," Kelly said.

"It's not going to help. He'll do what he thinks is right regardless."

"I know. It's so annoying. All of it." Kelly dropped the peeler and the potato and impulsively hugged her sister. "I'm glad you're here. I can't imagine going through this without you. Thank you for being my buffer. I'll do my best to be yours."

Olivia hugged her back. "We'll get through this," she promised. "Marilee doesn't have much of an attention span. Once this stops being fun, she'll leave."

"You are wise in the ways of the evil one," Kelly teased. "How often were you two in touch?"

Olivia turned to check on the oven. "Not that often. We texted and stuff. Met for dinner a few times."

Kelly felt a stab in her gut. Not jealousy, she told herself. She hadn't wanted anything to do with their mother. She'd been glad when Marilee had left. Okay, glad and filled with guilt that it was her fault. But never once had she wanted Marilee to return.

"You're right," she said firmly. "We'll get through this. And when she leaves, we'll celebrate with Jell-O shots and hot fudge sundaes."

"It's a date."

Kelly told herself no matter what happened at dinner, she was going to be calm, agreeable and quiet. She would smile, make pleasant, meaningless conversation, then escape. She would hide out in her room and binge watch something fun on her tablet.

She carried the bowl of mashed potatoes to the already set table. Olivia had sliced the pork tenderloin and put it on a serving platter. The roasted vegetables were in a bowl. As Kelly took her seat, she noticed there was only a single bottle of wine. No way that was going to be enough.

As if reading her mind, Olivia stepped close and whispered, "Second bottle on the buffet," she said as she pointed. "I've already opened it."

"Yay you."

They smiled at each other. Kelly appreciated knowing there was another person she could depend on in the house. Everything about her mother's visit creeped her out, and having her dad be so accepting of the situation wasn't the least bit reassuring.

Marilee strolled into the dining room. She'd changed into an off-the-shoulder dress that was way too fancy for an at-home dinner. Jeff had on his usual jeans and long-sleeved shirt. In deference to the warmer temperatures he'd replaced his winter plaid with a more seasonal light cotton.

He scanned the table. "This looks very nice."

There was an awkward moment as they all tried to decide where to sit. Kelly couldn't figure out which was worse—being next to her mother or being across from her. She settled on next to her. At least that way there wouldn't be any eye contact.

Jeff held out Marilee's chair, then took the seat across from her. Olivia sat across from Kelly. The awkwardness continued as everyone reached for serving plates and bowls only to draw back.

"I'll start," Kelly said firmly and picked up the bottle of wine.

She filled her glass, then passed the bottle to her sister. Olivia flashed her a smile. The need to giggle bubbled up.

There was only silence as the food was passed. The sound of flatware on china was excruciatingly loud. Kelly sliced off a bite of pork.

"It's delicious," she said. "Thanks for fixing this, Olivia."

"You cooked?" Marilee asked. "What a surprise. When did you learn to cook? Why am I always the last to know?"

Jeff shot Kelly a look, as if warning her not to say anything. Kelly did her best to look innocent.

"I've cooked for a while now, Mom," Olivia said.

"I didn't know that. How interesting."

Silence returned as the air thickened with all that was not being said. There weren't just elephants in the room, Kelly thought. There was the entire African savanna population. If they weren't careful, they were all going to get trampled.

Marilee reached for her wine. "This is so nice. It's been far too long since the four of us were together like this. Now when was the last time we all had dinner?"

Kelly told herself to be quiet. That in maybe twenty minutes, she could make her escape. That no one would be helped by her stating the obvious. She had every intention of not saying a word. But instead of filling her mouth with something safe like roasted Brussels sprouts she found herself blurting, "Probably the night before you took off, Mom. Unless you were out with one of your lovers. I can't remember. Olivia, do you remember?"

The words fell like bombs on the table. They exploded and in their aftermath, no one knew how to react. Jeff recovered first.

"Kelly, that's unnecessary."

"Oh, I don't know, Dad. It seems completely necessary to

me. Are we really going to do this? Simply pretend it's all fine? That nothing about this situation is strange or uncomfortable or twisted?"

She turned to look at her mother. "Why are you here? Why did you come back?"

Marilee's expression was calm and friendly. "I missed you and your father."

"It's been thirteen years. Why do you miss us now? What's different? You never bothered before. You never stayed in touch with me. So why now?"

Sympathy filled Marilee's eyes. "Is that what your outburst is about? Are you feeling ignored? Aren't you a little old for that, Kelly?"

"What? I'm not talking about now, I'm talking about before. Dear God, you left your family. Aren't you going to take any responsibility for that?"

"Kelly." Jeff's voice was sharp.

"No, Dad. We have to talk about this." She turned back to her mother. "What you did wasn't okay. It was selfish and heartless. We all paid the price for your behavior. You humiliated all of us. You were a terrible wife and mother and you don't get to come back here and act as if nothing ever happened."

Marilee shook her head. "I see you spoiled her. I'm surprised, Jeff. You were always able to control her when she was little. What happened?"

Jeff stood. "Stop it, both of you."

Kelly rose. "No, Dad, I won't." She pointed at her mother. "You're divorced. You shouldn't be in this house. Whatever game you're playing, it's not going to work."

Marilee raised her eyebrows. "That's not for you to say, is it? But while we're asking questions, what are you doing still living at home? Shouldn't you have your own life? Are you hiding, Kelly, and if so, from what?"

Kelly wanted to scream. "This isn't about me."

"Yet here we all are, talking about you." Marilee smiled at Olivia. "Interesting how the two of you aren't the least bit alike. I wonder why that is. Of course I've had a bigger influence on Olivia. Jeff, I hate to say it, but you've spoiled our oldest."

Olivia's head snapped up. "Mom, no."

Marilee shook her head. "I know what you're thinking but I can't help taking a little credit here. Jeff was always so convinced he was the better parent and yet it turns out it's really me." She glanced between him and Kelly. "Isn't Olivia impressive? So accomplished. She handles all the marketing at my real estate company and now she's doing staging. The clients just love her."

Kelly felt as if the floor had suddenly vanished and she was falling, falling, falling, not sure when she was going to hit bottom, or where it would happen. She couldn't breathe, couldn't think. Couldn't—

The careless words formed into sentences, then found meaning. Marilee's statements combined with what Olivia had said since she'd been back.

"You live in Phoenix?" she asked her mother.

"Where else? The real estate market has been a roller coaster, but I enjoy the challenge." She picked up her wine. "Yes, Kelly, your sister has been with me since she transferred to ASU. She lived with me those first couple of summers, then got her own place. She works with me. We're a team."

Kelly swung to face her sister. "You lied?"

Olivia sprang to her feet. "So what? You tossed me into boarding school. You abandoned me. Neither of you cared about me. I didn't have anyone. A friend's older sister helped me find Mom and I got in touch with her." Tears filled her eyes. "She cared about me and you never did."

"Girls."

They both ignored Jeff.

"I trusted you," Kelly breathed.

"I trusted *you* and look what it got me."

Kelly opened her mouth, then closed it. She walked toward the front door.

"Kelly," her father called, but she didn't answer. She grabbed her bag and walked out into the quiet of the night. She had no idea where she was going but it was going to be as far from here as possible.

20

Griffith knew that there was no way to read emotion in a text—especially one that was only four words long. Yet there was an ocean of feelings in Kelly's terse Can I come by? Tulpen Crossing was small enough that he'd already heard about Marilee's unexpected return.

Five minutes after texting back nothing more than Yes, he heard her truck pulling up next to his. He walked to the front door and waited. After several seconds she got out of the cab and walked to the house. From what he could tell, she hadn't been crying, but there was something going on.

He held open his arms. Kelly walked inside, dropped her purse on the floor and flung herself against him.

"I hate my mother," she whispered. "I'm sure it's wrong and I'll be burning in the fires of hell for saying it, but I hate her. She's a horrible person. She's a destructive creature, creating chaos wherever she goes. She honest to God doesn't think she did anything wrong. That her leaving was just fine and it's no big deal she abandoned her two children. She and I were never close, so fine. But what about Olivia? They were always a team and Marilee totally walked out on her, which should have been the worst of it, but it's not. Now I find out that Olivia's been with her this entire time. In Phoenix. They work together."

She raised her head and stared at him. "I trusted her. I believed her. I thought we were in this together, but we're not.

I can't trust either of them and my dad is useless. He won't say one bad thing about her."

Griffith was having a little trouble keeping up, but he was pretty sure the chaos here was Marilee and the one Kelly couldn't trust was her sister.

"What happened?" he asked.

Kelly drew back and sucked in a breath. "It all came out at dinner. Olivia had said she and Mom were in touch, but it's more than that. They're all tight and cozy in their shared business. She *lied* to me. When she got here and later. She never said anything about reuniting with Mom. Never told me the truth. Or Dad. She lied to him, too. Why not just say? But did she? Then Mom showed up and she pretended to be all shocked, like the rest of us."

She shook her head. "I believed Olivia. I was happy to have her back. I felt bad for what had happened before. I thought we were getting to know each other and all this time, she was lying. She's just like Marilee."

They had officially passed out of territory he could handle and into that scary netherworld of female emotion.

"Is it possible she didn't tell you the truth because she was afraid of what you'd think?"

"Maybe. I don't know." Kelly turned in a circle. "I don't know what's happening or what to think or who my family is. My dad is being soooo nice. It's incredibly frustrating. It's like when we were kids and he would never say anything bad about her even though we all knew about the affairs. Only now she's in the house. I have to do something."

"What did you have in mind?"

"Maybe I'll move out."

"Tonight?"

She managed a slight smile. "You're saying I might have trouble finding a rental?"

"You might have to wait until morning." He thought about

offering her a room in his house, but that could be misunderstood and Kelly didn't need any more stress in her life.

"I'm sorry to dump this on you."

He pulled her close and kissed her. "You're always welcome here. It's okay."

"You might have had hot plans for the night."

"Not possible. You weren't here."

She surprised him by pulling back and blinking. "I don't think I can handle you being nice."

"Then I'll stop. Are you ready to come inside or do you want to stay in the foyer for a while longer?"

She glanced around and groaned. "I didn't even get all the way into the house. I'm an idiot."

"You're not. You're kind of sweet. Did you eat? Are you hungry?" He didn't have much in the refrigerator but there was always frozen pizza.

Kelly flung herself at him and wrapped her arms around him. "Thank you. You're the best boyfriend ever."

"I know. I won the award just last year. I have a plaque. Want to see it?"

"I do."

Her hands felt good on his back. She smelled like flowers and some kind of lotion, because she would never wear perfume. Tonight there was no makeup, no girlie clothes. Tonight she was just Kelly in cargo pants and boots. His kind of girl.

He wanted her—that wasn't new. But he wasn't going to make his move. Not with her like this. Instead he would feed her, make her laugh and send her back home. Or offer her a bed in a guest room.

"Where's Ryan?" she asked.

"Out. I don't see much of him these days."

"He's still not cooperating on the work front?"

"Not even a little."

"I'm sorry."

"We'll figure it out. So pizza?"

She nodded. He stepped back and took her hand, then led her into the kitchen. They walked to the freezer and checked out the selection.

"Pepperoni, all meat, extra meat," he said.

"I'm sensing a theme."

He grinned. "You're not going to find anything with vegetables in the pizza selection, if that's what you're looking for."

"How shocking. How about the extra meat?"

"Perfect." He leaned in and lightly kissed her, then reached for the pizza. When he put it on the counter, she moved next to him and put her hand on his forearm.

"Griffith, wait."

He glanced at her.

"Let's go upstairs."

He waited, sure he'd misunderstood.

"Let's go upstairs," she repeated.

His dick immediately woke up and offered a yes vote. The rest of him was right there, as well. But his brain, oh, his stupid, sensible brain pointed out that Kelly was feeling battered and vulnerable and taking advantage of her was not only bad form but potentially dangerous for their relationship. He liked her—he wanted to take care of her—and this was not the way to do that.

"You're dealing with a lot," he began.

"I am." She bent down and unlaced her boots, then stepped out of them. "I'm thinking a distraction would be nice."

"Me, uh, too, but you need time to—"

She pulled off her T-shirt and walked out of the room. Griffith waited exactly three seconds before muttering, "This isn't my fault," and following up her the stairs.

Kelly knew her motivation was suspect. She mostly wanted to get lost and not have to think about everything going on and Griffith was the most effective, nicest, safest way she could think to make that happen.

When they reached his bedroom, she took in the cool colors, the large king-size bed, the thick carpet. The room was comfortable. Masculine enough to be his, but not so cutting-edge as to be trying too hard. She could get used to a room like this.

She crossed to the bed and pulled back the covers, then faced him. "Do you have a favorite side?"

"The one closest to you."

She smiled, then pulled off her socks. After unfastening her jeans, she pushed them down. Her bra and panties followed.

Before she could think more about the fact that she'd just stripped down in front of a man she didn't know all that well, he swore softly, crossed to her and pulled her into his arms.

She relaxed into his embrace and focused on how strong and tall he was. How his hands moved up and down her back. She breathed in the scent of him and the way he cupped her butt before shifting so he could caress her small breasts.

Sensations began to stir. Warmth and something that was nicely arousing. Her mind got fuzzy, which was the best reaction yet. They kissed. Hot, deep kisses with tongues and lips. That was good, too.

She tugged at his shirt until he pulled it off. His boots and socks followed, then his jeans and briefs. When they were both naked, she reached between them and stroked his erection. He flexed in her hand. She laughed.

"You have condoms, right?" she asked.

"In the nightstand."

"Good."

She shifted to the bed. He opened a drawer and pulled out a strip of condoms, then slid in next to her. He touched her everywhere, stroking her breasts and teasing her nipples. Heat built inside of her. He lowered his head to her breasts and kissed the tight peaks. She shivered as need raced to every part of her.

This was the good part, she thought happily. The before. When her body promised a thousand things.

He moved one hand between her legs. She parted for him. He explored her, paying special attention to the very core of her. He circled that spot, making her breathing quicken.

Her arousal continued building and building. She strained toward it, hoping this time she would be able to let herself go. Yet even as she reached, her mind intruded. So many thoughts. The fight with her mother, Olivia's betrayal. She pushed it all away but it returned and suddenly the feel of Griffith's fingers against her core was little more than pleasant. Her arousal faded as if it had never been and the awkwardness of this first sexual encounter loomed large.

Disappointment flooded her—sad but not surprising. It had always been like this. There was the good part and then there was nothing. Still, she knew how to move things along.

She opened her eyes and stretched out for the condom. "Be inside of me," she whispered.

"Are you sure?"

She nodded, then pulsed her hips, as if urging him along. Griffith did as she requested. He knelt between her legs and slowly eased inside of her. He filled her, stretched her and for a second, need returned. She sank into the sensation, willing it to continue before it drifted away.

He moved in and out. She wrapped her legs around his hips and kept pace with him. She consciously quickened her breathing. She wasn't going to fake it, exactly. Instead she would encourage him. Otherwise, guys liked to take forever and that only got uncomfortable for everyone.

"Kelly," he began.

She opened her eyes and found him watching her. "Don't hold back," she whispered. "Please, just go for it."

"But you—"

"It'll be better for me that way."

She arched her hips, pulling him in deeper, then breathed his name. He tensed as if doing his best to hold back, which wasn't going to work at all. When he pushed in again, she tightened her muscles around him and breathed, "Yes!" Seconds later, he came.

She sighed and held on to him. "That was wonderful. Thank you."

He drew back and studied her for a second. "Don't move," he told her.

He got off the bed and walked to the bathroom. When he returned, he sat on the mattress, facing her. "What's going on?"

Why did it always have to be like this? Why did they always have to care? It was her body—she should get to say what happened and what didn't happen.

"I don't understand," she said, then smiled. "I enjoyed that."

"Not enough." His voice was flat, his expression wary. "You didn't come."

"Oh, that." She waved her hand. "I liked what we did. It was enough for me."

"Uh-huh. What aren't you telling me?"

"Nothing. I had a great time, isn't that enough?"

"No." His gaze locked with hers. "Is it because it's our first time? Do you need to get comfortable? Or is this a regular thing?"

"I'm not entirely sure what you're asking, but if it's what I think it is, then not everyone is the same." She glanced down and found the weave of the sheets to be fascinating.

Griffith touched his fingers to her chin, forcing her to look at him. "You don't climax during sex?"

"No. I don't."

"Not ever?"

She held in a groan. "Nope. Which is totally fine."

"Not even by yourself?"

She flushed and jerked her head free of his light touch. "I don't do that."

"You should. A lot. Get to know your body. If you don't know what you like, how can you tell me what works best?"

Sven had been like this, she thought grimly. Determined to make things happen. After a few months he'd stopped trying so much and well, she'd gotten better at faking it. She supposed it spoke well for the men in her life that they cared about her pleasure. She just wished they would leave it be. She was fine. Happy. Content.

"You're making too big a deal out of this," she told him. "Not everyone needs to fly off into the universe. Some of us just like the closeness and intimacy. It's that way for me."

He didn't look convinced. "Having an orgasm is a physical response to stimulus. It's like sneezing. Unless there's a physical problem, you should be climaxing."

She groaned. "Can we please not talk about this? I beg you. Later, but not now. I have too much going on."

"You're right. I'm sorry." He leaned in and kissed her. "Thank you for tonight. Can you stay for a bit or do you have to get home?"

"Stay and do what?" she asked, trying not to sound wary. She so wasn't in the mood for him to take a stand, so to speak. The thought of a half hour of him trying various things on her body would be a nightmare.

"I thought I'd get back in bed and we'd cuddle. You can tell me everything you like about me and I'll bask in my wonderfulness. How does that sound?"

Her tension eased, which was probably the point of his humor. "Oh, could we?" She batted her eyes at him. "My hero."

"That's me. Your knight in shining armor."

She held up the sheet. He slid in next to her and pulled her against him. She rested her head on his shoulder.

"This is nice," he said. "You know what would make it perfect?"

She grinned. "Either sports or food."

"There's a Mariners game on, if that's okay."

Later she would have to deal with all the crap in her life. Later she would have to confront her sister and feel all the horrible emotions she was currently ignoring, but it wasn't later yet and she planned to enjoy every second of the reprieve.

She sighed and closed her eyes. "You go for it."

Helen had thought the time between declaring herself to Jeff and having him respond had been the longest two days in her life, but she'd been oh, so wrong. The time between finding out Marilee was back and having the chance to talk to him was at least seven lifetimes. When he did finally make it to the café, it was nearly two o'clock, but she had three customers who wanted to linger and then Delja wouldn't leave so it was forty minutes until they were able to sit down at one of the tables.

She felt sick to her stomach. Worrying about Marilee had been the best diet yet. She hadn't been able to eat or sleep. Every time she closed her eyes, she pictured them together. Marilee had always been beautiful and according to Kelly, that hadn't changed. Trying to eat had made Helen sick to her stomach. Even now she felt uneasy churning where lunch should have been.

"I'm sorry I haven't been able to come by," he told her. "Things have been complicated."

She was sure that was true, but she wasn't about to admit it to him. She and Jeff had become lovers, then his ex-wife had returned to town and she hadn't seen him since. If anyone was going to do the talking, it was him.

"I want to be clear," he said. "I had no idea she was going to show up and I'm not happy she's here."

Helen allowed some of her tension to ease.

"But," he said, and the tension returned, "I think this is a good thing. Kelly and Olivia need to spend time with their mother." He frowned. "Kelly does, at least. I'm still not clear on what Olivia has going on with Marilee. I knew they were in touch, but apparently they both live in Phoenix and work together." He shook his head. "Regardless, the three of them need time to be a family. They didn't have that before."

"Because Marilee left," she blurted before she could stop herself.

"You're right. But I still feel badly that Kelly didn't have a mother around as she went through high school. I wanted the two of them to stay in touch, but Marilee wasn't interested. She disappeared. I found her once and she told me if I came looking for her again, she would make sure she was never found. It didn't matter that I didn't want her back, that I wanted her for the girls. She was always one to go her own way."

Her own way? Was that what they were calling it?

"I made a lot of mistakes with my girls." He stared at the table. "I should have tried harder with Olivia. I shouldn't have let Marilee act the way she did."

"I'm not sure how you would have controlled her," Helen snapped before she could stop herself.

"You're right. I suppose I should have divorced her rather than waiting for her to run off." He looked at her. "The only thing I know I did right was to never bad-mouth their mother to my daughters. I haven't said a word against her and I won't. If she wants to spend time with them, then I'm in favor of that."

Helen waited for the rest of the sentence. The part where he explained that the reunion was going to happen from the safe distance of a hotel. She waited for him to say that he'd been missing her and thinking about her and even though they'd just become lovers, she was important to him and he didn't want to lose what they had. That he wanted her to know nothing was happening between him and his still-beautiful ex-wife who was sleeping *just down the hall in the damn guest room*!

But he didn't. Instead he looked at her and asked, "Are you okay?"

"Why wouldn't I be?"

Apparently the sarcasm was lost on him because all he said in response was, "I wanted to be sure." He gave her a smile, then rose. "I know you have to close out for the day and I need to get back to the office. I'm glad you're all right with this. I appreciate having one less thing to worry about."

Did he? How lovely. How great for him.

Fury built inside of her, but she ignored it and him. The need to throw something grew, but she resisted. After all, not only would she be stuck paying for whatever she broke, she would also have to clean it up. Because life sucked—especially hers.

He paused by the front door. "Helen?"

Hope fluttered. Happy, bright, maybe-he-wasn't-as-stupid-as-he-looked hope. "Yes?"

"Lock the door behind me."

That was it, and then he was gone.

Lock the door? Lock the *door*? Because someone sneaking in was the worst thing that could happen to her today?

"Asshole," she muttered as she went to the door and turned the lock.

As she returned to the counter, she passed a table with a vase on it. She reached for the perfect tulip, jerked it out of the water, then snapped its stem. After tossing it in the trash, she scooped out a bowl of ice cream, sank to the floor and started to cry.

21

Olivia felt the burn in her legs. She'd passed exhaustion two miles before and was now running on sheer force of will. That and the fact that she wasn't exactly sure where she was or how far she'd gone.

She'd gotten up at six, pulled on her running clothes and headed out. She hadn't warmed up or brought water or even her phone, all of which were stupid. Now she was dehydrated and potentially lost. Maybe she would pass out—not a normal goal, but if she was unconscious then she wouldn't have to think about what had happened the previous night. She wouldn't have to relive the fight with her sister and remember how hurt Kelly had looked when she'd learned the truth.

Olivia knew she had no one to blame but herself. Trusting Marilee was five kinds of stupid. Her mother *couldn't* be trusted—she knew that, but she'd done it anyway. She'd handed Marilee a weapon and then had been cut down not forty-eight hours later.

The ache in her legs turned to actual pain. She slowed to a walk and tried to catch her breath. Running had always been her escape but today she couldn't go fast enough or far enough to get away from what had happened.

She wasn't worried about her dad. He would understand and even if he didn't, he would forgive her for lying. But Kelly was different. She and Kelly were just getting to know each other.

They were becoming friends, which was different than being sisters. Now that had been blown and she didn't know how to fix it.

She heard a truck behind her. She thought briefly about waving her arms and asking for help, then told herself not to be foolish. Bad stuff happened everywhere, even in places like Tulpen Crossing.

But even without her flagging it down, the truck slowed. She turned and recognized the vehicle. Not Ryan's, thank God, but Sven's.

"You ran too far," he said after he'd rolled down the passenger window. "Are you all right?"

"No."

He leaned over and opened the door. "Get in. Have you had breakfast?"

Breakfast as in a meal or breakfast as in sex? Because she wasn't up for anything physical right now.

The question must have shown on her face. His expression gentled. "Breakfast, Olivia. Just food and maybe I listen while you talk."

Her eyes burned, but she blinked away the weakness before nodding. "Thank you."

"Anytime."

She could barely crawl into the seat. As soon as she sat down, her legs started shaking. He handed her a half-empty bottle of water.

"Sorry, that's all I have with me."

"It's okay."

She took a sip, careful to let her stomach absorb the fluid before taking a second sip. Her mouth was dry, as was her throat. Her body screamed at her for water, but she knew if she drank too much, too quickly, she would throw it all up and wouldn't that be pretty.

"I had to get a shipment off this morning," he said as they

drove back to his place. "There's a trucking company I use that's very reasonable, but the drivers like to make an early start. Did I tell you I'm growing blueberries? They're ripe and delicious. Blueberries are a good fruit. Lots of antioxidants."

The inane conversation should have bothered her but she had a feeling he was simply filling silence and giving her space to come to grips with whatever was wrong. She leaned back against the seat and closed her eyes. Her legs continued to shake as her muscles surrendered to exhaustion.

He pulled onto his property. "After breakfast, we'll go look in the barn. People have been dropping off items for your auction. You're going to have a lot to go through." He turned off the engine. "Don't try to walk. I'll come get you."

"I'm fine," she told him. She swallowed the last of the water, then opened the passenger door. Rather than try to step down, she slid off the seat. Her feet came in contact with the ground and she automatically braced her muscles to stay standing.

Nothing cooperated. Her knees gave way and she started to go down. Sven reached her in time to grab her.

"You're a stubborn woman."

"Sometimes."

He scooped her up as if she weighed nothing and carried her into the house. The back door was unlocked—of course. He took her through the mudroom and into the kitchen. He set her on one of the bar stools by the island.

"Don't move." His voice was stern.

He got a glass and poured her orange juice. "Drink this. It will help with the shaking. Your blood sugar is low and you're dehydrated. You could have collapsed."

Exactly what she'd been hoping for, she thought as she drank the fresh juice. Only in hindsight, it might not have been her best idea.

He started coffee, then began pulling ingredients out of the refrigerator. Instead of eggs, he collected fresh, thickly cut bread along with brie and ripe pears.

He put sandwiches together, then poured her coffee. While the panini pan heated, he got her water, then gently massaged her calves. The trembling had stopped, but she was still exhausted and knew she would be sore for days.

His large hands moved over her skin. His fingers and thumbs dug in to her muscles. There was nothing sexual about the actions, but she sensed his concern and kindness.

When the sandwiches were done, he sliced each of them in half and set them on a plate next to a small bowl of blueberries. She managed to hobble to the kitchen table and sank down next to him.

"Eat," he told her.

She took a bite. The combination of creamy, salty cheese with the tart pear and toasted bread nearly made her groan. She devoured half the sandwich before trying the blueberries. They were as perfect and ripe as he'd claimed. She inhaled the second half of her sandwich before reaching for her coffee.

Her blood sugar must have stabilized because she felt more alert. The emotional pain of the previous night was still there, but that would take a while to fade. Time and very possibly an apology.

She sighed. "My mother's back."

"I heard."

"I don't know how much you know about her past," she began, then hesitated, not wanting to go into it.

"I know enough."

"Good. Then you can imagine what a shock it was to everyone. I'm not sure she's even seen my dad since she walked out on us thirteen years ago. She hasn't seen Kelly, either. I don't think they talk at all."

"What about you?" His blue gaze was steady, as if he had all the time in the world for her.

She explained how she'd been sent to boarding school when she was fifteen and how alone she'd felt. "I didn't have anyone in the world. A friend's older sister helped me track down my mom and we got in touch. We met a few times. Different weekends. She flew me to New York once and we stayed at the St. Regis hotel. It was very fancy."

"And nice to have a secret."

She nodded. "We were friends more than mother and daughter. She was so fun, like a grown-up girlfriend."

She drew in a breath. "I went to TCU to be with Ryan. When he was drafted and left school to play for a triple A team, Mom suggested I transfer to ASU to be near her. Then when I graduated I went to work for her in her real estate firm."

She set down her coffee and rested her elbows on the table. "I never told my dad or Kelly any of that. Not when it was happening or later. Like you said, it was a nice secret. Mom and I were back together and we had each other. I told myself that was all I needed. Only it didn't work out."

"Why not?"

"She's…she's not like other mothers. Marilee lives her own life by her own rules and no one gets in the way. Not even her daughter. When I first went to work for her it was great but lately she's been difficult. I've been thinking of trying something different, of getting away. I took off the summer to figure out my next move. She knew I was coming home. I just never expected her to follow me."

"You're uncomfortable having your mother back here?"

"Yes, and I didn't tell my dad or Kelly about any of it. When she showed up, we agreed she wouldn't say anything."

"You lied to them."

There was no judgment in his voice but she felt the slap. "Not exactly." She hesitated then groaned. "Okay, yes, and it was stupid. Not only because I was wrong, but because I trusted her. Then she spills it all at dinner. Kelly's furious. I don't know what my dad's thinking, but he can't be happy. I didn't mean for it to happen, it's just I thought if they knew I was with Mom they…"

She reached for her coffee, not sure what she was trying to not say.

"You were afraid they wouldn't like you if they knew about your mother," Sven filled in. "That they would think less of you. Or worse, that they wouldn't welcome you. Because despite spending time with her all these years, you don't have her. Not the way you want to."

She nodded, too tired to be surprised by his insight. "I hurt Kelly. I betrayed her and I don't know how to fix that. Plus, when I think about what happened when we were kids, I get so mad. Kelly had Dad. He's the good parent. Mom is fun, but it's not like I could ever depend on her. She left me. I was twelve years old and she disappeared without warning. One day she was just gone and I didn't have anyone."

She wasn't aware she was crying but suddenly it was hard to see. She brushed at her cheeks and was surprised to find tears. Sven made a noise in the back of his throat and reached for her. Before she could figure out what was happening, she was on his lap with his arms around her.

She hung on and rested her cheek against his rock-hard shoulder. She couldn't remember the last time someone had been so willing to take care of her.

"I'm screwed up," she whispered.

"Yes, you are, but everyone is in one way or another."

"Kelly hates me."

"Kelly isn't the type of person to hate anyone. Apologize. She'll forgive you. You're safe, Olivia. Right this second, you're totally safe. Do you believe me?"

She nodded because speaking was impossible. Who was this man and why was he being so nice to her? Not a question she was going to ask, she told herself. Instead she was simply going to be very, very grateful.

★ ★ ★

Griffith stared at the computer screen and wished he'd put in a "no porn" filter before beginning his search. He mentally weeded out the obvious gross sites, then reluctantly clicked on a promising looking article.

Only text appeared, along with a couple of ads for a belt sander he'd been thinking of buying. Nothing a guy didn't want to see at eight on a Saturday morning. Not that he minded looking at a naked woman, but unless she was someone he was actually sleeping with, Griffith preferred to wait until his second cup of coffee.

He read the article twice, learned nothing new, then closed it and leaned back in his study chair. He didn't have a clue about what to do with Kelly. Or to her. Of all the things he'd thought might derail them, her not being able to have an orgasm hadn't even been in the top one thousand.

For the past three days he'd read enough to qualify himself as a semi-expert on the topic. He understood the stages of female arousal, he'd studied shockingly detailed diagrams of female anatomy. He could name all the parts, describe what it felt like when the G-spot was swollen, list fifteen different techniques to use during oral sex and he had a working knowledge of common physical reasons women didn't climax. While he found the information interesting, he had his doubts about any of it helping Kelly. He didn't think the problem was her body at all. He thought it was her head…and her mother.

In addition to reading and studying, he'd been doing a lot of thinking. Kelly's mom had been, to put it politely, promiscuous. She'd slept with more men than he would have thought possible in a town their size, including a few students. She hadn't been subtle about it and she'd humiliated her husband and her children. Griffith knew Kelly had been traumatized by her mother's behavior. Having Marilee walk out when Kelly was only fifteen had only compounded the problem.

Kelly didn't want to be like Marilee. Marilee liked sex, therefore Kelly couldn't.

He knew he was oversimplifying the problem and possibly getting it all wrong, but in his gut, he thought he was onto at least some part of the truth. He also guessed the issue might not be all about sex at all. That somehow love and commitment were woven into it. Why else would an otherwise fairly traditional twenty-eight-year-old woman be willing to enter into a long-term relationship where there was no promise of love and marriage?

He thought about what Sven had implied—that Kelly being quiet in bed had been a euphemism for something else. He wondered how hard the other man had tried to get her over the edge, then shook his head. Something else he didn't want to think about so early in the day. Or ever.

He reached for his coffee. Now that he'd defined the problem, he had to figure out how to solve it. He knew he was in way over his head, but hey, he knew all the stages of female arousal, so that was something. Maybe he would pinpoint where she derailed. Because he would have sworn she was doing just fine. And she'd been the one to initiate sex, so she wasn't opposed to the concept. It was the end that stalled her. Was it losing control? Did she slam on the brakes because she was afraid of what would happen?

He got up and walked to the kitchen to pour his third cup of coffee. Okay—he might or might not know the problem. He now had several new techniques to try. He was armed with information and a willing spirit, not to mention a dick that was very happy to take one for the team…over and over again.

As long as she was game, he was going to work to find the solution to the problem, and when they got there, he was going to have a hell of a good time saying "I told you so."

Kelly wrapped a towel around herself and stepped out of the shower only to find Olivia standing by their long, shared vanity.

Kelly came to a stop, not sure what to do. She'd been trying really hard to avoid being alone with Olivia. Okay, she'd actually been trying really hard not to see her sister at all, but run-ins were inevitable what with them living in the same house and sharing said bathroom.

"You can't avoid me forever," Olivia said, her arms folded across her chest, her gaze determined.

"I can try."

"That's mature."

"Trust me. Dealing with immature is going to be a whole lot easier for you than dealing with incredibly pissed off."

"You're mad at me."

"No, why would you say that?"

Kelly started to walk around her, but Olivia blocked her only way to her bedroom.

Kelly rolled her eyes. "Really? This is how you want to play it?"

"I'll play it any way I have to. We need to talk. You can listen easy or you can listen hard, but one way or the other, we're going to have a conversation."

"How do you listen hard?"

Olivia groaned. "You know what I mean."

"I do, but you really have to work on your communication skills." She realized she wasn't acting angry enough and glared. "Why on earth would I want to talk to you?"

"I didn't say talk, I said listen."

"You said we had to talk."

Olivia threw her hands in the air. "Dear God, will you stop? I know what I said and you're not going to distract me. I'm sorry I didn't tell you I was living in Phoenix with Mom." She sighed. "Not *living* with her, but working with her and spending time with her. I was afraid you'd be upset if you found out."

"Good call."

"I was afraid you wouldn't want me around."

"Again, excellent deductive skills."

Her sister leaned against the counter. "You can be as sarcastic as you want, but the truth is we're sisters. Marilee screwed us both. She left us both. I was just as abandoned as you, Kelly. Maybe more. I was younger and I didn't have Dad the way you did."

Kelly didn't want to think about that. She tightened her towel and tried not to feel sympathetic for the kid her sister had been.

She wanted to say that Olivia hadn't been alone—that she and her dad had been there for her, only she was pretty sure they hadn't been. She was pretty sure they'd been so confused and upset that she'd been forgotten.

Not her finest hour, she thought. Telling herself she'd only been fifteen didn't help. She should have looked out for her baby sister.

"I was really alone at boarding school," Olivia said, one shoulder raised. "I hated it and you and Dad." She held up a hand. "Don't apologize. That's not the point. I was there, I was trying to deal. One day I got the idea to get in touch with Mom. You know the rest."

"Why didn't you say anything?"

"I finally had her back. I finally had something you didn't. I wasn't alone. I liked having a secret." She sighed. "Pick one, pick all of them. When I went to college, you and I had that big fight."

Kelly closed her eyes and nodded. She'd been outraged that Olivia wanted to go to the same school as Ryan. It had been ridiculous and a huge waste of money. Their dad had said it was fine. She wondered now how much of his decision had been formed by guilt.

"When that didn't work out, Mom suggested I move closer to her so I transferred to ASU. From there, it was easy to get a job with her. I was still mad at you and Dad, so I kept the secret. Eventually I didn't know how to tell the truth anymore. Not without being the bad guy."

"And that spot was reserved for us."

Olivia nodded. "I had no idea she was going to show up here. You have to believe that. I've been…" Her mouth twisted. "It's hard to explain. Working with her is complicated. She's great and then she's not. Lately there's been a lot more not. I've been thinking about doing something else, but I couldn't figure out what. Coming here was supposed to give me time to think. You have to believe me. I was trying to get away from her, not lure her back."

Kelly didn't want to believe anything, but she couldn't help thinking maybe Olivia was telling the truth…about all of it.

"I'm sorry, too," she whispered, then couldn't figure out why she'd said that. Only she meant the words. "About what happened, about how I wasn't there for you."

"It wasn't us," her sister told her. "It was our parents. Both of them. They screwed us up big-time."

Kelly wanted to come to Jeff's defense, but knew Olivia was right. The adults in the family had been so focused on what they had going on, their daughters had been left to fend for themselves.

"I'm really sorry I didn't tell you about Mom," Olivia said.

"I'm sorry I had you sent away."

Olivia dropped her chin to her chest. "While it pains me to say this, it wasn't your decision." She straightened. "Can we be okay?"

Kelly thought about all the swirling emotion inside of her—how she'd felt so betrayed. That emotion could only have existed if her sister was starting to matter to her. She didn't want to lose what they'd had. Not because of something involving Marilee. "I'd like us to be."

"Me, too."

Kelly shifted from foot to foot. "I'd hug you, but I'm wearing a towel and that would be weird."

Olivia laughed. "I agree. But we're better?"

"Uh-huh. I'm still mad at Mom, though. You have to be okay with that."

"We'll form a team, get uniforms and a sponsor. How's that?"

Kelly laughed. "It's perfect."

22

"I can't believe you get paid for this," Olivia said on Sunday as she watched two five-week-old kittens try to scramble over her legs.

There were five kittens in all and a mother cat who seemed delighted to have someone take over babysitting, at least for a couple of hours. The family was camped out in Eliza's small apartment.

"Technically, today is my day off," Eliza told her. "It's Sunday. So I've brought my work home with me."

"Still." Olivia picked up a black-and-white kitten and petted her. "It beats having to figure out a quarterly report. Hey, you. Could you be cuter?"

The kitten looked at her and purred.

When Eliza had suggested lunch with a little kitten socialization thrown in, Olivia had offered to pick up takeout. Now as she sat on the living room floor, she wondered if she would have been able to make it through vet school.

"Thanks for coming over," Eliza said. "The kittens are old enough to be around people now so I need to make sure they're comfortable with being held so that they can be adopted."

"Do you take in a lot of strays?"

"I try not to. It would be easy to be inundated. The practice works with a local shelter. You'd be surprised how many people simply dump their animals off and run. But it's kitten season so I offered to be a foster mom."

"There's a season for kittens?"

"Late spring and summer." Eliza petted the momma cat. "She was abandoned by her family. She's very friendly and litter box trained. Once the kittens are ready to find their forever home, she'll be spayed and adopted out, as well."

"Tempted to keep one for yourself?"

Eliza wrinkled her nose. "I work a lot of hours. I'll foster again instead."

Olivia wondered if she had the right stuff to foster. Cats were pretty independent, which would help. Maybe next year she would be settled enough to try. In the meantime, she would make sure to hold each of the kittens. You know—for the sake of humanity, or in this case, kittendom.

"I brought my tablet," she said, reaching for her backpack. "I found a couple of really cool apps you're going to love. Now smile."

Eliza's expression was more startled than practiced. Olivia snapped a couple of pictures, then opened the app and uploaded them.

"I've been thinking about what you said before, about not looking old enough." Olivia turned the tablet to show Eliza the picture.

Her friend groaned. "I look like I'm twelve."

"Kind of. You need pet parents to take you seriously."

"Or at least not assume I'm some volunteer high school student."

"What do you wear at work?" Olivia asked as she entered information into the app. "Scrubs?"

"Mostly. They're comfy and practical."

"They make you look like a kid in pajamas."

"You don't know that."

"I can guess. You need to wear them for surgery and stuff,

but the rest of the time, and believe me I can barely mouth the words, you should be in tailored jeans and a T-shirt." She shuddered.

Eliza grinned. "Why is that bad?"

"Because you're a professional. Jeans and a T-shirt? But given what you do, it makes sense. Still, I'm not talking about one with the Seahawks logo. I'm talking plain and made out of a high-quality knit. I'll send you some links. Also, you need a shoe that gives you a little height." She held up a hand. "I get you won't be in Jimmy Choos, but there's no reason you can't wear a comfortable ankle boot with an inch or so of heel."

She turned the tablet so Eliza could see the outfit she'd put together. The mannequin had Eliza's slightly wide-eyed photo for a head. Olivia had chosen a long-sleeved round neck burgundy T-shirt, dark wash jeans and a cute Lucky Brand ankle boot.

"Under normal circumstances, I'd throw in a statement necklace, but with you handling animals, I'm guessing that would be bad." She smiled at her creation. "Put on a white coat and voilà—a professional doctor is born."

"I could try it," Eliza said, sounding doubtful.

"You will try it and you'll see I'm right. The fabrics are all machine washable. I know that's a big deal for you. Like I said—avoid the scrubs if at all possible. You'll look too young. Now, hair and makeup."

"Did I ask for this?"

"Yes, you did. Besides, I just made over my sister's wardrobe and I'm on a roll." She hit several buttons on the tablet, then smiled. "Oh, yeah, we're going classic."

She showed Eliza the picture. "Shoulder-length bob. It's simple, it flatters your features and you'll look older."

Eliza studied the image. "I've been thinking of cutting my hair. I like the style, but is it hard to manage?"

"I don't think so. Your hair is thick, so you could probably let it dry naturally most days and blow it out for special occasions.

I've been looking around for a good hairstylist. I have a couple of names I'll email you. A haircut will make a huge difference, but you're going to have to wear makeup."

"That's not happening. I have to be at work early most days. I don't have time."

"Like you're the first one to use that excuse. What if I could get you out of the bathroom in five minutes?"

"You can't."

Olivia set down the tablet and picked up a gray kitten. "Did you hear that total lack of faith?"

The kitten mewed. Olivia snuggled him close, then stood. "Come on. I'll prove it."

"With what?"

She grinned and pulled a small bag out of her backpack. "I went shopping. Come on."

They went into Eliza's bathroom. Olivia dumped out the contents of the bag.

"Liner, mascara, concealer, lip stain," she said. "Tie your hair back."

Eliza did as she was told.

"You're wearing sunscreen, right?" Olivia asked as she opened the package of eyeliner. "Even up here it's important."

"Every day," Eliza told her. "No matter what."

"Excellent. Now the trick to liner is to stay as close to the lash line as possible. Don't try to draw the whole line at once. Use short strokes."

Slightly more than five minutes later, Eliza had the makeup on. The concealer covered faint dark circles, while the liner and mascara brought out her big eyes.

"The lip stain will last most of the day," Olivia told her. "You don't have to worry about it wearing off in fifteen minutes. I would say apply it in the morning before you leave your apartment, then again after lunch."

Eliza studied herself. "I do look more sophisticated. Okay, I can do this."

Olivia pointed to the small bottle they'd yet to open. "Eye makeup remover," she said. "You'll need it to get everything off. Then wash your face like you usually do."

Eliza beamed at her. "You're so nice. Why don't I remember you being this nice in high school?"

"Because I wasn't."

She'd been more concerned with being popular and capturing Ryan's fickle attention than making and keeping real friends.

They returned to the living room and started a rousing game of string with the kittens. It didn't take long for the little guys to get tired out and head back to their mom. When the cat family was napping, Olivia and Eliza unwrapped sandwiches and chips.

"Is your sister going out with Griffith?" Eliza asked. "I heard a rumor."

"She is. Why?"

"He's dreamy." Eliza grinned. "Not that he's ever looked at me."

"Should I be worried that with your new look, you'll steal him away?"

"No. Kelly's all competent and cool. I could never be like that. But it would be nice to get involved with someone."

"No old boyfriend from college?"

Eliza flushed. "There was this one guy. Nelson. For a while I thought he liked me, but I guess not."

"Are you still in touch with him?"

"We text every couple of days. Talk about what's going on. He got a job at a practice in Seattle."

Olivia opened her bag of chips. "That's not far. Why don't you suggest getting together? See what happens."

"Wouldn't he ask me if he were interested?"

"Is he shy?"

Eliza smiled. "Yes. Very."

"Then go for it. I'm a big believer in going for it." She almost added that Eliza shouldn't put out on the first date, then reminded herself not everyone was her. Not that she and Sven were exactly dating. They were—

She frowned as she realized she had no idea what they were doing. It had pretty much been sex on demand until the last time she'd seen him. Then he'd just taken care of her. Something that rarely happened to her, which made it all the more special.

"Are you seeing Ryan?" Eliza asked, wrinkling her nose.

"There's an expression. Is that face about me, him or there being an us?"

Eliza's eyes widened. "I didn't mean anything by it. He's very handsome."

"And?"

"I don't know. Baseball? Really? Once it didn't work out, he didn't have another plan. He still doesn't have a plan." She put her hand over her mouth. "Sorry."

"Don't be. Ryan has a girlfriend. Autumn."

"I don't think I know her. Either way, you deserve someone special."

"I've been hanging out with Sven," she admitted.

Eliza sighed. "He's amazing. So strong and quiet. Those blue eyes. My mom would call him a hunk, and I think I'd have to agree."

"Okay, first Griffith and now Sven. Eliza, you have a slutty quality I knew nothing about. Go you."

Eliza giggled. "It's all in my head. You don't have to worry about me acting out."

"Too bad. I think you'd be fun acting out." She took a bite of her sandwich and chewed. "Okay, we've socialized kittens, had a mini makeover, discussed your impressively wanton side. I think we should tackle some really important world issue. We seem to be in the zone."

"How's the fund-raiser coming? Are you getting lots of do-nations?"

"I am. Sven's letting me borrow one of his barns and I'm fill-ing it up. There's so much there that I feel comforted. Even if no one comes to the fund-raiser, I can sell everything on eBay and make enough to replace the roof." She leaned forward. "What I don't have is a splashy finish. I have the bars in place for the silent auction, I have the tables for the dinner, the caterer, the tickets, an auctioneer. So we go through the various live auc-tion items and then what? We're indoors so fireworks are out. I feel like I need... I don't know what."

Dancers? A concert? Semaphore?

"What about a fashion show?" Eliza suggested. "Only show off what you're selling at the craft mall."

"It's antiques and tulip crap."

"So? Put the furniture on those flat dollies and wheel them across the stage. It will be unexpected and funny. Like a parade or something."

"A furniture fashion show. I like it."

Olivia raised her hand. Eliza slapped palms with her. Olivia grabbed Eliza's hand and stared at her nails. "What is it about this town and manicures?"

Eliza shook her head. "I draw the line at eye makeup," she said firmly. "No pun intended. I'm not getting a manicure."

"Now you sound like my sister."

"That's the nicest thing you've ever said to me."

Once again the temptation of throwing something crossed Helen's mind, cleanup be damned. Enough time had passed from when she'd last seen Jeff that she'd cycled through eight or ten *thousand* emotions, most of them bad. She was angry, hurt, en-raged, upset, broken, furious and the list went on. Worse, the moron hadn't been showing up for breakfast. There'd been zero happy visits before her customers arrived, no flowers, no smiles.

As she served lunch to her customers, she told herself she should be the adult in the room. Text him and ask him to stop by. Or go to the farm and slash his tires. While the former was more mature, she was confident the latter would be more satisfying. She'd never considered herself a vindictive or violent person before but was beginning to find uncharted depths deep in her soul.

Shortly before two she saw his truck pull into the parking lot. Her stupid, girlie heart got all warm and mushy. The rest of her glared with the fire of a scorned woman.

She debated ducking out the back, but realized she wanted to confront him and make him if not suffer, then at least feel really, really bad about himself. *Then* she would run away.

She busied herself with cleaning tables, ignoring Jeff as he settled at the counter in his usual seat. She continued to ignore him for twenty more seconds, in part to show him what was what and also because she'd had the horrifying realization that he had a usual seat. If things ended badly, she was going to have to have the stool completely removed. Or at the very least, emotionally cleansed by a shaman. She didn't know any shaman. Could you look for that sort of thing on Angie's List?

She shook off the question, grabbed a menu and walked over to face Jeff. Despite bracing herself, she was unprepared for the power of his full-on smile.

"Helen."

"Jeff."

"How are things going? I've missed seeing you at breakfast." He glanced around and lowered his voice. "You doing okay? Isaak called about us practicing today at three. Did he get in touch with you?"

She stared at him. That was it? That was all he was going to say? That he missed her and then they would return to their regularly scheduled lives?

She slapped down the menu she knew he didn't need and said,

"Excuse me," before walking to the cash register and taking the money from her last customers.

A quick glance into the kitchen told her Delja was finishing up. Helen went in to see if she needed anything. Delja smiled at her.

"Good day," she said.

"It was. Thanks for all your hard work."

They hugged, then the cook walked out the back door. Helen locked it behind her before returning to the front of the store.

Jeff studied her. "Are you upset about something?"

"What? Me?" She pressed both hands to her chest. "What a question. Why would you ask? What do I have to be upset about?"

"Helen, please tell me what's going on."

"No," she said forcefully. "You tell me. You've disappeared. I haven't heard from you in days. You've been coming in here for breakfast every morning. Every. Morning. For years! You've shown up with the flu and I had to send you home. But since your ex-wife returned, I haven't seen you. You sent your daughter to tell me the news and came by *once* and that's it. If we were just friends, I'd still be annoyed, but hey, more understanding. But we're not just friends, are we? There's a little bit more going on. At least in my mind. I sort of assumed I was the only one you're sleeping with. Maybe there are so many of us, I have to wait my turn on the information rotation."

She knew she had to stop talking, that not only did she need to breathe, there was the tiniest chance she was being unreasonable. Or overreacting. Not that she was going to give him a break. Maybe she should invite her ex-husband to move in for a few days and they could all see how Jeff liked it. Although the thought of having to see Troy again was horrifying, so she pushed that away and glared at the man in front of her.

"You haven't said anything. You haven't told me what's going on, so I'm left to wonder and figure it all out for myself. Are you getting back together? Are you tempted? And why on earth is she in your house? There are hotels in town. My God, Jeff, we slept together. I thought we were starting something, but apparently you only wanted to get laid."

His gaze was steady. She had no idea what he was thinking, which was probably for the best. She doubted it was overly flattering.

"Helen," he began. "I'm sorry you're upset."

"Don't," she snapped. "Do *not* start with that line. You don't get to be—" she made air quotes "—'sorry' I'm upset. That takes no responsibility. It's not an apology. It's a weasel thing to say and I expect better of you."

"All right." His tone was cautious. "I'm sorry you've been worried about Marilee and I apologize for not coming by sooner. I should have talked to you. There's been a lot going on and to be honest, I never thought you were upset about Marilee being back."

"She's not back. Back is seeing someone over coffee. She's *living* with you. Just down the hall. Not long ago you and I were just friends. We had one great night, I thought everything was different, then your ex-wife blew into town and you disappeared. What was I supposed to think?"

"You were supposed to trust me."

"Why?"

"You know me." He rose and glared at her. "Dammit, Helen, you've known me for years. We're friends. I'm a good guy. I do the right thing. Do you actually believe I would sleep with you, then sleep with my ex-wife?"

Yes. Yes! But she couldn't say that. She wanted to but understood there would be consequences.

"I'm scared," she admitted instead. "Marilee is so beautiful and you loved her once and we're so new and I'm just some girl in town and I don't understand anything that's happening."

He walked around the counter, stopped in front of her, pulled her close and held her. His strong arms felt good, as did the warmth of him. She liked the steady beat of his heart and how he didn't let go.

"You make me crazy," he murmured.

"That's nice."

He chuckled. "Maybe for you." He kissed her. "I'm sorry I didn't come see you or text or call. I should have. I wasn't thinking. Having Marilee back is a nightmare. I don't want her here, but I'm not going to tell her to leave."

"Why not? You should tell her. I can help."

He smiled. "Thank you, but this is bigger than us. I want Kelly to have time with her mother. Olivia, too, although she and Marilee are closer than I'd realized."

Helen wanted to point out that Kelly had no interest in spending time with Marilee but sensed that wasn't a good idea, so kept quiet. Jeff continued to hold her.

"Both girls were devastated when she left," he continued. "I was relieved for myself, but worried about my daughters. They missed out on a lot. I tried, but we both know I couldn't fill in for her, then I sent Olivia away."

Helen drew back. "You did the right thing."

"If I did, that was just dumb luck. I made the easy decision. I hurt Olivia. I don't want to make that mistake again. Marilee is nothing to me, but I love my girls and I want them to have time with their mother."

Which they could from a hotel, only saying that would make her seem petty and small. Thinking it made her that, too, but she was probably more forgiving of her flaws than Jeff would be.

"I know this happened at a bad time," he said, looking into her eyes. "We're at that scary new stage. I don't want to lose you. Please trust me, Helen. We've been friends a long time. You know me."

Something he'd said before, but it resonated with her now. She drew in a breath and knew she had to take a step of faith.

"I do trust you."

"Thank you."

He kissed her again, his mouth lingering this time. When he straightened, she was more than a little breathless.

"I'll be better about staying in touch," he promised. "I'll start coming in for breakfast again. I've been staying home to act as a buffer for the girls, but they can take care of themselves."

"Thank you. In return, I won't slash your tires."

He grinned. "That's my girl. Ready to go help a band find their sound?"

She nodded. She would rather stay here with him. Sex in the storeroom would be very healing. But a band waited and she didn't want to seem too needy. Something she would guess Marilee never had to worry about.

Life and ex-wives could be a real bitch.

23

Kelly slathered almond butter on her whole-grain waffle, then picked up a banana and carried it all to the table. Her dad was back to having breakfast at the café—at least she assumed he was. His truck had been gone when she'd gotten up. If she pretended Marilee wasn't in the guest room, Kelly could tell herself everything was back the way it had been.

She opened the fashion magazine her sister had given her, prepared to educate herself over breakfast. She'd barely gotten through several pages of ads when she heard her dad's truck in the driveway.

"Morning, Kitten," Jeff said as he came into the kitchen and poured himself a cup of coffee. "How's it going?"

"Good. Are you happy to be back in your routine?"

He grinned. "Yup. Nobody makes eggs like Delja." He picked up his mug and carried it to the table. "They up yet?"

"Olivia is. She's gone for a run. I don't know about the other one."

"You can call her your mother."

"I can call her a lot of things."

"Kelly." His tone was warning.

"What? Are you going to say I have to be nice to her? How long is she staying anyway?"

"I have no idea."

"You should ask. Better yet, you should ask her to move to a hotel."

Her dad's gaze sharpened. "Why would I do that?"

"To get her out of here."

"She's your mother. I'm not going to turn her away."

"Don't keep her on my account. I think this whole thing is ridiculous. You're never mad at her."

"How would that help?"

Most of the time Kelly was grateful her father was a calm, sensible kind of guy but every now and then she found him difficult.

"Dad, helping isn't the point. You're too nice when it comes to her." She held up her hand. "Please don't say it's because she's my mother. I'm incredibly aware of that fact."

His dark gaze settled on her face. "I worry about you."

"What? I'm fine."

"Are you? It's been thirteen years and you're still furious with her."

Apparently it was that obvious, Kelly thought, not totally surprised.

"I have reason to be. What kind of mother walks out on her two children? Did you notice that Olivia is the one who found Mom, not the other way around? Marilee doesn't care about anyone but herself. She never has. She's going to do whatever she wants and the consequences be damned. She doesn't care about who she hurts, but you won't say any of that, will you? You don't want to speak ill of her in front of me. Well, here's my news flash, Dad. I'm all grown up. I can take it."

"Old habits die hard."

"Just once I'd like you to admit she's a horrible person."

"That's not going to happen, but while we're on the subject of things we want in life…"

She waited, fairly confident she wasn't going to like whatever he was going to say. "Yes?"

"I'd like you to think about why you're so angry with her.

It's been a long time. You should have moved on." He lifted his mug. "I'm not saying you're wrong, Kelly, just that you should know why. Do you need closure? If you're waiting for an apology, it's not going to happen. She is who she is."

Good advice she didn't want to take. "I don't hate her."

"That's something." He sipped his coffee. "You're the one I worry about. She messed up your childhood. Don't let her mess up any more than that. I want you to be happy."

"I am."

He didn't say anything, but then he didn't have to. They knew each other well enough for her to figure out he didn't believe that. Not when it came to Marilee.

"I'll think about it," she grumbled.

"Thank you."

Before she could respond, she heard footsteps in the hall. As she hadn't heard the front door open, she had to brace herself for an early-morning appearance from their houseguest.

"Morning," Marilee said breezily as she walked into the kitchen. "Mmm, coffee. How wonderful."

Kelly stared at her mother. Marilee had obviously done her hair and put on makeup before emerging from her bedroom. But what got Kelly's attention the most was what she was wearing. A man's pajama top. Just the top.

The pale blue fabric covered in small tractors fell to mid-thigh. The shoulder seams were halfway down her upper arm. She looked adorable. Sexy, even.

Kelly's stomach sank. She looked at her father, who didn't seem the least bit shocked by his ex-wife's appearance. This despite the fact that Marilee was wearing *his* pajama top. Kelly knew that for sure because she'd bought the tractor-print pj's as a joke at Christmas.

What was her mother doing wearing them? Were they sleeping together?

The possibility of her parents having sex was bad enough but that it might lead to them getting back together made her feel sick. Breakfast sat very heavily and for a second she didn't know if she was going to throw up or cry.

She loved her dad and knew he'd been alone for a long time. He deserved someone special—someone who would care about him and be good to him. Someone normal and honest and faithful. Someone who wasn't Marilee.

"I need to get to work," Kelly said, coming to her feet.

"Oh, no," Marilee chirped. "Can you stay so we can talk?"

"Um, no. I'm late for a meeting."

"With whom? Your tulips?"

Her mother laughed at her own joke. Kelly dumped her coffee in the sink and bolted. She was halfway to the farm before her stomach calmed down, which left only tears, and those she would fight until the need passed.

Luck was on Kelly's side. When she arrived at the farm, she found that one of the greenhouse irrigation systems had clogged. Finding the problem and cleaning out the hosing had taken the better part of two hours. By then she was more herself and able to ignore whatever was happening between her parents. She had work, she reminded herself. The rest of it would take care of itself.

She went back to her office and cleared her email, then went into her private greenhouse to check on the progress of her test bulbs.

Two buds had appeared in the night. She took the small pots over to the desk by the door and booted the laptop there. She pulled a camera out of a desk drawer and took several pictures, then emailed them to herself to be included in her report.

The tight bud was brownish pink on the bottom, fading to pinkish mud-taupe on the top. She could see the individual petals were going to be very slim and pointed in an almost star pattern, but they looked to be different lengths, which could be a deliberate part of the design or an area of yet more concern.

After measuring the plant, she double-checked how long it had been in the greenhouse, then sat down to write her report.

The door opened and Griffith walked in. That was nearly as much of a surprise as the huge vase of flowers he was carrying. No, not flowers. Red roses.

She rose. "Hi. What are you doing here?"

"Bringing you these." He held out the roses. "It occurred to me that guys probably don't bring you flowers. What with you growing tulips and all."

He looked both proud and slightly apprehensive, as if he weren't sure of her reaction.

She smiled, then started to laugh. Big, beautiful red roses. It was crazy and yet really, really nice.

"You're right. No one's ever brought me flowers before," she admitted. "Thank you."

"You're welcome." He set them on the desk, then frowned at the tulip. "What is that? It's really ugly."

"You can't know that. It's barely a bud."

"The colors. What is that called? Muddy pink?"

She looked at the flower and sighed. "Sometimes the experiments don't work out. I'm not sure what the gradation was supposed to be but I'm pretty sure it wasn't this."

She touched one of the rose petals. They were perfectly shaped and deep red. The scent drifted to her. She turned to Griffith and put her hands on his shoulders.

"You're the sweetest man."

"I'm pretty great, huh? You're lucky to have me."

She laughed and pressed her mouth to his. His arms came around her. Just as she was settling in to the thrill of being held, she felt a strange burning in her eyes. In the second it took the feeling to register, her brain to process and the rest of her to say

"This is so not happening," it was too late. Tears fell and at the same time an ugly, primal sob worked its way out of her chest.

"Kelly?"

She turned away and struggled to get control of herself. The tears continued, along with the cries, until she couldn't catch her breath. She had no idea where all the emotion had been stored, but once released, it wasn't stopping for anyone.

Griffith pulled her close. She started to jerk away, then collapsed as his concern made itself felt in the way he stroked her back and murmured her name.

She had no idea if it had been seconds or minutes before she was finally able to breathe again. She drew back and wiped her face. He shocked her by holding out a snowy-white handkerchief.

"S-seriously?" she asked, her voice still broken.

He grinned. "My dad makes me. It's a thing for him. I never saw the point, until now. I'm going to have to call and tell him he was right. That will make him happy."

She took the handkerchief and wiped her face, then tucked it in her pocket. "I'll wash this before I return it."

"That's kind of the least of my worries. What's going on?"

His look of concern, his quiet voice, nearly had her sobbing again. She took a deep breath and told herself she was fine. Or she would be.

"I don't know," she admitted. "I'm not usually a crier."

"No surprise. You're tough. So whatever it is has you in knots. Let's talk about it."

He led her to the desk chair, then settled in the extra seat before leaning forward and taking her hand in his. She touched one of the roses again and marveled at their perfection.

"I don't want my parents to get back together." Not what she'd been thinking, at least not on the surface, she thought in some surprise. "I hate that she's here, that she's disrupted our lives. I want her to go away."

Griffith didn't speak.

She sniffed. "My dad wants me to have a relationship with her. He wants me to get to know her. As if."

One corner of his mouth turned up. "As if?"

She smiled. "You know what I mean. It's not going to happen. I hate her."

"No, you don't."

"I really do."

"Kelly, she's your mom. You may be angry at her and resent her actions. You may be frightened of being like her and worry that she's going to destroy the family you've made, but you don't hate her. You're not the kind of person who hates anyone, let alone your mother."

"I'm not excited about you being insightful."

His steady gaze never wavered. "You're going to have to deal with it."

"Fine. I want her to leave and I don't want her sleeping with my dad."

"Fair enough, but if it's going to happen, you can't stop it."

"Gross. I don't want to think about it." About them. She told him about the pj top. "She's just everywhere. I wasn't excited when Olivia came back, but that's different. Now I like having her around. We're sisters and we're finding our way back to that." She held up her hand. "By contrast, Mom hasn't said a word about what happened before or after she left. Until my mother is willing to admit what she did and ask for forgiveness, she doesn't get a second chance. I'll never trust her."

She half expected him to say she didn't have a choice. Instead he linked his fingers with hers and told her, "What's that old saying? Fool me once, shame on you, fool me twice, shame on me? It's not bad advice."

"So you're saying I shouldn't hate her but it's okay not to trust her?"

"Just my opinion."

"You're very fond of your opinion."

One shoulder rose slightly. "I can't help it. I'm a guy."

She laughed, then leaned forward and kissed him. "At the risk of stating the obvious, you're a pretty impressive guy."

"Tell me about it." His expression turned serious. "I want to talk about what happened the other night. With us."

What on earth was he—

She jerked her hand free, straightened and thought longingly of bolting for the door. "I'm fine."

"I'm not. We have to talk."

"Why? It was great. You were great. Fantastic."

She tried to sound as enthused as possible because if she didn't, he wouldn't believe her and then they would have an excruciating conversation about what had and hadn't worked and why she was the way she was and maybe he should just kill her now.

"I've been doing some reading," he began.

"What?" The word came out loud and at a higher pitch than she'd planned. She cleared her throat. "What do you mean you've been reading?"

"I'm not sure what's confusing about the sentence. I've been trying to figure out why you weren't able to climax. You never said that it was a first time thing, that after you relaxed, you'd be fine, which tells me that being with someone new isn't the problem."

She folded her arms across her chest, closed her eyes and wished she could just up and die.

"I don't think there's a physical problem," he continued. "With your anatomy. You would have mentioned that. Which means it's something else. Maybe you won't relax enough to let go. Maybe you're afraid of something. Maybe it's your mother."

Her eyes snapped open. "My *mother*? Are you telling me you think I can't have an orgasm because of my *mother*?"

"I think it's a possibility. You saw her behavior and you experienced the consequences. Maybe sex and devastation are linked in your head. I doubt it's that simple. I suspect there are a lot of reasons you're not willing to let go."

She once again glanced at the door, but it seemed incredibly far away and she had a bad feeling that Griffith wouldn't let her run away. He seemed determined to have it out with her, regardless of what she wanted. Still, she had to try.

"This isn't a conversation I want to be having."

"I'm sure."

She waited. "That's it?"

He leaned toward her. "Kelly, this is important. We have to figure out the problem and how to solve it."

"No, we don't. I'm fine. Completely happy."

"I want to believe that. Just to confirm what you said the other night, you've never climaxed, even by yourself?"

She covered her face with her hands. "Stop, I beg you."

"I'll take that as a no."

They weren't going to talk about this, she told herself as she straightened and glared at him. She was going to keep completely silent until he ran out of steam, then she was going to find a bar and start drinking. Even if it was barely noon.

"Do you like the touching?" he asked.

She pressed her lips together and refused to answer.

"When I stroke your breasts? Is that nice?"

She felt a whisper of sensation in the aforementioned body parts.

"Yes," she said grudgingly. "It's nice."

"Like you're aroused?"

She rolled her eyes.

"So maybe heat and tingles?"

She crossed her arms again. "I'm starting to think going out with you was a bad idea."

"What about oral sex? Do you like that?"

She felt herself blush. "Griffith!"

"It's a legitimate question. Do you like it?"

"I guess."

"Did you and Sven do that a lot?"

"Ask him," she blurted, only to realize Griffith probably would, leading to more humiliation, which she didn't need. "We did it a few times. It was nice."

"But not nice enough. Do you enjoy having your clitoris touched?"

She stood. "We're done."

He rose. "We can't be. Kelly, sex is important. Not just because it feels good, but because it makes it easier for us to bond as a couple. There are chemicals released during orgasm. We need them to make this work."

"Holy crap, how much reading did you do?"

"A lot. Is it the word? Clitoris? Is clit better?"

She sank back on the chair and rested her arms on the desk, then put her head on her arms. "I hate you."

"You hate a lot of people. So it's not the word?"

"No. Call it what you want. Touching it is fine." Sometimes it was better than fine. Sometimes she thought that maybe she was going to get there, but then something happened and she didn't. "Oral sex is fine. All of it is totally fine." She raised her head and looked at him. "Can we be done, please?"

He pulled her to her feet and kissed her. "We can be done talking about it for today, but aren't even close to finished with the subject."

"That's what I was afraid of."

Olivia had no idea what to expect with her meeting with Sally. The first time she and the quilt lady, as Olivia had come to think of her, had met, Olivia had gone over her booth space, explained what she thought the problem was, and had offered a couple of solutions. She'd been careful to talk about how wonderful the quilts were, how they weren't getting the attention they deserved and that she thought Sally would be selling a lot more with a different layout. Then she'd waited.

Sally had listened, thanked her and that had been that. Eight minutes of Olivia talking with virtually no response. She had no idea if Sally had been happy, offended or suffering from indigestion, so not actually listening.

She'd meant to sweat the problem for several days, only Marilee had blown into town and dropped the "why yes, Olivia and I *do* spend a lot of time together" bombshell, and all other issues had been forgotten. Until Olivia had received an email from Sally requesting a second meeting. That was it—just a date and time with no hint as to what the meeting was about.

Olivia dressed carefully in a sleeveless print dress that wasn't too short or low-cut. She added a short-sleeved shrug and low heels, then grabbed her briefcase and left the house.

It took her less than ten minutes to get to the craft mall. She was early so decided to walk around the booths. She took notes as she went, on the off chance that Sally had liked her advice and would give her name to other vendors. At five minutes to two, she went back to the mall entrance and found Sally waiting for her, along with another, slightly younger woman.

"This is Hannah," Sally told her. "She has two antiques booths in the mall. What do you think of the name Garden Variety?"

Olivia shook hands with the pretty brunette, then turned back to Sally. "For the craft mall?"

Sally nodded.

"I like it. I think The Dutch Bunch is cute and catchy, but the range of items sold isn't very specific. I'm concerned customers would expect a lot more Dutch and tulip-based inventory and be disappointed."

Sally and Hannah exchanged a look that Olivia couldn't read.

"I took your advice," Sally told her. "I rearranged my booth, took out most of the quilts, displayed the ones left and used the book of photographs, along with another book of sample quilting techniques." She grinned. "I've sold eight quilts in the past three days and I have five special orders that people want for the holidays. It's more than I've sold in any single month except December."

"Me, too," Hannah added, then laughed. "You gave Sally suggestions for one of my booths. I did what you said and I've doubled my sales."

Olivia's vague sense of apprehension faded. "I'm glad I could help."

"We appreciate your suggestions," Sally said. "For most of us, the booths are a second business, but we still have to make money. A couple of them are run by stay-at-home moms and they need all the help they can get. Hannah and I think you should offer to consult with all the booth owners. They probably don't have the money to pay you up front, but you could collect a percentage of the increased sales."

"A sliding percentage," Hannah added. "Say forty percent the first month, thirty the second, twenty the third. That's what I plan to pay you."

Olivia held up both hands. "I didn't ask to be paid. I was trying to help." To be useful and feel as if she belonged somewhere, she thought, careful not to say that. The nice women saying such lovely things about her didn't want to know how needy she was.

"Even so, it's only right." Hannah looked determined. "Can you draw up some kind of agreement? Nothing fancy—just a page spelling out the terms?"

"Of course. I'll do that tonight."

"Good." Sally smiled. "We'll speak with the other booth owners and get you their contact information. A few of them are old-fashioned and won't want to listen, but some will. I think after a few months, everyone is going to want your advice."

Wouldn't that be nice, Olivia thought. "I appreciate the vote of confidence."

Sally and Hannah exchanged another look. "There's one other

thing," Sally told her. "A few of us on the tourism board think we need a manager for the craft mall. Someone to make sure the rules are followed and to help with the marketing. Tourists should know about us and they don't. There's not a lot of money in the budget, but we should be able to afford someone part-time. I doubt the job would be more than a few hours a week. If you're interested, I'd like to take the idea to the committee."

Olivia did her best to keep from shrieking. "You're offering me a job?" she confirmed.

"Yes," Hannah said. "Maybe with you in charge, we can stop changing the name every few months. I love Vista Print but I don't need to be ordering new business cards every two months because we can't decide on a name."

"I'd be interested," Olivia told her. "Very much so." Talk about motivation to make the auction even more successful. A few of the extra dollars could go toward her salary, which would be very exciting.

She smiled at Sally. "I had no idea what you were thinking after our last meeting. I was afraid I'd insulted you and that you would be looking for someone else to run the fund-raiser."

Sally laughed. "I'll admit I was shocked by what you told me," she admitted. "I've had a booth here for years and I thought I was doing really well. At first I told myself you had no idea what you were talking about, but after a while I started to think about your suggestions. I gave it a weekend, just to prove you wrong. Then I found out it was me all along."

They made arrangements for Olivia to come to the city offices to fill out the required paperwork.

"There'll have to be a board vote," Hannah said. "I'm sending out an email later today to all the members telling them we need a meeting. I'm sure everyone will agree."

"I'll wait to hear from you."

On her way back to her car, Olivia did a little mental happy dance, only to stop when she realized she'd just made the decision to move back to Tulpen Crossing permanently. Who would have thought?

She could do it, she told herself. All she had to do was find another part-time job and then she was set. Oh, and give notice to her mother—not that she had the slightest idea of what to say. "Hey, Mom, you've been a real bitch, so I'm leaving," didn't seem like the best opening line.

"Not something I have to deal with today," she told herself as she got in her car. She started the engine and pulled out of the parking lot. Eventually she would head back to her dad's place, but first she had a stop to make. She was already on a roll—this was the time to take advantage of her momentum.

24

Griffith had an orgasm problem. Technically, the problem was Kelly's but he was involved. The thing was, he didn't know what to do first. Okay, yes, he had to get her back into bed, but then what? He could write a paper on a clitoral orgasm versus a vaginal one, including quoting scientists who said they were one and the same. He understood about stimulation (speed and pressure) along with the advantage of using a rest cycle. He could talk G-spot, anal stimulation, different angles of penetration and the advantages and disadvantages of using a vibrator. What he didn't know was which technique was going to work on Kelly, especially considering there was also an emotional component. He was both enthused and apprehensive. He felt like the kid who had overstudied for his final.

His mental hopscotch was interrupted when Olivia walked into his office.

"Hi, Griffith, do you have a few minutes?"

All thoughts of Kelly retreated, leaving him feeling vaguely guilty about thinking about Olivia's sister in that way, which made him smile.

"Sure," he told her. "What's up?"

A second too late, he braced himself to hear something about Ryan. His brother had been showing up more regularly, albeit grudgingly. He was also getting more work done, although today he'd called in sick.

She settled across from his desk. "I've been doing some re-search on tiny homes. The industry is growing quickly. The combination of the costs of construction, the rising price of land and a cultural shift toward owning less causes many economists to believe that micro housing has an excellent long-term future."

Griffith mentally shifted gears. So, not Ryan. "That's my understanding, as well."

"Good." She pulled out her tablet. "I stopped by a few weeks ago and Leo took me on a tour of the facility. I like what you're doing here. The quality work is impressive. You have six houses in various stages of completion for customers to see, and the cross section, but you don't have an actual display area."

"I've thought about it, but I'm not sure it's worth the money. Most people have a clear idea of what they want."

"What percentage?" she asked as she pulled out a pad of paper and a pen.

"About half."

"Do they change their minds as they go through the process?"

"Yeah. A lot. And when we get into picking out the materi-als to finish the house, there can be issues. A few know exactly how things should be but a lot of them are overwhelmed by the choices. I can give them direction on some things. There are some materials you want to stay away from."

"That's what I learned from my reading." She tapped on her tablet, then turned it so he could see the screen. "This is the basic floor plan of a twelve-by-twenty-four tiny home. It's something you'd have for a mother-in-law house or on undeveloped land."

"I'm familiar with the design," he said drily. "It's one of mine."

She flashed him a grin. "I'm so pleased you recognized it." She swiped to the next picture, an interior shot. Not a photo-graph, but a to-scale color rendering that was nearly as good.

The finishes were rustic, the furniture mostly fabric and wood. The floor was covered with wide planks. She showed him shots of the two lofts—one with a queen bed and one with two twins. There was another shot of the kitchen. Olivia had put in appliances, along with a few small touches, such as a built-in wine rack and two computer stations. She showed him where she'd found extra storage and finished with a big deck off the back.

"It's nice," he said, not sure where they were going.

She flipped to the next rendering. "A twelve-by-twenty-four tiny house with a loft," she said, then waited.

He stared at the interior. He knew the design front to back, knew he'd just seen it. Yet nothing he was looking at was the same. Oh, sure, there were the obvious placements. The kitchen, the bathroom. But this home was sleek and modern. The finishes were all chrome and glass. The windows were different, as was the furniture. Where the previous house would have fit in next to a lake or in the mountains, this one belonged in San Francisco, or Paris.

She flipped through to the kitchen. Again, the differences stunned him. These cabinets had a frosted glass finish with doors lifted up instead of to the side. The deck was on the roof, with gleaming stainless steel railings and a built-in fire pit.

"Holy shit," he murmured.

She smiled. "Thank you. Leo mentioned that there are customers who know what they want, but a lot of their ideas aren't practical for the space. There are other clients who want a tiny home but have no idea how to finish it. My suggestion is you expand your display area considerably."

She flipped to another rendering, this one of a showroom. There was a completed tiny house, his existing cross section, along with a wall of cabinets, appliances, fixtures and fabric swatches.

"I like it, but I don't have room for it."

"The storefront next to your warehouse is going to be available to lease at the end of the month. There's a huge parking lot out front for customers and in back for employees. You could rent that and have a permanent showroom. With the employee parking no longer taking up space, you could expand the second warehouse."

She slipped her tablet back in her bag. "Your company is privately held, so it's difficult to get hard numbers. From what I've been able to find out, you're doubling your sales every three years. I'm guessing you're turning business away. Why not expand, instead?"

He was doubling his business every 2.7 years, but her guess was a good one. As were her ideas.

"What do you get out of it?" he asked. "To run my showroom?"

"No, thanks. You don't really need someone to run it. Once it's set up, it's just there to give people ideas." She crossed her legs. "The bigger problem is time. You and Leo are busy enough without spending time with customers, especially when they can't decide if they want wallpaper or a flush toilet. Hire a salesperson to handle the sales and follow up on the orders. I'll oversee the renovation of the showroom and purchase the initial stock. I'll come in a few hours a month to change things around and order in new samples."

She drew in a breath. "As for the interior design work, I suggest you offer a package. Customers can order everything themselves or they can work with me. I'd be contract labor. When I'm needed, I'd be here. Otherwise, I'm not on the payroll."

His mind worked quickly to process her ideas. "Would they order the finishes and fixtures through me?"

"Why not? You'd be able to control quality that way and take a small markup. Even the pennies add up over time."

She was right about all of it, he thought, chagrined he hadn't thought of it himself. A showroom made sense. As for a salesperson, they'd needed one for a while. Leo had mentioned it more than once, but Griffith had been busy with other things.

He turned his attention to Olivia. "You're staying?"

"So it seems."

"Does Kelly know?"

"I haven't told her yet." She cleared her throat. "I haven't mentioned it to anyone. A few things have happened…" She shook her head. "It doesn't matter. I'm going to be living here and I think what you're doing is interesting and fun. I'd like to be a part of it. Shall I write up a formal proposal?"

Olivia had some balls on her, Griffith thought with a grin. "Sure. Give me a proposal for the remodel of the storefront, as well."

"You'll have it within a week," she told him. She rose and held out her hand. They shook. "Thank you for the opportunity."

"You're welcome. I look forward to seeing what you can do." He walked around his desk. "Oh, and you might want to tell your sister you're planning on sticking around."

"I will. The trick is to keep the information from my mother for as long as possible."

"Good luck with that."

"Thanks."

Kelly waited nervously for Griffith to pick her up. She hadn't seen him since their conversation about her, well, her *issues*, and she was more than a little apprehensive about the evening. She'd almost told him she couldn't make it, except they were going to see her dad and Helen play with a new band and she felt as if she hadn't seen her friend in forever.

She paced in the living room, checking out the front window. Everyone was gone. Her dad was already at the venue and Olivia and Marilee were somewhere, although Kelly doubted they were hanging out together. From what she could tell, Olivia was avoiding their mother as much as Kelly was.

Griffith arrived right on time. She went outside before he could come to the door.

"Hey, you," he said as she approached. "I'm supposed to come inside and explain my intentions to your disapproving father."

She laughed. "He's not here, so you're safe for the night."

"Lucky me."

Griffith pulled her close and kissed her. She knew that while they were kissing, he couldn't talk about her clit or any other part of her anatomy so she relaxed in his embrace. His mouth moved against hers in a slow, sexy way. She wrapped her arms around his neck and leaned in to him.

She was wearing one of her Olivia-purchased outfits. Slim pants, cute little flats and a halter top that left most of her back bare. The material was silky and felt kind of nice on her bare breasts. She'd curled her hair again, but had passed on the makeup her sister had bought her. It was still confusing, although she had used mascara.

Griffith moved his hands from her waist to her back. His fingers were warm and slightly rough against her skin and she shivered as he lightly traced her spine.

He drew back and smiled at her. "What's the musical theme tonight?"

"Eighties movies. Madonna's 'Who's That Girl' and that song from *Pretty in Pink*." She laughed. "Let's all pause and imagine how excited my dad is."

"I'm sure he can barely contain himself." Griffith put his arm around her and led her to his truck. "He's a good guy, doing what he does."

"I think he and Helen enjoy helping out the new bands. Every now and then they get to play with real musicians, so that's good."

There was a big crowd at the community center. "Everybody loves the eighties," he said as he parked.

"Why wouldn't you?" She slid to the ground. "I wonder if Olivia's here. I had the strangest email from her. She wants to meet with me at work tomorrow. She actually suggested a time, like there's some formal agenda. Then I have an unexpected tourism meeting in the afternoon. I have no idea what that's all about."

He held up both hands. "Don't look at me. I'm not on the board."

"It's the one place you didn't invade in your attempt to win me."

He took her hand. "Don't mock my tactics. They worked."

"They did, and doesn't that make you all smug."

"I'm only a little smug."

They walked inside and found seats in the back. The band was mostly men and women in their thirties and forties. Griffith had high hopes for them which were only slightly dashed with the first song.

"Madonna would not be happy," Kelly murmured as the drummer messed up the beat and the lead singer couldn't find the right key. She saw her dad and Helen exchange a private smile as the other two guitarists got lost in the bridge.

Just before intermission, Jeff and Helen took center stage with a duet of "If You Leave."

"I love this song," Kelly whispered to Griffith. He put his arm around her and pulled her close. As her dad and Helen began to sing, she became aware of Griffith moving his thumb along her upper arm. The movement was subtle, but steady. The contact felt nice.

She did her best to return her attention to the stage and her friend singing. When they were done, she and Griffith walked up to talk to Jeff and Helen.

"You sounded fantastic," Kelly told her friend as she hugged her. "I love that song."

"I know. We did it for you."

Kelly turned to her father. "Surviving the eighties?" she asked.

Her dad sighed. "I lived through them once. That was enough."

"I'm sure John Hughes would be very proud that you're celebrating his movies."

"He doesn't need me," Jeff grumbled, then nodded at Helen. "We're, ah, going to grab a bite after the show. Some, ah, friends are joining us so we might be late."

"No problem. I won't tell Mom."

Kelly meant the comment to be teasing, then realized too late it was probably in poor taste. Her father's mouth flattened and Helen turned away. Kelly guessed her friend was trying not to roll her eyes in public. Helen had always been supportive of Kelly's dislike of her mother, but she hadn't meant to remind her dad of what was happening at home.

"Sorry," she told him.

"It's fine. She can do what she likes. I don't care." He put his hand on the small of Helen's back. "I need to get this one some water. She has a big solo coming up."

Kelly sighed as they walked away. "I shouldn't have said that. About Mom."

"If it makes you feel any better, my brother's still not talking to me."

"I guess that helps a little. I just hate being socially awkward."

"You're not. Want to get out of here?"

She nodded and he led her back to his truck. He drove to his place and took her inside. After pouring them each a glass of wine, he sat next to her on the sofa.

"Still beating yourself up?" he asked.

"No. I wish my mom would go back home but that's all. Tell me what's new with you?"

"I'm thinking of expanding my business. I heard the storefront next door is going to be available. I've talked to the landlord and the price is good."

"What would you do there?"

"Have a showroom with different options for finishes, along

with a completed tiny house as well as my cross sections showing construction."

"That's a great idea."

"It wasn't even mine."

Before she could ask whose it was, he leaned in, took her wine from her and put it on the coffee table, then kissed her. She relaxed into his touch, letting herself absorb his nearness. When he stroked his tongue against her bottom lip, she parted for him. He slid inside and began that slow, sexy dance.

She liked how Griffith kissed. He moved his tongue against hers in a way that invited rather than took. His lips were firm yet soft. She felt his attention to detail and sensed he enjoyed the process. It was more than a pit stop, it was its own destination.

He drew back enough to nibble his way along her jaw, then down the side of her neck. The light scrape of his teeth on her skin made her shiver. Her small breasts grew more sensitive with every kiss and the silky fabric both aroused and irritated her nipples.

"This is one sexy top," he murmured as his hands moved up and down her arms. "It had me distracted all evening."

"That was the point."

"Then it's a success. From what I've been able to figure out, you're not wearing a bra underneath."

She smiled. "No. You'd be able to see it if I was."

"And these two hooks are the only thing holding it up."

"So it seems."

"Nice." He straightened. "Look at me."

She did as he requested. When their eyes locked, she felt his fingertips lightly touch her nipples. Not her breasts—just the tight, sensitive tips. Her breath caught as need and heat wove through her.

"I'm not going to say the C word," he began, "so you can relax."

"Thank you."

"I don't want you to have an orgasm."

She blinked. "Excuse me?"

"Not tonight. It would be too much pressure."

He lightly pinched her nipples between his thumb and forefinger. Sensation shot through her and she had to fight to keep from gasping.

"O-okay."

"Instead we're going to play. I want to try different things and you tell me if you like them. Sometime later we'll put it all together, but tonight is just one big experiment with no pressure."

While she liked the sound of that, she wasn't completely convinced it would go well. Not that it was easy to think when he kept touching her nipples. She loved what he was doing and couldn't helping thinking how much better it would feel if he undid her top and sucked on her. Hard.

The image filled her brain, of his head bent and his mouth closing over her. She wanted that. She wanted to feel his mouth on her and—

"Kelly?"

"Huh?"

"Is that okay?"

"Um, sure."

He dropped his hands to his lap. "What are you thinking?"

She felt herself blush and wanted to stomp her foot in frustration. Not just because there was a problem with her having an orgasm like a normal person but because she couldn't even *talk* about what she wanted him to do.

This was Griffith. He liked her. He wanted to please her—of course he would want to know what she was interested in. Dammit, she ran a successful multimillion-dollar business. She was smart, capable and there was no earthly reason why she couldn't simply tell the man she was dating that she wanted him to suck on her breasts.

Except the thought of doing that left her feeling humiliated and nauseous.

"I can't please you if I don't know what to do," he said gently.

"My breasts," she managed to say, motioning to the front of her chest.

He smiled. "I like them, too. Can you unfasten your top?"

She had a feeling the question was more about getting her to participate than him worrying about the closure. She nodded and reached behind to her neck and undid the hooks. The material fell, leaving her naked to the waist.

Griffith made a low, guttural sound in the back of his throat before leaning in and taking her left breast in his mouth. He sucked as deeply as she'd imagined, pulling pleasure from every part of her. He swirled his tongue and sucked again, then moved his fingers against her right breast. She arched into him and groaned.

He switched breasts and repeated the process, then drew back and blew air on her damp skin. The blast of cool made her laugh and break out in goose bumps. He pulled her to her feet.

"Let's take this upstairs."

They hurried to his bedroom. As he started to undress her, Kelly felt herself getting tense. She reminded herself of what Griffith had promised her. No pressure. Just an experiment, which she had to admit was going really, really well.

He waited while she stepped out of her shoes. Her pants followed, as did her bikini briefs. She was about to point out that while she was completely naked, he was still dressed, only he startled her by dropping to his knees.

The movement was so unexpected, she didn't know how to react. Before she could ask what was going on, he eased her legs apart, leaned close and kissed her. *There!*

Her breath caught. Yes, Sven had done that a couple of times and her college boyfriend had, too, but not for very long and never in that position. There was something about standing, or trying to stay standing while he licked her.

The sensation was delicious—more hint than full-on contact. She parted her legs a little more and wanted to hang on to something, only she was standing in the middle of the room, with no furniture around and grabbing onto Griffith's head seemed rude.

So she did her best to stay balanced as his tongue darted forward and back, lightly touching the very center of her. With each teasing second of contact, desire zinged through her, making it harder and harder for her to stay standing.

She swayed a little bit and had to consciously steady herself. Her muscles were far more interested in what was happening between her legs than in anything else, forcing her to point out that falling would not be pleasant for any of them.

She tried parting her legs more, wanting him to get to it, but nothing about his movements changed. The silly little whispers of his tongue on her clit made her groan and strain toward him. But it seemed as she moved closer, he moved away.

"Griffith," she breathed.

"Yes or no?" he asked.

"Yes."

"Good."

He stood and pulled off his shirt and jeans, but left on his briefs. She waited for him to move toward the bed, but instead he circled behind her and began kissing his way along her shoulders. His fingers moved from her hips to just below her breasts. They circled without touching anything good. One hand moved down and played between her legs, but again, on the periphery.

Need grew until her blood heated. She felt restless and achy. She knew what she wanted and that it wouldn't happen, but still. He could try. She wanted him to try.

She squirmed to get closer, but he was behind her and there was nowhere to go. She felt his erection against her rear—at least she knew he was as affected as she was, and while that was comforting, it didn't do anything for the tension building inside of her.

Finally, when she thought she was going to have to scream instructions, they moved to the bed. He touched every inch of her body, except where it really mattered. He stroked her arms, her cheeks, behind her knees. He tickled her feet, rubbed her thighs. He danced along her rib cage, her collarbone. He kissed her mouth but he didn't even bump into her breasts.

She felt herself starting to go mad. Her breathing came in pants as need thundered. She was aroused to the point of pain and the man wasn't doing anything. She wanted to grab him and shake him. She wanted to—

He nudged her wrist, moving her hand until her fingers rested on her upper thigh. She snatched it back and opened her eyes.

"Griffith," she began.

"Feedback loop."

"What?"

"You'll get a feedback loop. I won't. We're experimenting, remember. You said it was okay."

Her cheeks were on fire. "Not to do *that*."

"Give me three minutes, then we'll stop. Please. It's important to me."

She started to tell him she couldn't possibly. She'd never done that by herself, let alone in front of someone. Okay, that wasn't entirely true. A couple of times in college, she'd tried it and nothing had happened, so she'd given up. She simply wasn't built like everyone else and she was fine with that.

He pressed his hand on top of hers, moving her fingers in a slow circle. The pressure on her swollen clit captured her attention and she found herself minding slightly less that this was happening. Her eyes closed.

"Maybe faster," he whispered. "Or a bigger circle. You play. I want to do this."

This turned out to be slipping a finger inside of her. She liked how he moved in and out of her, how he went a little faster, then slower as if he were trying to keep time with…

Holy crap! She was doing it. She was touching herself. That was what he was trying to keep tempo with. Her! Because while she'd been thinking about him moving his finger in and out, she'd started rubbing, searching for the right rhythm that would… Okay, not make her come, but would feel the best.

She rubbed a little harder, feeling the very base of her swollen clit. She parted her legs and pushed down as Griffith slipped in again. There was something just out of reach. A feeling or sensation or promise. She wasn't sure she could get there, but she was determined to try until she couldn't anymore.

Her muscles tensed. Her breathing quickened. She didn't want to stop—not ever. She was terrified Griffith would get bored or have a cramp and if he did…if he did…

He shifted slightly and she nearly cried out to beg him not to move. Only then she felt his tongue on her breast. He licked the very tip of her nipple before drawing it in his mouth and sucking so deeply that the pleasure all connected from her breast to between her legs to the rest of her body. It filled her and awed her and made her—

There! She saw the goal. For the first time ever, she could understand what she was reaching for.

"I'm close!" she gasped. "Oh, Griffith, it's right there."

He didn't change anything. Not by a flicker of a lash did he stop what he was doing. She could barely breathe as she waited, moving her hand around and around—not faster, not slower, just the same. She waited and waited and just when she was sure it was never going to—

Her orgasm claimed her with a roar. It started in the very center of her and spread out like wildfire. It burned through every cell, leaving her gasping and crying and begging. She never wanted this amazing, wonderful feeling to stop. She wanted it to go on and on, but even as the thought formed, she felt the pleasure beginning to fade. Seconds later, it was gone, but in its place was a sense of relaxation and contentment unlike anything she'd ever known. It had finally, finally happened!

She opened her eyes and found Griffith watching her.

"Damn, you're hot. I nearly lost it a couple of times just watching you get close." His expression softened. "I felt it, too, Kelly. When you were coming. I could feel your muscles contracting. It was the best."

She couldn't seem to stop smiling. "It was. Can we do it again? Do you think I can? What about with you inside? Can I come that way?"

"Let's find out."

She nodded eagerly. She wanted to find out a lot of things. Could she come with him going down on her, or with him touching her? What about all those fun movie scenes? Could they re-create them? Ooh, what about her being on top?

She waited eagerly while he slipped on the condom, then guided him inside of her. He filled her completely, sending little jolts all through her body.

"Touch yourself," he said as he withdrew and pushed in again. "We know that works. Later we'll try other stuff, but for now, let's see if we can get you over the edge again."

"Okay." She moved her hand into place, not the least bit embarrassed anymore. She'd had an orgasm. She might have another. Honestly, normal had never looked so good.

25

Olivia prepared for her meeting with Kelly the way she would with any other prospective client. She did her research, organized a presentation and dressed for success. In this case, she had on black pants, flats and a lightweight sweater twinset. She was, after all, going to a working farm. A dress and heels would look ridiculous.

She was nervous—possibly more so because she was going to speak with her sister. Game face was required and she was determined to make a good impression. Luck was on her side— Marilee was out, allowing Olivia to leave the house without answering questions.

As she drove to the farm, she wondered what was going on with her mother. Marilee was gone a lot of the time but never mentioned where she went. Olivia wondered if she was hooking up with former lovers, then figured that wasn't anything she needed to know. Hopefully Marilee would get whatever she'd come home for and go back to Phoenix. Having her around was too uncomfortable.

At some point, they were going to have to have a conversation about Olivia quitting, and that was unlikely to go very well. Olivia's plan was to wait until they were both back in Phoenix, then hand in her letter of resignation. She would be packed up and ready to drive north so if her mother threw a fit, she could simply escape without looking back. There was an equal chance that her mother would be totally calm, explaining how she was minutes from firing Olivia and the resignation simply saved her the trouble. With Marilee, one never knew.

Olivia arrived at the farm and parked. Her dad's truck was gone, meaning he was, as well. Better and better. She and Kelly were less likely to be interrupted.

She went inside and found her sister sitting at her computer. Kelly smiled when she saw her.

"You're here. We had an appointment, right?" Kelly giggled. "We're sisters, Olivia. You didn't have to make an appointment."

Olivia came to a stop. "What's wrong?" she asked, then realized what she meant was *what's different?* Because something was.

Kelly appeared…softer. Okay, that wasn't the word, but it was close. Or maybe dreamy was better. Her eyes were a little unfocused, her skin flushed. She looked happy and content and just a little rumpled.

"I'm fine," Kelly told her. "A little tired. I got in late but I'm drinking coffee."

The smile returned. It was both knowing and timeless. Wow—whatever Griffith was doing, he was doing it right, Olivia thought. Of course she probably looked exactly like that after one of her sessions with Sven. The difference being Kelly and Griffith were dating, and she and Sven were, well, not dating.

Work, she told herself. She could deal with her non-relationship with Sven later.

Olivia sat across from her sister and set her faithful tote on her lap. "I made the appointment so we could talk about a few things."

Kelly smiled her smug I-got-some smile. "Whatever it is, I'll say yes."

"Yeah, I'm going to pretend you didn't say that." Olivia pulled out several sheets of paper. "Information for background purposes and you might want to brace yourself."

"I'm braced."

Olivia cleared her throat. "I'm not going back to Phoenix. I want to move back here. Permanently." She held up a hand. "You don't have to worry—I'm going to get my own place. I have savings so I won't be at Dad's too long. Mom and Dad don't know. I'm going to tell Dad privately, but I want to wait until Mom goes back to Phoenix and tell her there. It will be easier, I think."

Which sounded way more mature than her plan to resign and run.

Kelly's eyes widened and her smile broadened. "That's fantastic! I'm so excited. I can't wait to have you around all the time."

Olivia waited for the punch line. While she'd been fairly sure her sister wouldn't be overly pissed by the news, she hadn't imagined such…enthusiasm.

"Are you sure you're all right?"

"I'm fantastic, as is the news. Yay us."

"You're freaking me out a little."

"You'll have to deal." Kelly sighed. "Maybe we can get matching charm bracelets or something that we both wear."

"No. That's not happening."

"I'm just saying it could be nice."

"Not. Happening." Maybe her sister was hormonal from her period or something, Olivia thought. Whatever the cause, she'd slipped over the edge. "Anyway, I'm going to have to find a way to support myself here. Rather than look for a full-time job, which probably doesn't exist, I've decided to take on a few different projects and see where they lead me. The, ah, tourism board meeting you're going to is partially about me. Sally and Hannah want me to manage the craft mall. It's only a few hours a week, but I think I could—"

Before she could finish her statement, Kelly jumped to her feet and raced around her desk. She hugged Olivia, kissed her cheek, then hugged her again.

"It's perfect," she announced as she returned to her chair. "You'll do so great and we all know the craft mall needs some direction. Okay, so that's one of your jobs, what else?"

Olivia explained how she'd approached Griffith.

"He'll love everything you do," her sister said firmly. "You're in. I'm sure of it. What else?" Her eyes widened. "Oh, you have some ideas for me. Great. What are they?"

Olivia had hoped for an open mind, but maybe not one that was hanging out in the breeze.

"You're not taking any medication, are you?"

Kelly laughed. "Not even ibuprofen, I swear."

"All right, then I've been thinking of ways to bring more tourists to town in the off-season. I mentioned the planting before. I know you have your machines and your methods, but I think people would get a kick out of planting part of a field. However many bulbs they planted would mean they could come back and pick that many flowers in the spring, ensuring a return visit. I would also suggest you offer tours of the greenhouses on weekends. What you do there is really interesting."

"I don't know. It's bulbs in a bin. I care about it but does anyone else?"

"I think people will. Most of us don't think about where our food and flowers come from. You always have plants at some part of the growing cycle. We could include your private greenhouse on the tour. Visitors could learn about what you do there."

"They couldn't touch anything," Kelly said firmly.

"Easily managed. There would be a tour guide. I could be the first one. I could write up the material and figure out what people were most interested in. I'm thinking the charge would be fairly nominal. Unless you wanted to hook up with another business in town that sells something. Like a bakery or winery. We could have a tasting at the end and the charge could be a little higher."

She glanced at her notes. "If you're interested, I think we

should have some kind of gift shop where our visitors can buy tulip products. A few things that will remind them of the visit. T-shirts, fresh flowers, hot pads. All easy to customize."

Kelly's faraway look had returned. "I love gift shops. We should so have one."

Olivia had more to discuss. How the town needed to look at things like movie or music festivals and coordinating events between businesses, but this was obviously not the day. Whatever was going on with her sister had messed with her head.

"I've written up some notes and a proposal," she said, setting the folder on her sister's desk. "I'm going to follow up with you in a few days."

"I'd love that." Kelly's smile returned. "You're just so pretty."

Olivia nodded as she glanced toward the exit. "Ah, thanks. I'm going to go now."

"Thank *you* for coming by. Could you let Dad know I won't be home for dinner? I'm going to see Griffith later." She giggled. "He's my boyfriend."

"So I heard."

She made her escape, then paused by her car. To be completely honest, she wasn't sure what to think about her sister. Either she should think about getting a vaccination or maybe start drinking the water. She just couldn't decide.

Griffith figured that by any description, he was the man. He'd righted the ship, so to speak, pleased his woman in ways no one had before. He was good. No, he was better than good—he was a god among men—at least for now.

"You're not listening," Sven complained.

Griffith turned his attention back to the garden layout Sven proposed for the tiny house that was being delivered next week. They'd also agreed on some plants to spruce up the future showroom. He'd already decided to take the space. He wanted things to work out with Olivia, but even if they couldn't come to terms, her idea about a dedicated showroom had been a good one. He liked the idea of having samples on site. The space would also give him a permanent area to discuss designs, rather than trying to fit his clients into his sometimes messy office.

"How tall will they grow?" he asked, pointing to several bushes in pots.

"Not more than five feet. They'll flank the front door. I wouldn't recommend them for a house on wheels, but this one is permanent. If your customers prefer, they can be planted in the ground, but the pots add a visual element to the front of the house."

"I wouldn't have thought you were a 'visual element' kind of guy."

"I have hidden depths." Sven grinned.

Maybe, but he hadn't been able to please Kelly, Griffith thought, trying to keep from looking smug. That had been all him.

After the first time, they'd made love over and over again. Kelly had come more easily each time, and more vocally. His quiet farmer girl, it turned out, was a bit of screamer.

She'd been eager to try everything he could think of. Apparently figuring out how to have an orgasm had done the trick. From that moment on, she'd come pretty much every time they'd tried. Orally, with him inside of her, with her on top. He'd finally had to plead exhaustion, while she seemed ready to keep going forever.

It was, he admitted to himself, the absolute best problem ever.

"Hey, we're out of some of the plumbing fixtures."

Griffith turned and saw Ryan standing in the doorway to his office. His brother looked sullen and unhappy, as if being forced to speak.

"Leo's not here," Ryan added, his tone grudging. "I figured someone should know."

"Thanks for telling me. I'll find out what happened with the order."

His best guess was the replacement parts had arrived, but hadn't been unpacked yet. They were experiencing yet another increase in production and were at that awkward place of needing to hire more people. Yet another reason to get the showroom. He could move a lot of things over there, including his office. That would free up more space for building.

"Whatever," Ryan muttered, then left.

"Someone's not happy," Sven said. "He resents that he needs the job."

"He was meant for better things, at least in his mind."

"He has to find his way." Sven closed his laptop. "Is he still seeing Autumn?"

"I have no idea. Why?"

His friend avoided his gaze. "No reason. Just curious. Did you sell your tickets?"

"Jeez, yes." He held up his hand. "All of them."

Sven had insisted Griffith get rid of twenty tickets to the fund-raiser for the craft mall. Rather than deal with trying to find people who were willing to shell out the money to go, he'd bought them all himself, then given them away.

"Good. Olivia wants every seat full."

Griffith started to ask why Sven cared that much about Olivia, only to put the pieces together. "You and Olivia?" he asked.

Sven shook his head. "We're just friends."

Griffith thought about the question about Ryan's dating life. "It doesn't sound like friends."

"I can't help that."

He had another, less pleasant thought. "Does Kelly know?" he asked, only to realize it wasn't a question he wanted answered.

"There's nothing to know, but she wouldn't care. We should never have stayed together as long as we did. It wasn't right for either of us. How are things with the two of you?"

"Ah, good."

Better than good, but a gentleman didn't kiss and tell…so to speak.

He and Sven finished their business and the other man left. At five, the crews packed it up and headed out. Close to five thirty, Griffith closed his spreadsheet program and reached for his phone. He wanted to find out if Kelly wanted to get together tonight.

Before he could start his text, he heard footsteps in the warehouse. He left his office and saw Kelly walking toward him.

She'd come directly from the farm. She had on jeans, a short-sleeved T-shirt and work boots, all of which made her the sexiest woman ever. When she saw him, she smiled and quickened her step. He grinned and rushed forward. They met by the display home and hung on to each other.

"I missed you," he told her.

"Good, because I've been thinking about you all day."

"Me, or just my penis?"

She laughed. "Both."

They stared at each other. He felt the familiar heat explode inside. Her eyes darkened, even as she dropped a hand between them and rubbed his rapidly hardening erection.

"Is everyone gone?" she asked.

"They are."

"Good."

His mouth claimed hers as his mind searched frantically for the best place. His office? Acceptable but not overly original. Plus, the desk was a mess and the floor was too dirty. The front seat of his truck might work but it was still daylight outside and pulling it into the warehouse would take too much time. As it was, Kelly already had her shirt off. Her bra followed.

He put his hands on her breasts and stroked the way she liked. Her head fell back and she moaned.

He caught sight of the tiny house display and decided it would work. There was a small sofa and—

"Griffith, I really need you now," Kelly whispered. "Seriously, I'm dying here."

He pushed her to the tiny house. She stripped off the rest of her clothes faster than he would have thought possible, then helped him with his. At the last second, she pulled a condom out of her jeans pocket.

"I stopped at the store on the way here," she told him.

"Pretty and smart. Have I mentioned there's not one thing I don't like about you?"

"Thank you. I feel the same way."

They tumbled onto the sofa. Griffith sent up a mental apology to all the people who would sit there later, then slipped on the condom before finding his way home.

As he filled her, she wrapped her legs around him and pulled him in deeper.

"Just like that," she breathed, flexing her hips in rhythm with his movement.

Seconds later Kelly was clutching him, her eyes open, her breathing fast. "Now," she told him right before she began to climax. "Griffith, yes, yes. Yes!"

He watched her eyes glaze over and felt the rapid contractions. He went with her, filling her over and over until he lost himself in his own release.

When they were done, she followed him to the private bathroom off his office. When Kelly reached for her clothes, he stopped her.

"Give me a second," he told her. "I want to etch this moment in my memory so every time I'm in this room, I think of you standing there, naked."

She smiled and slipped a hand between her legs. "Want to picture me doing this?"

His dick stirred. Griffith swore. "You're deadly." He pulled her close and kissed her. "Can we go back to my place?"

"I have a tourism board meeting, but I can meet you at your house after that."

"I'm in."

"Good." She kissed him back before sighing. "I was thinking we could do it with you behind me. Think of all the things you could reach. Oh, and I want to go down on you tonight. I did some reading online and there are interesting techniques I've never tried."

Griffith had no idea why he'd won the sexual lottery, but he sure as hell wasn't going to complain. He kissed her again, then wrapped his arms around her. Emotions stirred. Emotions he wouldn't name or even acknowledge. They weren't part of the deal and he knew better than to try something he wasn't good at.

Kelly felt like Cinderella in the classic Disney movie—at any moment little birds were going to fly down from the sky and start singing and talking with her. She felt giddy and silly and happy and many other words ending with the letter *Y*.

In her sensible moments, she told herself it was just sex. What she was feeling wasn't real—it was hormones generated by dozens of orgasms. She was drunk on sex and smart enough to know that while she liked Griffith, she shouldn't confuse her climax-induced high with real feelings.

Still, the sky was bluer, the sun warmer and everyone she ran into was just so nice. She was going to go with the sense of well-being for as long as it lasted. And if a few woodland creatures smiled at her along the way, that was okay, too.

She pulled into the parking lot of the craft mall. The tourism board had a big pre-fund-raiser meeting that night. Two days before, Olivia had been voted as the new mall manager, something that had made Kelly feel oddly proud.

She made her way back to the community room and waved

when she saw Helen was already there. "I haven't seen you in forever," she said as she settled next to her friend. "How are you? How are things?"

Helen stared at her. "What happened?" She leaned close. "Are you glowing?"

Kelly felt herself blush. "Um, Olivia has me using some special products. There's a nightly peel. It really works. I'll get you the name."

Which was the best lie she could think of on such short notice. Ack! Now she was going to have to find a peel and buy it because there was no way she was going to admit her skin was dewy from all the sex she was having.

"Please. We should all look as good as you. So what's new?"

Kelly had to consciously press her lips together to keep from blurting out the truth. She loved Helen and they were close but there was no way she was going to admit her former "problem" to anyone.

"The usual," Kelly said as casually as she could. "Work, family crap. Things are good with Griffith."

"What family crap?" Helen's voice was sharp. "Your mom?"

A few of her happy bubbles popped. "Don't remind me and yes. Marilee is still everywhere. Sometimes she tries to be nice, which makes it all worse. I have no idea how long she's staying. Oh, and the other morning, she was wearing one of Dad's pajama tops. WTF? I have no idea what happened there."

Helen stared at her. "Do you think… Are they…" She cleared her throat. "Are they back together?"

"No." Kelly grimaced. "At least I hope not. Then she'll never leave. I've got to believe he's smarter than that. It's been thirteen years and she was awful to him when they were married. Why would he give her a second chance?"

"Men can be stupid sometimes. She's very beautiful."

"I know, right? But not my dad." Kelly didn't like thinking about the two of them together. "I wish he'd call her a bitch or something, but he won't. He's so reasonable about everything. It's annoying."

Olivia joined them. "Hey," she said. "How's it going?" She looked at Kelly. "Someone's rarely home these days. Mom or your hot boyfriend?"

"Both," Kelly admitted. "I sleep at home—I just get in late."

"Really late." Olivia turned to Helen. "Are you okay?"

Kelly saw that her friend had gone pale.

"I'm fine." Helen managed a wobbly smile. "It's my time of the month and I'm cramping."

Olivia fished a small makeup bag out of her tote. "I have some ibuprofen in here," she murmured. "One or two?"

"Two, please."

Olivia passed them over. Helen swallowed them dry.

"We were talking about Mom," Kelly told her sister. "I was complaining Dad won't say anything bad about her. You don't think they're getting back together, do you?"

"Of course not." Olivia wrinkled her nose. "Jeez, that would be awful. No. I don't think he would ever trust her again." She hesitated.

"What?" Kelly demanded. "You're thinking something."

"Just that Marilee still has a way with men. She pretty much gets whoever she wants. Guys find her sexy and appealing. There was this one time when—" Olivia pressed her lips together. "Oh, goody."

Kelly turned and saw Marilee walking into the community room. Her formfitting dress and high heels were out of place for the meeting, as were her perfect makeup and diamond earrings. Conversation stilled as everyone watched her make her way to her daughters.

"Hello, girls," Marilee said cheerfully. "I thought I'd come and see what you two were up to." She turned to Helen. "Hello. I'm Marilee, Jeff's wife. You must be Helen."

"Ex-wife," Kelly corrected, then frowned. "How do you

know who she is?" She and Helen had become friends as adults, long after Marilee had left town thirteen years ago.

"Oh, your father's mentioned her a few times." Marilee's smile relaxed. "I was expecting someone…different, but I see you're nothing like that."

Helen sucked in a breath and rose. "If you'll excuse me, I'm not feeling well."

Kelly stood. "Want me to drive you home?"

"No. I just need to, ah, lie down with a heating pad. I'll be fine."

Kelly hugged her. "Call me if you need anything."

"I will." Helen waved and left.

Kelly sat down, then looked at her mother. Had something just happened? Was there more going on than she realized? Before she could figure it out, Olivia pulled her tablet and a stack of handouts from her tote.

"We're okay on ticket sales," she murmured. "I have donations. The fund-raiser is going to be a huge success."

Marilee rolled her eyes. "You don't actually care, do you? You're never going to see this ridiculous little town again. Why does it matter if it's a success or not?"

"If it's so awful here, why do you stay?" Kelly asked, doing her best to make her voice as sweet as possible.

Marilee's expression turned knowing. "I would have thought that was obvious, darling. Your father is a very handsome man. I've missed him."

Kelly snorted. "Yeah, right. That's why you cheated, then left him. Am I missing anything?" She thought of the meeting she'd gone to with her dad the year after she graduated from college. The one that explained the structure of the farm and the family-held corporation that owned it. "Just so you know, you're still not eligible to claim any part of the business. The prenup was solid."

Marilee's smile twisted as her eyes narrowed. "Did he tell you that?"

"No, Mom. The lawyer did."

"There was a prenup?" Olivia asked, spinning to stare at Marilee. "Daddy made you sign that when you were pregnant?"

"Impressive, huh?" Kelly asked.

Marilee stood. "Be careful, girls. I'm a lot better at this than either of you." With that she turned and walked out.

Kelly shivered. "I want to say I don't care, but she's scary."

"Tell me about it." Olivia glanced at her notes. "On the bright side, I'm a lot less nervous about my presentation now."

"A death threat has a way of serving as a nice distraction."

"Tell me about it."

26

Helen's fake cramps faded as soon as she got home but the nausea lingered. She paced the length of her small house, trying to collect her thoughts or convince herself she'd misunderstood what Marilee had said, only she couldn't do either. The insult had been clear.

You're nothing like that. Whatever Marilee had meant, it wasn't good. Or nice. Or pleasant or any other positive word. Helen had a feeling what the beautiful ex-Mrs. Jeffrey Murphy had meant was fat. Or maybe fat and ugly. Because Marilee had taken one look at her and known everything. That Helen was in love with Jeff, that Jeff hadn't declared himself beyond wanting to sleep with her, and that Marilee was a threat.

While she was willing to admit she might be giving the other woman too much credit, Helen knew Marilee had figured out something. Otherwise, why bother to attack?

Helen decided she had to change the mental subject or go crazy. She walked over to the piano, then backed away. She was too agitated to play.

Her phone chirped. She looked at the screen and saw a text from Jeff.

You around? Want company?

Questions that made her both excited and nervous. Did she really want to see him after her close encounter? Was she too vulnerable?

"Maybe this is a good time to get answers," she muttered as she texted back a single, Yes.

She raced to the bathroom to check on her makeup, then spent five minutes trying to decide if she should change her clothes or not. If anything fun was on the menu, then an outfit slightly more accessible than jeans and a sleeveless shirt that buttoned could be a good idea, but under the circumstances, fun seemed unlikely.

She'd barely made her decision when she heard a knock on the front door. One of the downsides of living in a small town, she thought. It didn't take long to get anywhere.

She opened the door and let him in. As usual, Jeff looked too good to be true and just staring into his brown eyes had her heart and resolve both melting. He handed her a bottle of red wine and a box of brownies from a bakery she liked in Maryville, which meant he'd made a special trip to get them. She happened to know they closed at four, which meant he'd made that special trip earlier today.

Not sure what to do with that information, she crossed to the kitchen. "Want to open the wine?" she asked.

When he didn't answer, she turned to glance at him.

He stood just inside the kitchen, his arms at his side. But what really caught her attention was the stricken look in his eyes. Her melty heart froze. No. No! He was going to tell her he'd slept with Marilee. These weren't let's have sex brownies, they were an apology.

"Jeff?" She was proud of herself for being able to speak that single word. She wasn't totally broken. "What is it?"

He sucked in a breath. "I miss you, Helen. Every second of every day. I hate this. I hate having that woman in my house. I know it's important for my girls, but dammit all to hell I want her gone and I want to be back in your bed."

Time stood still long enough for her to indulge in an internal happy dance. She silently shrieked her victory call and gave the virtual finger to Marilee before crossing to the man who looked both hopeful and chagrined.

"Why didn't you say so?" she asked before leading him down the hall.

Kelly and Olivia walked into The Beer Garden shortly before seven thirty. Jeff and Helen's newest band project was making their debut here instead of at the community room in the craft mall. She hoped the music lived up to the improved venue.

She and her sister found a small table in the back, then each ordered a glass of wine. Olivia leaned back in her chair and sighed. "I'm exhausted. The fund-raiser is keeping me busy and avoiding Mom is an additional time suck. It seems like every time I turn around, she wants to have a heart-to-heart."

Not a problem Kelly had been having, she thought. So far Marilee had kept her distance and Kelly preferred it that way. She still wasn't sure how she felt about Olivia's confession on the mother front.

"Did she offer you the job while you were still in college?" she asked.

"Sort of. It was more of an understanding over time. She would talk about how things would be when I came to work for her." Olivia shifted in her seat. "Don't take this wrong, but I thought it was nice that she wanted me around, you know? She was there for me, or so I thought."

Kelly was fairly sure that Olivia's explanation should be taken at face value, even though that didn't erase the slight slap at the reminder of what had happened.

"At first it was great," Olivia continued. "We hung out, she helped me find my first apartment. Well, it took me a while to catch on to that. She helped me with my clothes and makeup. I felt so sophisticated and together and there I was, all of twenty-3o."

The server dropped off their wine. Kelly held up her glass. "To making interesting choices."

They touched glasses.

Olivia set hers back on the table. "I went to visit Ryan a couple of times," she confessed. "In the off-season. We had a great time, but he had no interest in moving to Phoenix and he never exactly asked me to stay, so I felt stuck."

"I didn't think you were seeing him. Isn't he with—" Kelly stopped herself in time and sipped her wine. "I mean how nice if you two get back together."

Olivia rolled her eyes. "You are the least subtle person I know. I have no idea if he's with Autumn or not and I sort of don't care. It's so strange—he's one of the reasons I came back this summer. I wanted closure with him. At first I was so hurt and pissed that he'd told me to come see him while he was dating someone else. But now I can't seem to summon any interest in him. He's just some guy I used to know."

"So it's over?"

"Yes." Olivia looked surprised, then grinned. "It's completely and totally over. How great is that?" She drank some wine. "I wonder if it's like that for Mom. If Dad is her Ryan and she's always wondered what would have happened." Her humor faded. "Of course she had a great marriage and totally blew it all on her own. There's a difference."

Kelly hated thinking that her parents might rekindle the flame, so to speak. While she wanted her dad to find someone and be happy, Marilee was not that person.

"You really don't know why she's here?" Kelly asked.

"Not a clue. She and her previous boyfriend aren't together, so that could be part of it. She might be hoping to get some money from Dad. Whatever's motivating her can't be good."

The band took their place on the small stage. They were all in their twenties and thirties but Kelly knew from experience that age didn't matter when it came to how bad a group could be. As far as she was concerned, guitars should come with warning labels and playing in public should require strict licensing.

"They look interesting," Olivia said, turning so she could see the stage more clearly.

"Ah, the optimism of youth."

"What are you—"

The band starting playing. It took Kelly a full minute to realize they were butchering OneRepublic's "Counting Stars." It was only when her dad and Helen joined in at the chorus that she could understand the words enough to pick out the tune.

When the song was over, there was a moment of stunned and grateful silence before everyone broke into applause. Olivia picked up her wine.

"I should have ordered something a lot stronger. How do you keep going to these?"

"They can be fun. Sometimes the bands aren't awful. Plus Dad and Helen usually have a duet and that's nice."

Four painfully played songs later, the band put down their instruments as Jeff moved closer to Helen. Three notes later, Kelly smiled.

"Helen does love the piano man," she told her sister as Helen and Jeff began to sing Billy Joel's "Just the Way You Are." She picked up her wine knowing she could relax for the next few minutes.

She glanced around the bar and saw most of the patrons looked equally relieved. Helen and Jeff were often the highlight of the showcases. She wondered if they'd ever thought of starting a band of their own. A good one that people wanted to listen to.

Olivia leaned toward her and laughed. "Okay, one worry we can let go."

"What are you talking about?"

Olivia pointed to the stage. "Them. There's no way Mom's getting Dad back in her bed. Not when he's so crazy about his girl. Why didn't you tell me about them? I would have slept a lot easier knowing we were safe from a parental reunion."

"What are you talking about?" Kelly asked, even as she looked at the couple performing.

Helen sat at the keyboard. Jeff stood close. Rather than look at the audience, they stared at each other. No. Not stared. There was a better word. Not gazed—it wasn't intense enough, but she couldn't think of anything that worked.

Helen finished her line and Jeff started singing his. Kelly had a feeling the rest of the room had disappeared and it was just the two of them. Although they weren't touching, the connection was obvious, as was the yearning. They looked like two people who couldn't wait to get back into bed together.

"I don't understand."

Kelly knew she'd spoken the words, but she had no memory of saying them. She couldn't think, couldn't make sense of any of it. Helen and her dad? It wasn't possible. Helen was her best friend. Her dad was...

She flinched as an image formed in her brain. No way. Her best friend could not be sleeping with her father. It was wrong. It was gross. But the proof was difficult to ignore.

Her stomach protested roiling emotions. Her heart gave a cry at the betrayal.

"Kelly?"

She saw her sister watching her.

"Are you okay?"

Kelly shook her head, then grabbed her bag and walked out of the bar. When she reached the parking lot, she realized Olivia had driven, so she didn't have her truck. Rather than go back inside, she started walking home. It was at least five miles but it wasn't as if she had somewhere else to be.

They'd lied. They'd both lied to her. Her father was less of

an issue—he'd never discussed his personal life. Kelly had assumed he had a girlfriend somewhere but if he didn't want to
talk about it, she was fine.

Helen was different. Helen was her friend. Her *best* friend.
They did everything together. When Sven had broken up with
her, Helen had been the first person she'd called. When Griffith
had shown interest, she'd told Helen. She'd thought Helen would
do the same with her. Was she wrong? Was it a one-sided friendship and she hadn't realized? How on earth could Helen not
have told her?

Kelly walked along the quiet road. She didn't know how far
she'd gone when a truck pulled up behind her. She turned and
saw Griffith getting out.

"Olivia texted and told me you were in trouble," he said as
he approached. When he reached her, he put his hands on her
shoulders. "Kelly, I'm the spectacular boyfriend, remember?
When you need something, I'm your first call."

She guessed he was trying to make her laugh, but in the last
few minutes, she'd forgotten how. She could only stare at him
and say, "Helen lied to me."

He drew her close. She went into his arms only to find herself
crying. She'd trusted Helen. She'd trusted her dad. What was
happening to everyone around her? Or was she the problem?

It took a few minutes, but she managed to pull herself together. When Griffith handed her a handkerchief, she was able
to summon a small chuckle.

"Is it the same one?"

"Probably."

She wiped her face. "At this rate, you're never going to believe
me when I once again say I don't really cry. It's not my thing."

He led her to the truck. "Come on. I'll take you back to your
place. You can pack a few things and spend the night with me."

"Thanks."

They pulled onto the road. Kelly stared out the passenger window.

"I don't get it," she said. "Why didn't Helen tell me? Has our friendship been a lie?"

Griffith didn't say anything. She glanced at him.

"You're thinking something."

"Maybe your reaction is the reason she didn't tell you."

His words, however true, stung. "I'm upset about the with-holding of information more than anything."

"Are you sure?"

She thought about the question. If Helen had come to her, what would she have said? She grimaced. "She's sleeping with my dad. That's gross."

Griffith was silent.

Kelly groaned. "I see your point. I should accept who my friend wants to hang out with. But it's my father. Come on. You have to admit there's an ick factor. Do you want to think about your parents having sex?"

"Nope."

"Helen and I talk about stuff. Intimate stuff."

"Did she know about you and Sven?"

It took Kelly a second to figure out what he meant. She flushed. "That I never climaxed?" She turned away. "I didn't mention that, no."

"Everyone keeps secrets, Kelly. Even you."

"I know, but…" She sighed. The mature response of a six-year-old. *Yes, but.*

He was right. They all had secrets, even Helen. Even her dad. She winced.

"I honestly have no idea what I'm supposed to think or tell her. The sex is part of it, and I get what you're saying about her worrying about what I would say or think, but still. She's with my dad and she never told me. This could have been going on for years. It makes our entire friendship a lie."

"You might want to reconsider that stance. You love Helen. She's a good friend and you'd miss her if things changed."

"I don't want things to change. I want them to go back to how they were."

Griffith was wise enough not to say anything and Kelly couldn't hide from what she hadn't said aloud. Things going back to how they'd been didn't mean how she thought they should be.

Sven ran his hands down Olivia's bare back. She lay on top of him, their bodies satiated, their breathing still ragged.

No matter how they made love, somehow they always ended up in this position—pressed tightly together. Around him she felt small and delicate. She supposed no matter how capable she wanted to be in the rest of her life, in bed with Sven she was safe enough to be feminine.

She sat up and straddled his waist, then pressed her hands on his chest. She could feel the power of his muscles. Now, like this, they blended together, but when he stood, they would be defined. He was a beautiful man, she thought absently.

"What are you thinking?" he asked.

"That I like looking at you."

He smiled. "I like looking at you, as well."

She groaned. "I'm sorry. I'm just not that comfortable prancing around naked after we have sex."

"I've never seen you prance." His eyebrows rose suggestively. "Can you demonstrate?"

She laughed and slid off the bed. "Not today, big guy." When she was standing, she stretched her arms up toward the ceiling, then bent over to press her palms flat on the floor. She shrieked when she felt teeth on her butt and spun to face him.

Sven shrugged. "I couldn't help myself. Open that." He pointed to the top dresser drawer.

Unexpected nerves fluttered in Olivia's chest as she crossed the carpet and pulled on the drawer. Inside it was empty except for a wrapped present the size of a shirt box. She returned to the bed and sat next to him.

"For me?"

He hesitated. "For both of us, I think."

While she was more than willing to try just about anything, she had to admit a sex toy would be just a little disappointing. She opened the box and saw he'd bought her lingerie. A light green lacy little thong with matching cropped T-shirt trimmed in the same lace.

"I like looking at your body," he said as he got out of bed. "You are uncomfortable naked. I thought this would please us both."

The unexpected gift was all the more precious because of his thoughtfulness.

"Thank you," she said, standing and giving him a quick kiss. "I love them both."

She pulled on the thong, then slipped on the T-shirt. The latter was way too low and tight, exposing more of her breasts than it covered, but she guessed that was the point. She turned slowly, wiggling her butt when her back was to him.

"What do you—"

Her sentence was cut off in a shriek as she found herself being flung onto the bed. Sven had her on her back in a nanosecond. Five minutes later, they were both on the edge of surrender.

"Remind me to buy you more lingerie," Sven said when they'd finished and were walking into the kitchen together.

She laughed. "It did seem to be a gift we could both enjoy."

She'd put her thong back on and felt both sexy and covered just enough to be comfortable. Sven was naked, although he tied an apron around his waist before he walked to the refrigerator. He collected marinating meat, cut-up watermelon, goat cheese and a few other ingredients. She set the table. When she was done, she settled on a stool by the island to watch him cook.

He'd already diced red onion and jalapenos. He had a couple of avocados by his cutting board. Watermelon and goat cheese salad went into a serving bowl next to a loaf of crusty French bread. Her stomach growled.

"Your cooking is possibly your second-best skill," she teased.

"I'm glad you think so." He poured orange juice into a tall, thin glass, added a single sugar cube, then filled it with champagne before passing it to her.

"You spoil me."

"I like making you happy."

An unusual and exciting characteristic in a man, she thought. He was nothing like the other men she'd known. Ryan was a complete selfish bastard when it came to anything—even sex. Or maybe that was "especially sex." All of which begged the question of why on earth she'd come home for him. She looked at Sven. Of course there had been compensations. He was one of them, as was reconnecting with her family.

Speaking of which… "Kelly's being a total butthead." She told him what had happened at the bar and how her sister had bolted. "Helen noticed. She looked upset. I'm not sure if I should stop by and talk to her. She's much more Kelly's friend than mine."

Sven stared at her. "Helen and Jeff?"

"Uh-huh."

He thought for a second. "I can see it. She's very beautiful and he's strong. She needs someone strong."

"You think Helen is beautiful?"

"Of course. Why are you surprised?"

Olivia felt trapped. "You're so into fitness," she hedged.

"You thought I'd judge her because she's heavy?"

"Maybe."

He shocked her by flashing a grin. "I doubt there's a man around who hasn't imagined what it would be like to have her in his bed. Her breasts, her hips. Who wouldn't want that?"

Olivia stood and put her hands on her hips. "Excuse me?"

He put down his spatula and crossed to her. "I am faithful, Olivia. I always have been. You're my woman. But when I was single, I briefly considered Helen before coming to the conclusion we were better as friends." He kissed her. "She'll be good for your dad and he'll be good for her."

She was still caught up in him calling her his woman. Was she? Were they? The possibility made her just the tiniest bit giddy.

"At least I don't have to worry about my parents getting back together," she said as he returned to the stove. "But Kelly is going to have to get over it."

"She's never liked change."

"Tell me about it." She sipped her mimosa. "So, big guy, who else did you consider to be your woman?"

"You want a list?"

"Yes, please. I need to go check out the competition."

"Jealous?"

She smiled. "Maybe just a little."

"Good."

27

Helen couldn't remember the last time she'd been in a fight with a girlfriend. Junior high? Earlier? She wasn't the kind of person who enjoyed conflict and even as a kid, she'd gone quiet rather than make trouble. That went a long way to explaining why it had taken her forever to confess anything close to her feelings for Jeff. But the stress of them finally getting together followed by his ex-wife moving into his house had both exhausted her and shown her the error of her ways. To make things better, she needed to be proactive, which was why after two days of not hearing from her friend, she made the decision to confront Kelly directly.

Helen hadn't realized anything was wrong until the end of her session with Jeff and the band. Kelly had left early, but Helen hadn't thought anything of it until Olivia had teased her about being with Jeff. Apparently their duet had given away their secret.

Jeff had said to give Kelly time to come to terms with what had happened. His advice had made sense, so she'd done as he'd suggested, but by this morning she'd realized the problem was bigger than either she or Jeff had realized. She and Kelly never went more than twenty-four hours without at least texting each other. The silence, to resort to a cliché, was deafening.

Helen drove to the farm and parked next to her friend's truck. She walked purposefully to Kelly's office and forced herself to simply go in without allowing herself a second to hesitate or chicken out. She was determined to be the adult in the room, and if she didn't feel especially grown-up, then she would fake it.

Kelly looked up as she entered. Her entire body stiffened and she glanced around, as if looking for an escape.

"I thought we should talk," Helen said, doing her best to sound friendly rather than sick to her stomach. She'd suspected Kelly was upset, but seeing her best friend so uncomfortable was disheartening.

"Okay." The single word was clipped. Kelly motioned to the chair by her desk. "You first."

There wasn't any give there, no sense of "Hey, we've known each other forever."

"I'm sorry you're upset with me," Helen began, only to have Kelly cut her off.

"You can't be serious. You're sorry I'm upset with you? That's it? Not that you're sorry you lied to me? You're dating my father." She slapped her hands on the desk. "No. You're *sleeping* with my father. You and my father have sex. You're supposed to be my best friend, Helen. I trusted you. I loved you. I thought you had my back. But none of that is true, is it? How could you keep a secret like that from me? It makes everything we were a sham."

Helen's eyes filled with tears. Her chest was tight and she was afraid she was going to throw up.

"Don't," she whispered. "Don't say that."

"Say what? That I don't know who you are anymore? Do you know what it's been like around here? First Olivia. She never said she and our mother were practically roommates. She'd been in touch with her for years and didn't say a word. Then Marilee shows up and that's been its own brand of hell and now this." Her gaze sharpened. "You've been sleeping with my father and didn't tell me. What else have you kept from me? And what the hell were you thinking? He's my dad—you're my best friend. It's disgusting."

Helen honestly didn't know where to start and even figuring that out, she had no idea what to say. *I didn't mean to lie to you?* Only she had lied—for years. There were reasons, but she wasn't sure they mattered.

A thousand thoughts flashed through her brain. They were all stupid or wrong or defensive. She supposed what it came down to was how she felt about her friend. Kelly was important and she'd let Kelly down.

"I didn't know how to tell you I was in love with your father," she admitted, her voice soft and shaky.

Kelly's eyes widened. "You're in love with him? It's not just sex?"

"Not for me." Helen brushed away tears. "Come on. Let's be real. I'm the one who hasn't dated since the divorce. I don't know how to date, and if a guy ever gets around to asking me out, I'm just a disaster." She swallowed against the tightness in the throat. "I'm sorry for hurting you and for keeping it a secret. I've been in love with Jeff for a couple of years now, only I didn't know how to tell him, or if he would care. I couldn't figure out what he thought of me. A few weeks ago, I just kind of went for it." She pressed her lips together, not wanting to say too much. "He doesn't know I'm in love with him."

She wanted to ask Kelly to not to mention that part to her dad, but figured her friend didn't feel all that loyal right now.

"Why didn't you say something?" Kelly demanded. "You never once hinted."

"Why do you think? I was scared."

"Of me?"

Helen shrugged. "Of what you'd think and say. What if you told me he secretly thought I was awful? What if you disapproved? What if you weren't willing to be my friend anymore? When Jeff and I finally took things to the, ah, next level, we both agreed not to make it public for a while. Not until we knew what was happening. But before we could get that far,

Marilee showed up and it's all a mess and you're mad and I never wanted to hurt you."

More tears fell. Helen covered her face with her hands. Kelly was silent for a long time, then a desk drawer opened and Kelly pushed a box of tissues toward her.

"I don't like that you didn't tell me," Kelly admitted. "It feels weird. Like you had this whole secret life I didn't know about."

"Would you have been more comfortable knowing I was crushing on your father?"

Kelly winced. "Probably not." She hesitated. "You really think he's hot?" She held up her hand. "No. Please don't answer that. I don't want to know. I'm not sure how to integrate my best friend having sex with my father."

"Probably best not to go there." Helen wiped her face and blew her nose. "If it makes you feel any better, I've been in hell since your mom showed up."

"It doesn't, which I guess makes me a decent person." Kelly sighed. "I don't know what to think or feel or anything. Everyone is keeping secrets."

"I'm sorry about mine."

"Thank you. I want to say it's okay, but I still don't know."

Not exactly the answer Helen wanted to hear, but it wasn't as if she could push or anything.

"I understand."

"I just need some time." Kelly sounded defensive. "I'm not saying anything is different, but it's a lot to think about."

"Sure." Helen rose. "I'll talk to you soon."

Kelly nodded.

Helen walked back to her car. She felt as if a pile of rocks were sitting in her stomach. Kelly might not be willing to admit that anything was different, but Helen knew everything had changed. What she didn't know was if they could ever get back to where they'd been.

★ ★ ★

While Kelly didn't like fighting with Helen, she enjoyed spending time with her mother even less, so she wasn't happy to get home after talking with her friend to find Marilee hanging out in the kitchen.

"You look awful," her mother said as Kelly tried to sneak past her and bolt for her bedroom. "Haven't you been sleeping?"

Kelly thought about the past two nights. "Not really." She'd stayed with Griffith the first night only to realize that her tossing and turning kept him up. It seemed kinder to take her crabby self home. Now she surrendered to what seemed to be a case of bad timing and walked into the kitchen.

"I have a lot on my mind," she admitted as she crossed to the refrigerator and pulled out the pitcher of iced tea. "Work," she added, not sure why she was lying. Okay, she knew exactly why she was lying. What was she supposed to say? "I'm upset because my best friend is sleeping with my father, your ex-husband. By the way, why are you walking around in his pajama tops every morning?"

A conversation she was in no way prepared to have. As it was, she would gladly pay large sums of money to get the visual permanently erased from her brain.

She put ice in her glass, then poured in the tea. As she took a sip she wondered if maybe her day would be brighter if she started adding vodka to her liquids.

"Is your father seeing anyone?" Marilee asked.

Kelly swore as the glass started to slip from her fingers. She caught it, but at the price of cold tea spilling down the front of her shirt. Worse, it was one of the new ones Olivia had bought for her.

"How would I know?" she demanded as she made her way to the sink. "He's my father. The thought of him dating anyone is inherently icky."

"I just wondered."

"What part of gross wasn't clear?" Kelly asked as she dabbed at the front of her shirt.

"So you're not sure? He mentions Helen all the time, but I met her and that's not happening."

Kelly turned to her mother. It was one thing for her to be mad at Helen, but quite another for Marilee to say anything. "Why not? Helen's my best friend. She's great. Pretty and smart and funny and kind."

Marilee rolled her eyes. "Please. She's fat. Jeff would never be interested in her. He's not that desperate."

"She's not fat. She's curvy. I think she's fabulous."

Marilee looked Kelly up and down. "Yes, we should all rely on your sense of what's attractive."

Kelly gasped at the insult. "You know what, Mom? You think what you want. Helen's amazing and Dad would be lucky to have her. Plus, she's got what, twenty years on you?"

Marilee gasped. Kelly took that as the best she was going to get for the day and bolted for her room.

"Hey, Mom," Griffith said as the call connected.

"Griffith!" His mother's voice became muffled as she covered the receiver with her hand and yelled, "Mark, it's Griffith. Pick up the other phone."

The ritual made Griffith smile. God forbid his parents get a speakerphone, which he'd suggested more than once. But it was too fancy—they were simple people, as they liked to remind him. His father could easily pick up an extension.

"Hello, son," His father's voice was familiar. A little gravelly, but full of affection.

"Hey, Dad. How's it going?"

"We should ask you the same question," his mother said. "You're calling us in the middle of the week. Is something wrong?"

The downside of a regularly scheduled Sunday morning call,

he thought with a shake of his head. Any variation in routine was cause for alarm. Unfortunately, this time he did have something he needed to talk to them about.

"I need your advice," he admitted. What he really needed was their blessing, but he didn't want to say that.

"What's happened?" his father asked. "You hurt?"

"I'm fine, Dad. Everything is great."

"Good. We're glad. You're so successful and you're doing what you love. That's what we wanted for you. For both our boys."

"Yeah, well, that brings me to the reason for my call. I need to talk about Ryan. He's fine," he added hastily. "But I don't know what to do about him."

"What is it?" his dad asked.

Griffith braced himself for parental disappointment and disapproval. "Ryan's still being a problem on the floor." He detailed how his brother rarely showed up for work on time and was calling in sick a couple of times a week. How even after Griffith told Leo to treat him like everyone else and his brother's paycheck reflected his actual hours, little had changed.

"If it was just him, I might be able to deal with it," he continued. "But it's not. Some of the other guys on his team are picking up bad habits."

There was a moment of silence. He pictured his parents in their small kitchen exchanging a look and private conversation.

"You know what you have to do," his father told him. "Ryan's an adult. He's had some bad luck and he's going to have to learn how to adjust. You've done the best you could to help him out. He hasn't appreciated the effort and now he's dragging you down. You have to cut him loose."

His mother sighed. "Your father's right, Griffith. I hate to say it, but it's time to fire Ryan. He's a good boy and I can't help thinking in his heart he knows he's wrong."

Griffith thought their tenderhearted mother was giving Ryan too much credit but he wasn't going to say that to her.

"Thanks for understanding," he said instead. "I know it's my decision to make but I wanted your advice. I worry that I'm too close to the situation."

"He's your brother, but you're not wrong," his mother said. "I'm sorry it turned out like this."

"Me, too."

"How are you otherwise?" she asked. "How's Kelly?"

He thought of the last night they'd spent together and grinned. "Good. She's doing good."

"Is that bitch Marilee still around?"

Griffith raised his eyebrows. "Mom, that's kind of surprising talk from you."

"I know but I won't apologize. There isn't another word to describe her."

"She's still here."

"I hope Jeff is smart enough to avoid her. He's a good man and deserves someone nice in his life."

"I think he knows to avoid his ex-wife," Griffith said, careful not to mention the Jeff–Helen revelation. He knew Kelly was still upset and didn't think the information had gone public. He loved his mom but if he told her that juicy tidbit, she would be on the phone with every person she knew in Tulpen Crossing and he was pretty sure she knew them all.

"When are you going to marry that girl?" his father asked bluntly.

Griffith nearly dropped the phone. "Dad, I told you. It's not like that. We're not interested in taking things that far. This is enough."

"That's crap and you know it. Griffith, you've always made me proud of you. You're smart, determined and you're doing a hell of a job with your company, but when it comes to women, you're an idiot."

"Mark!"

"You know I'm right, Melinda. You've said so yourself."

"I'm right here," Griffith muttered, trying not to imagine what else his parents had been discussing about his life.

"You fell off the horse," his father continued. "Granted your divorce was painful, but it happens. I want to say it was all Jane, but you have flaws and part of the responsibility for the failure of your marriage falls to you."

"You never should have made that poor girl move to Africa," his mother chimed in. "That was never part of the deal. For some women it would have been fine, but not Jane. I don't know how she kept from killing you in your sleep."

Sometimes his mother's willingness to speak her mind was charming—other times, not so much.

"I know what you're thinking," his dad added. "That you failed. Well, so what? What if you'd given up the first time you hadn't been able to solve a math equation? Should we have pulled you out of elementary school and sent you to work in the fields?"

"Dad," he began, only to have his mother *tsk* him into silence.

"Your father is right," she said firmly. "Things have come too easily to you. You're making a mistake, Griffith. Love is important. Marriage is important and anything worth having is worth working for. Don't give up so easily. You're better than that. Now your father and I have to go to water aerobics and you have to fire your brother. We love you and we'll talk on Sunday. 'Bye."

There was a click, then nothing. Griffith put his cell phone on the desk and shook his head. For a second he thought about pounding it on the desk, but he knew he would regret the action later, even if it felt good in the moment.

His parents were wonderful people and he'd been lucky to have them in his life, but every now and then…

Better not to think about what they'd said on the Kelly front, he told himself. They didn't know what he'd gone through with Jane. The divorce had been—

What? Devastating? Not really. He'd been surprised and angry and hurt, but he'd kept going. If he were completely honest, a part of him had been relieved. Because neither of them had been happy for a long time.

He stood and then sat back down. Now, looking back, he could see that someone like Kelly was a much better fit for him, but he hadn't known that then. He'd thought he'd loved Jane. He'd thought they were going to be together forever.

Was it possible that he'd gotten it wrong? He'd assumed the problem was that he wasn't good at marriage and love. Maybe the issue had been his choice instead. And if that were true, didn't it change everything?

"Damn," he muttered, not sure what to do with the information. Not that he had to do anything right now. He would sit with it. Of course if it were true, then what about Kelly—what about them?

Questions he couldn't answer and he still had his brother to fire.

He walked into the warehouse and found Ryan lounging against the wall. When his brother saw him, he straightened.

"Hey, bro, how's it going?"

"Can I talk to you for a second?"

Ryan rolled his eyes, but fell into step. When they reached the office, Griffith shut the door behind them.

He'd planned a couple of different speeches where he explained how he'd tried to give his brother a place to regroup only to have it bite him in the ass. He wanted to say that Ryan had been given more chances than he deserved and if he'd been anyone else, he would have been tossed out his first week. Which meant he was waiting for his brother to get it—for Ryan to say "Hey, wow, I've been a dick. Sorry." That was never going to happen.

He walked to his desk and pulled an envelope out of the top drawer. "You're fired," he said, handing it to his brother. "Clean out your locker. This is two weeks' pay, which is more than you deserve. You can stay in the house for three months while you figure out what you want to do with the rest of your life, then I'm having the locks changed."

"What? You can't do this to me."

"You didn't leave me a choice. You're not doing your job and you're bringing the team down with you. This is a small company, Ryan. I can't afford to take the hit."

"So you're going to screw me instead." Ryan glared at him. "Some brother you are."

"Back at you."

"Autumn thinks she's pregnant. What am I supposed to tell her now?"

Griffith's gut twisted. There was a disaster waiting to happen. And if Ryan took off, Griffith had a sinking feeling about who would be picking up the pieces.

"Tell her whatever you want," he said with a carelessness he didn't feel.

Ryan gave him the finger, then walked out. Griffith sank onto his chair. He supposed it could have gone worse, but he didn't see how.

He picked up his cell and hit a couple of buttons. Kelly answered on the first ring.

"How did it go?" she asked.

"Not great."

"I'm coming over. You need a hug and then we'll go get ice cream."

Despite everything, he smiled. "I'm not five."

"The ice cream was for me."

"That's my girl."

"You know it."

28

Kelly's life had become segmented. There were the happy bits—hanging out with Griffith or her dad or even, surprisingly, Olivia. Then there were the confusing parts which were mostly about Helen, and then there was the horror of having her mother still in the house.

Kelly missed her old life where everything had been pretty much the same. There was something to be said for predictable. Yes, the sex was better now, but it was a high price to pay for—

She looked at herself in the bathroom mirror and smiled. Who was she kidding? The sex was so great and worth nearly everything. So she would put up with her awful mother and assume that settled her account with the universe. As for Helen—that remained a question she couldn't answer.

Kelly left her bedroom and walked into the kitchen. She needed coffee, then to start her day. She poured coffee, only to yelp when she saw Marilee sitting at the kitchen table.

"What are you doing here?"

"I live here." Marilee was already dressed and wearing makeup. She stretched as she stood. "I never get to see you, darling and you're one of the reasons I came back to this wretched little town. I want us to spend the day together."

That would be a nightmare, Kelly thought grimly. "I have to work."

"Don't be ridiculous. We both know your father would happily give you the day off. I was thinking we'd go get your sister and the three of us will have some quality girl time." She wrinkled her nose. "I don't suppose there's a halfway decent day spa anywhere around here." Her expression brightened. "Oh, I know. Let's drive into Seattle. We can check into a hotel and stay the night. Just the three of us. We'll shop at Nordstrom and have a delicious dinner, go to a spa." She sighed. "Just like civilized people."

Or they could rub hot pokers all over their bodies and jump into bubbling tar. Kelly did her best to smile normally. "I'm not kidding, Mom. I have to work."

"You grow tulips. They do it all themselves. It's not like you have to be there to encourage them."

"Thanks for dismissing my work so completely."

"I'm sorry, but the truth is a monkey could do what you do, Kelly. And not a very bright one."

The slap shouldn't have stung and yet it did. Kelly put down her coffee. "Thanks for making it easier to say I'm not spending the day with you, Marilee."

She turned to leave. Her mother hurried after her.

"Wait. I'm sorry. That came out wrong. If you won't do the day, at least have lunch with me. I really want to spend time with you. I mean it."

"Why?"

"You're my daughter. My firstborn. We have a special bond. Please?"

It was all crap and she was being manipulated for reasons she couldn't understand. At the same time she found it more difficult than she'd thought to say no. In fact, what came out of her mouth instead was, "Fine. Lunch. But not at the café."

She might not be speaking to Helen at this moment, but there was no way she was going to force her friend to serve Marilee lunch.

They settled on a time and place. Before Kelly started her

truck, she texted her sister about the lunch date and asked that she be there, as well. Marilee was better in small doses and having a third person there would lighten the load.

"Is this really the nicest we could do?" Marilee asked as they settled in a booth at Tulip Burger. "Is that a bowling alley across the street? How do you stand it here?"

Kelly looked across at her sister. Olivia offered a sympathetic smile. Oh, yeah, this was going to be a stellar lunch.

"They have the best burgers this side of the Cascades," Olivia said.

"As if that's something to brag about. Still…" Marilee smiled. "I'm with my two favorite girls." She picked up the menu, then put it down. "I wish your father had joined us."

Kelly held in a groan.

"Have you heard from Roger lately?" Olivia asked. "He was so nice."

"I have no idea what you're talking about." Marilee's tone was icy. "Roger and I barely dated." She turned to Kelly. "Men can sometimes be a problem. You smile at them and they get the wrong impression."

"You and Roger were practically living together," Olivia said, then grinned at Kelly. "Mom was supposed to spend the summer with him at his place in Colorado." She looked back at Marilee. "What happened? I thought you said he was ready to propose." She lowered her voice. "Was it ED?"

Kelly struggled to keep from bursting into hysterical laughter. She'd been wary about having her sister back but she had to admit Olivia was great to have around. She was smart and funny and when she got on a roll, you needed to stay out of the way.

"It wasn't anything to do with that," Marilee said, her voice low and sharp. "He was no one. It's over. I've moved on."

"Dad has, too." Kelly smiled. "It's great that both of you have full lives without each other. I always think it's kind of pathetic when one person can't let go."

"Oh, me, too." Olivia's expression was innocent. "Don't you feel sorry for them? There's nothing sadder than living in the past. Mom would never do that, would you, Mom?"

"I think we all know I could have any man I want."

"Except Roger," Olivia muttered.

Kelly covered her laugh with a cough. Marilee glared at each of them in turn. When their server came over to take their order, Kelly had the thought that lunch with her mother wasn't going to be so horrible, after all, and it was all thanks to Olivia.

Olivia's good mood lasted all afternoon. Lunch with her mom and Kelly had turned out much better than she'd expected. For the first time since she'd come home, she felt that she and Kelly were a team.

Eliza had texted about getting together with a couple of women they'd both known in high school. Olivia's first instinct had been to refuse the invitation. Back in high school, neither of the women had been someone she could trust, despite the fact that they'd hung out together. They'd been more frenemy than friendly and she'd heard they'd both dated Ryan within seconds of her leaving town.

Then she'd reminded herself that over a decade had passed, that she was looking to make a fresh start and girlfriends were a part of that. So she'd texted back happy emojis with her acceptance and had spent the afternoon figuring out what to wear to a casual happy hour reunion.

She'd settled on cropped pants and a tank top in bright orange with a crocheted loose off-the-shoulder sweater on top. Her makeup was light but pretty, her jewelry simple. She looked casually sophisticated. She'd passed on heels, thinking flats would make a quick getaway easier, if it came to that.

Krissie and Caitlyn had both been popular back in high

school. They'd ruled the sophomore class like the queen bees they were. Not that Olivia could complain—she'd been right in the middle of mean-girl land with them.

She saw the three women sitting at a table. Actually she saw Eliza in her new haircut and barely registered the other two. Eliza rushed over to hug her.

"Do you love it?" her friend asked, her voice full of enthusiasm. "I wasn't sure. My hair's been long my whole life, but I love it so much. It's easier and faster after my shower and I've been getting so many compliments." She swung her head back and forth so her short, sassy bob moved. "Thank you for suggesting the style."

"You look amazing. You were cute before and now you're gorgeous."

Eliza flushed. "You're so nice to me. Thank you for that." She glanced back at the table. "Um, Krissie and Caitlyn are really excited to see you. Be careful."

There was no time to ask what Eliza meant before they were at the table and there were squeals and hugs all around.

"How *are* you?" Caitlyn asked enthusiastically. "Oh, my God! I can't believe you're back."

"Here I am." Olivia tried not to show her surprise at the changes in Caitlyn. The woman was still blonde but at least forty pounds heavier. Krissie's big change was her obvious pregnancy. Olivia smiled at her. "Congratulations."

"Oh, thanks. This is my second." She rested her hand on her belly. "I swear, Derek has so much testosterone in his system, he only has to look at me and I get pregnant."

"I have two kids, too," Caitlyn added, as they all sat down. "Olivia Murphy. I can't believe you're really here."

A server came over. Krissie ordered cranberry juice with club soda, Eliza and Olivia each asked for a glass of white wine while Caitlyn got a vodka martini, straight up.

Krissie leaned forward. "Tell us everything about what you've been up to." She grabbed Olivia's left hand. "No ring, I see. Still having trouble getting your man?" She giggled. "Let's see, Derek and I married a year after high school. You remember Derek, don't you? He was one of the football captains. Just the most handsome guy. So masculine. He's an EMT." She wrinkled her nose. "That means he's gone twenty-four hours at a time, which is hard with a little one and a baby on the way, but I manage. Caitlyn helps me."

"We live close," Caitlyn added. "Like sisters."

Olivia was still stuck back on the comment about her being unable to get her man. Had Krissie really said that? Was she imagining the insult?

"My Justin and I bought the Burnett gas station a few years back," Caitlyn continued. "It's doing so incredibly well. Justin negotiated them down on the price and now we're just swimming in money." She smiled. "Do you have a job, Olivia?" She covered her mouth with her fingers. "Oops. Sorry. I didn't mean to say that. Of course you're doing something, aren't you?" She looked at Krissie.

"Running the fund-raiser," Krissie said brightly. "We're all so excited. We've bought tickets." She leaned close. "I hear it's going to be fancy."

"I think you'll enjoy the meal," Olivia murmured, not sure what she was supposed to think. Had these women been like this back in high school or was this show just for her? "The caterer has won awards. There are a lot of great auction items and it's all for a good cause."

"I sure hope you can make enough to pay for expenses. The town can't afford to cover your mistakes."

Olivia met her gaze. "I have it handled."

Krissie cleared her throat. "Caitlyn, she'll do fine. Oh, remember that time back in high school when we—" She paused. "Oh, wait. That was after you were sent away. We're so sorry that happened. We missed you desperately. Have you seen Ryan since you've been back? You know he's dating Autumn, right? She's a sweet girl. Not the brightest bulb, but a lot of men aren't that into women with brains. Are you seeing anyone?"

Olivia was saved from answering by the return of their server. Drinks were passed around and a toast offered.

"To old friends," Krissie said with a smile. "They're just the best."

"I'm sorry," Eliza said for the fourth time as they walked to the car. "I'm so sorry."

"Stop apologizing."

"It was my idea that we get together." Eliza sounded miserable. "I was never that close to the two of them but I don't remember them being like this before. So hateful."

"I'm not surprised at the behavior, I just can't figure out why it's directed at me."

Eliza stopped walking and stared at her. "You're kidding, right?"

"No. They're both married and have kids. Their husbands are successful. By nearly every standard, they have way more than me. You'd think they could afford to be generous. But I guess outgrowing the bitch gene isn't easy."

Eliza shook her head. "You really don't get it, do you? They don't have it all, Olivia. The only reason Justin married Caitlyn is because she got pregnant. He cheats on her all the time and they could only afford the gas station because of some unexpected inheritance. He's not a great negotiator—the Burnetts felt sorry for them. As for Krissie, she once told me she always dreamed of moving away and having a glamorous career, only she wasn't willing to even try to go to college, so she's stuck here. Now she's married with kids and she's never going to be able to do any of the things she imagined. Her small life is getting smaller and she only has herself to blame."

Information that almost made her feel sorry for them, Olivia thought. "Then why be pissed at me?"

"Look at you. You're glamorous and successful. Whatever you're doing here, you had a good job in Phoenix. You've lived all over the country, you've seen things. And you've been back in town all of five minutes and you're practically running things. I understand they're envious but they shouldn't have been so mean."

Olivia hugged her friend. "Thank you. You're the best friend ever."

"I'm not. A good friend would have punched one of them in the nose."

"Can you reach that high?"

Eliza stepped back and laughed, then her humor faded. "I really am sorry."

"Stop saying that. I don't want to hear it again. Come on. Let's go get takeout and head back to your place. I'd invite you over, but my mother is there and I like you too much to subject you to that."

Kelly stood on Helen's front porch, a bag from the drugstore in her hand. She knew her dad was at home—she'd left him there with Marilee not fifteen minutes before, so was reasonably confident that Helen was alone.

It had been too many days since they'd spoken. Too many days of her not knowing what to say. Helen was her best friend and with them not talking, she had a Helen-sized empty space in her chest and no idea how to fill it.

She knocked, then waited. A couple of seconds later, Helen opened the door. Her eyes widened in surprise. "Kelly, hi."

"Hi, back." She held up the bag. "Olivia has shamed me about the state of my nails. I've explained I farm for a living but then she pointed out I don't actually dig in dirt, so there's no excuse. I went and bought supplies and thought maybe we could do manicures together. I have no idea how, but I thought you might be able to teach me the basics."

Helen hesitated only a second. "Sure. Come on in."

They walked into the kitchen and sat at the table. Kelly unloaded the items she'd purchased. She'd bought manicure scissors and nippers, a package of files, an orange stick which wasn't close to orange, three different colors of nail polish, a base coat, a top coat and pads that were supposed to take it all off.

"You weren't kidding," Helen said. "Did you watch any YouTube videos?"

"A couple. They were pretty basic. I'm not looking to create nail art. Just, you know, get Olivia off my back."

"It's hard to compete with a beautiful sister."

"Tell me about it. I swear, she wakes up with great hair. It's not right."

They smiled at each other, then their smiles faded. They both looked away.

Kelly reached for the package of nail files, then dropped it back on the table. "I don't know what to say. Or think. I'm confused about everything that's happened."

"Me, too," Helen admitted. "I'm sorry I didn't tell you about Jeff. In my heart of hearts, I didn't know how."

"I get that. He's my dad and older and it's weird. Are you really in love with him?"

Helen nodded. "He doesn't know. Right now things are fairly casual."

Kelly opened her mouth, then closed it. She sighed. "So this is what makes it hard. Normally I would ask what that means. I would want details. But I don't want to know more. Can you understand that?"

Helen nodded. "It's hard for me, too, because you're my best friend and if I don't tell you, who do I tell?"

A question that made Kelly feel small and selfish.

"I want this to work," she said. "For both of us. I think I just need time."

"Okay."

"What does that mean? Okay, I get what you're going through and it's fine, or okay, be that way?"

Helen picked up a bottle of nail polish and turned it over in her hands. "It means I understand you're not comfortable, but I wish you'd at least try to see things from my point of view. I'm going through something huge and I can't talk to the one person I always thought would be there for me."

"You're saying I'm not being a good friend."

"I'm saying you're not being *my* friend."

"Are you being mine? You're sleeping with my father."

"What does that have to do with us being close?"

A reasonable question, Kelly thought, fighting guilt. "I don't know, but it does. Helen, you changed everything. I need some time to catch up."

"If I were with Sven, would this be an issue?"

"What? No." Kelly paused. "It would be a little weird because I was with him for so long, but not a big deal." She stared at Helen. "Do you think I don't want you to be happy? That I resent you having someone?"

"I don't know. Do you?"

"No! Of course not. This is about my father, Helen. I swear. Just my dad. I want you to be with someone wonderful. Someone who will cherish you and take care of you. Someone who believes you're the best thing to ever happen to him and—"

Kelly stared at her friend. Oh, no. She was describing her father. She knew him, possibly better than anyone, and he was that guy. He was decent and honest and loyal. If he fell for Helen, he would be all in. And based on what she'd just said, she should really, really want that for her friend. No, she *did* want that for her friend. So what the hell was the problem?

Tears burned. Kelly blinked them away. She stood. "I'm

sorry," she said as she fought emotions she couldn't define, let alone control. "I should be a better person. I want you to be with someone great and if that's my dad, then yay you. I just need more time to deal with everything. Please don't hate me for that."

She ran out of the house and climbed into her truck. She drove a few blocks, then pulled over and picked up her phone.

Griffith answered right away. "What's up? I thought you were going to talk to Helen."

"I did." She sniffed. "It didn't go well. Can I come over?"

"I'd say yes, but Ryan is here with a bunch of his buddies and it's loud. Want me to sneak into your place?"

She managed a smile. "You don't have to sneak. I'm over twenty-one."

"Are you really? Damn. I thought I was dating a teenager. Now I have to rethink everything." She heard movements, then he said, "My keys are in my hands. I'll meet you at the house in ten minutes."

"Thank you. Want to bring a bag? You can stay the night."

"I just might do that."

Kelly got there first and waited for him. Griffith pulled up and she ran to him.

"I'm a terrible person," she admitted as she hung on.

"You're not. You're processing."

"I'm sure Helen would tell me to process faster." She raised her head and looked at him. "I'm very flawed. Do you still like me?"

"I like you a lot." He kissed her nose. "To prove that, I'm going to take you into your bedroom and make incredibly quiet love to you."

"I texted Olivia and she said it was fine for you to stay the night as long as you leave the toilet seat down. It's because we share a bathroom."

"I figured." He reached in the truck for a backpack and slung it over his shoulder. "It'll be just like college. Me sneaking into a girl's room, then sneaking out in the morning."

She laughed. "There's no sneaking. You keep saying that. Everyone will know."

"You're determined to take the fun out of this, aren't you?"

Instead of answering, she took his hand in both of hers. "Thank you," she whispered. "For everything."

"You're welcome." He pulled her close and kissed her on the mouth. When he straightened he said, "Kelly, you're not wrong or bad or any of those things. You're genuinely trying to work through some things. It's okay that it takes time. Helen will understand."

"I hope you're right."

Because while he sounded sure, she was less so.

29

Helen had a restless night. Even giving herself a manicure with Kelly's supplies hadn't made her feel any better. Logically she could understand what her friend was going through, but the rest of her felt angry and betrayed.

She was awake before her alarm and knew she was going to be exhausted all day. Hopefully work would be busy and time would go quickly, then she could go home and catch a quick nap.

As she approached the café, she saw a truck parked in front. Not Jeff's truck, she thought as she studied it. Griffith's.

Sure enough, as she reached the front door he got out. Sven stepped down from the passenger side and they both walked toward her.

Their faces were unreadable, their eyes concerned. Her mouth went dry and her chest tightened.

"What?" she demanded. "Was there an accident?"

The two men exchanged a look.

"We should go inside," Sven said. "Everyone is fine. There was no accident. We have to talk to you."

Helen felt her body stiffen. She had trouble getting the key in the lock. Griffith took it from her and opened the door, then locked it behind them.

Lights were already on. Delja would have arrived at two. Helen called out a shaky greeting, then faced the two men.

"What is it?"

Griffith led her to a table for four and urged her to sit. He and Sven sat down as well, then Griffith cleared his throat.

"I spent the night with Kelly last night. At her place."

Helen glanced between the two of them. What on earth were they talking about? "I know you're having sex. What's the point of this? If you're trying to scare me, you're doing a really good job."

Sven reached for her hand. Helen wanted to snatch it back—despite using Sven as an example the previous evening, she'd really never been interested in him that way. But something warned her that in a few minutes she might welcome the human contact. She braced herself both physically and emotionally, then looked at Griffith.

"Tell me?"

Griffith was obviously struggling. He opened his mouth, then closed it. He looked ready to run. Helen couldn't figure out what would—

No. No! She knew, even as she refused to believe. Her fingers tightened on Sven's hand.

"I spent the night at Kelly's," Griffith began. "Around midnight, I got up to get a glass of water. Marilee was in the kitchen. She was wearing a man's pajama top and fixing a sandwich. She said—"

He looked at Sven who nodded encouragingly.

Helen's stomach rose up in her throat. Had she eaten, she would have thrown up. As it was, she was terrified she was going to start retching, although maybe that wouldn't be so bad. At least it would be a distraction for everyone.

Time slowed, or maybe her brain sped up. She noticed how the second hand on the wall clock barely seemed to be moving. She registered that it was five in the morning and that Sven was with Griffith. Obviously he'd put a call in to his friend because he'd wanted moral support. No, that wasn't the reason. He'd done it so she could have someone else to...to...

Someone else to hang on to when he said what she knew he was going to say.

"She said sex always made Jeff hungry. That she was fixing him a sandwich and wondered if Kelly shared that characteristic."

Griffith hung his head. "I'm sorry, Helen. I didn't know what to do except tell you."

Sven's hold on her hand tightened. She gripped him just as hard, hoping the pain would distract her. Tears filled her eyes and fell down her cheeks but that was nothing compared with the awful ripping in her heart. It was as if she were being torn in two and then tossed to the floor.

She didn't remember moving, but suddenly she was on her feet, being held. Both men hung on to her, offering comfort and supporting her as she tried to suck in air.

He'd betrayed her. She'd trusted him and he'd betrayed her. Had anyone else told her, she would have had doubts, but not Griffith. He was a good guy. He would never tell her something that wasn't true.

"I'm sorry," he whispered. "I couldn't not say something."

"It's okay," she managed, wiping her face. "It's horrible, but I'd rather know." She sniffed and turned to Sven. "Thank you for coming with him."

"You're a good girl. You don't deserve this. I can beat him up for you."

She managed a strangled laugh. "I'm sure you could, but that would create a lot of trouble in our little community. Plus, you're too handsome for prison."

Sven raised a shoulder. "You're right. I would be very popular."

They hugged her again. She tried to control herself, but emotions overwhelmed her.

"Child."

She turned and saw Delja walking toward her. She hurried to the tiny woman and began crying again. Strong hands held her tight.

"I heard," Delja said, then spoke in Russian. Helen had no idea what she was saying, but it sounded mean and violent.

"You go home," Delja told her. "You need time. I'll get in someone else."

Helen started to protest, then nodded. "You're right. Thank you."

"We'll walk you back to your place," Sven told her. "Make sure you get there okay."

She wiped her face. "I appreciate that, but I'm going to stay here and set up." Once one of the other servers arrived, she would duck out. When she was in her own house, she could figure out how to deal with the gaping hole inside her heart.

Neither man moved. Helen walked to the door and opened it. "You were great. I appreciate you telling me what you saw. Sven, thank you for being there for me. I'm not okay, but I will be. Seriously. You can go."

They started for the door. Sven paused and kissed her cheek. "Call me if you want me to come over and cook something."

She managed a smile. "I will. Thank you."

Griffith hugged her. "I didn't tell Kelly. I didn't know if you'd want me to, so I waited."

"Thanks. I think it's better if she doesn't hear about this just yet." Kelly was already conflicted about everything going on and if she knew, she might feel she had to defend her father. That would be more than Helen could handle.

They left and she went to work. At five thirty, one of her servers arrived and she was able to escape to the back.

"I'm going to text him and tell him I have food poisoning," she told Delja. "If I say anything else, he'll want to stop by."

She thought her friend might tell her she was being a coward, but Delja only nodded. "Just make sure you're clear it wasn't my cooking."

For the first time since hearing the news, Helen laughed. "I swear. I'll blame that fast-food place by the freeway."

Delja hugged her again. "You're a good girl. I love you."

"I love you, too."

She collected her bag and left, careful to circle around the parking lot. The last thing she wanted to do was to run into Jeff.

As soon as she got home, she texted him the lie, then went to her room and curled up on the bed. But no matter how tightly she pulled her knees to her chest, she couldn't stop the bleeding. There was nothing to do but wait it out. Over time she would stop feeling stupid, hurt and betrayed. In time she would find her mad, then she would start to heal. But until then, there were only tears and the sense of having been the world's biggest fool.

Kelly found her sister at the small desk in her bedroom. There was paperwork strewn across every possible surface—the desk, the bed, both nightstands and the window seat. Olivia was on the phone. As she spoke, she entered information on a spreadsheet. She smiled at Kelly, then indicated she would only be a minute.

"Let's say between three and three thirty. Uh-huh. I'll have a room set up for you. It's not huge, but it opens to the outside for walks. Yes, of course you can use the bathroom for the cats. That's perfect. I'll see you then. Thank you so much."

She pushed a button on her phone, then pulled off her headset and sighed. "A local animal rescue center has offered puppies and kittens for the grand finale fashion walk, which is fantastic. No one will be expecting it and hey, I'm all in favor of a surprise ending, but the fund-raiser is in less than a week and I wasn't actually looking for one more thing."

Guilt rippled through Kelly, making her uncomfortable. "I haven't asked how it's going. Do you need help? Is everything set?"

Olivia stood and stretched. "I'm good. A little frantic, but good. Sally and Hannah provided me with a list of volunteers. They're mostly high school kids who need their volunteer hours.

Sven's been letting me store silent auction items in his barn and Griffith sent over a few guys to help me sort through them. The decorations are going to be pretty basic. With the tickets all sold out, I had a bigger budget than I'd first planned and I've given the caterers a bit more money, so what we lack in balloons and flowers, we'll make up for in food."

"This is going to be a big deal, isn't it?" Kelly asked. "You're going to raise a lot more than roof money."

"I hope so." Olivia grinned. "If that happens, I'm going to ask Sally for a raise."

Kelly had been so caught up in dealing with having her mother around and having amazing sex with Griffith that she'd totally forgotten about Olivia's fund-raiser.

"I should have been helping. I'm sorry."

"I'm fine," Olivia told her, then sighed. "Okay, *fine* might be a stretch, but I'm okay. Only until Friday, then it's done."

"What can I do to make things easier?"

"On Friday morning I'll need help getting the silent auction items into the craft mall, so if you and your hunky boyfriend could spare a couple of hours, that would be great."

"Done." Kelly remembered why she'd come to see her sister. "I had a call from the mayor, which let me say, doesn't ever happen."

"We have a mayor?"

"Of course. Mayor America wanted your cell number. I hope it's okay that I gave it to him."

"Our mayor's last name is America?"

"He's Delja's son." At Olivia's blank look, Kelly added, "Delja who works at Helen's café and does all the baking."

"Oh, wow. I keep forgetting what a small town this is. Should I be worried that the mayor wants to talk to me?"

"He wants to set up a meeting to discuss starting First Fridays as a way to draw in tourists." When Olivia didn't speak, she continued. "That's when local businesses hold special events and stay open late to entice tourists."

"I'm clear on the First Friday concept," Oliva said, taking her seat. "I'm just..." She stared at Kelly. "Why does everyone keep offering me jobs before the fund-raiser? After, sure. It's going to be a success and then all this will make sense. But before? What if it's a disaster?"

"It won't be." Kelly cleared off a place on the bed and sat down. "I'm glad you're staying. I hope you can be happy here."

Olivia grinned. "Isn't there an old song about being happy down on the farm? I think I could. There's not much for me in Phoenix. I think I can cobble together a few jobs here." Olivia tucked her hair behind her ears. "That probably sounds really strange, but it's appealing to me. I like the idea of doing different things in my day."

"You're going to need more space than this." Kelly motioned to the bedroom. "And a filing system."

They both laughed.

"I'm going to find a place," Olivia told her. "Office space can't cost too much, right?"

"I know somewhere." The statement was impulsive. Kelly gave herself a second to reconsider, then added, "At the farm. We have a few empty offices and one of them is huge. You could use it for your business."

Olivia's eyes widened. "You're sure about that?"

"Very. Dad and I have already talked. We also want you to come up with a marketing plan that focuses on tourists and help us develop some kind of tour for the farm." Kelly grinned. "You're going to be quite the entrepreneur."

"I'll build an empire."

Kelly thought about all that had happened in the past few months. "I wish you'd come home sooner. Or that I'd gone to see you."

"Not that," her sister said quickly. "Mom would have turned

that into a disaster. But I know what you mean. We lost a lot of sister time."

Kelly stood and crossed to her. Olivia rose and they hugged.

"We'll make up for it," Kelly promised.

"Yes, we will."

Olivia's good mood lasted through to Tuesday. By noon she'd confirmed, double-checked and was thinking any triple checking should wait until maybe Thursday. The addition of puppies and kittens had been a bit of a twist, but they would add an "aw" factor to the antiques runway walk. She had tables and chairs, linens, food, drinks, items to sell and sold tickets. She could, maybe, take a breath.

Which was how she found herself staring at a real estate listing online.

She shouldn't, she told herself. It was ridiculous. Not expensive and from the pictures, really nice, but still. Buying a place didn't make any sense. What if she hated it here? Better to rent. Yet the duplex appealed on so many levels.

For one thing, the houses were connected by their garages, rather than by the living areas, limiting any noise issues. The backyards were big, the roof new and the other unit was rented with a two-year lease.

She had the money for the down payment. The trick would be qualifying for a loan—that might take some doing, especially with her newly self-employed status, although a tenant with a lease would help. She had to admit, she was tempted...

She grabbed her cell and dialed the broker, telling herself if no one answered, she would take it as a sign. The Realtor picked up on the first ring.

Thirty minutes later Olivia parked in front of the duplex. The yard was pretty, the exterior freshly painted. The agent, an attractive, friendly woman named Sherry, met her out front.

"You're going to love this property," Sherry told her. "The

owners have maintained it really well and the location is great. The renters are an older couple with grown children in the area. They travel a fair amount. The duplex is their home base. They're very willing to sign a four-year lease with the new buyer, so you'd have steady income from that. Come on inside and I'll show you around."

Olivia followed her into the right side of the duplex. The entryway led to an open concept kitchen/great room with a small formal dining room beyond. To her right was a den. The hardwood floors needed refinishing and the interior walls could use a coat of paint but it was clean and the appliances had been updated.

The kitchen cabinets were in great shape. Olivia eyed the tile countertops and quietly groaned. Not her style, but a solid surface would completely change the look. She liked the big windows. Come winter and the very short days, getting in as much light as possible was important.

There was a big pantry and a laundry room with the entrance to the garage off the kitchen. She wouldn't need space for two cars, so she could use the second bay for storage.

They walked down the short hall. There was a tiny half bath, an en suite second bedroom, then a nice-sized master with a sliding door that opened to a small patio. The attached bathroom needed to be redone, but it was functional and the closet was happily large.

Olivia returned to the great room and closed her eyes. She breathed in deeply, trying to get a feel for the space. Some houses looked great but had an uncomfortable vibe about them. As if something bad had happened or the people who lived there had been desperately unhappy. She wasn't a big woo-woo person, but had been in enough houses to pay attention to the feel of a home. This one was happy, she thought as she turned to Sherry.

"You're right. It's really nice. It needs updating and it might be bigger than I need, but I'm going to think about it."

Sherry handed over her card. "Let me know if you have any questions."

"I will. Thanks."

Olivia returned to her car and headed home. She'd liked the duplex a lot. She should talk to her dad. He might know a local banker who would be sympathetic to her situation and be willing to take a chance on her. With the tenants in place and a shiny new four-year lease, she could swing the payments. It was a risk, but a good one. Now that she'd decided to stay she was going to—

There was no way to avoid it. She was going to have to tell her mother she was quitting.

There's a conversation that's going to go smoothly, she thought as she got out of her car and closed the door. In theory Marilee should be pleased. It wasn't as if they'd been getting along. But having Olivia quit was very different—it was someone else making the decision and Marilee wasn't going to like that at all.

Olivia eyed the house and wondered if she should just get it over with. Do it fast—like ripping off a bandage. Then she thought about all she had to get through in the next few days. The fund-raiser was Friday. Was it wrong to wait until that was over?

Before she could decide, a truck pulled up next to her car and Ryan got out. He was tall, handsome and when he smiled at her, all she felt was a strong need to escape...and maybe a little guilt.

She hadn't seen Ryan in ages and she hadn't much thought of him, either. She remembered that first night, when she'd dressed up and had done her best to entice him. Embarrassment heated her cheeks as she got out of the car. She'd been an idiot.

"Hey, babe," he said as he walked toward her. He grabbed her around her waist and drew her close, then kissed her.

She pushed him away before stepping back. "What are you doing?" she snapped, glancing around, hoping no one had seen them. Guilt and annoyance merged—the former because of Sven and the latter because she wasn't a girl who felt guilt over very many things and certainly not Ryan.

"I haven't seen you. I thought we could get together."

He moved toward her but she held him off with a glare. "And Autumn?"

"We're done."

She rolled her eyes. "Right."

"I mean it, Olivia." He actually looked stricken. "It's your fault, too. I've been thinking about you all the time. Autumn figured it out and dumped me." He reached for her and drew her close. "Come on. You know it was always good between us. Things have gotten in the way before, but now we're both free. It could be like it was." He leaned in to kiss her.

She ducked away and stared at him. "Like it was before?" she repeated. "You mean back in college when you only had time for me when it wasn't baseball season?"

He flinched. "That's low. You know I can't play anymore. I'm stuck being just like everyone else. Don't worry—I've got nothing but you."

She thought maybe he meant that as a good thing, but it sure didn't sound that way.

"So we're going to start dating now?" she asked. "I want to make sure I understand how things are."

He brightened. "Sure. We can start right now. Come home with me." He winked. "I remember how you like it."

"Uh-huh." There was no way she was going anywhere with him. But why after all this time was he seeking her out? "What aren't you telling me?"

He looked down, then back at her. "Nothing. It's great. I quit that stupid job with Griffith. I've got some ideas about what to do next. I'm thinking I might start my own business. I'm good at a lot of things, you know. But Griffith doesn't see that. He's an asshole."

Olivia translated the handful of sentences. If she had to guess she would say Ryan had been fired and was looking for work.

While it was unlikely his brother would have thrown him out at the same time, he might have put a time limit on how long Ryan could mooch room and board. Ryan was looking for a meal ticket and he figured Olivia was a better bet than Autumn.

"Did you really break up with her or is that going to happen if I say yes?"

He shoved his hands in his front jeans pockets. "We're done, I swear. She, ah, might be pregnant, but I think she's lying about it. You know, to trap me."

Olivia circled around to the driver side of her car. "Get away from me, Ryan. I wasn't interested in you before and I'm sure not now. Go back to Autumn and make things work."

"I don't want to." He took a step toward her. "Olivia, you've always been the one. You have to know that."

She knew a lot of things and one of them was when to save herself.

The front door opened and Marilee stepped out. "Olivia? I thought I heard you drive up." She spotted Ryan and smiled. "Oh, my. Who's your friend?" She walked toward him, her hand extended. "I'm Marilee. I don't believe we've met." They shook hands.

"Ryan, Marilee. Marilee, Ryan. He's Griffith's younger brother. He used to be my boyfriend."

Marilee looked him up and down. "I do like having a handsome young man around. Were you two on your way out?"

"Nope, he's all yours."

Marilee linked her arm through Ryan's. "I was just about to make a pitcher of martinis. Would you like to join me?"

Ryan looked at Olivia. His expression turned smug. "Sure." He paused, as if waiting for her to protest.

"You two kids have fun," she called as she got in her car, then backed out of the driveway.

She drove around the corner before pulling over and texting her sister that she might want to avoid coming home for a couple of hours.

Ryan's having martinis with Mom, if you can believe it.

Kelly's response came immediately. I can't. You okay?

Olivia thought about her ex-boyfriend. She had no idea why he'd been such a draw, then realized it hadn't been him at all. Instead she'd wanted what he represented. Her past, possibilities, a sense of belonging. None of which she needed him for.

Never better, she texted back, then sent a message to Sven, asking him if he'd like a little company that evening.

Naked company?

She laughed out loud before replying, Absolutely.

30

Wednesday morning Helen was done hiding. She braced herself for the hell that would be her day and arrived at the café
promptly at five. She greeted Delja, who hugged her harder
than usual, then went about the work that was getting ready
for customers.

Jeff arrived close to five thirty. She saw him pull in and told
herself she was strong enough to get through whatever he had
to say. She had to believe in herself because there was no one
else to do it for her. Whatever they'd had together, it had ended
when he'd slept with Marilee.

She watched him walk up to the front door, then step inside. As always, the sight of him made her melt. Anger and hurt
could do a lot of things, but they couldn't kill love. At least not
in forty-eight hours. She accepted she was an idiot and a fool,
but she wouldn't be treated like either.

Jeff's expression of concern softened to pleasure when he saw
her. "You *are* here. When I didn't get a text saying you were still
sick, I hoped you would be. How are you feeling? I wanted to
come by and check on you but you were adamant about being
left alone." He reached for her, but she stepped back.

"Don't. I can't..." She stopped and swallowed, not sure what
she couldn't do. Talk? Talk and not cry? She'd never been a
screamer—in bed or in fights—and she wasn't about to start now.

The concern returned. "Helen, what's going on?"

Despite her best intentions, tears filled her eyes. "You have to ask?" She shook her head. "Of course you do. Because you think I don't know. Well, I do. I know all of it."

His gaze was steady. "I have no idea what you're talking about."

She wanted to throw something at him. "You're going to pretend ignorance? I would have expected better, only I shouldn't, should I? Not anymore." She circled around the counter so there was a physical barrier between them. "Fine. I'll tell you. Griffith spent the night at your place Sunday. Or at least most of it. When he went into the kitchen around midnight, Marilee was there. They had a nice talk about how hungry you get after sex."

She slapped her hands down on the counter and glared at him. "You're sleeping with her, Jeff. You gave me this whole song and dance about how there was nothing going on and you were just being a nice guy, trying to get your daughters and their mother to be friends. And you know what? I bought it. I believed you. I should have trusted my instincts, but no. More fool me."

Tears spilled down her cheeks. She brushed them away, but it didn't matter. He knew he'd hurt her. There was no pride saving anymore.

"No," he growled. "No! That's not what happened. I never slept with her. I have no interest in her. You're the one I want to be with. Dammit, Helen, she's lying. This is her idea of a sick game. You have to believe me."

"Actually, I don't." She pointed at the door. "You should go."

"Don't do this. Don't throw us away. She's not worth it. Everything she's doing is a game to her. You're the one I want to be with. Nothing happened."

She desperately wanted to believe him, which made her beyond pathetic.

"I can't trust you," she whispered. "Not anymore. You're living with her. She's right down the hall and you used to be married to her. You had children with her."

Jeff turned away and swore, then looked back at her. "I'm

going to move into a hotel right now. I won't sleep in that house again while she's there. You have to believe me. I never touched her. I don't even like her. Helen, you're the one I want to be with. Only you. Can't you entertain the possibility that she was lying?"

Oh, how she wanted to. She desperately needed to have him say all these things to her. She wanted to surrender to his pleading and have him tell her everything was fine. Only she knew better.

"You should go," she told him.

"That's it? You're not going to even consider I might be telling the truth? Helen, of the two of us, who is more likely to lie?"

"You should go," she repeated, pointing to the door.

"You know me," he insisted. "Come on. This is ridiculous. I didn't sleep with her."

Helen turned her back on him. There weren't any more words and she only had a few minutes to compose herself before her customers started arriving.

For a few seconds there was nothing, then she heard footsteps on the floor, followed by the door opening, then slamming shut. She sucked in a breath. Delja rushed out of the kitchen and hugged her so tightly she couldn't breathe. Helen hung on to her friend and told herself that with time, she would figure out how on earth she was going to survive.

Olivia told herself that throwing up was not an option. Nerves were fine—nerves would give her an edge, but vomiting was just unpleasant for everyone. And if that funny little pep talk didn't work, there was always reality. It was too late to do anything. They were at T minus thirty minutes until the event started.

Olivia walked the silent auction area for what she hoped was the last pre-guest time. Everything was in place. Yes some of the displays were amateur, but hey, this was her hometown. People would understand she'd been working on a very tiny promo budget. But everything was laid out in what she thought was an orderly fashion and there was even a section of extra fancy silent auction items right by the bar.

The caterer had banned her from the dining area after she'd started refolding napkins about an hour before. The puppies and kittens were safely in their quiet space, dozing before their moment of fame at the end of the auction, and the antiques that would also be part of the big finale were on rolling pallets.

The event was sold out, the bars were stocked, the tables set up, the food delivered. She was done. Okay, not done-done, but as ready as she could be, which made throwing up just silly. She should be celebrating, which she would…as soon as her stomach stopped flipping over and over.

Sven entered the auction area and glanced around. When he caught sight of her, he started toward her, his blue eyes bright with pleasure.

It turned out he was the perfect upset tummy antidote—or maybe it was the way he looked in a tailored navy suit, white shirt and tie.

As he approached, Olivia realized she'd only ever seen him in jeans, or shorts…or naked. Sven was a casual guy who didn't care much for affectations. He grew things for a living, he took care of his body, he enjoyed making love. But the man who stopped in front of her before leaning in and lightly kissing her could have passed for a blond, Nordic James Bond.

His normally curly hair had been cut and tamed. He'd shaved and she'd already swooned over the suit.

"You look amazing," she breathed.

"Thank you. Tonight's important for you and I wanted to dress right." He looked around. "The room is ready, Olivia. You've done all you can. The evening is going to be a success and it's all because of you. Now go get changed."

Because she was still wearing jeans and a T-shirt. She'd done her makeup and left her hair in hot curlers that had long since cooled, but there'd been no time to remove them. She'd stashed her dress and heels in a storage closet next to the women's restroom by the back exit.

She handed him her tablet. "I'm trusting you with this. If there's any problem, come get me. Or text me. I'm not that far away."

"You're going to do great. You'll have money for the roof and even more left over. You'll have to start a charity."

That made her laugh. "It's not my money, but it's a nice thought." She touched his arm. "You've been so supportive through all of this. I don't think I've thanked you enough. Not just for the use of your barn, but for all of it." She was horrified when she realized her eyes were filling. She couldn't cry. Not only wasn't it her, but she couldn't risk her makeup. Still, he'd been there for her. He was a great guy and—

"We'll talk about this later," he told her, giving her a little push. "Go get changed."

"You're so bossy."

She hugged him, then hurried down the hallway and cut through the back of the craft mall. She grabbed her dress, heels and a tote bag, then went into the restroom and pulled out the curlers. Fifteen minutes later she was dressed, fluffed, hairsprayed and as ready as she was going to be. She tucked everything she didn't need back into the closet, then headed for the event.

It was five minutes to five. For one horrifying, heart-stopping second she wondered what she would do if nobody showed up. If the items went unsold and food went uneaten and the—

"Breathe," she told herself. "Just breathe. You'll be fine."

A lie, but one she could live with. Faking it until she knew what she was doing was a skill she'd learned the hard way. It had started that first day at boarding school when she'd known no one and had been faced with not only being the new girl but the reality of having lived in a small, insignificant town her entire life. She'd gone from queen bee to target in less than twenty-four hours.

She'd done her best to put on a brave face and over time that brave face had become real. She'd had to learn the lesson all over again when Ryan had walked away from her when he'd been recruited for a Triple A farm team and she'd transferred colleges in her sophomore year. Now she was going to do it again—back where she'd started. Maybe this was the cycle of life, maybe it was fate with a sense of humor. Regardless, she was going into the event with her head held high. Worst-case scenario, she could eat a hundred and fifty desserts tonight.

She walked toward the back of the craft mall only to stop in surprise as she saw the line of people waiting to get in. There were dozens. Tens of dozens. She saw her sister and Griffith, Eliza and a couple of girlfriends along with other people she'd met while canvasing for donations.

Her stomach righted itself and she gave a brief whisper of thanks. Everything was going to be okay.

Kelly stared at a delicate necklace for sale at the silent auction. She liked the small silver chain and the way the polished stones were strung like beads. The piece was handmade and not anything she would have bought a year ago, but she was different now. The colors would go with several of the shirts Olivia had bought her. Accessories had always been a mystery, and while they still were, she was thinking it was time to take the plunge.

Griffith returned with a glass of white wine for each of them and glanced at the necklace. "Do you like it?"

"I do. I'm not a jewelry person, but this piece is pretty. I think I might bid on it."

She reached for her cell phone. They'd both downloaded the bidding app when they'd checked in. While the live auction at dinner would have an auctioneer, the silent auction was managed through technology.

Griffith covered her hand with his. "Allow me," he said and put down his wine, then typed on his phone.

"You can't buy that for me."

He tucked it back in his suit pocket and picked up his wine. "Too late."

"How do you know you won? The auction isn't over for another forty minutes."

"I paid the 'buy it now' price." He sounded smug. "Did I mention my auction competitive streak?"

"You didn't. Should I be worried?"

He smiled at her. "You should say thank you for the necklace."

She moved closer and pressed her lips to his cheek. "I'll say thank you later," she whispered.

His body tensed. "That works, too."

She chuckled, then drew back a little and glanced around. "Olivia must be thrilled. The room is packed. I heard all the tickets sold."

"I heard the same thing. She's going to have money for the roof plus extra."

"The mayor wanted to talk to her about starting a First Friday program in town." Kelly knew her sense of pride was silly— she'd had nothing to do with her sister's success—yet she felt herself beaming with pleasure. "She's done so great."

Not just with the event, Kelly thought, smoothing the front of her dress. Olivia had helped her pick out the perfect outfit for the evening. The tight, plunging, dark red sheath had terrified her on the hanger but once she put it on, she knew it was magical. The fabric had a slight weave to it and a glow without being shiny. The fit took advantage of her lack of breasts, and gave her the illusion of curves elsewhere. The red-and-black pumps she'd bought actually cost more than the dress but they were so sexy, she couldn't help herself. Her feet already hurt and she would probably walk with a limp for a week, yet she didn't care.

She sipped her wine and scanned the crowd. The room had filled up and from what she could tell, they were buying.

"I'm going to claim us a couple of seats," Griffith told her. "Want to come with me or stay and shop?"

"I see Helen," she said, spotting her friend. "Save a seat for her and Dad, too, please."

"Will do." He kissed her. "Don't go flirting with anyone else while I'm gone."

"As if."

Griffith was so amazing, she thought as she made her way toward her friend. Kind and funny and caring. To think she'd actually resisted getting involved with him. They were so right for each other. So—

Something nibbled at the back of her mind. Not a worry exactly, but the beginning of a revelation. She enjoyed being around Griffith. A lot. More than a lot. She liked everything about their relationship and she never wanted it to end. In fact—

"Is your dad here?"

Helen's question jerked Kelly out of her musings. She grinned. "You would know that better than me." She saw her friend's pale face and strained expression. "What's wrong? Don't you feel well?"

"No. I mean I'm not sick, it's just…" She sucked in a breath, then exhaled. "I shouldn't have come. This is insane. It's just I promised Olivia and I'm supposed to walk in the fashion show at the end." Her mouth twisted. "With an armoire. That's sexy."

"I have a kitten," Kelly said. "We'll trade. You'll feel better with a kitten. Helen, what's going on? I saw you over the weekend and everything was fine. We've been texting and you haven't hinted at anything." She opened her mouth, then closed it as the obvious occurred to her. "Are you and my dad fighting?"

Her friend stared at her. "You really don't know? I thought you weren't saying anything because you felt caught in the middle of the situation." Helen shook her head, then looked away. "No, we're not fighting. That would require us to be together."

Tears filled Helen's eyes. She blinked them back. "I don't know what to do. I have to be here and I don't think I can stand it. I just want to go home."

Kelly pulled her friend to the side of the room, away from the other guests. "Tell me what happened."

"Griffith didn't mention anything?"

"Why would he? How is he involved?" She'd assumed the reason she didn't know was her dad. "I'm confused. What's going on and how can I help?"

Helen wrapped her arms around herself and seemed to shrink into the wall. "You can't. It's not like that. I just..." She started to cry. "Your dad slept with Marilee. When Griffith spent the night, he saw her, you know, after. Griffith felt he had to tell me and he was right to. I just never thought... Of course I was worried, but I never thought Jeff was really like that."

Kelly hugged her friend, but had no idea what to say. Her mind raced. Why hadn't Griffith said something to her? He should have told her first. Could her dad really have slept with Marilee? Worse, could he have really cheated on Helen?

"What did my dad say when you talked to him?" she asked.

"He denied it all. He said he'd made a mistake to have her stay in the house and that he would move to a hotel." She looked up, her expression hopeful. "Did he?"

Kelly felt as if someone had stabbed her in the gut...or the heart. "Not that I know of. I'm sorry."

Helen whimpered. "I should go home."

"If that's what you want, I'll take you and stay with you. Griffith can hang out here and walk with the kitten and the armoire." Olivia would understand, Kelly told herself.

"No, you have to stay."

"What's going on?"

Kelly turned and saw Griffith had joined them. He moved to Helen and put his arm around her.

"How are you holding up?"

"I'm a little shaky."

Griffith squeezed her. "I want you to look at me and think happy thoughts. Then I want you to fake laugh. Now."

Helen sniffed, then did as he asked.

"Good," he told her. "Marilee is here and she was looking this way."

"That's it," Kelly said firmly, deciding this was the time to worry about her friend. She would deal with Griffith and her father later. "We're taking you home."

Helen hesitated, then squared her shoulders. "No. I'm staying. I don't care that she's here. I bought my ticket and I'm going to support the craft mall. This is my town, too."

"I already saved us seats," Griffith said.

"Thank you." Helen wiped her face. "I have to go tidy up. I'll be back in a couple of minutes."

"I'll come with you," Kelly said quickly.

Kelly stayed close through the restroom visit and sat next to Helen at dinner. When her friend leaned away to talk to the couple on the other side of her, Kelly turned to Griffith.

"When did you find out?" she asked, her voice low. "About my dad and mom?"

"Last Sunday when I stayed."

"Is that why you left so early?"

"I needed to tell Helen."

She tried not to show her turmoil, but she had a bad feeling her confusion showed on her face.

"You're upset," he said gently.

"Yes, and pissed. You should have said something to me. I had the right to know what was happening in my own house."

"Why?"

An unexpected question. "Because it's my dad and my best friend."

"You weren't sure how you felt about Helen dating Jeff and I didn't know if you were ready to be supportive. Trust me, telling her was not fun. The last thing she needed was you being ambivalent. I figured I'd let Helen tell you when she was ready. I wasn't keeping secrets from you, I was keeping secrets *for* her."

Her outrage grew. "I would have been there for her. I was tonight. It wasn't your decision to make." She couldn't believe he'd kept this from her.

His gaze was steady. "Yes, it was, Kelly. Helen is my friend, too."

But we shouldn't keep secrets from each other. The thought formed, but she didn't speak the words, mostly because she wasn't sure they were true. Of course they kept secrets. They hadn't known each other that long and while they'd agreed to be a couple, it wasn't as if they were on the road to falling in love and getting married. In fact Griffith had pretty much promised that would never happen.

"I love Helen," she said instead. "I would never hurt her."

"You love your dad, too. What about him? Besides, you weren't exactly supportive when you found out about their relationship, were you?"

She looked at him and didn't know what to say.

"I'm sorry if you're mad at me," he told her. "I won't apologize for telling Helen and I won't apologize for not telling you. That's between you and her."

The servers set salads in front of them, Helen turned back and the chance to continue the conversation was lost.

Ignoring the fact that Helen was devastated and Kelly alternated between shame and hurt, the evening went perfectly. The auction items, including a year's worth of tulips, went for way more than Kelly would have expected. When she got up to go backstage for the fashion show, she spotted her parents sitting together. Marilee looked dazzling while her dad seemed more resigned. She had no idea what might or might not have happened and couldn't begin to figure out how to handle the situation. There was only one thing she knew for sure.

She turned to Helen. "I'm sorry. I was wrong not to be more supportive when I found out about you and my dad. I'm sorry I wasn't the kind of friend you felt you could tell from the beginning. I love you and I want to be there for you. Please forgive me and help me do better."

Helen started to cry and Kelly did, as well. They hung on to each other until Olivia raced over.

"What are you two doing? Stop it this second. There's an antique furniture and pet fashion show about to start and you're both in it. Stop it right now!"

Kelly held out one arm. "Group hug," she announced.

"Fine. Then no more tears. I mean it."

The three of them hugged, then straightened. Olivia wiped each of their faces, pronounced them camera ready and motioned for them to get in place. Kelly pulled an armoire on a wheeled pallet while Helen held a small black-and-white kitten in her arms. She nuzzled the sweet baby.

"You're right," she said when they were backstage again. "This is really helping."

"I'm glad." Kelly stopped. "If you and my dad get back together, I want you to know I'll be really happy for you. I want you to tell me everything." She wrinkled her nose. "Unless it's about sex and if you get married, there's no way I can call you Mom. Otherwise, I'm game for anything. Deal?"

Helen nodded and tried to smile. "Deal."

31

Kelly waited in the kitchen for her dad to wake up. They'd both had a late night with the fund-raiser. She didn't know about him, but she sure hadn't slept well. There'd been a lot on her mind. Not just what had happened between him and Helen, but how it had been handled. While she understood why Griffith hadn't told her, she didn't like the implication—that she was a bad friend.

She loved Helen. They were there for each other, depended on each other, yet all this time, Helen had kept a really big secret from her and based on how she'd reacted, her friend hadn't been wrong.

Kelly didn't like what that said about her as a person. She'd always thought she was a good and thoughtful friend. That she was dependable. It was kind of a shock to find out that wasn't actually true.

She poured herself a second cup of coffee. She had to come up with an action plan, or at the very least, vow to do better so she could be the kind of friend she'd always imagined herself to be.

She heard footsteps in the hallway and got another mug from the cabinet, then handed coffee to her father as he walked in the kitchen.

He looked tired, as if he, too, hadn't been sleeping well. She supposed if she were a better person, she would be sympathetic, but she wasn't. Right now she had to be Team Helen all the way.

"Dad, we need to talk."

Her father sat at the kitchen table and sighed. "I figured we'd get to that. You found out what your mother said."

She settled across from him. "Let me be clear. What you do in your personal life is your business. I get that. You're an adult and you're my father. There are things we don't talk about. Which is fine, but I'm not here as a member of your family right now, I'm here as Helen's friend."

She stared at him. "She's my best friend, Dad, and you hurt her. You led her on and humiliated her. How could you do that? She's wonderful and doesn't deserve that."

He hung his head. "Nothing happened. Not that night, not any night. I haven't so much as kissed your mother. She's staying here for you and Olivia, not me."

Kelly desperately wanted to believe him, but she wasn't completely sure. "Then why aren't you at a hotel? You told Helen you'd move into one a few days ago."

His head snapped up. "Because I can't get a goddamn room. Do you think I haven't tried? It's summer, Kelly. We might not be a tourist destination here in Tulpen Crossing, but everywhere else is. It's warm and sunny and I can't get a room for thirty miles. Don't believe me? You go spend an hour on any travel website you like. Find me a room and I'll move out."

Sweet relief eased some of the tightness in her chest. "Really? That's the reason?"

"Of course it's the reason. Otherwise I would have been gone. I told Helen I would—I care about her. I'm not going to lie to her. She matters to me. I figured it would be okay—that your mother would get bored and leave."

Kelly stared at him. "Then tell Mom to go."

He shook his head. "Her being here isn't about me."

"Oh, my God! Are you serious? Are you still trying to give me time with my mother? I don't want time with her. I don't even like her."

"Kelly Ann, don't say that. She's your mother."

"Don't 'Kelly Ann' me. She's a horrible person. The only reason I don't say I hate her *is* because she's my mother, but that's all she gets. I'm going to tell her to get her ass out of this house right now."

"No, you won't." Her father sounded sterner than she'd ever heard. "You will not. Tonight, when everyone is up, we'll have a family meeting and discuss it. You're not going to go yell at her on my behalf. Not when you're upset about Helen."

Kelly glared at him. "You're still defending her. I don't get it."

He touched her hand. "I'm not defending her. I'm making sure you don't say a lot of things you'll regret later. The last thing you want to have to do is apologize."

She opened her mouth, then closed it. There was the tiniest possibility that he might be right. Which was annoying.

"Fine," she grumbled. "I'll wait until tonight."

"Thank you."

She sighed. "Relationships are hard."

"Tell me about it."

"You have to make things right with Helen."

"I'm still working on that one."

Sven put a plate in front of Olivia. "You have to eat."

She stretched and yawned. "I don't but I will. I'm still tired."

"You've been doing too much, getting everything ready."

"Maybe, but it was worth it." She looked at the perfect omelet with fluffy eggs, cheese, avocado and bacon. "You sure know how to dazzle a girl. Thank you for breakfast."

"Thank you for coming over."

She took a bite, then wrinkled her nose. "I wasn't very good company."

The event had ended just after nine, but Olivia had stayed until nearly eleven to help with the cleanup. Sven had driven her back to his place, where she'd crashed on his bed and hadn't stirred until about twenty minutes ago. Probably not the romantic evening he'd had planned.

"Just let me eat and I'll rally and then we'll go back to bed and have some fun."

He crossed to the table and sat across from her. His blond hair was mussed, his blue eyes concerned. Even more upsetting, the man was dressed in jeans and a T-shirt. She liked her Sven cooking naked.

She was about to say that when he spoke first.

"This isn't just about sex, Olivia." His voice was low and stern. "Don't you know that?"

"I, ah, just thought…"

"You were wrong," he said firmly, returning to the stove and flipping his own omelet.

He wanted her for more than sex? Wasn't that nice to hear? She tried to remember the last time a man had said that to her only to realize the reason she couldn't was no one had. Not ever. She wasn't the girl you took home to meet your folks. She was the girl you did in the back of your car.

Emotions threatened to overwhelm her. She carefully pushed them down to be dealt with another day. She was tired and this wasn't the time for any kind of serious discussion. Her entire goal for this particular Saturday was to do as little as possible, then start fresh tomorrow.

"Thank you," she said, then deliberately switched topics. "I think we're going to clear over a hundred thousand dollars."

"That's wonderful. More than a roof."

"A lot more than a roof. I'm sure the tourism board has some thoughts, but I've prepared a list of ideas anyway."

He chuckled and joined her at the table. "I'm sure you have." He picked up his fork. "When we first met I thought you were nothing like your sister, but I've started to see similarities. You're both strong and creative, in your own way."

And while she appreciated the compliment, it was kind of a strange thing to say.

"Kelly? Really? Do you know her that well?" She waved her hand. "I get it's a small town and all, but are you two friends?"

She'd never seen them together and couldn't remember her sister mentioning Sven more than in passing.

He stared at her. "What are you talking about? Of course I know Kelly. We were together for five years."

The fork slipped from Olivia's fingers and clattered to the plate. Her mind went blank, then regretfully rebooted and she was forced to absorb the information.

"Wh-what?"

"We dated." He frowned. "We broke up six months ago. It was common knowledge, Olivia. I thought you knew."

"I didn't." She sprang to her feet. The bit of omelet she'd eaten sat heavily in her stomach. The room spun a couple of times before settling down. "Oh, *God.* This is bad." She glared at him. "You never once thought to mention it, just to be sure?"

"Like I said, I thought you knew. Why is this a problem?"

"Because she's my *sister.* I can't date her ex. I never mentioned you—not that we were..." She waved her hand between them, realizing she had no idea how to characterize their relationship.

"Kelly and I are long over. She's fine with it."

"She doesn't know about it. You don't understand. We've barely become friends. She might have been fine if I'd asked, but I didn't. She's going to think I went behind her back. Oh, this is bad, Sven. Really, really bad. Can you please take me to my car? I have to find her and tell her."

He shook his head. "You're making more of this than it is, but fine. I'll take you to your car."

"Thank you." She hugged him. "You're the best." Then she punched him in the stomach which, given his muscle mass, was a meaningless gesture. "You still should have told me. Sisters? Come on. What is this? Porn?"

He winked. "I can be kinky."

"We'll deal with that later."

Kelly finished the last of her emails, then switched programs and waited for her orders to boot. It was time she reviewed them anyway. The office was quiet and—

She heard the front door open followed by the sound of running feet. She'd barely stood when Olivia burst into her office.

"Who works on Saturday?" her sister demanded. "I raced home only to be told you were here. It's the weekend. Stop working."

Olivia was wide-eyed and breathing hard, as if she'd run miles.

"What's going on?" Kelly asked, not sure she could deal with another crisis. Her apprehension turned to dread when her sister twisted her fingers together and tears filled her eyes.

"I didn't know! I swear, I didn't know. No one said a word. Not one person. We can talk about the minutiae of everyone's lives, but no one saw fit to mention that you'd dated Sven for five years? It's so unfair. I mean it, Kelly. No one. Not Dad or Helen or Griffith or the guy at the grocery store who knows everything."

Kelly assumed Olivia meant the guy knew everything and not the grocery store but figured this wasn't the time to mention that.

"I have no idea what you're talking about."

"I'm sleeping with Sven."

The four words hung in the room for what felt like a really long time. Kelly collapsed into her seat.

"You're—"

"Sleeping with Sven. Yes." Olivia perched on the chair opposite. "I didn't know. It just happened. We met and I thought he was cute and one thing led to another and I've been seeing him and dammit, it's not my fault. I would have told you or asked or said something. I really, really didn't know."

Sven and Olivia? Kelly had to admit it made sense. They were both gorgeous and they would have a lot in common. There was a weird factor and if she thought about it too much, she could see herself getting angry, but first…

"I thought you were dating Ryan."

"God, no. Yuck. He's a disaster."

"But you came back for him."

Olivia shifted in her seat. "Maybe at first. Or maybe he was the excuse. I don't know. But I haven't been seeing him. Besides, even if I was interested, he has a girlfriend." She sucked in a breath. "I'm sorry about Sven. I would have talked to you. I know it could really make you uncomfortable to have us together so if you want me to break up with him, I will. I'll never see him again."

Kelly knew Olivia was telling the truth. This was her way of saying their new, closer relationship was more important. Kelly poked at her heart, trying to figure out if there was any genuine anger or hurt. She and Sven had been together a long time—she should feel something. Only she didn't. Amazement that she hadn't known, but other than that—

"It's fine," she said. "I mean it. I'm kind of shocked but Sven and I were never right for each other."

Olivia stared at her as if waiting for there to be more.

Kelly smiled. "It's okay. He's great. I can see the two of you together. Kind of. I don't actually want to think about it too much."

"You're sure?"

Kelly thought about all that had happened the night before—with Helen. She'd hurt her friend by not being there for her. By not being the kind of person Helen could trust. She never wanted that to happen again with anyone she loved.

"I'm very sure."

Olivia flew around the desk and pulled Kelly to her feet, then hugged her. "Thank you. Thank you, thank you, thank you." She danced in place. "Isn't he wonderful? He's so sexy. Didn't you love how he always walks around naked after sex? It's like my own private show. I sure can't get enough of that. And the cooking. The things that man can do with a blintz. He's so steady and strong and, well, I don't have to sell you."

Olivia hugged her again. "You're the best. Okay, I'm going back over there now."

"Back over."

"I spent the night. I told Dad where I was going to be. Didn't he mention it?"

"He didn't." Probably because they weren't exactly speaking. Not after their fight this morning.

"He knew." She waved. "I'll be back tonight."

"See you then."

Olivia ran out of the office. Seconds later the front door opened and closed. Kelly leaned back in her chair and closed her eyes. While it was weird that her ex-long-term boyfriend and her sister were together, she was, as she'd said, fine with it. Family was complicated, she thought, turning to look out the window. As were relationships. Even with Helen, which still made her feel bad. The only easy place in her life was with Griffith. He was great. They fit together so much better than she would have imagined possible. Just thinking about him made her smile. Her feelings for him were so different than her feelings for Sven had ever been. Funny how before she could have gone a couple of weeks without seeing Sven and she'd been fine with it, but when it came to Griffith, it had only been a handful of hours and she was already missing him.

Thoughts swirled and danced, moved and settled. She watched more than participated and when the truth became too big to ignore, she sucked in a breath and let herself accept the possibility.

She was in love with Griffith. She wanted to be with him—

not just as his girlfriend but as the most important person in his life. She wanted to spend time with him, plan a future with him, grow old with him.

She wanted everything he'd promised wouldn't happen. She wanted forever. She loved him.

Kelly wasn't sure if she should laugh or cry, then she decided there'd been enough tears and she would try to see the humor in the situation. And if not the humor, then at least the irony. Because hey, why was she even surprised? This was so how her life had always gone.

Kelly checked in on Helen who was heading to Delja's house for a big dinner then, out of excuses and reasons to avoid her own home, left the office about two. Her father's truck was gone and of course Olivia wasn't there. No doubt her sister was watching Sven parade naked through the kitchen while he made blintzes.

"Bitterness is not attractive," she told herself as she parked her truck. "You love your sister and Sven makes her happy. He didn't make you happy. Them being together is nice."

Which she actually believed—something she could be proud of, she thought as she walked into the house.

First she was going to get herself some ice cream, then she was going to retreat to her bedroom and find something girly to binge watch until the family meeting that night.

"There you are!" Marilee stood in the living room, a dress in each hand. "Everyone's abandoned me. I need your opinion on these. Which one do you think your father will like best?"

Kelly put her tote bag on the table by the door, drew in a breath and reminded herself that she was a good person and she should act like it.

"What are you doing here, Mom? I don't mean why are you picking out dresses, I mean why are you here in town? Why did you come back?"

Marilee set the dresses on the back of the sofa. "To see my girls, of course. And your father. Why would you ask?"

Kelly fought against a series of swear words. Yelling wouldn't accomplish anything.

"You left him thirteen years ago. In fact, you left all of us. You didn't care then and you don't care now. Tell me honestly, why are you here?"

"That's not your business, is it?" Her mother looked smug. "This is still your father's house and Jeff is happy to have me here."

"No, he's not."

"Then he should say so."

Frustration built. "You know he won't. He has some dumb-ass idea that he shouldn't speak ill of his daughters' mother. I have no idea what that is, but it exists. I don't get it. I honestly don't get it. Why now? Why *this* summer?"

Marilee played with one of the buttons on the dress and didn't answer.

Kelly stared at her. "No way," she breathed. "Because of Olivia? You came back because she came back? Is that it? Were you afraid we were going to accept her as one of the family?"

Marilee rolled her eyes. "Hardly."

"That's it, isn't it? You couldn't stand for her to be a part of the family again. You liked it better when she was with you." Kelly couldn't begin to understand the hows and whys of her parents' marriage, but she knew she was close to the truth.

"You're being vindictive. You're here so Dad doesn't win Olivia back. Yet from everything I've heard, you don't want her anymore. What is wrong with you?"

Marilee's gaze narrowed. "I'm your mother, Kelly. You'll do well to remember that."

"I can't seem to forget it, although I'd like to." She told herself to stay in her head, to not let her emotions run wild. That would only lead to disaster.

She drew in a breath and gentled her voice. "Mom, you had your chance with us and you don't get a second one. Not from me or Olivia or Dad. More important, you don't even want one. You'd never be happy here. This town is too small for you. You always hated it. It's time for you to leave."

"Not your call," her mother chirped. "I'll leave when your father says I should." She smiled. "He's never been able to resist me. That hasn't changed. Your little friend thinks she's all that, but she's completely wrong."

Something inside of Kelly snapped. "You leave Helen out of this. She's so much better than you in every way. We are all lucky to have her in our lives. As for my father, you know what? Let's go ask him. Right now. I'll drive. We'll go see Dad and ask him flat out if he's interested in you sticking around or if he'd like nothing better to have you gone." She grabbed her tote bag. "Come on, Mom. Then we'll both know where we stand."

Her mother's pleasant expression slipped, revealing cold, ugly rage. "You little bitch! You're not going to win this one, you hear me?"

Kelly wanted to take a step back but she knew in her gut that showing weakness would be a disaster. "I take it that's a no?" she asked, pretending not to be affected by her mother's vitriol. "Too bad. It would have been a fun conversation."

Marilee grabbed her dresses and stalked down the hall. Kelly took a step toward her own room only to realize she was trembling and couldn't actually walk. She took a couple of deep breaths before trying again. On the bright side, she would guess the family meeting had just been canceled.

32

Work was a great way to escape from the horror of her life, Helen told herself Monday morning. Jeff didn't show up for his pre-opening chat, but that was hardly a surprise. She hadn't expected him to—only she had hoped and now there wasn't even that.

"Dramatic much?" she muttered to herself as she put dirty dishes into the bins, then reminded herself that her customers didn't care about her issues. They had plenty of their own to deal with.

She took three more orders and turned them over to Delja. The cook smiled at her and Helen instantly felt better. Her love life might suck but her friends were great. Delja and her family had kept her busy all yesterday afternoon and evening. Kelly was constantly in touch. She was loved by everyone but one stupid guy. Things could be worse.

Kelly stopped by during the midmorning lull and told her about the blowout she'd had with Marilee the day before.

"I think she's going to be leaving soon."

Helen pretended to be pleased by the news, mostly because Kelly looked so hopeful and was trying so hard. But in truth, it wouldn't matter. Jeff obviously didn't care about her. Not enough to make things right.

"Want to go to dinner this week?" Kelly asked as she was leaving. "Just hang out?"

Helen hugged her. "That would be great."

"I'll text you later and we'll figure something out." She hesitated.

Helen smiled and pushed her toward the door. "I'm fine. Go grow tulips. The world is waiting for your beautiful flowers."

Kelly laughed, waved and left. When the door closed behind her, it was all Helen could do not to collapse on the floor and give in to hopelessness.

But wallowing and doing nothing wasn't on her to-do list, so it would have to wait, she told herself as she cleared the last of the tables and began to set up for lunch.

By noon, the café was completely full. She and the other two servers were scrambling to keep up with orders. Everyone wanted to talk about the fund-raiser and how great it had been. Most were hoping it would be an annual tradition. All the puppies and kittens had been adopted and most of the antique furniture sold.

Helen was happy for Olivia. She'd worked hard and it had paid off—reaffirming world order and a sense of justice. That was nice to know. It could give her hope.

She heard the front door open and automatically reached for the pad by the cash register. They were going to have to start taking names until tables became available. She was halfway to the door before she looked up and saw Jeff standing in front of her.

She had no idea what to do or say, which turned out not to be a problem because he walked past her to the center of the room and spoke.

"If I could have your attention, please," he said loudly.

The café went quiet as everyone looked at him.

"Rumors are flying and I'd like to set the record straight." He turned to Helen. "I'm not sleeping with my ex-wife. I know her being back in town has been intriguing to many of you and has hurt some of you. I'm sorry about that, Helen. More sorry than I can say."

She felt herself blushing but couldn't seem to move from her spot on the floor.

His gaze was steady as he continued. "To be honest, I don't like her very much. I know what I saw in her all those years ago and it had nothing to do with her character."

"Tell me about it," one man yelled.

Jeff didn't smile. "I married her and I stayed true to her, but I wasn't sorry when she left. I was relieved. Time went by and I realized our marriage had been a mistake from the beginning. The only good thing to come out of it was our girls. But while I no longer cared about Marilee, I respected that she was their mother and I vowed never to speak ill of her. That was a mistake, because in keeping that vow, I hurt someone I care about very much."

He continued to hold her gaze. "I didn't get a hotel room because I couldn't find one. It's summer. That's the only reason I stayed in the house. But I see it was a mistake. I should have moved into the office."

"You could have stayed with us," an older man called.

Jeff ignored him and focused on Helen. "That's the truth but it's not an excuse. I hurt you, Helen, and I apologize for that. You deserved so much better. You're wonderful and honest and kind and sexy as hell and I'm an old fool."

He walked toward her. "Please forgive me and give me another chance. I'm hopelessly, desperately in love with you. I have been for a long time only I was too stupid to see it. You're the best thing that ever happened to me. I know you could do better, but I hope you won't try."

The room spun. Sound grew louder, then faded to silence. She was confused and shocked and deep, deep inside, trying to believe this was really happening.

Jeff stopped in front of her and took her hands. "Any chance we can give this a go? I mean it, Helen. I love you."

She stared into his eyes and felt herself starting to melt. Loving Jeff had always been the best part of her. Being with him, even just as friends, had always made her happy. How much better to have his heart, as well.

"It's time to forgive him, child." Delja moved into view, then gave her a little push. "Men can be stupid. We know this and we love them anyway."

Helen laughed, then threw herself at Jeff. He caught her and held her tight.

"I'm never letting go," he whispered. "Not for a second."

"Me, either."

Olivia sorted through the items that hadn't sold at the silent auction. There were a few salvageable things and the rest had been questionable at best. Fortunately she'd thought to have all the donors sign a release so that she could dispose of the leftovers as she saw fit. The good stuff she would donate to a local women's shelter. The rest was going to be recycled or tossed.

She had the double doors open in Sven's barn. The day was sunny and warm, which fit her happy mood. All was well in her world. Kelly was okay with her seeing Sven—that was huge. She would have broken up with him for her sister, but was so grateful she didn't have to.

While she didn't know all the details, rumor had it her dad had declared himself for Helen, right in the middle of The Parrot Café. She would have given anything to be there for that… or maybe not. She wasn't sure how she would feel about the happily-ever-after kiss. Helen was cool, but her dad was still her dad and parental heavy kissing was kind of gross to see.

Regardless of the when and where, it was done. They were hanging out at Helen's until things settled with Marilee, because while everyone wanted her gone, no one had yet gathered the courage to force her out. Kelly had made a run at it and deserved kudos for the effort. Olivia supposed it was going to come down to her doing the deed.

She was pretty much ready. She'd written her letter of resignation, so that part was done. Her plan was to finish up here, then head home, confront her mother, quit her job and celebrate with Eliza and a nice, cold bottle of champagne.

She was already working out a plan for wrapping up her life in Phoenix. She would fly back, rent a moving van and pack what she wanted to bring here. There were her staging supplies and her furniture. She figured she could hire movers for a day to help her load, then drive back herself. It would only take two days. She was hoping she could store everything here, in Sven's barn, until she figured out her next housing step. If the duplex was still for sale when she got back, she was going to put in an offer and see if she could figure out the financing. Maybe she could talk to her dad about him loaning her the money she needed rather than trying to make it work with a bank. She could pay him a bit above the going rate, give him her down payment and do whatever else was necessary to make it a real loan.

Something to think about, she told herself. She could work out the details on the drive back from Phoenix. There would be time. Maybe she should ask Sven if he would like to come along with her. They could hang out and he would be excellent company on the long trip. His muscles would be helpful for moving, but they were secondary in her mind.

Speak of the devil, she thought happily as the man on her mind walked into the barn. She smiled and moved toward him only to stop when she caught sight of his face. His expression was more stern than she'd ever seen—his blue eyes were glacial, his mouth an angry, straight line.

"What's wrong?" she asked.

He stopped in front of her, close enough that she had to look up to meet his gaze. Had he been anyone else, she would have assumed he was using his size to try to intimidate her.

"So I'm just your fuck buddy?" The harsh words were in keeping with the low, angry growl in his voice.

She supposed she could have stepped back, but while she might be confused, she wasn't afraid. Not of Sven.

"What on earth are you talking about?"

"You and me. This." He pointed to himself, then her. "I should have seen you were nothing but a whore."

She flinched, then squared her shoulders. "You don't get to talk to me like that. Whatever you think I did, I don't deserve that." She planted her hands on her hips. "We'll get to you apologizing later. Right now I want to know what has your panties in a bunch."

She had to admit, she was a little proud of herself. She was being strong and rational, she was asking questions instead of reacting emotionally. On the inside she was one quivering mass of hurt, terror and confusion. She wasn't afraid he would hurt her—no, the real fear was that he would leave her. Sven mattered. *They* mattered. So what had happened?

He turned and stalked to the far side of the barn, then returned to stand in front of her. Not so close this time, but that was hardly good news. His glower was plenty intimidating on its own.

"I knew about Ryan," he told her. "Kelly had mentioned the two of you stayed in touch. So the first time I saw you, I understood you might be open to using me to make him jealous. I decided it didn't matter. I wanted you and when you said yes, I was okay with however things started."

All of which sounded great, but then what?

"I thought things changed," he told her.

"I did, too."

"Right." His voice burned with scorn. "You've been seeing him all this time."

"What?" The word was a yelp. "I haven't. I've run into him maybe once and I never sought him out. I haven't had anything to do with him. Even if I was interested, which I'm not, he's with Autumn, who might be pregnant, by the way."

"I want to believe you, but I can't. I saw Ryan an hour ago. He says he's moving back to Phoenix with you. He's going to learn real estate. His exact quote was 'when a Murphy woman tells you she wants you, you'd be a fool not to go.'"

"I didn't say that." Olivia wanted to stomp her foot on the floor. "I'm not going back to Phoenix, I don't sell real estate and I've been here all morning." She motioned to the barn. "Look at all the work I've done. There's no way I could have snuck off and talked to anyone." She moved toward him. "Sven, you have to believe me."

"Why? I knew you were using me and I trusted you anyway. I thought you were changing. I thought we had something."

"I am and we do." She reached for him, but he backed away. "Just go."

"No." She glared at him. "No. You don't get to give up on me like that." Technically he could do anything he wanted, but she was willing to bluff her way through the moment. "I won't accept it. I didn't do anything wrong. You have to believe me."

He turned away. "Goodbye, Olivia."

Panic seized her and she couldn't move, couldn't breathe. No! Not like this. It so wasn't fair. She hadn't done anything wrong. She refused to lose Sven to something that wasn't her fault.

"You're an idiot," she said as she grabbed her bag and ran past him. "And I'm going to prove it. I'm going to find Ryan and make him tell the truth on camera." She waved her phone. "Then you'll have to believe me."

He didn't say anything. He didn't call her back or ask her to wait or say he hoped he was wrong. She supposed she shouldn't be surprised, only she was. No. That wasn't the word. She was devastated. This was a hell of a time to figure out that some-time when she hadn't been looking, she'd totally fallen for Sven.

Olivia sat in her car and tried to figure out where she could find Ryan. If Sven had talked to him an hour ago, then he wasn't at work. She shook her head. Of course he wasn't at work—he'd been fired. So where would he be? Home, maybe?

It was a place to start, she told herself as she backed out of the driveway and headed in that direction. When she arrived she didn't see any cars out front, but the house had a big four-car garage off to the side. She shouldn't assume he wasn't home.

She ran up to the front door and knocked. When there was no answer, she figured she was already in trouble so why not go for it. She checked and the door was open. Not a surprise in this small town, she thought as she raced through the downstairs, then went to the second floor. She heard noises—very specific noises. Good, she thought, pulling her phone out of her bag and punching the camera icon. No doubt he was boinking Autumn so the conversation wouldn't go well, but she didn't care. She wasn't leaving until she got Ryan on video admitting they hadn't been involved at all. Maybe having a furious Autumn hating on him would make him more talkative.

She walked to the end of the hall where a bedroom door stood open. She went inside and opened her mouth, closed it, then felt her jaw drop.

Ryan was in bed, all right. With a woman. But it wasn't Autumn. It was Marilee.

They were going at it, Marilee on top, bouncing and scream-ing. Ryan's eyes were closed as he moaned—possibly in pain, it was difficult to tell. Olivia knew she would carry the image of them for the rest of her life. Fine, later she would get therapy, but right now she needed a picture.

She snapped two, just to be safe. At the sound, they both turned.

"Hey, Mom."

Marilee didn't even look embarrassed. "Darling, what are you doing here?"

"Long story. I won't bother you with it, or ask what you're doing here. It's pretty obvious."

Ryan's eyes widened, but he didn't speak. She was pretty sure he couldn't. She would guess he also couldn't stay hard because Marilee glared at him, before sliding off and casually pulling the sheet up to cover herself.

"Is there a point to this visit?" her mother asked, sounding bored.

Later Olivia would process all that had happened this morning. She had a bad feeling that if she stopped to think about any of it, she would become immobilized, so she decided to just keep moving forward.

"There is," she told her mother. "I quit. I'm not going back to Phoenix. I'm staying here. I'll email you my resignation."

"You're supposed to give me two weeks' notice."

Olivia waved the camera. "Yeah, that's not going to happen and you're going to be fine with it. You're leaving today, right?"

Marilee sniffed. "Ryan and I were already planning to go back to Phoenix together. As you can see, I'm sleeping with your boyfriend."

"He's not my boyfriend, but it's nice you thought he was." Olivia looked at Ryan. "Let me guess. She's going to teach you the real estate business."

"I can't stay here," he said grudgingly. "Autumn's not pregnant and I have to get away while I can."

"I can see that. Good luck." She jerked her head toward Marilee. "Watch your back, get a lawyer to read your contract and make sure she doesn't stiff you on the money."

"Olivia! How can you say that about me?"

"You have to ask?"

Ryan smiled and put his hands behind his head before leaning back on the headboard. "Olivia, don't worry. It's me. I'll be fine."

He would be an idiot, but none of this was her problem. She'd warned him. He would listen or not.

She returned her attention to her mother. "I'll delete these when you're gone. If you don't leave or if you make any trouble for Kelly or Dad, I'll figure out a way to humiliate you with them."

"Blackmail, Olivia? Isn't that a little low rent?"

"I learned from the master, Mom." She smiled. "I probably won't drop by while I'm getting my stuff, so this is goodbye. Good luck with everything. You, too, Ryan."

"Sorry it didn't work out," he called after her as she walked down the hall.

She didn't know what to say to that, so didn't bother answering. She made it all the way to her car before she started shaking. She managed to fall into the seat before her body went into complete shock and she worried she was going to faint.

A few minutes of slow breathing helped, as did sipping water from the bottle in her console. She told herself that she would get through all this and later that night there were so going to be cocktails, then she started her car and headed back to confront Sven.

33

"You had the wrong Murphy," she said, handing him her phone. She'd found him in his house, sitting in the living room. He'd looked surprised to see her, as if he hadn't expected her to come back so quickly. Or maybe at all. Not that many women were willing to return to the place of being called a whore.

"My mother uses her maiden name now, but Ryan wouldn't know that. He would still think of her as Marilee Murphy, you bastard. I *told* you I hadn't been seeing him. I *told* you I wasn't going back to Phoenix. What do you think all this was? That I would be with you the way I was and then go to him? Oh, wait. Of course you did, because I'm a whore."

He went pale as he looked from the pictures to her. "Olivia," he began.

"No! No. Don't you dare apologize. You didn't trust me. After all we've been through, you assumed the worst about me. WTF? How could you? I've been here with you. I've cared about you, I've—"

She'd what? Slept with him the second time she'd met him? They'd been each other's booty call. There'd never been a discussion of them having a relationship beyond sex. They'd never once talked about liking each other or being a couple. It had been nothing but convenient. They'd been using each other and there was absolutely no reason to think he should trust her at all.

She sank onto the sofa opposite his. "Oh, no," she whispered.

Her chest tightened and she couldn't breathe, which was perfectly fine, as long as she didn't cry. There was no way she was going there. No tears. Not one.

"We were using each other." She tried to speak louder but couldn't. "You and I. We were taking advantage. We never talked about any of this."

He moved to sit next to her. "We talked about everything."

"Not us. Not what we were doing. No wonder you didn't trust me."

"I was wrong, Olivia. I'm sorry." He stared at her and grimaced. "What a stupid thing to say. I'm sorry. How does that make it better? You're right—I assumed the worst and I insulted you. I apologize because I know that's important, but I understand that your forgiveness will have to be earned with more than words."

They were screwed, she thought grimly. Totally screwed. "We did this all wrong. If I'd known you were going to be so great, I wouldn't have slept with you right away. It was dumb. It ruined everything."

"It's not ruined."

She jumped to her feet and moved away from him. "How are we supposed to get back together now? We don't have a relationship. Not really. We never had a plan. You're supposed to have a plan. People date and then sleep together and fall in love. Some of them fall in love before sex, but that's not the point. It's ruined."

He stood in front of her. "It's not ruined," he repeated.

"How do we fix it? I'm falling in love with you and you called me a whore."

"I'm sorry." He took her hands in hers. "I care, too. That's why I was so hurt when I thought you'd been with Ryan all this time. It wasn't just that you were leaving, but that you'd been playing me."

She wanted to believe him but the timing was too convenient. "You never said anything."

"You didn't, either." He rubbed her fingers and held her gaze. "Olivia, I cooked for you. I've never cooked for a woman I was seeing before."

"I didn't get pissed that you'd been with my *sister* for five years, so don't get all righteous on me."

He smiled. "You're tough."

"I have to be."

She'd been on her own since she was fifteen. No one had cared about her—not enough to be there. Maybe she'd built a lot of barriers, but they'd been necessary.

He pulled her against him. She resisted for a second, then gave in because being held by Sven was the best feeling in the world.

"I'm sorry," he whispered. "So incredibly sorry. I was wounded and I lashed out. That's an explanation, not an excuse."

"Thank you for saying that. I probably should have told you I hadn't been seeing Ryan." She sniffed and drew back. "What happens now?"

"I don't know. Maybe we just start over."

"Do you think that's possible?"

"How about if we find out?"

Kelly got home from work on Monday and noticed the rental car was gone. While she wanted to believe that was good news, it seemed unlikely.

She found her father at the kitchen table. He waved a note. "Your mother left."

"Really?" Hope filled her as she went back to the guest room and looked inside.

The bed hadn't been made, but all Marilee's personal effects were gone. The drawers were empty, as was the closet. She returned to the kitchen and hugged her dad.

"Hallelujah."

He passed her note. "There's more."

She picked it up and scanned the words. Then read it again because it wasn't possible that—

"She ran off with Ryan?" Kelly asked, reading it for the third time. "They're going back to Phoenix together? She had a wonderful time and hopes we can do it again?" Her voice rose with each word until she was shrieking. "I honest to God don't know what to say."

"Me, either."

Marilee and Ryan? "Does Olivia know?"

"She does and she seems less upset than I would have thought." He cleared his throat. "Marilee is your mother and if you want to see her, that's great, but I won't let her stay here again."

Kelly sighed in relief. "Thank God. It was a nightmare."

"It was. I was a fool to think I was doing the right thing. I've never spoken ill of your mother and that's not going to change, but I carried things too far. I hurt Helen."

"Have you two made up?"

His eyes brightened and he smiled. "We have." His expression sobered. "Kelly, I'm in love with Helen. I'm not asking for permission, I'm simply letting you know. She's your best friend and that may make things awkward, but we're both adults and I hope we can—"

She didn't let him finish. Instead she flung herself at him and hugged him tight.

"Oh, Daddy, I'm so happy. Yes, it will be weird, but that's okay." She drew back. "I didn't take it well when I first found out and that's on me. I was wrong and I've apologized to Helen. I promise that will never happen again." She grinned. "So, you're in love. Are you going to marry her?"

"I want to. If she'll have me."

Kelly laughed. "Wow. That was direct. Okay. I'm not calling her Mom. Not ever, just so we're clear. It's going to be very confusing to have my best friend be my stepmother, but what the hey. We'll challenge stereotypes."

They were getting married. She felt a faint twinge of regret that she and Griffith weren't in the same place. Loving someone who didn't love you back was both wonderful and awful. Still, she was thrilled for her dad.

"I need to find a place," she announced.

"Kelly, no. This is your home and it's plenty big for all of us."

She laughed again. "I don't think so, Dad. I'm going to be twenty-nine. Don't you think it's time I was on my own? Besides, you're going to have a new bride in the house. You're not going to want your grown daughters around."

"Yes, well, Olivia's moving out. She's found a duplex she wants to buy. I'm loaning her the money and she's paying me back. I want you to stay, but if you insist on your own place, I'll make the same offer to you."

"That's very generous. Thanks." She got up and headed for her room. "Go be with your soon-to-be fiancée. Oh and, Dad? Buy her a really big ring. After having to wait out Mom, she deserves the bling."

"I will."

Kelly walked to her sister's open door and found Olivia at her desk.

"Can I interrupt?" Kelly asked.

Olivia turned in the chair. "Sure. Come on in. Did you hear Mom's gone? Isn't that the best?"

"It's great." Kelly settled on the bed. "It's wonderful and I'm afraid to believe it."

"Oh, she's gone and she won't be back. Trust me on that."

"She took Ryan. Are you okay with that?"

Olivia's smile took on an impish quality. "I would say it made the whole situation better."

"So you're not upset?"

"Not about Mom and Ryan." She sighed. "I'll admit he was

part of the reason I came back, but once I was here, I never saw him. It's as if he disappeared into the landscape. I don't want him back."

"Good. He was a bit of a jerk. Anyway, did Dad tell you about Helen?"

"That they're in love? He did." Olivia's expression turned cautious. "I, um, think this means we have to move out."

"I know. He said you found a place."

"A duplex. It's cute and the other side has great renters." She bit her lower lip. "Did you want me to see if I can break the lease so you can move in?"

"Sweet offer, but no. I think it's time for me to be on my own. I'll rent a place for a while until I figure out my next step."

"Or marry Griffith." Her voice was teasing.

Kelly did her best not to react to the statement. "We're not exactly talking marriage." Or anything long-term. He'd been clear on that.

"But you're in love with him."

Kelly nearly fell off the bed. "How did you know?"

"Oh, please. I'm your sister. It wasn't hard to figure out." She tilted her head. "I take it from your reaction that he doesn't know."

"I doubt he has even a hint of a clue."

"Men. They're all idiots. When are you going to tell him?"

"What? I'm not. It wouldn't go well. I'm going to keep things the way they are."

Olivia didn't say anything but the word *chicken* seemed to fill the room.

"He's not that into me," Kelly hedged. "He's not looking to get married."

"No one said anything about marriage. I'm talking love. If you love him, you should tell him. Not saying the words doesn't take away their power or make you less. I think he'd want to know."

Which all made perfect sense, Kelly thought, but what hap-

pened when he ran for the hills? She would be left devastated
and alone. Of course loving him and not saying anything made
her a coward, which wasn't good. She'd vowed to be a better
person—hadn't she best get going on that?

Kelly wrestled with the Griffith problem for two days. On the
third, she was tired of thinking about it and tired of wondering
why everyone was emotionally strong but her. Determined to
get things settled once and for all, she texted him and asked him
to meet her at his house. With Ryan in Phoenix, they wouldn't
have to worry about being interrupted.

They arrived at the same time. He kissed her before they
climbed up the porch stairs.

"How's my best girl?" he asked.

"Still reeling from all that's happened. Have you heard from
Ryan?"

He held open the unlocked front door and followed her inside. "Not a word, which is fine by me." He stood in the middle of the living room. "What's up? Or did you lure me here to
play escaped prisoner and the warden's wife?"

Here it was. The moment of truth. She could avoid it by falling into bed with him and having amazing, wonderful sex for
the next few hours, or she could grow a pair—so to speak—and
be self-actualized.

The sex option was incredibly appealing, but she reminded
herself she was here on a mission.

"I'm in love with you," she said, her voice clear. "I don't expect you to do anything with that information, I just wanted
you to know."

Griffith's face was a caricature of stunned surprise. "What?"

"I'm in love with you," she repeated. "I have been for a while.
I don't know exactly when it happened, but here we are. I know
you don't want me to change things, that you don't want to be
in love or any of that, although I have to tell you, your reasons

are really dumb. I mean you won't love anyone because you're not good at it? What's up with that?"

She pressed her lips together and told herself to stay on topic. "Anyway, I'm not going to be afraid or staid or anything else that I've been doing these past few years. I'm going to be my own person and that person is in love with you."

She noticed it was getting easier to say. Maybe it was the repetition. Maybe it was the fact that he seemed unable to speak.

"I'm going to be living my life to the fullest, every day. I'd like that to be with you, but if not, I'll keep moving forward."

She paused, hoping he would say something, but when he didn't, she wasn't sure what to do. Yell? Leave? Tell him he was an idiot?

She went with the easiest. "You're an idiot if you let me get away. I'm good for you and we're good together. We fit and it's fun and we have each other's backs. That's important. You get me and I get you." She glared at him. "Are you going to say anything?"

He was still another second, before telling her, "Wait right here." Then he turned and ran up the stairs.

What on earth? She still didn't know what to do but decided to wait. She was scared and hopeful and determined to get this right, even if it meant walking away. She stood alone in the living room for several seconds, before he returned and held out his hand.

There was a brooch on his palm. A bouquet of flowers. The stems were silver tone and the flowers were different colors of glass. It was obviously old and not especially attractive.

"I found this at the craft mall," he told her. "A few weeks ago. I was waiting for the right time to give it to you."

"I don't get it."

"It's a pin," he said moving toward her. "Because you're my girl."

He pinned the brooch on her shirt, then cupped her face and

kissed her. "You're always one step ahead of me. I hope that never changes. You're right. I would be an idiot to let you go because having you love me is a gift I don't deserve." He grinned. "I'm going to accept it anyway."

His smile faded and he stared into her eyes. "Someone I know took me to task recently and got me to thinking about a lot of things. Why my marriage failed and what I could have done differently. There's been so much going on with work and Ryan and everything else, but you've been the best part of me since the day you agreed to go out with me. I'm not an idiot, Kelly. I'm in love with you."

Relief mingled with joy mingled with disbelief and a million other emotions she couldn't name just then because he was kissing her and when Griffith kissed her it was difficult to think about anything but what the man did to her body.

"You really love me?" she asked when they came up for air.

"I do."

"Why didn't you say something?"

"I was still figuring it out."

She rolled her eyes. "And everyone assumes men are stronger. It's total crap."

"You know it." He pulled her close and nibbled on her neck. "Now about that game we were going to play…"

Kelly and Helen were sprawled on Kelly's bed. Olivia appeared in the doorway wearing a light green summer dress.

"It's pretty," Kelly said. "But low-cut. I'm not saying it doesn't look great. You're always fabulous, but it's not what you said you wanted."

"Okay. I've got another option."

"Explain this to me," Helen said when Olivia had ducked back into her room. "She doesn't want to be sexy?" As she spoke her gaze stayed locked on the very impressive diamond solitaire on her left hand.

"Apparently she and Sven are starting over. They're dating now and tonight is the first date. They're going to get to know each other before taking things to the next level."

"I'm still confused."

Kelly laughed. "That's because you can't stop staring at your engagement ring."

Helen blushed and tucked her hand behind her back. "I know. I'm sorry. It's just so new and shiny, I can't help myself."

"Don't apologize. I think it's wonderful."

Helen beamed.

Kelly enjoyed her friend's happiness. Jeff had proposed two days before. They were getting married at home at the end of August, which was going to be a scramble but also a lot of fun for everyone. Olivia's offer on her duplex had been accepted and she would close just before the wedding. She would fly down to Phoenix while Jeff and Helen were on their honeymoon and be all moved out by the time they returned.

Kelly had found a cute apartment not too far from work and even closer to Griffith. He'd wanted her to move in with him and, while she knew she would eventually, she thought it was a good idea for her to be on her own for a few months first. She fingered the pin she wore every day and smiled.

Olivia returned wearing a white dress that was relatively high at the neck and came down to her knees.

"It's perfect," Kelly told her. "You can't help being sexy, but everything is covered."

"Good. That's what I want." She joined them on the bed. "He's taking me out to dinner."

"How long are you going to make the poor man wait for sex?" Helen asked.

"Three dates." Olivia laughed. "I'm trying to be traditional."

"Maybe I should wait to get married," Helen said. "We could have a triple ceremony."

Olivia plugged her ears with her fingers. "Don't say that. You'll jinx everything."

Kelly shook her head. "Helen, I love you like a sister, but I am not getting married with my dad."

"Oh, right." Helen stared at her ring. "I didn't think of that."

Olivia lowered her arms to her side. "I love you guys. Thanks for being my family."

"I love you, too," Kelly said.

"Me, three!"

They laughed, then hugged.

Olivia got up to finish getting ready. Helen was staying in with Jeff and Kelly was heading over to Griffith's place.

"Look at us," Kelly said. "We're all so happy. This is the best day ever."

Helen shook her head. "I hate to break it to you, but it's only the beginning. Things are going to get a whole lot better."

Olivia winced. "She's already talking like a mom."

"I know. It's disconcerting."

"I'm not," Helen protested, then laughed. "Okay, maybe a little." Her expression turned stern. "I hope you two girls are using protection."

"Us? What about you?" Kelly asked, then shook her hands. "I meant that in a joking way. I don't want to actually know."

She kissed Helen's cheek, then Olivia's. "I'm out of here. Have fun everyone."

As she walked to her truck, she fingered the brooch Griffith had given her. Being his girl was the best thing ever. She'd been blessed with happiness and planned to hang on with both hands.

epilogue

It turned out that the end of the year was a busy season for tulip farmers. Olivia hadn't realized that until this year. Apparently there was tight timing what with getting the Christmas tulips shipped and the Valentine's Day ones planted. Her fingers still hurt from pushing bulbs onto little spikes. The work had been challenging but Kelly paid well and Olivia had wanted the money.

Fortunately all the tulips were planted and thriving and they, along with the humans, had all gotten through Christmas. The holiday had been fairly low-key, what with them planning for the wedding held on the Saturday between Christmas and New Year's.

Olivia helped Helen position the dress so Kelly could duck into it. The three of them had decided, given the huge petticoat the dress required, stepping into the gown wasn't going to work at all.

"A princess dress," Olivia said in a pretend grumble. "It's so not you."

"I know. I couldn't help myself. It was love at first sight."

After Griffith had proposed in October, the Murphy women, as they called themselves, had gone to Seattle for a few days to dress shop and wedding plan. With the wedding less than three months away, Kelly had needed a dress off the rack. She'd tried on elegant sheaths, a couple of mermaid styles and had finally looked at a strapless ball-gown style.

The latter had won her heart, shocking the heck out of Helen and Olivia.

The gown was white, with a modified sweetheart neckline. Beading and pearls covered the corseted bodice and were scattered across the skirt. The only flaw in an otherwise flawless outfit was the ridiculous pin Kelly insisted she wear. Olivia had gotten her to compromise by fastening it at her waist on the side that would face away from the guests during the actual wedding.

The ceremony and reception were being held at the craft mall—in the community room. Olivia had been in charge and given their dad's generous budget, she'd made a real party out of it. She'd used the caterers from the fund-raiser and had picked beautiful linens. There were flowers, a professional band and tons of food.

Nearly the whole town was coming. Marilee had sent her regrets, which was a huge relief to everyone. Ryan had flown up to be there for Griffith. From what Olivia could tell, he was thriving in Phoenix.

Helen reached for the veil and secured it on Kelly's head. Olivia had already done her makeup and pinned up her hair. On the table was the bridal bouquet—white roses with exotic tulips, of course, and similar but smaller bouquets for Olivia and Helen, with peach-colored roses instead of white.

Olivia and Helen were Kelly's only attendants. They wore matching knee-length mint cocktail dresses that were sleeveless and empire style. Olivia would have been happy with something more fitted but with Helen nearly five months pregnant, they'd needed to go flowy.

Jeff walked into the dressing room. "How's it going?" he asked, walking up to Kelly. "You're beautiful. The photographer wants to get started. Can I send her in?"

"You can," Olivia said. "Make sure Griffith isn't lurking nearby. He can't see the bride yet."

"I will."

She noticed her dad seemed a little more interested in Helen than Kelly. He was especially doting these days, what with her being pregnant and all. Plus they'd just found out the baby was a boy and Jeff was over the moon.

Most people had assumed Helen was giving up the chance to be a mother when she married a man Jeff's age. But he'd made it clear he was more than willing to enjoy fatherhood again.

The photographer came in and started taking pictures. When she was done with everyone but the bride, Olivia ducked out to find Sven.

Her sexy man looked good in his dark tux. He would stand up with Griffith, along with Ryan. The starting over and going slow thing had worked for them. Over Thanksgiving, Sven had proposed.

Not wanting to overshadow Kelly's upcoming wedding, Olivia and Sven had kept things quiet. They'd stolen away for a long weekend in Seattle where they'd bought their matching wedding bands and he'd given her a beautiful engagement ring she only wore when they were together. Next week, while Kelly and Griffith were honeymooning in Hawaii, Olivia and Sven were going to elope to Las Vegas. Neither of them wanted a big wedding. As busy as everything had been with her starting her various businesses and working her different jobs, they hadn't had a whole lot of time together. She wanted to get married, then retreat to a gorgeous room for five days of being with the man she loved.

He pulled her close and smiled at her. "You're beautiful."

"So are you."

"We leave in less than forty-eight hours. I can't wait to make you mine."

"I feel exactly the same way."

He kissed her palm. "Are you still planning on moving in when we get back?"

She laughed. He'd asked her to come live with him several times, but she'd been firm about keeping her own place until they were married. Being unconventional had gotten them into trouble. She was determined to be very ordinary until they said "I do."

"I'm already packed."

"Good. I need you in my life, Olivia. For always."

She smiled at him. Helen stepped out of the bride's room.

"We're ready to start," she said.

Olivia stepped back. "I'll see you at the altar," she told Sven.

"Yes, you will."

Olivia joined Helen and her sister. She adjusted Kelly's dress, then handed her the bouquet.

"You're stunning."

Kelly drew in a breath. "I'm nervous. What if I trip in my heels?"

"You'll do fine."

"I love you," Kelly told her, then turned to Helen. "You, too."

Helen's lower lip trembled.

Olivia put her hands on her hips. "No crying. You'll ruin your makeup. This is a happy day. Weddings and babies. What could be better?"

Kelly smiled. "Having my sister and best friend with me. That's the very best of all."

★ ★ ★ ★ ★

Secrets of the Tulip Sisters

Book Club Discussion Questions
and Menu Suggestions

Book Club Discussion Questions

1. In *Secrets of the Tulip Sisters*, everyone has a secret (or two). What secret is each character hiding at the beginning of the book? Whose secret did you think had the most potential to create problems, and why? Were you right?

2. Susan Mallery is known for creating complex interpersonal relationships with characters in very true-to-life situations. Neither Kelly nor Olivia was wrong or right, but they were certainly in conflict with each other. How would you describe the conflict between the sisters? How did it start? Was it relatable for you? How do you think the sisters felt about each other when the story began, and how did their feelings change throughout the book?

3. Discuss the external plot of this story—the events that moved the story along. (For example, the ailing tourism industry in Tulpen Crossing.)

4. Each character is connected to the others in multiple ways, making for a multilevel storyline. Talk about the ways in which these characters' relationships are intertwined: Kelly, Griffith, Olivia, Ryan, Jeff, Helen, Sven, and Marilee.

5. What did you think of the way Jeff and Marilee raised the girls? Did their mistakes make you dislike both of them? Did you forgive them by the end of the book? Why or why not?

6. What did you think of Griffith's plan to have a semi-serious, committed, monogamous relationship, but not to fall in love? Do you think a relationship like that could ever work?

7. Helen fell in love with Jeff long before she confessed her feelings to him. How would you feel if you found out one of your closest friends was secretly dating your father? Do you think a relationship with a significant age difference can work? Were you happy with the way this story line ended?

8. Were you surprised by the way Olivia's relationship with Sven developed? Did anyone in your group take the time to look up www.Sven-the-viking-god.com?

9. How did Olivia's life differ by not spending her adolescence in Tulpen Crossing? What experiences did she have that Kelly, who lived her entire childhood and most of her adult life with their father, never had?

10. How did the characters view themselves differently by the end of the book? Were you satisfied with the ending? Why or why not?

Book Club Menu Suggestion

SVEN'S BLUEBERRY CHEESE BLINTZES

These can be made ahead of time, and then just complete the final step while your book club arrives so they're nice and fresh. These make a great breakfast, too! Makes about 12 blintzes.

FILLING:

1 lb cottage cheese
8 oz cream cheese
1 egg
1 tsp vanilla

BLUEBERRY SYRUP:

16 oz blueberries, fresh or frozen
¾ cup water
½ cup sugar
Zest and juice of half a lemon
1 tsp corn starch

1. Blend all filling ingredients in a bowl until smooth. Refrigerate until ready to use.

2. Stir together the blueberries, water, sugar and lemon juice in a heavy-bottomed pan.

3. Heat over low-medium heat until it reaches a simmer, then reduce heat and simmer for five minutes, stirring frequently.

4. Spoon a few tablespoons of the mix into a small bowl and whisk in the corn starch. Add the corn starch mixture back to the pan and continue to simmer until the syrup thickens.

BLINTZES:

1 cup flour
1 tsp sugar
½ tsp salt
¼ tsp cinnamon
4 eggs
1 cup milk
2 Tbsp melted butter
Butter for the pan, plus peanut oil for frying

1. Sift together the dry ingredients. In a separate bowl, mix the eggs, milk and butter. Add the wet ingredients to the dry ingredients and whisk until smooth.

2. Heat a six-inch sauté pan over medium heat. When it's hot, add a sliver of butter and turn the pan to coat the bottom. Pour 2–3 tbsp of batter into the pan and turn quickly to coat the bottom. Cook until brown on the bottom. Do not flip over—you'll cook the other side in the final step. Place onto waxed paper or parchment paper and allow to cool.

3. To assemble the blintzes, scoop 3 tbsp of filling onto the center of the cooked side of a wrap, then roll up like a burrito (bottom up, sides in, then roll). Set them seam-side down on a plate. You can prepare all of the blintzes to this point, and then cover and refrigerate until it's time for the final step.

4. Just before you're ready to eat, heat half an inch of peanut oil in a large pan over medium heat. Fry the blintzes until brown on one side, then flip. Drain on paper towels. Serve with warm blueberry syrup.

Read on for a sneak peek of YOU SAY IT FIRST,
the first book in the exciting new HAPPILY INC *series*
from #1 New York Times *bestselling author Susan Mallery!*

CHAPTER ONE

"Don't take this wrong, but I really need you to take off your shirt."

Pallas Saunders winced as she said the words—this was so not how she usually conducted an interview. But desperate times and all that.

Nick Mitchell raised his eyebrows. "Excuse me?"

A valid semiquestion and certainly better than simply bolting which, hey, he could have done.

"It's an emergency," she said, waving her hand in what she hoped was a *can we please move this along* gesture.

"I'm going to need more than that."

"Fine." She drew in a breath, then began talking. Fast. "I have a wedding in less than an hour and I'm one Roman soldier short. J.T. ran off to LA because his agent called about an audition. Note to self. Do *not* hire actors during pilot season. Anyway, I need a Roman soldier. You're about the same height as the other guys and you're here because you need a job, so take your shirt off, please. If you look halfway decent, I'll sponge tan you and you'll carry a very skinny girl in on a palanquin."

"On what?"

"One of those sedan chair things. I swear, she probably doesn't even weigh a hundred pounds. I don't think she's eaten in three months. You look strong. You'll do great. Please? There's a check at the end."

Not a very big one, but money was money. And Nick Mitchell had answered her ad for a part-time carpenter, so he must be at least a little desperate for money. A feeling Pallas could so relate to.

"You want me to carry a girl in on a palanquin for her wedding?"

Why were the pretty ones always dumb, she wondered with a sigh. Because Nick certainly qualified as pretty. Tall with dark hair and eyes. His shoulders were broad and from what she could see, he looked to be in shape, so what was the big deal?

"The name of my business is *Weddings in a Box*." She gestured to the walls around them. "This is boxlike. People come here to get married. I do theme weddings. The couple today want a Roman wedding. You'd be stunned at how popular they are. The Roman wedding includes the palanquin for the bride. Please, I beg you. Take off your shirt."

"You're weird," Nick muttered as he unbuttoned his shirt and tossed it onto her desk.

Hallelujah, she thought, walking around to view him from the back. As she'd hoped, he looked good—with broad shoulders and plenty of muscle. No massive tattoos, no ugly scars. Not that she objected to tattoos, but so few of them were Roman wedding appropriate and she really didn't have time to do her thing with concealer. As it was, Nick would fit in with the other guys perfectly.

"You're hired, but we have to hurry."

She grabbed him by the hand and dragged him down the hall toward the male cast dressing room. Because themed weddings required a cast of, if not thousands, then at least three or four. Roman weddings had the palanquin carrying crew and all the servers were dressed in togas. Not original, but the clients were happy and that was what mattered.

She pulled Nick into the large, plain room with racks of costumes at one end and a counter with lit mirrors above at the other. Three guys in various states of undress were already there. Two were stepping into white togas while the third was studying himself in the mirror.

Alan glanced up from his self-appraisal and smiled. "Hello, stranger."

"Not for long," Pallas muttered. "Please help Nick get ready for the wedding. Nick, Alan. Alan, Nick." She glanced at her watch and shrieked. "We have less than an hour, people." She turned to Nick. "Ever done fake tanning?"

"Do I look like I do fake tanning?"

Until that second, the man in front of her had been little more than a capable shoulder upon which she could rest one quarter of a bride. Now she actually *looked* at him. At the dark eyes watching her with a combination of disbelief and wariness. The firm set of his oddly attractive mouth. He had big hands, she noted absently, then did her best not to laugh.

Big hands? Seriously? Because she had time for *that* in her life?

She walked over to the counter and opened a drawer. Inside were gloves sealed in plastic. Gloves coated with fake tanning product she could buy in bulk for a very happy price.

"I'm about to rock your world," she told him cheerfully. "Let's go."

NICK MITCHELL FELT as if he'd stepped into an alternate universe. One where the crazy people ruled and the rest of the citizens were left to stumble along, trying to keep up.

Before he knew what was happening, the woman who was supposed to be interviewing him for a carpentry job was rubbing some weird-ass glove thing up and down his back.

"Even strokes," she said as she worked. "It takes five minutes to dry, then you check for streaks. Do your arms and chest, then your legs. Front and back, please."

She slipped off the gloves and held them out to him. "Can you do this?"

Her expression was two parts earnest and one part frustrated—as if the world conspired to make her day more difficult.

He thought about repeating that he was just there for the carpentry job, but realized she already knew that. Okay, then—fake-tanned Roman soldier it was. If nothing else, he would have a good story to tell his brothers.

He put on the gloves and began rubbing on the fake tan goop. It was less gross than he'd thought. Pallas showed him his toga costume and asked the other guys to get him in place.

"I have to go get changed," she said as she hurried to the door. "If you need anything, ask Alan. He knows all."

Alan winked at her. "That's true." Once the door was closed, Alan turned back to him. "And your story is?"

Nick took off the gloves, wiped his hands on a towel sitting on the counter, then stepped out of his jeans. "I'm a carpenter. I answered an ad." He put the gloves on again, bent over and rubbed up and down his legs.

"I see. Want some help with that?"

Nick didn't bother looking up. "I'm good."

"Well, I'm Alan, as you heard. Those two are Joseph and Jonathan. I call them the J's. They're high school students earning money on a Saturday. They play football."

One of the teens looked up. "It's basketball, Alan. We keep telling you."

"Whatever. It's sports and they're all the same." Alan turned back to Nick. "I've been on Broadway. That's how I met Gerald. He was my mentor, and then he retired and moved here. I came for the winter weather and stayed. After Gerald died, I moved to LA, but when I'm here, I do this because it's fun."

As he spoke, Nick realized that the other man was a lot older than he'd first thought. At least in his late forties.

"People really have Roman weddings?" he asked.

"You have no idea. There are cowboy weddings, too, but I don't do those." He shuddered. "Horses are the worst! And they smell. I do like a good princess wedding though. I'm a very handsome courtier, if I do say so myself. But today we're Romans. All hail Caesar."

Ten minutes later, Nick stared at himself in the mirror. He was wearing an honest to God toga. Or at least a costume. The short white skirt came to midthigh. The top tied over one shoulder and Alan had given him a circlet of grape leaves to stick on his head. Now, as he laced up sandals, he thought maybe he wouldn't be telling his brothers what he'd done, after all. They would never let him live it down.

"It's very simple," Alan told him when he was dressed. "The bride sits on the palanquin. We lift it up, carry her in. She gets off and we carry it out. The J's and I also serve at the reception, but I doubt Pallas expects that of you. So you're free to go."

Nick didn't bother pointing out that he'd yet to have his interview. To be honest, he was having his doubts about the job. He'd wanted something to fill his day while he figured out what he was going to do about his commission. While this place offered plenty of distraction, it wasn't exactly what he was looking for.

Pallas returned. She'd replaced her jeans and T-shirt with a simple dark green dress that brought out her hazel eyes. Her long brown hair was still in its fancy braid and he didn't think she was wearing any makeup. Of course she wasn't the bride— she was here to make the bride's dreams come true.

She walked up to him and nodded in approval. "You look great. Thank you for doing this. I would be in so much trouble if you hadn't agreed to help out. Did Alan tell you what was going to happen?"

"We carry in the bride, then quietly leave."

"Right. Oh, we still have to do our interview. I have no excuse for scheduling it so close to a wedding except to say I must have gotten the days wrong. There's just so much to do."

Emotions filled her eyes. He read worry, panic and more than a little determination. An interesting combination.

She squared her shoulders. "One crisis at a time, as Gerald always said. We are ready for the wedding. Gentlemen, if you'll take your positions, please."

She led the way downstairs. Nick wasn't sure what to expect, but quicker than he'd anticipated, they were in a room with a frazzled-looking bride, several bridesmaids dressed in what he would guess were Roman-inspired gowns and an honest-to-God palanquin.

He moved closer to the sedan chair and studied the carving on the sides. They were hand done, then attached to what he guessed was a lightweight metal frame.

Pallas got everyone in position. The bride took her seat. Alan took the front right position, which Nick would guess meant he was in charge.

"On three, gentlemen. We lift slowly, in unison and with our knees." Alan smiled at the bride. "Not that we have to worry about you, darling. You're no bigger than a minute and so lovely in your gown. It's designer, isn't it? Lucky, lucky you."

The bride visibly relaxed. "Thank you. I love my dress."

"It loves you back. Shall we? On three."

Nick waited for the count, then raised the bride. The crossbar had a padded, curved notch for his shoulder. He found he only had to use his hand to steady it, not support it. As Pallas had promised, the bride was light and the weight easy to bear.

He went with the others down the hall. A photographer snapped pictures. Huge double doors opened for them and they walked into a massive room with at least a twenty-foot ceiling.

Guests lined up on either side of the large aisle and a groom in a fancier version of toga waited up at the carved altar. Despite the fact that it was the middle of the afternoon, flickering torches provided light.

They reached the end of the aisle. Alan directed them to lower the bride. When she was with her Roman groom, they carried the palanquin back out. Alan ushered them to a huge outdoor courtyard set up for the reception. The palanquin was set down in a corner.

"People love climbing all over it for pictures," Alan told Nick. "All right, you're free to go." He pointed to a door. "Go through there. You'll find a staircase that will take you up to the second floor. The dressing room is at the end, on the right."

"Thanks."

Nick followed his directions. When he went inside, he saw the staircase. Before he reached it however, he spotted a partially open door.

"No way," he murmured as he moved closer.

He opened the door wider, swore under his breath and stepped inside.

Several large carved wooden panels hung from tracks where they could slide into place. He stepped to the side and visually followed the track. He would guess it led to the big ballroom he'd just been in.

These panels—easily ten feet tall and twice as wide—were exquisite works of art. The carvings depicted what he would guess was early palace life. There were several tableaux of a royal court and a few outdoor country scenes. Sure, the arrangements were cheesy, but the carving was incredible. Each of the characters in the first relief seemed ready to come to life. He traced the etched lines that created dimension in a few elegant strokes only to feel rough edges. He looked more closely and saw the panels were dinged, dry and in need of some serious TLC. Was this the job Pallas wanted a carpenter for?

He went back out the way he'd come, circling around the now-empty courtyard. He crept into the back of the ballroom and saw the carved Roman panels in place on the walls. They were as brilliant as the other ones and even from a distance, cried out to be restored.

And here he'd thought Pallas was looking for someone to repair windows or build cabinets. To work on something like this… Had Atsuko known about the panels? Was that why she'd suggested Nick apply for the job? Because while he'd grown up working with glass, in the past decade he'd fallen for wood.

Glass was cold and mercurial, but wood was alive. Wood had a soul.

He retreated back the way he'd come and headed up the stairs. The whole carry-a-bride-after-being-fake-tanned thing had put him off the part-time job, but now that he'd seen the panels, he knew he didn't have a choice. He had to restore them and make sure they were in good enough shape to last for future generations.

Dramatic much, he thought to himself as he entered the dressing room. Except the panels were worth the drama and oddness that was Pallas's wedding business. They deserved the very best of him and he was determined that they would get it. As much as he might want to deny it, he was, down to his bones, an artist. His father's blood ran through him and with it came the need to create. Or in this case, restore.

PALLAS RARELY SCHEDULED more than one wedding on a weekend. It was simply too difficult to set up everything and then break it down in time. The only exception was when a wedding party wanted a Friday event—then she could handle a second one on Sunday. Still, even with that option, and the slightly lower cost for choosing "off hours," most brides and grooms wanted the traditional Saturday night party. Which meant she had most Sundays off.

Bright and early Monday morning she made her way to Weddings in a Box and walked the property. The main building was three sided, in a U shape with a courtyard in the middle. At the west end was the small lobby with a fairly traditional facade done with a slight Italian villa flair. The north side was finished with stone and resembled a medieval castle. The south side was covered with wooden siding—giving it a ranch-like, Old West, rustic feel.

One building, three options that could easily be fluffed to fit nearly a dozen wedding themes. Quirky, yes, but she loved every fake brick and nonworking window.

She checked for damage to the building and fence—because there was that one time a groomsman had run his car into the gate—and lost or abandoned property. Celebrations went late, liquor ran freely and more than one shoe, bra or pair of panties had been found on the lawn.

What was it about weddings and irresponsible sex? Sure, the bride and groom were likely to get some but that was tradition. Everyone else should wait until they got home—only they rarely did. Fortunately today all she found was a streamer and a few flower petals. No need for protective gloves to pick up those.

She made her way inside and headed for the business office on the second floor. She'd only moved into what she still thought of as Gerald's office a few weeks before. For the first month after his death—after learning that he'd left her his business—she'd been in shock. For the next two months, she'd been unwilling to make any changes. Last month she'd realized that running from her desk to his fifty times a day was just plain dumb. Gerald wouldn't have given her Weddings in a Box if he didn't want her to keep it going. So she'd moved into his office.

Instead of feeling sad, she'd realized that being where she always pictured him had made her feel closer to him. He'd been like a second father to her, and while she missed him every day, she knew he would be happy with what she was getting done.

Now she checked her calendar while carefully avoiding the pile of bills in her inbox. Weddings in a Box might be a happy, interesting place, but it was also hanging on by a financial thread. One that was constantly in danger of snapping. Theme weddings didn't come cheap, but neither did the venue and the special touches.

Tomorrow, she promised herself. She would be brave tomorrow. She checked her email and saw that two more brides had sent back signed contracts. That was good news. She would review them before—

"Good morning."

She looked up and saw a man in the doorway to her office. Not just any man—Nick Mitchell.

Several emotions collided. Gratitude for how he'd rescued her on Saturday, slight embarrassment at how she'd stripped him down and fake-tanned him, major embarrassment after she'd figured out who he was and disappointment that she was still going to have to keep looking for a part-time carpenter. Oh, and confusion as to why he was here.

She rose, ignoring the fact that he was the best-looking man she'd had in her office in oh, forever, and smiled. "Hi. How can I help you?"

He leaned against the door frame. "I thought we could have that interview now."

Because she'd accidently scheduled the last one right before a wedding. Only there was no way he would want to work for her now, was there? "I really appreciate how you helped me out on Saturday."

"You're welcome. It's not every day a guy gets to be a Roman soldier."

"Unless you work here, then it happens way too often." She hesitated. "I'm sorry about how everything played out."

"I'm not. It was an experience I can talk about for a long time."

"I'm relieved you're not mad. Alan said you were a nice guy. He's generally a good judge of character."

"Glad to hear it."

"You're not threatened by Alan?" Because a lot of straight guys were.

"Not even close." He flashed her a grin. "I work with a chain saw. It takes a lot to threaten me."

"That certainly puts things in perspective." She shifted her weight from foot to foot and decided to just say it. "I don't mean to be rude, but there's no point in us having an interview. When I set up our appointment I hadn't done more than pencil in a name on my calendar. I looked you up yesterday."

One eyebrow rose. "Google or Bing?"

She smiled. "Both, and they said the same thing." Her smile faded as she remembered everything she'd read. Nick Mitchell wasn't anything close to an out-of-work carpenter. He was a world-renowned artist who had won awards. Yes, he worked with wood, but on a completely different level. It would be like asking a successful race car driver to teach someone to drive.

"I don't know what my friend Atsuko was thinking when she gave me your name. You're some famous artist guy and I'm a small business owner who needs some repairs done. On the cheap." She tried not to wince over the last word because someone like Nick Mitchell wouldn't understand what it was like to scramble for every penny to keep her business open.

"But I appreciate you coming by," she added. "And you being a good sport about the whole fake tanning thing."

"It was fun. I enjoyed myself. The tanning was...interesting."

"Not an experience to be repeated?"

"Um, no."

She stood by her desk, waiting for him to leave, but he didn't seem in a hurry to go.

"What did you want done?" he asked.

Why did he care? "Nick, I'm serious. I was going to pay a few dollars above minimum wage. That's all I can afford."

"Is it the wood panels?"

"Yes, but—"

He nodded toward the hallway. "Let's go see them."

She was more than a little confused, but okay. They went down the stairs and through the large, empty ballroom toward the storage areas on the side. She pulled open the big doors and flipped on the lights, then waited while Nick examined the panels hanging in place.

The rectangles of wood were huge—tall and wide, completely carved on one side. As she watched, Nick moved to the first one and placed his hands on the wood. He half closed his eyes as he traced the carvings with his fingers. Pallas had the oddest sense of watching something intensely personal, which was uncomfortable and more than a little fanciful.

"What do you know about these?" he asked, still studying them.

"Not much. They were here long before I started working for Gerald. To be honest, I never thought much about them except as decorative backdrops. When he died and left me the business, I did an inventory of everything. That was the first time I'd really looked at the panels. I realized they were in rough shape."

"They are. They're old, and the dry air is both preserving them and causing them to split. You can see the workmanship. Someone took a long time to create these. Someone with talent."

"I wish I knew more about them," she admitted. She should have asked Gerald about them, but it had never come up. She'd never realized what his plans were. In her mind, she'd been an employee and he'd been a great friend. The inheritance, an unexpected and unbelievably generous gift, had caught her off guard.

"My brothers work in glass," he said without looking at her. "They talk about the beauty, the cleanness of it. The purity. Glass can be anything. It doesn't exist until we bring it to life. But wood is alive. Wood has a soul—it tells the artist what it's supposed to be. You can ignore what it says, but if you do, the carving will never turn out right."

He turned to her, his dark gaze intense. "I want to work on these."

She stared at him. "What? No, that's ridiculous. You've been in *People* magazine."

He chuckled. "Why does that matter?"

"It just does." She was going to ignore the fact that he'd been in their Sexiest Man Alive issue and that the picture had been impressive. "I'm going to find some carpenter to—"

"No. Not a carpenter. These are incredible, Pallas. They deserve to be revered. I'll do it for whatever you were planning to pay. I want the job."

"Why?"

He turned back to the panels and placed his hands on them. "They told me they trusted me." He dropped his arms to his sides and faced her. "Don't worry. I'm not going off the deep end. This kind of work is rare. I'll enjoy it. I'm between projects right now, so I have the time."

He paused as if considering how much to tell her. "I'm up for a commission in Dubai. I'll know in the next couple of months if I'm going to get it. I doubt there's much question, but until I hear, I don't want to commit to anything big."

"Dubai?"

"A hotel wants to hire me to create a piece for its lobby. I would be there about two years."

"That's a long time."

"I know, but it would be an interesting experience. These will keep me busy until then." He smiled. "I promise to take good care of your panels."

"I don't doubt your ability," she admitted. "Or your commitment. But I'm serious about what I could pay."

"It's not about the money."

Right. Because a guy like Nick didn't necessarily work for the money, she reminded herself. Wouldn't that be nice?

"Take advantage of me," he urged. "You'll like it."

She knew exactly how he meant the comment but for one brief second, she pretended he was coming on to her. In a boy-girl kind of way. Because it had been forever since anyone had bothered.

She knew the reasons for that were complicated. She was perfectly normal looking with an average body and no habits that were outside of social norms. In theory she should be able to find some nice guy to date and take to bed. But while there had been the occasional man in her life, there hadn't been anyone close to "the one." Or even "the right now."

Part of it was where she lived. Happily Inc was a relatively small town and in her part of it, there weren't that many single guys. The ones she knew happened to be relatives, so ick. There was also the fact that she had a way of holding herself back, emotionally. She knew why—what she didn't know was how to change. Which meant being propositioned was rare and something to be treasured. Not that Nick had. He'd been talking about—

"Pallas?"

"Huh?" Oh, right. He wanted an answer. "If you're willing to accept my sad little hourly paycheck, then I'm happy to offer it," she told him.

"It's a deal." He held out his hand.

She shook it, ignoring how *large* it was and the brief heat she felt. Nick was so far out of her league as to be an extraterrestrial. Still, he was nice to look at. She would enjoy the show while it lasted.

"You can work whatever hours you want," she told him. "As long as you're not interfering with a wedding. I'll give you a time sheet for you to keep track of your hours. You'll get paid twice a month. Do you need tools or supplies or anything?"

"I'll bring my own."

"Good." Because she wouldn't know where to start. "Then I guess I'll see you around."

"You can count on it."

If only that were true, she thought humorously. She wondered how wrong it would be to ask him to work shirtless. Because he'd made a fine Roman soldier.

Maybe one of her brides would want a Garden of Eden wedding where the attendants would be naked. Nick could be an extra. A fantasy to brighten her day, she thought as she returned to her office. One she would be sure to remember.

CHAPTER TWO

NICK HANDED HIS brother a beer. The evening was clear and promised to be cold, but for now it was warm enough. They sat on Mathias's back patio, overlooking the sixteenth hole of the golf course to the right. To the left was, well, definitely an open, grassy area. It wasn't the landscape that required an explanation so much as the residents.

"You'll get used to it," Mathias offered as Nick stared at the shapes moving in the near twilight. "They head in for the night."

"To what? A barn?"

"I've never asked," Mathias admitted. "Something. My guess is they get out of the open to avoid predators."

Nick didn't bother pointing out there weren't any predators—at least not that he knew about. Instinct was instinct and he'd long since learned there was no arguing with nature.

A couple miles southwest of town, just beyond the golf course, were hundreds of acres of grassland. If you kept going, you got to the city dump—a high-tech, ecofriendly kind of place where everything that could be recycled or reclaimed was. But the most interesting part wasn't the fact that Happily Inc had one of the lowest trash-to-resident ratios in the country, it was the animals that made the grasslands between the dump and the golf course their home.

So far Nick had seen zebras, gazelles and something that looked a lot like a water buffalo. All grazing animals. In the past few days, he would swear he'd seen a giraffe strolling around, but that could have been a trick of the light.

"It's odd," he muttered, then took a drink of his beer.

"We grew up in Fool's Gold," Mathias pointed out. "We don't get to say any other town is odd."

That was probably true, Nick told himself. And a reason why he was already comfortable in Happily Inc. Once you'd lived in a weird place, it was hard to settle for normal.

But there were differences. Fool's Gold was in the foothills of the Sierra Nevada. Happily Inc was on the edge of the desert. There were mountains in both towns, but the ones here seemed newer, with sharper peaks and more edges. As interesting to his artist's eyes were the changes in colors. Dawns were a mix of oxblood and carnelian with umber and sepia for shading.

He'd been in town for three weeks. Mathias owned a ridiculously large house on the edge of the golf course and had offered him a place to stay until he figured out what he wanted to do.

"Why'd you move here?" Nick asked. "Why not Sedona or some artists' village in Tennessee?"

"Atsuko was already selling our work," Mathias said, mentioning the gallery owner in town. "She wanted us to meet, and when she heard we were leaving Fool's Gold, she suggested we stop by and visit her. One thing led to another and here we are."

His brothers had a sweet setup, Nick thought. Atsuko had contacts all over the world. With her acting as broker, they didn't have to bother with the business side of what they did. Instead they could focus on their art. Their studio was large and open. They had each other for company and yet plenty of space.

While Mathias lived here, by the golf course and the zebras, Ronan had a house up in the mountains. Built mostly of stone and native materials, the structure blended perfectly with the surroundings. There was even a large studio out back, when Ronan didn't want to make the drive into town.

When Nick had figured out it was time for him to get somewhere else, he'd considered a lot of options, but Happily Inc had been the obvious choice. Especially with the Dubai commission looming.

Twilight turned to night. There were a million stars out here. Nick studied the sky and wondered if they were far enough south for it to be different from what he was used to. Probably not.

"Any regrets about leaving?" Nick asked.

"No."

Because of their father, Nick thought grimly. Ceallach had made an impression on all of them. Some good and a lot bad.

There were five Mitchell sons. The oldest two hadn't been blessed—or was it cursed?—with any form of Ceallach's talent. They had been mostly ignored by their father, while the younger three had gotten the brunt of his attention.

"Ronan okay?" he asked. Their youngest brother had had the most to deal with.

"We don't talk about it."

"Still?"

"Always."

Which had to be a bear. Mathias and Ronan had always been tight. Probably because they were twins—or they used to be.

Neither of them would want to talk about that so he changed the subject. "How was your date Saturday night?"

Mathias looked at him over his beer bottle. "It wasn't a date."

"You didn't take a woman to dinner, and then have sex with her?"

"Yeah, sure, I did that."

"How is it not a date?"

"I'll never see her again."

"I guess that does change the definition."

Since moving to Happily Inc, Mathias had started taking up with the various bridesmaids that came into town. He hooked up with them for a night or two, then they were gone.

Nick enjoyed women as much as the next guy, but he'd never been that into volume, or variety. He liked the idea of having someone in his life—as long as he could keep things under control. He wanted enough passion for things to be interesting, but not so much that he was consumed. Sometimes that balance was difficult to find so he erred on the side of not doing.

"Just be careful," Nick warned. "You don't want some woman coming back in six months and saying she's madly in love with you."

"Not gonna happen."

Nick hoped he was right.

"Atsuko says you're going to be working for one of the wedding venues," Mathias said.

"Yup. Weddings in a Box."

His brother frowned. "Doing what? Folding napkins?"

"I've never folded napkins. It could be interesting."

Mathias stared at him. "Do I have to worry about you?"

"I don't know. Do you?"

His brother's stare turned into a glare. Nick laughed. "I'm going to be restoring two sets of wooden panels. They're old and in bad shape. The work is brilliant. I need to do some research to see if I can figure out who made them."

"You should ask Atsuko. She knows things and has a lot of connections in the art world."

"That's a good idea. I'll take some pictures and see if she can show them around."

He'd only known the gallery owner a few weeks but he was already impressed. The fiftysomething woman had buyers everywhere. She drove a hard bargain, got an excellent price, then handled shipping. He'd sold more through Atsuko in the past three weeks than in the past three years.

His father's philosophy had always been to let the art buyer come to him. Nick was beginning to believe that was a very shortsighted way of doing business.

"Heard anything on the Dubai commission?" Mathias asked.

"No. It's going to be a couple of months until they decide. Then I'll have to figure out what I want to do. Two years is a long time."

"Is this where I point out you don't have the job yet?"

Nick grinned. "Hey, it's me. Who else would they give it to?"

"Someone with talent."

"You're jealous."

"Not of you, big brother."

Nick laughed and turned his attention back to the night. "Any bats around here?"

"Scared?"

"Intrigued. I keep getting flashes of a piece that has a lot of bats in it."

Mathias shook his head. "There's something wrong with you."

"Probably."

"Bats. Fruit or vampire?"

"Fruit. I think. I should do some research."

"On bats." Mathias took a drink of beer. "Do you think Mom dropped you on your head when you were little?"

Nick laughed. "Not as often as she did you."

WHILE PALLAS ENJOYED lunch out with friends as much as the next woman, lunch with her mother was a completely different animal. First there were the logistics involved. They didn't trade off picking restaurants. Instead the command performance always occurred in the bank's executive dining room. A fancy title for a slightly nicer than average display of tables and chairs in a square, windowless room. There wasn't a kitchen, so food was brought in. Still, there was an assigned server and white tablecloths were the norm. All of which meant changing from her usual jeans and T-shirt into a dress.

As she drove across the river to the north side of town, Pallas told herself she would be fine. She'd been dealing with her mother for twenty-eight years. She knew how to get through the conversations with a minimum of pain and judgment. She just had to smile and nod and say what was expected. No big deal.

Except it always was a big deal—one way or another.

All her life Pallas had wanted desperately to please her mother, which shouldn't have been a problem. Libby Saunders loved rules. The most sensible plan would have been for Pallas to follow said rules and voilà—motherly love. Only it hadn't worked out that way. Not even once.

Perhaps it had something to do with the old saying about the road to hell and good intentions. Or the fact that Pallas had felt torn between wanting to make her mother happy and wanting to make herself happy. Whatever the reason, her childhood had been an ongoing battle—one she'd never won. Not for a lack of trying.

Cade, her twin brother, had been much smarter. He'd simply withdrawn from the field of conflict and had gone his own way. Emotionally *and* physically. Pallas still remembered their shared fifth birthday. Libby had asked her children if they wanted to work in the bank when they grew up. Pallas had immediately said she did, even though she had no understanding of what "working in the bank" meant. All she knew was that her mom went there every day and it was important and that working in the bank would make her mom love her enough that she didn't feel scared inside.

Cade had smiled that happy smile of his and said, "No. I'm going to grow up to be a cowboy."

Libby had been unamused, but Cade stood firm. He loved horses, not stuffy banks. He'd never once wavered. At eighteen, Pallas had dutifully gone off to college to major in finance and

Cade had taken off to learn his trade at a famous breeding farm in Kentucky. Five years later, he'd moved on to Texas.

They stayed in touch, and from everything he'd told her, he was blissfully happy. Life away from Libby and the bank was, apparently, very good. Pallas wouldn't know. She was still trying to prove herself to the stern matriarch of the family.

Pallas parked in the customer parking lot, careful to take a spot at the far end so as not to inconvenience anyone, then walked into the bank.

Her great-great-grandfather had established California First Savings and Loan in 1891. It wasn't the first S and L in the state by a long shot, or even the second, but it was still standing and she figured that had to be a point of pride. A lot of people thought that if she came from a banking family, she must be rich. Alas, no. While her grandfather had been the only one to inherit, he'd produced seven daughters, all of whom had children. Not only was Pallas's sliver incredibly tiny, she wouldn't inherit anything until she was thirty-nine. Because if nothing else, Grandpa Frank had a sense of humor.

So making her own way in the world wasn't an option and she had the student loans to prove it. She also had Gerald's business, which wasn't exactly the shining example of flush.

It was early April. Except for one oddly vacant date in June, she had a wedding booked every weekend from now until late September. If all went well, she would be able to pay her bills, make a few repairs and continue to take a small salary herself. Assuming she kept the business. Because as much as she loved Gerald and appreciated his completely unexpected gift, she'd never planned on making Weddings in a Box her life's work. She'd always thought she would go to work with her mother at the bank.

Pallas walked into the old, Spanish-style building. The combination of high ceilings and dark wood made her feel as if she were stepping back to a more elegant time. A floor-to-ceiling mural depicting the desert at sunrise dominated the east wall. It had been an old WPA project paid for by the government during the Great Depression in the last century. For reasons not clear to Pallas, her mother had always hated the mural, but there was nothing to be done. It was as much a part of the bank as the marble floors and old-fashioned teller windows.

She passed through the lobby and headed toward the executive suites. Despite her brisk steps, she felt a growing need to bolt for the door. Her stomach clenched and her chest tightened. When Pallas was ten feet from the door to her mother's office, Libby stepped out into the hall and gave her a tight smile.

Pallas instantly felt as if she were eight years old and had broken a treasured plate. Or tracked mud on the floor. Or been responsible for one of a million transgressions that had marked her childhood.

"Hello, Pallas."

"Mom."

Libby offered her cheek for the expected brief kiss. The Saunders clan weren't much for hugging.

Pallas had inherited her brown hair and average height from her mother. She knew she had her father's hazel eyes, but other than that, Libby's genes dominated. Their smiles were the same, as was the way they walked. As a teenager, Pallas had hated looking so much like her mother. Eventually she'd surrendered to the fact and had tried to appreciate that despite the passing years, Libby never seemed to age. At least that was something to look forward to.

As always, her mother wore a dark suit and a white blouse—appropriate attire for her senior vice president position. Her hair was pulled back into a tight bun at the nape of her neck. Her makeup was light and tasteful, her jewelry elegant and simple. Pearl studs and, despite being a widow for eighteen years, a gold wedding band.

"Thank you for being able to make lunch," Libby said as she led the way to the small dining room.

Pallas didn't know what to say to that. "My pleasure" wasn't exactly the truth and "You're welcome" seemed oddly snarky. She settled on a noncommittal throat noise.

As per usual, the table was set with china and crystal. Two large delivery bags sat on the sideboard. As a kid, Pallas had been so impressed to learn that any restaurant in town would happily bring in food for lunch. Now she wondered why Libby couldn't simply go get a sandwich or bring her lunch from home like the rest of America.

She also noted the lack of server, which was not a good sign. Not that she needed anyone plating her food—it was more that Libby didn't want anyone else overhearing their conversation. Pallas spent a couple of seconds trying to figure out what she'd done wrong this time, before giving up. No way could she guess. Besides, Libby would tell her over and over again, when she was ready.

"Would you like to dish us up?" Libby asked, taking her seat.

"Sure."

Pallas brought the bags to the table and opened them.

Inside the first were green salads, broiled chicken and a side of vegetables. The second bag contained bottled iced tea and one roll, along with a single, tiny square of butter. The latter were for her, Pallas thought, not sure if she should be amused or not. Libby wouldn't eat carbs at lunch.

Pallas put the food onto plates, and then collected ice from the small refrigerator in the corner. Her mother poured the iced tea and they sat across from each other.

Pallas told herself that there was no need to feel defiant, yet she took two spoonfuls of salad dressing to her mother's delicate drizzle. What was it about being around Libby that made her feel like a cranky preadolescent?

"I'm so pleased you've finally finished your degree," her

mother said with a smile. "I'm sorry it took you so long, but that's water under the bridge."

Pallas put her fork down and told herself to just breathe. Time would pass and she would get to leave. Or she could throw something or scream. That would work, too.

While Libby had paid for Pallas's college in Southern California, there had been several stipulations. First, that Pallas maintain a B+ GPA. Second, that Pallas earn her own spending money. Pallas had gotten a job working at nearby Disneyland. She'd loved it so much, she'd taken on extra hours, and in her third semester, her GPA had fallen to a B-. Within hours of finding out, Libby had sent an email explaining she would no longer be paying for college, her dorm room or anything else. Pallas was completely on her own. Permanently.

With less than thirty dollars to her name, Pallas had been forced to return to Happily Inc and move in with a girlfriend while she figured out what to do. She'd eventually gone to work for Gerald at Weddings in a Box and had put herself through community college, then a state school. It had taken eight and a half years, but she'd done it. She was now the proud owner of a degree in finance.

Her mother looked at her. "I assume you've learned your lesson."

"I don't even know what that means, Mom."

"That you won't be foolish again."

Pallas wanted to point out she'd simply gotten a C in geology. That she hadn't been arrested, done drugs or even dated inappropriately. But there was no point. Libby wouldn't care. The rules had been broken and there were always consequences. For everything.

"I'm pretty sure everyone but you is foolish every now and then," she said instead. "Regardless, yes, I have my degree."

"Excellent." Her mother smiled. "Then it's time. Pallas, I'm delighted to offer you a position here at the bank. You can start in two weeks."

There it was. The one thing she'd wanted since she was a little girl. The chance to work here—with her mother.

Pallas waited for the wave of excitement or even a sense of satisfaction. *Finally.* Finally she would gain respectability. Stability. She would be part of the family legacy. She was thrilled. Really.

Or not. Because in truth what she felt was...nothing.

Her mother frowned. "What's the problem? I thought you would be overjoyed."

"I am. I appreciate the offer..."

"Do not say *but* to me, Pallas. I mean it. I've been waiting for this for almost a decade. If you hadn't screwed around at college, you wouldn't have wasted the last eight years of your life."

"It was one C, Mom. Because I was working extra hours."

"At Disneyland," her mother said between clenched teeth.

"I loved my job there and I learned a lot. For the record, I don't consider my life a waste, but thanks for the vote of confidence."

Libby's expression turned impatient. "Then what is your problem? You should be jumping at this opportunity."

"I can't leave Weddings in a Box in the next two weeks. I have weddings booked through September. I have employees who are depending on their paychecks."

"Dear God, you can't be serious. Are any of your employees full-time? Isn't there someone else who can handle the weddings? It's people getting married. How hard can it be?"

It was one thing for Pallas to wonder about making Weddings in a Box a success, but it was another to hear her mother denigrate the business. Her hackles went up and she went from mildly irritated to seriously annoyed.

"I owe Gerald," she said, doing her best to keep her voice low and calm. "He left me his life's work and I am going to do my best to honor his gift."

"The man is dead. He doesn't care one way or another."

"That's harsh, even for you."

"It's practical." Libby's brown eyes snapped with anger. "I absolutely can't believe this. What is it about you, Pallas? You simply will not do what is expected. You've always been this way. Defiant. Stubborn. You get it from your grandfather."

Something Pallas had heard her whole life. She found it difficult not to roll her eyes. Plus, she really loved Grandpa Frank, so where was the bad?

"So how long do you plan to keep that ridiculous business open?" her mother asked.

"You may not like what I'm doing, Mom, but that doesn't give you the right to mock Weddings in a Box. It's a legitimate firm that makes people happy. Even you should see the value in that."

Libby pressed her lips together. "All right. How long do you plan to work there?"

"I'm not sure. As I said, I have weddings booked through September. I was thinking I would sell it then." Maybe to Alan, not that he'd ever expressed any interest in owning the company.

"That's a long way from now. I can't promise there will be an opening then. Or ever." Her mother's stern expression returned. "This may be a one-shot deal, Pallas. Are you willing to give up everything you've worked for because of a worthless inheritance?"

And there it was—the Libby-like ultimatum. She shouldn't be surprised. Or hurt. And yet...

"It's not worthless to me." Pallas still remembered how stunned she'd been to find out her boss had left her Weddings in a Box. She'd known they were friends and that he cared about her but to leave her the business—just like that—had been incredible.

"There will be consequences for this decision," her mother warned.

"There always are."

She looked at her plate and realized there was no way she was going to be able to eat anything.

"If there's nothing else, I'm going to go," Pallas said as she tossed her napkin on the table. "I'm sorry I've upset you."

"You're mistaken. I'm not upset. I'm disappointed. There's a difference."

A familiar one, Pallas thought grimly. Because she'd always been the disappointing child.

"Goodbye, Mom."

Libby only sighed.

As Pallas walked back to her car she wondered why it was always like this between her mother and herself. No matter the circumstances, they clashed. Libby ended up disappointed and Pallas was left questioning the fact that she continually had to earn her mother's love. Nothing was freely given. It wasn't that way for Cade or any of her cousins, but it had always been like that for her. She had no idea why, and was equally clueless on how to get things to change.

Love it? YOU SAY IT FIRST is on sale September 2017—
pre-order your copy now!